William

from P. 6 Sep 45

The Novels and Plays
of
SAKI

The Novels and Plays

of

SAKI

(H. H. MUNRO)

COMPLETE IN ONE VOLUME

NEW YORK

The Viking Press

1944

PUBLISHED, JULY, 1933
SECOND PRINTING, OCTOBER, 1933
THIRD PRINTING, NOVEMBER, 1935
FOURTH PRINTING, DECEMBER, 1940
FIFTH PRINTING, NOVEMBER 1943
SIXTH PRINTING, NOVEMBER 1944

SECOND "OMNIBUS" VOLUME
COPYRIGHT, 1933, BY THE VIKING PRESS, INC.

PRINTED IN THE UNITED STATES OF AMERICA
BY THE VAIL-BALLOU PRESS, INC., BINGHAMTON, N. Y.

CONTENTS

The Unbearable Bassington

First published, 1912

INTRODUCTION

by MAURICE BARING

SAKI'S works were the prelude to his work, which was to live and die in the war.

The Unbearable Bassington seems to me the key of that work as well as of all his works. "Bassington," an acute critic once wrote to me, "is what Saki might have become and mysteriously didn't."

It is, for this reason I think, the most interesting, because the most serious and most deeply felt, just as from a literary point of view, it is likewise the most "important," because the most artistically executed of his books.

It is a tragic story; and it might have deserved as a work of art a still higher place, among the Tragedies of fiction, with Turgenev's *Fathers and Sons;* Meredith's *Feverel;* Maupassant's *Une Vie,* had there been in the book—for the *story* is as tragic as possible—a stronger dose of that without which a tragedy is not a tragedy: pity. But in the category of books that deal with the misfits, failures, misunderstandings and the minor victims of misunderstandings it is a masterpiece: worthy of a place with Daudet's *Jack,* Anstey's *Pariah,* and *Misunderstood.*

It is not that there is no pity in the book, the pity is there, but it is not strong enough to counter-balance and to mitigate the misery, nor to sweeten the bitterness of the misery.

In *The Unbearable Bassington* you see nearly all sides of Saki's peculiar talent; the only salient quality among those that distinguish and differentiate him as a writer from other writers, which is absent in this book, is his vein of macabre supernatural fantasy. There is a hint, but not more than a hint of this, in the farewell dinner party given to Comus.

He had the power of inspiring horror by a touch of the supernatural, but I doubt whether it was one of his most valuable gifts. It was perhaps in his hands too cruel.

The qualities of earlier stories are all to be met with in this book, and such limitations as were their inevitable complement. *The Unbearable Bassington* was hailed when it first came out in 1913, by the critics, as one of the "wittiest books, not only of the year but of the decade." It was called clever, brilliant, ironic, witty, sombre, elegant, grim. It is all these things, but let us try and be a little more precise.

In the first place Saki could draw and create characters. The gift, in his case, is the result of a superfine sensibility and response to subtle and delicate shades of character and feeling. He could draw men, women, boys, children and even animals, and make them live. He understood the English character, especially the English female character, and best of all, the English of the county families, the well-to-do prosperous men and women who live in the Shires and hunt in the Midlands and play Bridge in Belgravia.

Since John Oliver Hobbes, with whose work that of Saki has affinities, although it is possible that he never read Mrs. Craigie's books, nobody has drawn such vivid crayons or has created so many men and women of that category and belonging to that class. Saki not only creates real people of that kind, but he names them as happily as some people name race-horses, or as Adam and Eve named the animals in Eden. For instance, Merla Blathlington,

"Merla was one of those human flies that buzz." . . .

Lady Caroline Benaresq . . . Miss Ada Spelvexit, who said while playing Bridge,

" 'I can't tell you the impression his words leave.' . . .
" 'At least you can tell us what you intend to make trumps,' broke in Lady Caroline gently." . . .

Or Mr. Lonkins . . . the American at the foreign hotel,

"What Mr. Lonkins wants is a real *deep* cherry-pie."

This gift of happy and unexpected nomenclature is to be found throughout Saki's work.

His men especially, his prigs and his bores, are as sharply

drawn as his women. The characterization in both cases is effected often by some little touch that reveals not only the character, but throws light on a fundamental trait in human nature; for instance, when at the beginning of the book Francesca Bassington is writing to her son Comus asking him to be kind to her friend Emmeline Chetrof's little boy—Emmeline Chetrof's good-will being seriously and financially necessary to her future comfort—after she has written the letter and sealed it, her brother Henry—a prig—says to her,

" 'Perhaps it would be wiser to say nothing about the boy to Comus. He doesn't always respond to directions, you know.'
"Francesca did know, but the woman who can sacrifice a clean unspoiled penny stamp is probably yet unborn."

In describing a bore Saki can give you the impression of infinite riches of boredom, in a little room—in a short sentence. For instance, Colonel Springfield's story of what happened to a pigeon cote in his compound at Poona.

"And there, dear lady," concluded the Colonel, "were the eleven dead pigeons. What had become of the bandicoot no one ever knew."

Sometimes the bore is made sharply to stand out by a shaft of wit:

"Stephen Thorle recounted a slum experience in which two entire families did all their feeding out of one damaged soup-plate.
" 'The gratitude of those poor creatures, when I presented them with a set of table crockery apiece, the tears in their eyes and in their voices when they thanked me, would be impossible to describe.'
" 'Thank you all the same for describing it,' said Comus."

Next to his power of characterization, which is the most important gift a novelist can possess, I should put his wisdom, his gift of light-hearted irresponsible nonsense, and his wit; his barbed, sometimes bitter and sometimes cruel satire; underneath and behind all these gifts there looms a permanent sadness. His wisdom is revealed over and over again in a broad gravity of outlook which foresees the inevitable consequences of folly, that effect can but follow a cause; the rare gift of seeing that a moral "two and two" make four; sometimes it appears in a passing comment or passage. For instance, two schoolmasters are arguing:

" 'Nonsense, boys are Nature's raw material.'

" 'Millions of boys are. There are just a few, and Bassington is one of them, who are Nature's highly finished product when they are in the schoolboy stage, and we, who are supposed to be moulding raw material are quite helpless when we come in contact with them.'

" 'But what happens to them when they grow up?'

" 'They never do grow up,' said the housemaster; 'that is their tragedy. Bassington will never grow out of his present stage.'

" 'Now you are talking in the language of Peter Pan,' said the form-master.

" 'I am not thinking in the manner of Peter Pan,' said the housemaster."

Here is the matter in a nutshell. Not only the subject of this book but perhaps the essence of Saki's work, his character: himself.

He sometimes talks, dreams, improvises, jokes, revels in the manner of Peter Pan, *but he does not think in the manner of Peter Pan*. And this contradiction and conjunction of opposites make for tragedy.

Now for his wit. I have already quoted a characteristic example of his wit (as I think), at its best. (The passage about Mr. Thorle and the soup-plate.) Every page, or almost every page of this book is starred either with epigrams, felicitous phrases, pointed comments or verbal pyrotechnics.

At its worst, it is mere verbalism, an indulge in epigram more for the sake of the sound than the sense, or for the fun of twisting phrases or juggling with words and syllables and antitheses; this is cheaper, it is the cardinal defect of his quality; he is tempted in all his books to do it. But in this book, *The Unbearable Bassington*, the level of Saki's wit and the dexterity of his phrasing is high, and he might possibly, had he lived longer, have gradually discarded his more facile verbalisms: this kind of thing: "The art of public life consists to a great extent of knowing exactly where to stop and going a bit further." His stories are rich in phrases of this kind; this is all right where it comes, but the trick is easy; many people can do it, and it tires in the long run.

But his phrasing is for the greater part on a higher level; instances are too numerous to quote; they will be found on every page.

There is often a lining of seriousness to his wit: a silver cloud, as he would say, with an ominous fringe.

"To see her standing at the top of an expensively horticultured staircase receiving her husband's guests was rather like watching an animal performing on a music-hall stage. One always tells oneself that the animal likes it, and one always knows that it doesn't."

To approach the particular, this book, *The Unbearable Bassington*, I said at the beginning it is a tragic story. The author at the beginning tells us the story has no moral; he states an evil and suggests no remedy—but just as *Vice Versa* was called "A Lesson to Fathers," so this book might have been called "A Lesson to Mothers" or "Mother and Son." There may not be one moral in it, there are very likely fifty morals or more, for mothers, sons and every one else. It is the story of a misunderstanding, of a mistake, and of a wasted life: of a life which is wasted partly because of a misunderstanding, and partly because of an ingrained egotism and lack of consideration which has for its inevitable effect the retribution of an isolated death.

Francesca Bassington lives for her furniture, or thinks she does. "Francesca Bassington, if pressed in an unguarded moment to describe her soul, would probably have described her drawing-room." She finds out when it is too late, that drawing-rooms, household gods and even a Van der Meulen round which all the other household gods centre, do not matter.

Her son Comus is good-looking, irresponsible, irrepressible, petulant, wilful; his own enemy against whom he carries on a reckless and ceaseless warfare. The result of this strife we see is inevitable from the start; but third parties who interfere with the best intentions, make it still more so, and of these third parties the chief and most formidable antagonist of Comus is his mother.

It is not that they do not love each other, or could not love each other. Mrs. Bassington

"was, in her own way, fonder of Comus than of anything in the world, and if he had been browning his skin somewhere east of Suez she would probably have kissed his photograph with genuine fervour every night. . . . But with the best-beloved installed under her roof, occupying an unreasonable amount of cubic space, and demanding daily sacrifices instead of providing the raw material for one, her feelings were tinged with irritation rather than with affection. She might have forgiven Comus generously for misdeeds of some gravity committed in another continent, but she could never overlook the fact that out of a dish of five plovers' eggs he was certain to take three. . . . The absent may be wrong, but they are rarely in a position to be inconsiderate.

"Thus a wall of ice had grown up gradually between mother and son, a barrier across which they could hold converse, but which gave a wintry chill even to the sparkle of their lightest words."

This is the tragedy of the book. The wall is nearly broken; it is nearly made to melt once or twice, but never quite. The opportunities are misused. The mother is tied to her possessions. She sees ahead of her and foresees all too clearly the day when she may have to be shorn of them. A rich marriage for Comus becomes more than a desirability, a possibility, for he falls in love with Elaine de Frey, a rich heiress who is like one of the pictures in the narrow gallery at the Louvre attributed to

Leonardo da Vinci. And she more than likes him. She is attracted but doubtful—and Comus throws away the game. He cannot, not even, or rather especially when everything is at stake and in his favour, bring himself to be *considerate* even for one moment. Consideration never like an angel comes. He takes away from the doubtful and hesitating girl at a critical moment and before her eyes her silver butter-dish—half as a joke, but under protest, at a moment when she is not inclined to see a joke, and that joke less than any. When she is still sore, ruffled, hesitating and dubious, he borrows a ridiculously small sum of money from her at the crucial moment, and by so doing wounds her pride mortally, "besides alarming her sense of caution," so that Elaine de Frey marries out of pique the rising, showy but really unsatisfactory and shallow politician Courtenay Youghal, whom she does not love, and Saki makes it clear to us that she has made an irretrievable mistake. The scene at the Zoological Gardens (earlier in the book) of the final interview between Youghal and a former flame, an outdoor country hunting girl is superlatively skilful, and throws a flood of light on the whole drama.

Comus having made a mess of everything is sent to West Africa.

" 'Couldn't he grub about for a living in England?' he asks. His mother shook her head. 'And as we have no money available, and can scarcely pay our own debts it is no good thinking about it.'

" 'Can't we sell something?' said Comus.

"He made no suggestion as to what should be sacrificed, but he was looking straight at the Van der Meulen."

This was the apple of his mother's eye, the cream and centre of her collection, the idol in chief among all the household gods. Comus goes to Africa, gets fever, and a telegram comes to Mrs. Bassington saying he is stricken, and then in a terrible last chapter she goes for a walk in St. James's Park, and there she waits for what she knows must come, and there she meets Lady Caroline Benaresq who understands—at a glance—what she is waiting for.

" 'I wish I could say something, I can't.' Lady Caroline spoke in a harsh grunting voice that few people had heard her use."

The telegram is awaiting Francesca when she gets home. It confirms the worst, and on the top of that she is told by her priggish brother that an expert whom she had invited to see the Van der Meulen says it is a copy. It is the fate of the mother as much as, and perhaps still more than that of the son which is the tragedy in the book. The son, Comus, one feels, is doomed from the beginning. He dies unhappy, and in frightful loneliness; but he was probably a little bit dazed; the mother is not dazed, and she has to live on, knowing what she knows and what she has done.

A critical friend once said to me that the description of the last walk in St. James's Park seemed to him to be the crown of miserable writing, unmitigated unhappiness. I agree. The same critic also said that where the human tragedy was so great the ironic discovery of the failure of the picture at the end, indeed the whole episode of the picture, was in this book too heavily emphasized—if not superfluous. It would have been in its place in *The Chronicles of Clovis*. It would, he thought, have been better if the picture had proved to be genuine and that Mrs. Bassington no longer cared. But the book as it is is an ironic tragedy on a high level; and it is full of wit that has had time to turn to tinsel, but has not been tarnished.

Saki is a worthy descendant of John Oliver Hobbes and the author of *Sybil* and *Endymion*. Perhaps, like Lord Beaconsfield, he thought life was more important than art, and whether he thought it or not, he proved it by living and dying as a corporal in the trenches. *Ave atque Vale*.

THE UNBEARABLE
BASSINGTON

CHAPTER I

FRANCESCA BASSINGTON sat in the drawing-room of her house in Blue Street, W., regaling herself and her estimable brother Henry with China tea and small cress sandwiches. The meal was of that elegant proportion which, while ministering sympathetically to the desires of the moment, is happily reminiscent of a satisfactory luncheon and blessedly expectant of an elaborate dinner to come.

In her younger days Francesca had been known as the beautiful Miss Greech; at forty, although much of the original beauty remained, she was just dear Francesca Bassington. No one would have dreamed of calling her sweet, but a good many people who scarcely knew her were punctilious about putting in the "dear."

Her enemies, in their honester moments, would have admitted that she was svelte and knew how to dress, but they would have agreed with her friends in asserting that she had no soul. When one's friends and enemies agree on any particular point they are usually wrong. Francesca herself, if pressed in an unguarded moment to describe her soul, would probably have described her drawing-room. Not that she would have considered that the one had stamped the impress of its character on the other, so that close scrutiny might reveal its outstanding features, and even suggest its hidden places, but because she might have dimly recognized that her drawing-room was her soul.

Francesca was one of those women towards whom Fate appears to have the best intentions and never to carry them into practice. With the advantages put at her disposal she might have been expected to command a more than average share of

feminine happiness. So many of the things that make for fret-
fulness, disappointment and discouragement in a woman's life
were removed from her path that she might well have been
considered the fortunate Miss Greech, or later, lucky Francesca
Bassington. And she was not of the perverse band of those
who make a rock-garden of their souls by dragging into them
all the stony griefs and unclaimed troubles they can find lying
around them. Francesca loved the smooth ways and pleasant
places of life; she liked not merely to look on the bright side
of things, but to live there and stay there. And the fact that
things had, at one time and another, gone badly with her and
cheated her of some of her early illusions made her cling the
closer to such good fortune as remained to her now that she
seemed to have reached a calmer period of her life. To undis-
criminating friends she appeared in the guise of a rather selfish
woman, but it was merely the selfishness of one who had seen
the happy and unhappy sides of life and wished to enjoy to the
utmost what was left to her of the former. The vicissitudes of
fortune had not soured her, but they had perhaps narrowed
her in the sense of making her concentrate much of her sympathies on things that immediately pleased and amused her,
or that recalled and perpetuated the pleasing and successful incidents of other days. And it was her drawing-room in particular that enshrined the memorials or tokens of past and present
happiness.

Into that comfortable quaint-shaped room of angles and bays
and alcoves had sailed, as into a harbour, those precious personal possessions and trophies that had survived the buffetings
and storms of a not very tranquil married life. Wherever her
eyes might turn she saw the embodied results of her successes,
economies, good luck, good management or good taste. The
battle had more than once gone against her, but she had somehow always contrived to save her baggage train, and her complacent gaze could roam over object after object that represented the spoils of victory or the salvage of honourable defeat.
The delicious bronze Fremiet on the mantelpiece had been the
outcome of a Grand Prix sweepstake of many years ago; a
group of Dresden figures of some considerable value had been

THE UNBEARABLE BASSINGTON 13

bequeathed to her by a discreet admirer, who had added death
to his other kindnesses; another group had been a self-bestowed
present, purchased in blessed and unfading memory of a wonderful nine-days' bridge winnings at a country-house party.
There were old Persian and Bokharan rugs and Worcester
tea-services of glowing colour, and little treasures of antique
silver that each enshrined a history or a memory in addition
to its own intrinsic value. It amused her at times to think of
the bygone craftsmen and artificers who had hammered and
wrought and woven in far distant countries and ages, to produce the wonderful and beautiful things that had come, one
way and another, into her possession. Workers in the studios
of medieval Italian towns and of later Paris, in the bazaars of
Bagdad and of Central Asia, in old-time English workshops
and German factories, in all manner of queer hidden corners
where craft secrets were jealously guarded, nameless unre-
membered men and men whose names were world-renowned
and deathless.

And above all her other treasures, dominating in her estimation every other object that the room contained, was the
great Van der Meulen that had come from her father's home
as part of her wedding dowry. It fitted exactly into the central
wall panel above the narrow buhl cabinet, and filled exactly its
right space in the composition and balance of the room. From
wherever you sat it seemed to confront you as the dominating
feature of its surroundings. There was a pleasing serenity about
the great pompous battle scene with its solemn courtly war-
riors bestriding their heavily prancing steeds, grey or skewbald
or dun, all gravely in earnest, and yet somehow conveying the
impression that their campaigns were but vast serious picnics
arranged in the grand manner. Francesca could not imagine
the drawing-room without the crowning complement of the
stately well-hung picture, just as she could not imagine herself
in any other setting than this house in Blue Street with its
crowded Pantheon of cherished household gods.

And herein sprouted one of the thorns that obtruded through
the rose-leaf damask of what might otherwise have been Francesca's peace of mind. One's happiness always lies in the future

rather than in the past. With due deference to an esteemed lyrical authority one may safely say that a sorrow's crown of sorrow is anticipating unhappier things. The house in Blue Street had been left to her by her old friend Sophie Chetrof, but only until such time as her niece Emmeline Chetrof should marry, when it was to pass to her as a wedding present. Emmeline was now seventeen and passably good-looking, and four or five years were all that could be safely allotted to the span of her continued spinsterhood. Beyond that period lay chaos, the wrenching asunder of Francesca from the sheltering habitation that had grown to be her soul. It is true that in imagination she had built herself a bridge across the chasm, a bridge of a single span. The bridge in question was her schoolboy son Comus, now being educated somewhere in the southern counties, or rather one should say the bridge consisted of the possibility of his eventual marriage with Emmeline, in which case Francesca saw herself still reigning, a trifle squeezed and incommoded perhaps, but still reigning in the house in Blue Street. The Van der Meulen would still catch its requisite afternoon light in its place of honour, the Fremiet and the Dresden and Old Worcester would continue undisturbed in their accustomed niches. Emmeline could have the Japanese snuggery, where Francesca sometimes drank her after-dinner coffee, as a separate drawing-room, where she could put her own things. The details of the bridge structure had all been carefully thought out. Only—it was an unfortunate circumstance that Comus should have been the span on which everything balanced.

Francesca's husband had insisted on giving the boy that strange Pagan name, and had not lived long enough to judge as to the appropriateness, or otherwise, of its significance. In seventeen years and some odd months Francesca had had ample opportunity for forming an opinion concerning her son's characteristics. The spirit of mirthfulness which one associates with the name certainly ran riot in the boy, but it was a twisted wayward sort of mirth of which Francesca herself could seldom see the humorous side. In her brother Henry, who sat eating small cress sandwiches as solemnly as though they had been ordained in some immemorial Book of Observances, fate had been undisguisedly kind to her. He might so easily have married some pretty helpless little woman, and lived at Notting Hill Gate, and been the father of a long string of pale, clever, useless children, who would have had birthdays and the sort of illnesses that one is expected to send grapes to, and who would have painted fatuous objects in a South Kensington manner as Christmas offerings to an aunt whose cubic space for lumber was limited. Instead of committing these unbrotherly actions, which are so frequent in family life that they might almost be called brotherly, Henry had married a woman who had both money and a sense of repose, and their one child had the brilliant virtue of never saying anything which even its parents could consider worth repeating. Then he had gone into Parliament, possibly with the idea of making his home life seem less dull; at any rate it redeemed his career from insignificance, for no man whose death can produce the item "another by-election" on the news posters can be wholly a nonentity. Henry, in short, who might have been an embarrassment and a handicap, had chosen rather to be a friend and counsellor, at times even an emergency bank balance; Francesca on her part, with partiality which a clever and lazily-inclined woman often feels for a reliable fool, not only sought his counsel but frequently followed it. When convenient, moreover, she repaid his loans.

Against this good service on the part of Fate in providing her with Henry for a brother, Francesca could well set the plaguy malice of the destiny that had given her Comus for a son. The boy was one of those untamable young lords of misrule that frolic and chafe themselves through nursery and preparatory and public-school days with the utmost allowance of storm and dust and dislocation and the least possible amount of collar-work, and come somehow with a laugh through a series of catastrophes that has reduced every one else concerned to tears or Cassandra-like forebodings. Sometimes they sober down in after-life and become uninteresting, forgetting that they were ever lords of anything; sometimes Fate plays royally into their hands, and they do great things in a spacious manner, and are thanked by Parliaments and the Press and acclaimed by gala-day crowds. But in most cases their tragedy begins when they leave school and turn themselves loose in a world that has grown too civilized and too crowded and too empty to have any place for them. And they are very many.

Henry Greech had made an end of biting small sandwiches, and settled down like a dust-storm refreshed, to discuss one of the fashionably prevalent topics of the moment, the prevention of destitution.

"It is a question that is only being nibbled at, smelt at, one might say, at the present moment," he observed, "but it is one that will have to engage our serious attention and considera-tion before long. The first thing that we shall have to do is to get out of the dilettante and academic way of approaching it. We must collect and assimilate hard facts. It is a subject that ought to appeal to all thinking minds, and yet, you know, I find it surprisingly difficult to interest people in it."

Francesca made some monosyllabic response, a sort of sym-pathetic grunt which was meant to indicate that she was, to a certain extent, listening and appreciating. In reality she was reflecting that Henry possibly found it difficult to interest peo-ple in any topic that he enlarged on. His talents lay so thor-oughly in the direction of being uninteresting, that even as an eye-witness of the massacre of St. Bartholomew he would prob-ably have infused a flavour of boredom into his descriptions of the event.

"I was speaking down in Leicestershire the other day on this subject," continued Henry, "and I pointed out at some length a thing that few people ever stop to consider——"

Francesca went over immediately but decorously to the ma-jority that will not stop to consider.

"Did you come across any of the Barnets when you were down there?" she interrupted; "Eliza Barnet is rather taken up with all those subjects."

In the propagandist movements of Sociology, as in other arenas of life and struggle, the fiercest competition and rivalry is frequently to be found between closely allied types and spe-cies. Eliza Barnet shared many of Henry Greech's political and social views, but she also shared his fondness for pointing things out at some length; there had been occasions when she had extensively occupied the strictly limited span allotted to the platform oratory of a group of speakers of whom Henry Greech had been an impatient unit. He might see eye to eye with her on the leading questions of the day, but he persistently wore mental blinkers as far as her estimable qualities were concerned, and the mention of her name was a skilful lure drawn across the trail of his discourse; if Francesca had to listen to his eloquence on any subject she much preferred that it should be a disparagement of Eliza Barnet rather than the prevention of destitution.

"I've no doubt she means well," said Henry, "but it would be a good thing if she could be induced to keep her own personality a little more in the background, and not to imagine that she is the necessary mouthpiece of all the progressive thought in the countryside. I fancy Canon Besomley must have had her in his mind when he said that some people came into the world to shake empires and others to move amendments."

Francesca laughed with genuine amusement.

"I suppose she is really wonderfully well up in all the subjects she talks about," was her provocative comment.

Henry grew possibly conscious of the fact that he was being drawn out on the subject of Eliza Barnet, and he presently turned on to a more personal topic.

"From the general air of tranquillity about the house I presume Comus has gone back to Thaleby," he observed.

"Yes," said Francesca, "he went back yesterday. Of course, I'm very fond of him, but I bear the separation well. When he's here it's rather like having a live volcano in the house, a volcano that in its quietest moments asks incessant questions and uses strong scent."

"It is only a temporary respite," said Henry; "in a year or two he will be leaving school, and then what?"

Francesca closed her eyes with the air of one who seeks to shut out a distressing vision. She was not fond of looking intimately at the future in the presence of another person, especially when the future was draped in doubtfully auspicious colours.

"And then what?" persisted Henry.

"Then I suppose he will be upon my hands."

"Exactly."

"Don't sit there looking judicial. I'm quite ready to listen to suggestions if you've any to make."

"In the case of any ordinary boy," said Henry, "I might make lots of suggestions as to the finding of suitable employment. From what we know of Comus it would be rather a waste of time for either of us to look for jobs which he wouldn't look at when we'd got them for him."

"He must do something," said Francesca.

"I know he must; but he never will. At least, he'll never stick to anything. The most hopeful thing to do with him will be to marry him to an heiress. That would solve the financial side of his problem. If he had unlimited money at his disposal, he might go into the wilds somewhere and shoot big game. I never know what the big game have done to deserve it, but they do help to deflect the destructive energies of some of our social misfits."

Henry, who never killed anything larger or fiercer than a trout, was scornfully superior on the subject of big game shooting.

Francesca brightened at the matrimonial suggestion. "I don't know about an heiress," she said reflectively. "There's Emmeline Chetrof, of course. One could hardly call her an heiress, but she's got a comfortable little income of her own, and I suppose something more will come to her from her grandmother. Then, of course, you know this house goes to her when she marries."

"That would be very convenient," said Henry, probably following a line of thought that his sister had trodden many hundreds of times before him. "Do she and Comus hit it off at all well together?"

"Oh, well enough in boy and girl fashion," said Francesca. "I must arrange for them to see more of each other in future. By the way, that little brother of hers that she dotes on, Lancelot, goes to Thaleby this term. I'll write and tell Comus to be specially kind to him; that will be a sure way to Emmeline's heart. Comus has been made a prefect, you know. Heaven knows why."

"It can only be for prominence in games," sniffed Henry; "I think we may safely leave work and conduct out of the question."

Comus was not a favourite with his uncle.

Francesca had turned to her writing cabinet and was scribbling a letter to her son in which the delicate health, timid disposition and other inevitable attributes of the new boy were brought to his notice, and commended to his care. When she had sealed and stamped the envelope Henry uttered a belated caution.

"Perhaps on the whole it would be wiser to say nothing about the boy to Comus. He doesn't always respond to directions, you know."

Francesca did know, and already was more than half of her brother's opinion; but the woman who can sacrifice a clean unspoiled penny stamp is probably yet unborn.

CHAPTER II

LANCELOT CHETROF stood at the end of a long bare passage, restlessly consulting his watch and fervently wishing himself half an hour older with a certain painful experience already registered in the past; unfortunately it still belonged to the future, and what was still more horrible, to the immediate future. Like many boys new to a school he had cultivated an unhealthy passion for obeying rules and requirements, and his zeal in this direction had proved his undoing. In his hurry to be doing two or three estimable things at once he had omitted to study the notice-board in more than a perfunctory fashion and had thereby missed a football practice specially ordained for newly-joined boys. His fellow-juniors of a term's longer standing had graphically enlightened him as to the inevitable consequences of his lapse; the dread which attaches to the unknown was, at any rate, deleted from his approaching doom, though at the moment he felt scarcely grateful for the knowledge placed at his disposal with such lavish solicitude.

"You'll get six of the very best, over the back of a chair," said one.

"They'll draw a chalk line across you, of course, you know," said another.

"A chalk line?"

"Rather. So that every cut can be aimed exactly at the same spot. It hurts much more that way."

Lancelot tried to nourish a wan hope that there might be an element of exaggeration in this uncomfortably realistic description.

Meanwhile in the prefects' room at the other end of the passage, Comus Bassington and a fellow-prefect sat also waiting on time, but in a mood of far more pleasurable expectancy. Comus was one of the most junior of the prefect caste, but by no means the least well known, and outside the masters' common-room he enjoyed a certain fitful popularity, or at any rate admiration. At football he was too erratic to be a really brilliant player, but he tackled as if the act of bringing his man headlong to the ground was in itself a sensuous pleasure, and his weird swear-words whenever he got hurt were eagerly treasured by those who were fortunate enough to hear them. At athletics in general he was a showy performer, and although new to the functions of a prefect he had already established a reputation as an effective and artistic caner. In appearance he exactly fitted his fanciful Pagan name. His large green-grey eyes seemed for ever asparkle with goblin mischief and the joy of revelry, and the curved lips might have been those of some wickedly-laughing faun; one almost expected to see embryo horns fretting the smoothness of his sleek dark hair. The chin was firm, but one looked in vain for a redeeming touch of ill-temper in the handsome, half-mocking, half-petulant face. With a strain of sourness in him Comus might have been leavened into something creative and masterful; fate had fashioned him with a certain whimsical charm, and left him all unequipped for the greater purposes of life. Perhaps no one would have called him a lovable character, but in many respects he was adorable; in all respects he was certainly damned.

Rutley, his companion of the moment, sat watching him and wondering, from the depths of a very ordinary brain, whether he liked or hated him; it was easy to do either.

"It's not really your turn to cane," he said.

"I know it's not," said Comus, fingering a very serviceable-looking cane as lovingly as a pious violinist might handle his Strad. "I gave Greyson some mint-chocolate to let me toss whether I caned or him, and I won. He was rather decent over it and let me have half the chocolate back."

The droll lightheartedness which won Comus Bassington such measure of popularity as he enjoyed among his fellows did not materially help to endear him to the succession of masters with whom he came in contact during the course of his schooldays. He amused and interested such of them as had the saving grace of humour at their disposal, but if they sighed when he passed from their immediate responsibility it was a sigh of relief rather than of regret. The more enlightened and experienced of them realized that he was something outside the scope of the things that they were called upon to deal with. A man who has been trained to cope with storms, to foresee their coming, and to minimize their consequences, may be pardoned if he feels a certain reluctance to measure himself against a tornado.

Men of more limited outlook and with a correspondingly larger belief in their own powers were ready to tackle the tornado had time permitted.

"I think I could tame young Bassington if I had your opportunities," a form-master once remarked to a colleague whose House had the embarrassing distinction of numbering Comus among its inmates.

"Heaven forbid that I should try," replied the housemaster.

"But why?" asked the reformer.

"Because Nature hates any interference with her own arrangements, and if you start in to tame the obviously untamable you are taking a fearful responsibility on yourself."

"Nonsense; boys are Nature's raw material."

"Millions of boys are. There are just a few, and Bassington is one of them, who are Nature's highly finished product when they are in the schoolboy stage, and we, who are supposed to be moulding raw material, are quite helpless when we come in contact with them."

"But what happens to them when they grow up?"

"They never do grow up," said the housemaster; "that is their tragedy. Bassington will certainly never grow out of his present stage."

"Now you are talking in the language of Peter Pan," said the form-master.

"I am not thinking in the manner of Peter Pan," said the other. "With all reverence for the author of that masterpiece I should say he had a wonderful and tender insight into the child mind and knew nothing whatever about boys. To make only one criticism on that particular work, can you imagine a lot of British boys, or boys of any country that one knows of, who would stay contentedly playing children's games in an underground cave when there were wolves and pirates and Red Indians to be had for the asking on the other side of the trap door?"

The form-master laughed. "You evidently think that the 'Boy who would not grow up' must have been written by a 'grown-up who could never have been a boy.' Perhaps that is the meaning of the 'Never-never Land.' I daresay you're right in your criticism, but I don't agree with you about Bassington. He's a handful to deal with, as any one knows who has come in contact with him, but if one's hands weren't full with a thousand and one other things I hold to my opinion that he could be tamed."

And he went his way, having maintained a form-master's inalienable privilege of being in the right.

.   .   .   .

In the prefects' room, Comus busied himself with the exact position of a chair planted out in the middle of the floor.

"I think everything's ready," he said.

Rutley glanced at the clock with the air of a Roman elegant

in the Circus, languidly awaiting the introduction of an expected Christian to an expectant tiger.

"The kid is due in two minutes," he said.

"He'd jolly well better not be late," said Comus.

Comus had gone through the mill of many scorching casti-
gations in his earlier schooldays, and was able to appreciate
to the last ounce the panic that must be now possessing his
foredoomed victim, probably at this moment hovering miserably outside the door. After all, that was part of the fun of
the thing, and most things have their amusing side if one knows
where to look for it.

There was a knock at the door, and Lancelot entered in
response to a hearty friendly summons to "come in."

"I've come to be caned," he said breathlessly; adding by
way of identification, "my name's Chetrof."

"That's quite bad enough in itself," said Comus, "but there
is probably worse to follow. You are evidently keeping something back from us."

"I missed a footer practice," said Lancelot.

"Six," said Comus briefly, picking up his cane.

"I didn't see the notice on the board," hazarded Lancelot
as a forlorn hope.

"We are always pleased to listen to excuses, and our charge
is two extra cuts. That will be eight. Get over."

And Comus indicated the chair that stood in sinister isolation in the middle of the room. Never had an article of furniture seemed more hateful in Lancelot's eyes. Comus could well
remember the time when a chair stuck in the middle of a
room had seemed to him the most horrible of manufactured
things.

"Lend me a piece of chalk," he said to his brother prefect.

Lancelot ruefully recognized the truth of the chalk-line
story.

Comus drew the desired line with an anxious exactitude
which he would have scorned to apply to a diagram of Euclid
or a map of the Russo-Persian frontier.

"Bend a little more forward," he said to the victim, "and
much tighter. Don't trouble to look pleasant, because I can't

see your face anyway. It may sound unorthodox to say so, but this is going to hurt you much more than it will hurt me."

There was a carefully measured pause, and then Lancelot was made vividly aware of what a good cane can be made to do in really efficient hands. At the second cut he projected himself hurriedly off the chair.

"Now I've lost count," said Comus; "we shall have to begin all over again. Kindly get back into the same position. If you get down again before I've finished Rutley will hold you over and you'll get a dozen."

Lancelot got back on to the chair, and was re-arranged to the taste of his executioner. He stayed there somehow or other while Comus made eight accurate and agonizingly effective shots at the chalk line.

"By the way," he said to his gasping and gulping victim when the infliction was over, "you said Chetrof, didn't you? I believe I've been asked to be kind to you. As a beginning you can clean out my study this afternoon. Be awfully careful how you dust the old china. If you break any don't come and tell me, but just go and drown yourself somewhere; it will save you from a worse fate."

"I don't know where your study is," said Lancelot between his chokes.

"You'd better find it or I shall have to beat you, really hard this time. Here, you'd better keep this chalk in your pocket, it's sure to come in handy later on. Don't stop to thank me for all I've done, it only embarrasses me."

As Comus hadn't got a study Lancelot spent a feverish half-hour in looking for it, incidentally missing another footer practice.

.   .   .   .

"Everything is very jolly here," wrote Lancelot to his sister Emmeline. "The prefects can give you an awful hot time if they like, but most of them are rather decent. Some are Beasts. Bassington is a prefect, though only a junior one. He is the Limit as Beasts go. At least, I think so."

Schoolboy reticence went no further, but Emmeline filled in

the gaps for herself with the lavish splendour of feminine imagination. Francesca's bridge went crashing into the abyss.

CHAPTER III

ON the evening of a certain November day, two years after the events heretofore chronicled, Francesca Bassington steered her way through the crowd that filled the rooms of her friend Serena Golackly, bestowing nods of vague recognition as she went, but with eyes that were obviously intent on focusing one particular figure. Parliament had pulled its energies together for an Autumn Session, and both political Parties were fairly well represented in the throng. Serena had a harmless way of inviting a number of more or less public men and women to her house, and hoping that if you left them together long enough they would constitute a *salon*. In pursuance of the same instinct she planted the flower borders at her weekend cottage retreat in Surrey with a large mixture of bulbs, and called the result a Dutch garden. Unfortunately, though you may bring brilliant talkers into your home, you cannot always make them talk brilliantly, or even talk at all; what is worse you cannot restrict the output of those starling-voiced dullards who seem to have, on all subjects, so much to say that was well worth leaving unsaid. One group that Francesca passed was discussing a Spanish painter, who was forty-three, and had painted thousands of square yards of canvas in his time, but of whom no one in London had heard till a few months ago; now the starling-voices seemed determined that one should hear of very little else. Three women knew how his name was pronounced, another always felt that she must go into a forest and pray whenever she saw his pictures, another had noticed that there were always pomegranates in his later compositions, and a man with an indefensible collar knew what the pomegranates "meant." "What I think so splendid about him," said a stout lady in a loud challenging voice, "is the way he defies all the conventions of art while retaining all that the conventions stand for." "Ah, but have you noticed—"

put in the man with the atrocious collar, and Francesca pushed desperately on, wondering dimly as she went what people found so unsupportable in the affliction of deafness. Her progress was impeded for a moment by a couple engaged in earnest and voluble discussion of some smouldering question of the day; a thin spectacled young man with the receding forehead that so often denotes advanced opinions, was talking to a spectacled young woman with a similar type of forehead, and exceedingly untidy hair. It was her ambition in life to be taken for a Russian girl-student, and she had spent weeks of patient research in trying to find out exactly where you put the tea-leaves in a samovar. She had once been introduced to a young Jewess from Odessa, who had died of pneumonia the following week; the experience, slight as it was, constituted the spectacled young lady an authority on all things Russian in the eyes of her immediate set.

"Talk is helpful, talk is needful," the young man was saying, "but what we have got to do is to lift the subject out of the furrow of indisciplined talk and place it on the threshing-floor of practical discussion."

The young woman took advantage of the rhetorical full-stop to dash in with the remark which was already marshalled on the tip of her tongue.

"In emancipating the serfs of poverty we must be careful to avoid the mistakes which Russian bureaucracy stumbled into when liberating the serfs of the soil."

She paused in her turn for the sake of declamatory effect, but recovered her breath quickly enough to start afresh on level terms with the young man, who had jumped into the stride of his next sentence.

"They got off to a good start that time," said Francesca to herself; "I suppose it's the Prevention of Destitution they're hammering at. What on earth would become of these dear good people if any one started a crusade for the prevention of mediocrity?"

Midway through one of the smaller rooms, still questing for an elusive presence, she caught sight of some one that she knew, and the shadow of a frown passed across her face. The object of her faintly signalled displeasure was Courtenay Youghal, a political spur-winner who seemed absurdly youthful to a generation that had never heard of Pitt. It was Youghal's ambition—or perhaps his hobby—to infuse into the greyness of modern political life some of the colour of Disraelian dandyism, tempered with the correctness of Anglo-Saxon taste, and supplemented by the flashes of wit that were inherent from the Celtic strain in him. His success was only a half-measure. The public missed in him that touch of blatancy which it looks for in its rising public men; the decorative smoothness of his chestnut-golden hair, and the lively sparkle of his epigrams were counted to him for good, but the restrained sumptuousness of his waistcoats and cravats was as wasted efforts. If he had habitually smoked cigarettes in a pink coral mouthpiece, or worn spats of Mackenzie tartan, the great heart of the voting-man, and the gush of the paragraph-makers might have been unreservedly his. The art of public life consists to a great extent of knowing exactly where to stop and going a bit farther.

It was not Youghal's lack of political sagacity that had brought the momentary look of disapproval into Francesca's face. The fact was that Comus, who had left off being a school-boy and was now a social problem, had lately enrolled himself among the young politician's associates and admirers, and as the boy knew and cared nothing about politics, and merely copied Youghal's waistcoats, and, less successfully, his conversation, Francesca felt herself justified in deploring the intimacy. To a woman who dressed well on comparatively nothing a year it was an anxious experience to have a son who dressed sumptuously on absolutely nothing.

The cloud that had passed over her face when she caught sight of the offending Youghal was presently succeeded by a smile of gratified achievement, as she encountered a bow of recognition and welcome from a portly middle-aged gentleman, who seemed genuinely anxious to include her in the rather meagre group that he had gathered about him.

"We were just talking about my new charge," he observed genially, including in the "we" his somewhat depressed-looking listeners, who in all human probability had done none of the talking. "I was just telling them, and you may be interested to hear this——"

Francesca, with Spartan stoicism, continued to wear an ingratiating smile, though the character of the deaf adder that stoppeth her ear and will not hearken, seemed to her at that moment a beautiful one.

Sir Julian Jull had been a member of a House of Commons distinguished for its high standard of well-informed mediocrity, and had harmonized so thoroughly with his surroundings that the most attentive observer of Parliamentary proceedings could scarcely have told even on which side of the House he sat. A baronetcy bestowed on him by the Party in power had at least removed that doubt; some weeks later he had been made Governor of some West Indian dependency, whether as a reward for having accepted the baronetcy, or as an application of a theory that West Indian islands get the Governors they deserve, it would have been hard to say. To Sir Julian the appointment was, doubtless, one of some importance; during the span of his Governorship the island might possibly be visited by a member of the Royal Family, or at the least by an earthquake, and in either case his name would get into the papers. To the public the matter was one of absolute indifference; "who is he and where is it?" would have correctly epitomized the sum total of general information on the personal and geographical aspects of the case.

Francesca, however, from the moment she had heard of the likelihood of the appointment, had taken a deep and lively interest in Sir Julian. As a Member of Parliament he had not filled any very pressing social want in her life, and on the rare occasions when she took tea on the Terrace of the House she was wont to lapse into rapt contemplation of St. Thomas's Hospital whenever she saw him within bowing distance. But as Governor of an island he would, of course, want a private secretary, and as a friend and colleague of Henry Greech, to whom he was indebted for many little acts of political support (they had once jointly drafted an amendment which had been ruled out of order), what was more natural and proper than that he should let his choice fall on Henry's nephew Comus? While privately doubting whether the boy would make the sort of secretary that any public man would esteem as a treasure, Henry was thoroughly in agreement with Francesca as to the excellence and desirability of an arrangement which would transplant that troublesome young animal from the too restricted and conspicuous area that centres in the parish of St. James's to some misty corner of the British dominion overseas. Brother and sister had conspired to give an elaborate and at the same time cozy little luncheon to Sir Julian on the very day that his appointment was officially announced, and the question of the secretaryship had been mooted and sedulously fostered as occasion permitted, until all that was now needed to clinch the matter was a formal interview between His Excellency and Comus. The boy had from the first shown very little gratification at the prospect of his deportation. To live on a remote shark-girt island, as he expressed it, with the Jull family as his chief social mainstay, and Sir Julian's conversation as a daily item of his existence, did not inspire him with the same degree of enthusiasm as was displayed by his mother and uncle, who, after all, were not making the experiment. Even the necessity for an entirely new outfit did not appeal to his imagination with the force that might have been expected. But, however lukewarm his adhesion to the project might be, Francesca and her brother were clearly determined that no lack of deft persistence on their part should endanger its success. It was for the purpose of reminding Sir Julian of his promise to meet Comus at lunch on the following day, and definitely settle the matter of the secretaryship, that Francesca was now enduring the ordeal of a long harangue on the value of the West Indian group as an Imperial asset. Other listeners dexterously detached themselves one by one, but Francesca's patience outlasted even Sir Julian's flow of commonplaces, and her devotion was duly rewarded by a renewed acknowledgment of the lunch engagement and its purpose. She pushed her way back through the throng of startling-voiced chatterers fortified by a sense of well-earned victory. Dear Serena's absurd *salons* served some good purpose after all.

Francesca was not an early riser, and her breakfast was only just beginning to mobilize on the breakfast-table next morning when a copy of *The Times*, sent by special messenger from her brother's house, was brought up to her room. A heavy margin of blue pencilling drew her attention to a prominently-printed letter which bore the ironical heading: "Julian Jull, Proconsul." The matter of the letter was a cruel disinterment of some fatuous and forgotten speeches made by Sir Julian to his constituents not many years ago, in which the value of some of our Colonial possessions, particularly certain West Indian islands, was decried in a medley of pomposity, ignorance and amazingly cheap humour. The extracts given sounded weak and foolish enough, taken by themselves, but the writer of the letter had interlarded them with comments of his own, which sparkled with an ironical brilliance that was Cervantes-like in its polished cruelty. Remembering her ordeal of the previous evening Francesca permitted herself a certain feeling of amusement as she read the merciless stabs inflicted on the newly-appointed Governor; then she came to the signature at the foot of the letter, and the laughter died out of her eyes. "Comus Bassington" stared at her from above a thick layer of blue pencil lines marked by Henry Greech's shaking hand.

Comus could no more have devised such a letter than he could have written an Episcopal charge to the clergy of any given diocese. It was obviously the work of Courtenay Youghal, and Comus, for a palpable purpose of his own, had wheedled him into forgoing for once the pride of authorship in a clever piece of political raillery, and letting his young friend stand sponsor instead. It was a daring stroke, and there could be no question as to its success; the secretaryship and the distant shark-girt island faded away into the horizon of impossible things. Francesca, forgetting the golden rule of strategy which enjoins a careful choosing of ground and opportunity before entering on hostilities, made straight for the bath-room door, behind which a lively din of splashing betokened that Comus had at least begun his toilet.

"You wicked boy, what have you done?" she cried reproachfully.

"Me washee," came a cheerful shout; "me washee from the neck all the way down to the merrythought, and now washee down from the merrythought to——"

"You have ruined your future. *The Times* has printed that miserable letter with your signature."

A loud squeal of joy came from the bath. "Oh, Mummy! Let me see!"

There were sounds as of a sprawling dripping body clambering hastily out of the bath. Francesca fled. One cannot effectively scold a moist nineteen-year-old boy clad only in a bath-towel and a cloud of steam.

Another messenger arrived before Francesca's breakfast was over. This one brought a letter from Sir Julian Jull, excusing himself from fulfilment of the luncheon engagement.

CHAPTER IV

FRANCESCA prided herself on being able to see things from other people's points of view, which meant, as it usually does, that she could see her own point of view from various aspects. As regards Comus, whose doings and non-doings bulked largely in her thoughts at the present moment, she had mapped out in her mind so clearly what his outlook in life ought to be, that she was peculiarly unfitted to understand the drift of his feelings or the impulses that governed them. Fate had endowed her with a son; in limiting the endowment to a solitary offspring Fate had certainly shown a moderation which Francesca was perfectly willing to acknowledge and be thankful for; but then, as she pointed out to a certain complacent friend of hers who cheerfully sustained an endowment of half a dozen male offsprings and a girl or two, her one child was Comus. Moderation in numbers was more than counterbalanced in his case by extravagance in characteristics.

Francesca mentally compared her son with hundreds of other young men whom she saw around her, steadily, and no doubt happily, engaged in the process of transforming themselves from nice boys into useful citizens. Most of them had occupations, or were industriously engaged in qualifying for such; in their leisure moments they smoked reasonably-priced cigarettes, went to the cheaper seats at music-halls, watched an occasional cricket match at Lord's with apparent interest, saw most of the world's spectacular events through the medium of the cinematograph, and were wont to exchange at parting seemingly superfluous injunctions to "be good." The whole of Bond Street and many of the tributary thoroughfares of Piccadilly might have been swept off the face of modern London without in any way interfering with the supply of their daily wants. They were doubtless dull as acquaintances, but as sons they would have been eminently restful. With a growing sense of irritation Francesca compared these deserving young men with her own intractable offspring, and wondered why Fate should have singled her out to be the parent of such a vexatious variant from a comfortable and desirable type. As far as remunerative achievement was concerned, Comus copied the insouciance of the field lily with a dangerous fidelity. Like his mother he looked round with wistful irritation at the example afforded by contemporary youth, but he concentrated his attention exclusively on the richer circles of his acquaintance, young men who bought cars and polo ponies as unconcernedly as he might purchase a carnation for his buttonhole, and went for trips to Cairo or the Tigris valley with less difficulty and finance-stretching than he encountered in contriving a week-end at Brighton.

Gaiety and good looks had carried Comus successfully and, on the whole, pleasantly, through schooldays and a recurring succession of holidays; the same desirable assets were still at his service to advance him along his road, but it was a disconcerting experience to find that they could not be relied on to go all distances at all times. In an animal world, and a fiercely competitive animal world at that, something more was needed than the decorative *abandon* of the field lily, and it was just that something more which Comus seemed unable or unwilling to provide on his own account; it was just the lack of that something more which left him sulking with Fate over the numerous breakdowns and stumbling-blocks that held him up on what he expected to be a triumphal or, at any rate, unimpeded progress.

Francesca was, in her own way, fonder of Comus than of any one else in the world, and if he had been browning his skin somewhere east of Suez she would probably have kissed his photograph with genuine fervour every night before going to bed; the appearance of a cholera scare or rumour of native rising in the columns of her daily news-sheet would have caused her a flutter of anxiety, and she would have mentally likened herself to a Spartan mother sacrificing her best-beloved on the altar of State necessities. But with the best-beloved installed under her roof, occupying an unreasonable amount of cubic space, and demanding daily sacrifices instead of providing the raw material for one, her feelings were tinged with irritation rather than affection. She might have forgiven Comus generously for misdeeds of some gravity committed in another continent, but she could never overlook the fact that out of a dish of five plovers' eggs he was certain to take three. The absent may be always wrong, but they are seldom in a position to be inconsiderate.

Thus a wall of ice had grown up gradually between mother and son, a barrier across which they could hold converse, but which gave a wintry chill even to the sparkle of their lightest words. The boy had the gift of being irresistibly amusing when he chose to exert himself in that direction, and after a long series of moody or jangling meal-sittings he would break forth into a torrential flow of small talk, scandal and malicious anecdote, true or more generally invented, to which Francesca listened with a relish and appreciation that was all the more flattering from being so unwillingly bestowed.

"If you chose your friends from a rather more reputable set you would be doubtless less amusing, but there would be compensating advantages."

Francesca snapped the remark out at lunch one day when she had been betrayed into a broader smile than she considered the circumstances of her attitude towards Comus warranted.

"I'm going to move in quite decent society tonight," replied Comus with a pleased chuckle; "I'm going to meet you and

Uncle Henry and heaps of nice dull God-fearing people at dinner."

Francesca gave a little gasp of surprise and annoyance.

"You don't mean to say Caroline has asked you to dinner tonight?" she said; "and of course without telling me. How exceedingly like her!"

Lady Caroline Benaresq had reached that age when you can say and do what you like in defiance of people's most sensitive feelings and most cherished antipathies. Not that she had waited to attain her present age before pursuing that line of conduct; she came of a family whose individual members went through life, from the nursery to the grave, with as much tact and consideration as a cactus-hedge might show in going through a crowded bathing tent. It was a compensating mercy that they disagreed rather more among themselves than they did with the outside world; every known variety and shade of religion and politics had been pressed into the family service to avoid the possibility of any agreement on the larger essentials of life, and such unlooked-for happenings as the Home Rule schism, the Tariff-Reform upheaval and the Suffragette crusade were thankfully seized on as furnishing occasion for further differences and subdivisions. Lady Caroline's favourite scheme of entertaining was to bring jarring and antagonistic elements into close contact and play them remorselessly one against the other. "One gets much better results under those circumstances," she used to observe, "than by asking people who wish to meet each other. Few people talk as brilliantly to impress a friend as they do to depress an enemy."

She admitted that her theory broke down rather badly if you applied it to Parliamentary debates. At her own dinner table its success was usually triumphantly vindicated.

"Who else is to be there?" Francesca asked, with some pardonable misgiving.

"Courtenay Youghal. He'll probably sit next to you, so you'd better think out a lot of annihilating remarks in readiness. And Elaine de Frey."

"I don't think I've heard of her. Who is she?"

THE UNBEARABLE BASSINGTON

"Nobody in particular, but rather nice looking in a solemn sort of way, and almost indecently rich."

"Marry her" was the advice which sprang to Francesca's lips, but she choked it back with a salted almond, having a rare perception of the fact that words are sometimes given to us to defeat our purposes.

"Caroline has probably marked her down for Toby or one of the grand-nephews," she said carelessly; "a little money would be rather useful in that quarter, I imagine."

Comus tucked in his underlip with just the shade of pugnacity that she wanted to see.

An advantageous marriage was so obviously the most sensible course for him to embark on that she scarcely dared to hope that he would seriously entertain it; yet there was just a chance that if he got as far as the flirtation stage with an attractive (and attracted) girl who was also an heiress, the sheer perversity of his nature might carry him on to more definite courtship, if only from the desire to thrust other more genuinely enamoured suitors into the background. It was a forlorn hope; so forlorn that the idea even crossed her mind of throwing herself on the mercy of her *bête noire*, Courtenay Youghal, and trying to enlist the influence which he seemed to possess over Comus for the purpose of furthering her hurriedly conceived project. Anyhow, the dinner promised to be more interesting than she had originally anticipated.

Lady Caroline was a professed Socialist in politics, chiefly, it was believed, because she was thus enabled to disagree with most of the Liberals and Conservatives, and all the Socialists of the day. She did not permit her Socialism, however, to penetrate below stairs; her cook and butler had every encouragement to be Individualists. Francesca, who was a keen and intelligent food critic, harboured no misgivings as to her hostess's kitchen and cellar departments; some of the human side-dishes at the feast gave her more ground for uneasiness. Courtenay Youghal, for instance, would probably be brilliantly silent; her brother Henry would almost certainly be the reverse.

The dinner party was a large one, and Francesca arrived

late with little time to take preliminary stock of the guests; a card with the name "Miss de Frey," immediately opposite her own place at the other side of the table, indicated, however, the whereabouts of the heiress. It was characteristic of Francesca that she first carefully read the menu from end to end, and then indulged in an equally careful, though less open, scrutiny of the girl who sat opposite her, the girl who was nobody in particular, but whose income was everything that could be desired. She was pretty in a restrained nut-brown fashion, and had a look of grave reflective calm that probably masked a speculative unsettled temperament. Her pose, if one wished to be critical, was just a little too elaborately careless. She wore some excellently set rubies with that indefinable air of having more at home that is so difficult to improvise. Francesca was distinctly pleased with her survey.

"You seem interested in your *vis-à-vis*," said Courtenay Youghal.

"I almost think I've seen her before," said Francesca; "her face seems familiar to me."

"The narrow gallery at the Louvre: attributed to Leonardo da Vinci," said Youghal.

"Of course," said Francesca, her feelings divided between satisfaction at capturing an elusive impression and annoyance that Youghal should have been her helper. A stronger tinge of annoyance possessed her when she heard the voice of Henry Greech raised in painful prominence at Lady Caroline's end of the table.

"I called on the Trudhams yesterday," he announced; "it was their Silver Wedding, you know, at least the day before was. Such lots of silver presents, quite a show. Of course there were a great many duplicates, but still, very nice to have. I think they were very pleased to get so many."

"We must not grudge them their show of presents after their twenty-five years of married life," said Lady Caroline gently; "it is the silver lining to their cloud."

A third of the guests present were related to the Trudhams.

"Lady Caroline is beginning well," murmured Courtenay Youghal.

"I should hardly call twenty-five years of married life a cloud," said Henry Greech lamely.

"Don't let's talk about married life," said a tall handsome woman, who looked like some modern painter's conception of the goddess Bellona; "it's my misfortune to write eternally about husbands and wives and their variants. My public expects it of me. I do so envy journalists who can write about plagues and strikes and Anarchist plots, and other pleasing things, instead of being tied down to one stale old topic."

"Who is that woman and what has she written?" Francesca asked Youghal; she dimly remembered having seen her at one of Serena Golackly's gatherings, surrounded by a little court of admirers.

"I forget her name; she has a villa at San Remo or Mentone, or somewhere where one does have villas, and plays an extraordinary good game of bridge. Also she has the reputation, rather rare in your sex, of being a wonderfully sound judge of wine."

"But what has she written?"

"Oh, several novels of the thinnish ice order. Her last one, *The Woman who wished it was Wednesday*, has been banned at all the libraries. I expect you've read it."

"I don't see why you should think so," said Francesca coldly.

"Only because Comus lent me your copy yesterday," said Youghal. He threw back his handsome head and gave her a sidelong glance of quizzical amusement. He knew that she hated his intimacy with Comus, and he was secretly rather proud of his influence over the boy, shallow and negative though he knew it to be. It had been, on his part, an unsought intimacy, and it would probably fall to pieces the moment he tried seriously to take up the *rôle* of mentor. The fact that Comus's mother openly disapproved of the friendship gave it perhaps its chief interest in the young politician's eyes.

Francesca turned her attention to her brother's end of the table. Henry Greech had willingly availed himself of the invitation to leave the subject of married life, and had launched forthwith into the equally well-worn theme of current politics.

He was not a person who was in much demand for public meetings, and the House showed no great impatience to hear his views on the topics of the moment; its impatience, indeed, was manifested rather in the opposite direction. Hence he was prone to unburden himself of accumulated political wisdom as occasion presented itself—sometimes, indeed, to assume an occasion that was hardly visible to the naked intelligence.

"Our opponents are engaged in a hopelessly uphill struggle, and they know it," he chirruped defiantly; "they've become possessed, like the Gadarene swine, with a whole legion of——"

"Surely the Gadarene swine went down-hill?" put in Lady Caroline in a gently inquiring voice.

Henry Greech hastily abandoned simile and fell back on platitude and the safer kinds of fact.

Francesca did not regard her brother's views on statecraft either in the light of gospel or revelation; as Comus once remarked, they more usually suggested exodus. In the present instance she found distraction in a renewed scrutiny of the girl opposite her, who seemed to be only moderately interested in the conversational efforts of the diners on either side of her. Comus, who was looking and talking his best, was sitting at the farther end of the table, and Francesca was quick to notice in which direction the girl's glances were continually straying. Once or twice the eyes of the young people met and a swift flush of pleasure and a half-smile that spoke of good understanding came to the heiress's face. It did not need the gift of the traditional intuition of her sex to enable Francesca to guess that the girl with the desirable banking account was already considerably attracted by the lively young Pagan who had, when he cared to practise it, such an art of winning admiration. For the first time for many, many months Francesca saw her son's prospects in a rose-coloured setting, and she began, unconsciously, to wonder exactly how much wealth was summed up in the expressive label "almost indecently rich." A wife with a really large fortune and a correspondingly big dower of character and ambition, might, perhaps, succeed in turning Comus's latent energies into a groove which would provide him, if not with a career, at least with an oc-

cupation, and the young serious face opposite looked as if its
owner lacked neither character nor ambition. Francesca's speculations took a more personal turn. Out of the well-filled coffers
with which her imagination was toying, an inconsiderable sum
might eventually be devoted to the leasing, or even perhaps
the purchase of, the house in Blue Street when the present
convenient arrangement should have come to an end, and
Francesca and the Van der Meulen would not be obliged to
seek fresh quarters.

A woman's voice, talking in a discreet undertone on the
other side of Courtenay Youghal, broke in on her bridge-
building.

"Tons of money and really very presentable. Just the wife
for a rising young politician. Go in and win her before she's
snapped up by some fortune hunter."

Youghal and his instructress in worldly wisdom were looking straight across the table at the Leonardo da Vinci girl with
the grave reflective eyes and the over-emphasized air of repose.
Francesca felt a quick throb of anger against her matchmaking
neighbour; why, she asked herself, must some women, with
no end or purpose of their own to serve, except the sheer love
of meddling in the affairs of others, plunge their hands into
plots and schemings of this sort, in which the happiness of
more than one person was concerned? And more clearly than
ever she realized how thoroughly she detested Courtenay Youghal. She had disliked him as an evil influence, setting before
her son an example of showy ambition that he was not in the
least likely to follow, and providing him with a model of extravagant dandyism that he was only too certain to copy. In
her heart she knew that Comus would have embarked just
as surely on his present course of idle self-indulgence if he
had never known of the existence of Youghal, but she chose
to regard that young man as her son's evil genius, and now
he seemed likely to justify more than ever the character she
had fastened on to him. For once in his life Comus appeared
to have an idea of behaving sensibly and making some use of
his opportunities, and almost at the same moment Courtenay
Youghal arrived on the scene as a possible and very dangerous

rival. Against the good looks and fitful powers of fascination
that Comus could bring into the field, the young politician
could match half a dozen dazzling qualities which would go
far to recommend him in the eyes of a woman of the world,
still more in those of a young girl in search of an ideal. Good-
looking in his own way, if not on such showy lines as Comus,
always well turned-out, witty, self-confident without being
bumptious, with a conspicuous Parliamentary career alongside
him, and Heaven knew what else in front of him, Courtenay
Youghal certainly was not a rival whose chances could be held
very lightly. Francesca laughed bitterly to herself as she remembered that a few hours ago she had entertained the idea
of begging for his good offices in helping on Comus's wooing.
One consolation, at least, she found for herself: if Youghal
really meant to step in and try and cut out his young friend,
the latter at any rate had snatched a useful start. Comus had
mentioned Miss de Frey at luncheon that day, casually and
dispassionately; if the subject of the dinner guests had not come
up he would probably not have mentioned her at all. But they
were obviously already very good friends. It was part and par-
cel of the state of domestic tension at Blue Street that Francesca should only have come to know of this highly interesting
heiress by an accidental sorting of guests at a dinner party.

Lady Caroline's voice broke in on her reflections; it was a
gentle purring voice, that possessed an uncanny quality of being
able to make itself heard down the longest dinner table.

"The dear Archdeacon is getting *so* absent-minded. He read
a list of box-holders for the opera as the First Lesson the other
Sunday, instead of the families and lots of the tribes of Israel
that entered Canaan. Fortunately no one noticed the mistake."

CHAPTER V

ON a conveniently secluded bench facing the Northern
Pheasantry in the Zoological Society's Gardens, Regent's
Park, Courtenay Youghal sat immersed in mature flirtation
with a lady, who, though certainly young in fact and appear-

ance, was some four or five years his senior. When he was a schoolboy of sixteen, Molly McQuade had personally conducted him to the Zoo and stood him dinner afterwards at Kettner's, and whenever the two of them happened to be in town on the anniversary of that bygone festivity they religiously repeated the programme in its entirety. Even the menu of the dinner was adhered to as nearly as possible; the original selection of food and wine that schoolboy exuberance, tempered by schoolboy shyness, had pitched on those many years ago, confronted Youghal on those occasions, as a drowning man's past life is said to rise up and parade itself in his last moments of consciousness.

The flirtation which was thus perennially restored to its old-time footing owed its longevity more to the enterprising solicitude of Miss McQuade than to any conscious sentimental effort on the part of Youghal himself. Molly McQuade was known to her neighbours in a minor hunting shire as a hard-riding conventionally unconventional type of young woman, who came naturally into the classification, "a good sort." She was just sufficiently good-looking, sufficiently reticent about her own illnesses, when she had any, and sufficiently appreciative of her neighbours' gardens, children and hunters to be generally popular. Most men liked her, and the percentage of women who disliked her was not inconveniently high. One of these days, it was assumed, she would marry a brewer or a Master of Otter Hounds, and, after a brief interval, be known to the world as the mother of a boy or two at Malvern or some similar seat of learning. The romantic side of her nature was altogether unguessed by the countryside.

Her romances were mostly in serial form, and suffered perhaps in fervour from their disconnected course what they gained in length of days. Her affectionate interest in the several young men who figured in her affairs of the heart was perfectly honest, and she certainly made no attempt either to conceal their separate existences, or to play them off one against the other. Neither could it be said that she was a husband hunter; she had made up her mind what sort of man she was likely to marry, and her forecast did not differ very widely from that formed by her local acquaintances. If her married life were eventually to turn out a failure, at least she looked forward to it with very moderate expectations. Her love affairs she put on a very different footing, and apparently they were the all-absorbing element in her life. She possessed the happily constituted temperament which enables a man or woman to be a "pluralist," and to observe the sage precaution of not putting all one's eggs into one basket. Her demands were not exacting; she required of her affinity that he should be young, good-looking, and at least moderately amusing; she would have preferred him to be invariably faithful, but, with her own example before her, she was prepared for the probability, bordering on certainty, that he would be nothing of the sort. The philosophy of the "Garden of Kama" was the compass by which she steered her barque, and thus far, if she had encountered some storms and buffeting, she had at least escaped being either ship-wrecked or becalmed.

Courtenay Youghal had not been designed by Nature to fulfil the *rôle* of an ardent or devoted lover, and he scrupulously respected the limits which Nature had laid down. For Molly, however, he had a certain responsive affection. She had always obviously admired him, and at the same time she never beset him with crude flattery; the principal reason why the flirtation had stood the test of so many years was the fact that it only flared into active existence at convenient intervals. In an age when the telephone has undermined almost every fastness of human privacy, and the sanctity of one's seclusion depends often on the ability for tactful falsehood shown by a club page-boy, Youghal was duly appreciative of the circumstance that his lady fair spent a large part of the year pursuing foxes, in lieu of pursuing him. Also the honestly admitted fact that, in her human hunting, she rode after more than one quarry, made the inevitable break-up of the affair a matter to which both could look forward without a sense of coming embarrassment and recrimination. When the time for gathering ye rosebuds should be over, neither of them could accuse the other of having wrecked his or her entire life. At the most they would only have disorganized a week-end.

On this particular afternoon, when old reminiscences had been gone through, and the intervening gossip of past months duly recounted, a lull in the conversation made itself rather obstinately felt. Molly had already guessed that matters were about to slip into a new phase; the affair had reached maturity long ago, and a new phase must be in the nature of a wane.

"You're a clever brute," she said suddenly, with an air of affectionate regret; "I always knew you'd get on in the House, but I hardly expected you to come to the front so soon."

"I'm coming to the front," admitted Youghal judicially; "the problem is, shall I be able to stay there? Unless something happens in the financial line before long, I don't see how I'm to stay in Parliament at all. Economy is out of the question. It would open people's eyes, I fancy, if they knew how little I exist on as it is. And I'm living so far beyond my income that we may almost be said to be living apart."

"It will have to be a rich wife, I suppose," said Molly slowly; "that's the worst of success, it imposes so many conditions. I rather knew, from something in your manner, that you were drifting that way."

Youghal said nothing in the way of contradiction; he gazed steadfastly at the aviary in front of him as though exotic pheasants were for the moment the most absorbing study in the world. As a matter of fact, his mind was centred on the image of Elaine de Frey, with her clear untroubled eyes and her Leonardo da Vinci air. He was wondering whether he was likely to fall into a frame of mind concerning her which would be in the least like falling in love.

"I shall mind horribly," continued Molly, after a pause, "but, of course, I have always known that something of the sort would have to happen one of these days. When a man goes into politics he can't call his soul his own, and I suppose his heart becomes an impersonal possession in the same way."

"Most people who know me would tell you that I haven't got a heart," said Youghal.

"I've often felt inclined to agree with them," said Molly;

"and then, now and again, I think you have a heart tucked away somewhere."

"I hope I have," said Youghal, "because I'm trying to break to you the fact that I think I'm falling in love with somebody."

Molly McQuade turned sharply to look at her companion, who still fixed his gaze on the pheasant run in front of him.

"Don't tell me you're losing your head over somebody useless, some one without money," she said; "I don't think I could stand that."

For the moment she feared that Courtenay's selfishness might have taken an unexpected turn, in which ambition had given way to the fancy of the hour; he might be going to sacrifice his Parliamentary career for a life of stupid lounging in momentarily attractive company. He quickly undeceived her.

"She's got heaps of money."

Molly gave a grunt of relief. Her affection for Courtenay had produced the anxiety which underlay her first question; a natural jealousy prompted the next one.

"Is she young and pretty and all that sort of thing, or is she just a good sort with a sympathetic manner and nice eyes? As a rule that's the kind that goes with a lot of money."

"Young and quite good-looking in her way, and a distinct style of her own. Some people would call her beautiful. As a political hostess I should think she'd be splendid. I imagine I'm rather in love with her."

"And is she in love with you?"

Youghal threw back his head with the slight assertive movement that Molly knew and liked.

"She's a girl who I fancy would let judgment influence her a lot. And without being stupidly conceited I think I may say she might do worse than throw herself away on me. I'm young and quite good-looking, and I'm making a name for myself in the House; she'll be able to read all sorts of nice and horrid things about me in the papers at breakfast-time. I can be brilliantly amusing at times, and I understand the value of silence; there is no fear that I shall ever degenerate into that fearsome thing—a cheerful talkative husband. For a girl with money and social ambitions I should think I was rather a good thing."

"You are certainly in love, Courtenay," said Molly, "but it's the old love and not a new one. I'm rather glad. I should have hated to have you head-over-heels in love with a pretty woman, even for a short time. You'll be much happier as it is. And I'm going to put all my feelings in the background, and tell you to go in and win. You've got to marry a rich woman, and if she's nice and will make a good hostess, so much the better for everybody. You'll be happier in your married life than I shall be in mine, when it comes; you'll have other interests to absorb you. I shall just have the garden and dairy and nursery and lending library, as like as two peas to all the gardens and dairies and nurseries for hundreds of miles round. You won't care for your wife enough to be worried every time she has a finger-ache, and you'll like her well enough to be pleased to meet her sometimes at your own house. I shouldn't wonder if you were quite happy. She will probably be miserable, but any woman who married you would be."

There was a short pause; they were both staring at the pheasant cages. Then Molly spoke again, with the swift nervous tone of a general who is hurriedly altering the disposition of his forces for a strategic retreat.

"When you are safely married and honeymooned and all that sort of thing, and have put your wife through her paces as a political hostess, some time, when the House isn't sitting, you must come down by yourself, and do a little hunting with us. Will you? It won't be quite the same as old times, but it will be something to look forward to when I'm reading the endless paragraphs about your fashionable political wedding."

"You're looking forward pretty far," laughed Youghal; "the lady may take your view as to the probable unhappiness of a future shared with me, and I may have to content myself with penurious political bachelorhood. Anyhow, the present is still with us. We dine at Kettner's tonight, don't we?"

"Rather," said Molly, "though it will be more or less a throat-lumpy feast as far as I am concerned. We shall have to drink to the health of the future Mrs. Youghal. By the way, it's rather characteristic of you that you haven't told me who

she is, and of me that I haven't asked. And now, like a dear
boy, trot away and leave me. I haven't got to say good-bye to
you yet, but I'm going to take a quiet farewell of the Pheasantry. We've had some jolly good talks, you and I, sitting on
this seat, haven't we? And I know, as well as I know anything,
that this is the last of them. Eight o'clock tonight, as punctually
as possible."

She watched his retreating figure with eyes that grew slowly
misty; he had been such a jolly comely boy-friend, and they
had had such good times together. The mist deepened on her
lashes as she looked round at the familiar rendezvous where
they had so often kept tryst since the day when they had first
come there together, he a schoolboy and she but lately out of
her teens. For the moment she felt herself in the thrall of a
very real sorrow.

Then, with the admirable energy of one who is only in
town for a fleeting fortnight, she raced away to have tea with
a world-faring naval admirer at his club. Pluralism is a merciful narcotic.

CHAPTER VI

ELAINE DE FREY sat at ease—at bodily ease, at any
rate—in a low wicker chair placed under the shade of a
group of cedars in the heart of a stately spacious garden that
had almost made up its mind to be a park. The shallow stone
basin of an old fountain, on whose wide ledge a leaden-
moulded otter for ever preyed on a leaden salmon, filled a conspicuous place in the immediate foreground. Around its rim
ran an inscription in Latin, warning mortal man that time
flows as swiftly as water and exhorting him to make the most
of his hours; after which piece of Jacobean moralizing it set
itself shamelessly to beguile all who might pass that way into
an abandonment of contemplative repose. On all sides of it a
stretch of smooth turf spread away, broken up here and there
by groups of dwarfish chestnut and mulberry trees, whose
leaves and branches cast a laced pattern of shade beneath them.
On one side the lawn sloped gently down to a small lake,

whereon floated a quartet of swans, their movements suggestive of a certain mournful listlessness, as though a weary dignity of caste held them back from the joyous bustling life of
the lesser waterfowl. Elaine liked to imagine that they re-
embodied the souls of unhappy boys who had been forced by
family interests to become high ecclesiastical dignitaries and
had grown prematurely Right Reverend. A low stone balus-
trade fenced part of the shore of the lake, making a miniature
terrace above its level, and here roses grew in a rich multitude.
Other rose bushes, carefully pruned and tended, formed little
oases of colour and perfume amid the restful green of the
sward, and in the distance the eye caught the variegated blaze
of a many-hued hedge of rhododendron. With these favoured
exceptions flowers were hard to find in this well-ordered garden; the misguided tyranny of staring geranium beds and beflowered archways leading to nowhere, so dear to the suburban
gardener, found no expression here. Magnificent Amherst
pheasants, whose plumage challenged and almost shamed the
peacock on his own ground, stepped to and fro over the emerald turf with the assured self-conscious pride of reigning sul-
tans. It was a garden where summer seemed a part-proprietor
rather than a hurried visitor.

By the side of Elaine's chair under the shadow of the cedars
a wicker table was set out with the paraphernalia of afternoon
tea. On some cushions at her feet reclined Courtenay Youghal,
smoothly preened and youthfully elegant, the personification
of decorative repose; equally decorative, but with the showy
restlessness of a dragonfly. Comus disported his flannelled person over a considerable span of the available foreground.

The intimacy existing between the two young men had
suffered no immediate dislocation from the circumstance that
they were tacitly paying court to the same lady. It was an intimacy founded not in the least on friendship or community of
tastes and ideas, but owed its existence to the fact that each
was amused and interested by the other. Youghal found Comus, for the time being at any rate, just as amusing and interesting as a rival for Elaine's favour as he had been in the *rôle*
of scapegrace boy-about-town; Comus for his part did not

wish to lose touch with Youghal, who among other attractions possessed the recommendation of being under the ban of Comus's mother. She disapproved, it is true, of a great many of her son's friends and associates, but this particular one was a special and persistent source of irritation to her from the fact that he figured prominently and more or less successfully in the public life of the day. There was something peculiarly exasperating in reading a brilliant and incisive attack on the Government's rash handling of public expenditure delivered by a young man who encouraged her son in every imaginable extravagance. The actual extent of Youghal's influence over the boy was of the slightest; Comus was quite capable of deriving encouragement to rash outlay and frivolous conversation from an anchorite or an East End parson if he had been thrown into close companionship with such an individual. Francesca, however, exercised a mother's privilege in assuming her son's bachelor associates to be industrious in labouring to achieve his undoing. Therefore the young politician was a source of unconcealed annoyance to her, and in the same degree as she expressed her disapproval of him Comus was careful to maintain and parade the intimacy. Its existence, or rather its continued existence, was one of the things that faintly puzzled the young lady whose sought-for favour might have been expected to furnish an occasion for its rapid dissolution.

With two suitors, one of whom at least she found markedly attractive, courting her at the same moment, Elaine should have had reasonable cause for being on good terms with the world, and with herself in particular. Happiness was not, however, at this auspicious moment, her dominant mood. The grave calm of her face masked as usual a certain degree of grave perturbation. A succession of well-meaning governesses and a plentiful supply of moralizing aunts on both sides of her family, had impressed on her young mind the theoretical fact that wealth is a great responsibility. The consciousness of her responsibility set her continually wondering, not as to her own fitness to discharge her "stewardship," but as to the motives and merits of people with whom she came in contact. The knowledge that there was so much in the world that she could buy, invited speculation as to how much there was that was worth buying. Gradually she had come to regard her mind as a sort of appeal court before whose secret sittings were examined and judged the motives and actions, the motives especially, of the world in general. In her schoolroom days she had sat in conscientious judgment on the motives that guided or misguided Charles and Cromwell and Monck, Wallenstein and Savonarola. In her present stage she was equally occupied in examining the political sincerity of the Secretary for Foreign Affairs, the good-faith of a honey-tongued but possibly loyal-hearted waiting-maid, and the disinterestedness of a whole circle of indulgent and flattering acquaintances. Even more absorbing, and, in her eyes, more urgently necessary, was the task of dissecting and appraising the characters of the two young men who were favouring her with their attentions. And herein lay cause for much thinking and some perturbation. Youghal, for example, might have baffled a more experienced observer of human nature. Elaine was too clever to confound his dandyism with foppishness or self-advertisement. He admired his own toilet effect in a mirror from a genuine sense of pleasure in a thing good to look upon, just as he would feel a sensuous appreciation of the sight of a well-bred, well-matched, well-turned-out pair of horses. Behind his careful political flippancy and cynicism one might also detect a certain careless sincerity, which would probably in the long run save him from moderate success, and turn him into one of the brilliant failures of his day. Beyond this it was difficult to form an exact appreciation of Courtenay Youghal, and Elaine, who liked to have her impressions distinctly labelled and pigeon-holed, was perpetually scrutinizing the outer surface of his characteristics and utterances, like a baffled art critic vainly searching beneath the varnish and scratches of a doubtfully assigned picture for an enlightening signature. The young man added to her perplexities by his deliberate policy of never trying to show himself in a favourable light even when most anxious to impart a favourable impression. He preferred that people should hunt for his good qualities, and merely took very good care that as far as possible they should never draw blank; even in the matter of selfishness, which was the anchor-sheet of his existence, he contrived to be noted, and justly noted, for doing remarkably unselfish things. As a ruler he would have been reasonably popular; as a husband he would probably be unendurable.

Comus was to a certain extent as great a mystification as Youghal, but here Elaine was herself responsible for some of the perplexity which enshrouded his character in her eyes. She had taken more than a passing fancy for the boy—for the boy as he might be, that was to say—and she was desperately unwilling to see him and appraise him as he really was. Thus the mental court of appeal was constantly engaged in examining witnesses as to character, most of whom signally failed to give any testimony which would support the favourable judgment which the tribunal was so anxious to arrive at. A woman with wider experience of the world's ways and shortcomings would probably have contented herself with an endeavour to find out whether her liking for the boy outweighed her dislike of his characteristics; Elaine took her judgments too seriously to approach the matter from such a simple and convenient standpoint. The fact that she was much more than half in love with Comus made it dreadfully important that she should discover him to have a lovable soul, and Comus, it must be confessed, did little to help forward the discovery.

"At any rate he is honest," she would observe to herself, after some outspoken admission of unprincipled conduct on his part, and then she would ruefully recall certain episodes in which he had figured, from which honesty had been conspicuously absent. What she tried to label honesty in his candour was probably only a cynical defiance of the laws of right and wrong.

"You look more than usually thoughtful this afternoon," said Comus to her, "as if you had invented this summer day and were trying to think out improvements."

"If I had the power to create improvements anywhere I think I should begin with you," retorted Elaine.

"I'm sure it's much better to leave me as I am," protested Comus; "you're like a relative of mine up in Argyllshire, who spends his time producing improved breeds of sheep and pigs and chickens. So patronizing and irritating to the Almighty, I should think, to go about putting superior finishing touches to Creation."

Elaine frowned, and then laughed, and finally gave a little sigh.

"It's not easy to talk sense to you," she said.

"Whatever else you take in hand," said Youghal, "you must never improve this garden. It's what our idea of heaven might be like if the Jews hadn't invented one for us on totally different lines. It's dreadful that we should accept them as the impresarios of our religious dreamland instead of the Greeks."

"You are not very fond of the Jews," said Elaine.

"I've travelled and lived a good deal in Eastern Europe," said Youghal.

"It seems largely a question of geography," said Elaine; "in England no one really is anti-Semitic."

Youghal shook his head. "I know a great many Jews who are."

Servants had quietly, almost reverently, placed tea and its accessories on the wicker table, and quietly receded from the landscape. Elaine sat like a grave young goddess about to dispense some mysterious potion to her devotees. Her mind was still sitting in judgment on the Jewish question.

Comus scrambled to his feet.

"It's too hot for tea," he said; "I shall go and feed the swans."

And he walked off with a little silver basket-dish containing brown bread-and-butter.

Elaine laughed quietly.

"It's so like Comus," she said, "to go off with our one dish of bread-and-butter."

Youghal chuckled responsively. It was an undoubted opportunity for him to put in some disparaging criticism of Comus, and Elaine sat alert in readiness to judge the critic and reserve judgment on the criticized.

"His selfishness is splendid but absolutely futile," said Youghal; "now my selfishness is commonplace, but always thoroughly practical and calculated. He will have great diffi-

culty in getting the swans to accept his offering, and he incurs
the odium of reducing us to a bread-and-butterless condition.
Incidentally, he will get very hot."

Elaine again had the sense of being thoroughly baffled. If
Youghal had said anything unkind it was about himself.

"If my cousin Suzette had been here," she observed, with
the shadow of a malicious smile on her lips, "I believe she
would have gone into a flood of tears at the loss of her bread-
and-butter, and Comus would have figured ever after in her
mind as something black and destroying and hateful. In fact,
I don't really know why we took our loss so unprotestingly."

"For two reasons," said Youghal; "you are rather fond of
Comus. And I—am not very fond of bread-and-butter."

The jesting remark brought a throb of pleasure to Elaine's
heart. She had known full well that she cared for Comus, but
now that Courtenay Youghal had openly proclaimed the fact
as something unchallenged and understood matters seemed
placed at once on a more advanced footing. The warm sunlit
garden grew suddenly into a heaven that held the secret of
eternal happiness. Youth and comeliness would always walk
here, under the low-boughed mulberry trees, as unchanging as
the leaden otter that for ever preyed on the leaden salmon on
the edge of the old fountain, and somehow the lovers would
always wear the aspect of herself and the boy who was talking
to the four white swans by the water steps. Youghal was
right; this was the real heaven of one's dreams and longings,
immeasurably removed from that Rue de la Paix Paradise
about which one professed utterly insincere hankerings in
places of public worship. Elaine drank her tea in a happy silence;
besides being a brilliant talker Youghal understood the rarer
art of being a non-talker on occasion.

Comus came back across the grass swinging the empty
basket-dish in his hand.

"Swans were very pleased," he cried gaily, "and said they
hoped I would keep the bread-and-butter dish as a souvenir of
a happy tea-party. I may really have it, mayn't I?" he continued in an anxious voice; "it will do to keep studs and things
in. You don't want it."

"It's got the family crest on it," said Elaine. Some of the happiness had died out of her eyes.

"I'll have that scratched off and my own put on," said Comus.

"It's been in the family for generations," protested Elaine, who did not share Comus's view that because you were rich your lesser possessions could have no value in your eyes.

"I want it dreadfully," said Comus sulkily, "and you've heaps of other things to put bread-and-butter in."

For the moment he was possessed by an overmastering desire to keep the dish at all costs; a look of greedy determination dominated his face, and he had not for an instant relaxed his grip of the coveted object.

Elaine was genuinely angry by this time, and was busily telling herself that it was absurd to be put out over such a trifle; at the same moment a sense of justice was telling her that Comus was displaying a good deal of rather shabby selfishness. And somehow her chief anxiety at the moment was to keep Courtenay Youghal from seeing that she was angry.

"I know you don't really want it, so I'm going to keep it," persisted Comus.

"It's too hot to argue," said Elaine.

"Happy mistress of your destinies," laughed Youghal; "you can suit your disputations to the desired time and temperature. I have to go and argue, or what is worse, listen to other people's arguments, in a hot and doctored atmosphere suitable to an invalid lizard."

"You haven't got to argue about a bread-and-butter dish," said Elaine.

"Chiefly about bread-and-butter," said Youghal; "our great preoccupation is other people's bread-and-butter. They earn or produce the material, but we busy ourselves with making rules how it shall be cut up, and the size of the slices, and how much butter shall go on how much bread. That is what is called legislation. If we could only make rules as to how the bread-and-butter should be digested we should be quite happy."

Elaine had been brought up to regard Parliaments as something to be treated with cheerful solemnity, like illness or family reunions. Youghal's flippant disparagement of the career in which he was involved did not, however, jar on her suscepti-bilities. She knew him to be not only a lively and effective debater but an industrious worker on committees. If he made light of his labours, at least he afforded no one else a loophole for doing so. And certainly the Parliamentary atmosphere was not uninviting on this hot afternoon.

"When must you go?" she asked sympathetically.

Youghal looked ruefully at his watch. Before he could an-swer, a cheerful hoot came through the air, as of an owl joy-ously challenging the sunlight with a foreboding of the coming night. He sprang laughing to his feet.

"Listen! My summons back to my galley," he cried. "The Gods have given me an hour in this enchanted garden, so I must not complain."

Then in a lower voice he almost whispered, "It's the Persian debate tonight."

It was the one hint he had given in the midst of his talking and laughing that he was really keenly enthralled in the work that lay before him. It was the one little intimate touch that gave Elaine the knowledge that he cared for her opinion of his work.

Comus, who had emptied his cigarette-case, became sud-denly clamorous at the prospect of being temporarily stranded without a smoke. Youghal took the last remaining cigarette from his own case and gravely bisected it.

"Friendship could go no farther," he observed, as he gave one-half to the doubtfully appeased Comus, and lit the other himself.

"There are heaps more in the hall," said Elaine.

"It was only done for the Saint Martin of Tours effect," said Youghal; "I hate smoking when I'm rushing through the air. Good-bye."

The departing galley-slave stepped forth into the sunlight, radiant and confident. A few minutes later Elaine could see glimpses of his white car as it rushed past the rhododendron bushes. He woos best who leaves first, particularly if he goes forth to battle or the semblance of battle.

Somehow Elaine's garden of Eternal Youth had already become clouded in its imagery. The girl-figure who walked in it was still distinctly and unchangingly herself, but her companion was more blurred and undefined, as a picture that has been superimposed on another.

Youghal sped townward well satisfied with himself. Tomorrow, he reflected, Elaine would read his speech in her morning paper, and he knew in advance that it was not going to be one of his worst efforts. He knew almost exactly where the punctuations of laughter and applause would burst in, he knew that nimble fingers in the Press Gallery would be taking down each gibe and argument as he flung it at the impassive Minister confronting him, and that the fair lady of his desire would be able to judge what manner of young man this was who spent his afternoon in her garden, lazily chaffing himself and his world.

And he further reflected, with an amused chuckle, that she would be vividly reminded of Comus for days to come, when she took her afternoon tea, and saw the bread-and-butter reposing in an unaccustomed dish.

CHAPTER VII

TOWARDS four o'clock on a hot afternoon Francesca stepped out from a shop entrance near the Piccadilly end of Bond Street and ran almost into the arms of Merla Blathlington. The afternoon seemed to get instantly hotter. Merla was one of those human flies that buzz; in crowded streets, at bazaars and in warm weather, she attained to the proportions of a human bluebottle. Lady Caroline Benaresq had openly predicted that a special fly-paper was being reserved for her accommodation in another world; others, however, held the opinion that she would be miraculously multiplied in a future state, and that four or more Merla Blathlingtons, according to deserts, would be in perpetual and unremitting attendance on each lost soul.

"Here we are," she cried, with a glad eager buzz, "popping

in and out of shops like rabbits; not that rabbits do pop in
and out of shops very extensively."

It was evidently one of her bluebottle days.

"Don't you love Bond Street?" she gabbled on. "There's
something so unusual and distinctive about it; no other street
anywhere else is quite like it. Don't you know those ikons and
images and things scattered up and down Europe, that are supposed to have been painted or carved, as the case may be, by
St. Luke or Zaccheus, or somebody of that sort; I always
like to think that some notable person of those times designed
Bond Street. St. Paul, perhaps. He travelled about a lot."

"Not in Middlesex, though," said Francesca.

"One can't be sure," persisted Merla; "when one wanders
about as much as he did one gets mixed up and forgets where
one *has* been. I can never remember whether I've been to the
Tyrol twice and St. Moritz once, or the other way about; I
always have to ask my maid. And there's something about the
name Bond that suggests St. Paul; didn't he write a lot about
the bond and the free?"

"I fancy he wrote in Hebrew or Greek," objected Francesca; "the word wouldn't have the least resemblance."

"So dreadfully non-committal to go about pamphleteering
in those bizarre languages," complained Merla; "that's what
makes all those people so elusive. As soon as you try to pin
them down to a definite statement about anything you're told
that some vitally important word has fifteen other meanings in
the original. I wonder our Cabinet Ministers and politicians
don't adopt a sort of dog-Latin or Esperanto jargon to deliver
their speeches in; what a lot of subsequent explaining away
would be saved! But to go back to Bond Street—not that
we've left it——"

"I'm afraid I must leave it now," said Francesca, preparing
to turn up Grafton Street. "Good-bye."

"Must you be going? Come and have tea somewhere. I
know of a cozy little place where one can talk undisturbed."

Francesca repressed a shudder and pleaded an urgent engagement.

"I know where you're going," said Merla, with the resentful buzz of a bluebottle that finds itself thwarted by the cold unreasoning resistance of a windowpane. "You're going to play bridge at Serena Golackly's. She never asks me to her bridge parties."

Francesca shuddered openly this time; the prospect of having to play bridge anywhere in the near neighbourhood of Merla's voice was not one that could be contemplated with ordinary calmness.

"Good-bye," she said again firmly, and passed out of earshot; it was rather like leaving the machinery section of an exhibition. Merla's diagnosis of her destination had been a correct one; Francesca made her way slowly through the hot streets in the direction of Serena Golackly's house on the far side of Berkeley Square. To the blessed certainty of finding a game of bridge, she hopefully added the possibility of hearing some fragments of news which might prove interesting and enlightening. And of enlightenment on a particular subject, in which she was acutely and personally interested, she stood in some need. Comus of late had been provokingly reticent as to his movements and doings; partly, perhaps, because it was his nature to be provoking, partly because the daily bickerings over money matters were gradually choking other forms of conversation. Francesca had seen him once or twice in the Park in the desirable company of Elaine de Frey, and from time to time she heard of the young people as having danced together at various houses; on the other hand, she had seen and heard quite as much evidence to connect the heiress's name with that of Courtenay Youghal. Beyond this meagre and conflicting and altogether tantalizing information, her knowledge of the present position of affairs did not go. If either of the young men was seriously "making the running," it was probable that she would hear some sly hint or open comment about it from one of Serena's gossip-laden friends, without having to go out of her way to introduce the subject and unduly disclose her own state of ignorance. And a game of bridge, played for moderately high points, gave ample excuse for convenient lapses into reticence; if questions took an embarrassingly inquisitive turn, one could always find refuge in a defensive spade.

The afternoon was too warm to make bridge a generally popular diversion, and Serena's party was a comparatively small one. Only one table was incomplete when Francesca made her appearance on the scene; at it was seated Serena herself, confronted by Ada Spelvexit, whom every one was wont to explain as "one of the Cheshire Spelvexits," as though any other variety would have been intolerable. Ada Spelvexit was one of those naturally stagnant souls who take infinite pleasure in what are called "movements." "Most of the really great lessons I have learned have been taught me by the Poor," was one of her favourite statements. The one great lesson that the Poor in general would have liked to have taught her, that their kitchens and sickrooms were not unreservedly at her disposal as private lecture halls, she had never been able to assimilate. She was ready to give them unlimited advice as to how they should keep the wolf from their doors, but in return she claimed and enforced for herself the penetrating powers of an east wind or a dust-storm. Her visits among her wealthier acquaintances were equally extensive and enterprising, and hardly more welcome; in country-house parties, while partaking to the fullest extent of the hospitality offered her, she made a practice of unburdening herself of homilies on the evils of leisure and luxury, which did not particularly endear her to her fellow-guests. Hostesses regarded her philosophically as a form of social measles which every one had to have once.

The third prospective player, Francesca noted without any special enthusiasm, was Lady Caroline Benaresq. Lady Caroline was far from being a remarkably good bridge player, but she always managed to domineer mercilessly over any table that was favoured with her presence, and generally managed to win. A domineering player usually inflicts the chief damage and demoralization on his partner; Lady Caroline's special achievement was to harass and demoralize partner and opponents alike.

"Weak and weak," she announced in her gentle voice, as

she cut her hostess for a partner; "I suppose we had better play only five shillings a hundred."

Francesca wondered at the old woman's moderate assessment of the stake, knowing her fondness for highish play and her usual good luck in card holding.

"I don't mind what we play," said Ada Spelvexit, with an incautious parade of elegant indifference; as a matter of fact she was inwardly relieved and rejoicing at the reasonable figure proposed by Lady Caroline, and she would certainly have demurred if a higher stake had been suggested. She was not as a rule a successful player, and money lost at cards was always a poignant bereavement to her.

"Then as you don't mind we'll make it ten shillings a hundred," said Lady Caroline, with the pleased chuckle of one who has spread a net in the sight of a bird and disproved the vanity of the proceeding.

It proved a tiresome ding-dong rubber, with the strength of the cards slightly on Francesca's side, and the luck of the table going mostly the other way. She was too keen a player not to feel a certain absorption in the game once it had started, but she was conscious today of a distracting interest that competed with the momentary importance of leads and discards and declarations. The little accumulations of talk that were unpent during the dealing of the hands became as noteworthy to her alert attention as the play of the hands themselves.

"Yes, quite a small party this afternoon," said Serena, in reply to a seemingly casual remark on Francesca's part; "and two or three non-players, which is unusual on a Wednesday. Canon Besomley was here just before you came; you know, the big preaching man."

"I've been to hear him scold the human race once or twice," said Francesca.

"A strong man with a wonderfully strong message," said Ada Spelvexit, in an impressive and assertive tone.

"The sort of popular pulpiteer who spanks the vices of his age and lunches with them afterwards," said Lady Caroline.

"Hardly a fair summary of the man and his work," protested Ada. "I've been to hear him many times when I've been depressed or discouraged, and I simply can't tell you the impression his words leave——"

"At least you can tell us what you intend to make trumps," broke in Lady Caroline gently.

"Diamonds," pronounced Ada, after a rather flurried survey of her hand.

"Doubled," said Lady Caroline, with increased gentleness, and a few minutes later she was pencilling an addition of twenty-four to her score.

"I stayed with his people down here in Herefordshire last May," said Ada, returning to the unfinished theme of the Canon; "such an exquisite rural retreat, and so restful and healing to the nerves. Real country scenery; apple blossom everywhere."

"Surely only on the apple trees!" said Lady Caroline.

Ada Spelvexit gave up the attempt to reproduce the decorative setting of the Canon's home-life, and fell back on the small but practical consolation of scoring the odd trick in her opponent's declaration of hearts.

"If you had led your highest club to start with, instead of the nine, we should have saved the trick," remarked Lady Caroline to her partner in a tone of coldly gentle reproof; "it's no use, my dear," she continued, as Serena flustered out a halting apology, "no earthly use to attempt to play bridge at one table and try to see and hear what's going on at two or three other tables."

"I can generally manage to attend to more than one thing at a time," said Serena rashly; "I think I must have a sort of double brain."

"Much better to economize and have one really good one," observed Lady Caroline.

"*La belle dame sans merci* scoring a verbal trick or two as usual," said a player at another table in a discreet undertone.

"Did I tell you Sir Edward Roan is coming to my next big evening?" said Serena hurriedly, by way, perhaps, of restoring herself a little in her own esteem.

"Poor dear good Sir Edward! What have you made trumps?" asked Lady Caroline, in one breath.

"Clubs," said Francesca; "and pray, why these adjectives of commiseration?"

Francesca was a Ministerialist by family interest and allegiance, and was inclined to take up the cudgels at the suggested disparagement aimed at the Foreign Secretary.

"He amuses me so much," purred Lady Caroline. Her amusement was usually of the sort that a sporting cat derives from watching the Swedish exercises of a well-spent and carefully thought-out mouse.

"Really? He has been rather a brilliant success at the Foreign Office, you know," said Francesca.

"He reminds one so of a circus elephant—infinitely more intelligent than the people who direct him, but quite content to go on putting his foot down or taking it up as may be required, quite unconcerned whether he steps on a meringue or a hornet's nest in the process of going where he's expected to go."

"How can you say such things!" protested Francesca.

"I can't," said Lady Caroline; "Courtenay Youghal said it in the House last night. Didn't you read the debate? He was really rather in form. I disagree entirely with his point of view, of course, but some of the things he says have just enough truth behind them to redeem them from being merely smart; for instance, his summing up of the Government's attitude towards our embarrassing Colonial Empire in the wistful phrase 'Happy is the country that has no geography.'"

"What an absurdly unjust thing to say!" put in Francesca; "I daresay some of our Party at some time have taken up that attitude, but every one knows that Sir Edward is a sound Imperialist at heart."

"Most politicians are something or other at heart, but no one would be rash enough to insure a politician against heart failure. Particularly when he happens to be in office."

"Anyhow, I don't see that the Opposition leaders would have acted any differently in the present case," said Francesca.

"One should always speak guardedly of the Opposition leaders," said Lady Caroline, in her gentlest voice; "one never knows what a turn in the situation may do for them."

"You mean they may one day be at the head of affairs?" asked Serena briskly.

"I mean they may one day lead the Opposition. One never knows."

Lady Caroline had just remembered that her hostess was on the Opposition side in politics.

Francesca and her partner scored four tricks in clubs; the game stood irresolutely at twenty-four all.

"If you had followed the excellent lyrical advice given to the Maid of Athens and returned my heart we should have made two more tricks and gone game," said Lady Caroline to her partner.

"Mr. Youghal seems pushing himself to the fore of late," remarked Francesca, as Serena took up the cards to deal. Since the young politician's name had been introduced into their conversation the opportunity for turning the talk more directly on him and his affairs was too good to be missed.

"I think he's got a career before him," said Serena; "the House always fills when he's speaking, and that's a good sign. And then he's young and got rather an attractive personality, which is always something in the political world."

"His lack of money will handicap him, unless he can find himself a rich wife or persuade some one to die and leave him a fat legacy," said Francesca; "since M.P.'s have become the recipients of a salary rather more is expected and demanded of them in the expenditure line than before."

"Yes, the House of Commons still remains rather at the opposite pole to the Kingdom of Heaven as regards entrance qualifications," observed Lady Caroline.

"There ought to be no difficulty about Youghal picking up a girl with money," said Serena; "with his prospects he would make an excellent husband for any woman with social ambitions."

And she half sighed, as though she almost regretted that a previous matrimonial arrangement precluded her from entering into the competition on her own account.

Francesca, under an assumption of languid interest, was watching Lady Caroline narrowly for some hint of suppressed knowledge of Youghal's courtship of Miss de Frey.

"Whom are you marrying and giving in marriage?"

The question came from George St. Michael, who had strayed over from a neighbouring table, attracted by the fragments of small-talk that had reached his ears.

St. Michael was one of those dapper, bird-like, illusorily-active men, who seem to have been in a certain stage of middle-age for as long as human memory can recall them. A close-cut peaked beard lent a certain dignity to his appearance—a loan which the rest of his features and mannerisms were continually and successfully repudiating. His profession, if he had one, was submerged in his hobby, which consisted of being an advance-agent for small happenings or possible happenings that were or seemed imminent in the social world around him; he found a perpetual and unflagging satisfaction in acquiring and retailing any stray items of gossip or information, particularly of a matrimonial nature, that chanced to come his way. Given the bare outline of an officially announced engagement, he would immediately fill it in with all manner of details, true or, at any rate, probable, drawn from his own imagination or from some equally exclusive source. The *Morning Post* might content itself with the mere statement of the arrangement which would shortly take place, but it was St. Michael's breathless little voice that proclaimed how the contracting parties had originally met over a salmon-fishing incident, why the Guards' Chapel would not be used, why her Aunt Mary had at first opposed the match, how the question of the children's religious upbringing had been compromised, etc., etc., to all whom it might interest and to many whom it might not. Beyond his industriously-earned pre-eminence in this special branch of intelligence, he was chiefly noteworthy for having a wife reputed to be the tallest and thinnest woman in the Home Counties. The two were sometimes seen together in Society, where they passed under the collective name of St. Michael and All Angles.

"We are trying to find a rich wife for Courtenay Youghal," said Serena, in answer to St. Michael's question.

"Ah, there I'm afraid you're a little late," he observed, glowing with the importance of pending revelation; "I'm afraid you're a little late," he repeated, watching the effect of his words as a gardener might watch the development of a bed of carefully tended asparagus. "I think the young gentleman has been before you and already found himself a rich mate in prospect."

He lowered his voice as he spoke, not with a view to imparting impressive mystery to his statement, but because there were other table groups within hearing to whom he hoped presently to have the privilege of re-disclosing his revelation.

"Do you mean——?" began Serena.

"Miss de Frey," broke in St. Michael hurriedly, fearful lest his revelation should be forestalled, even in guesswork; "quite an ideal choice, the very wife for a man who means to make his mark in politics. Twenty-four thousand a year, with prospects of more to come, and a charming place of her own not too far from town. Quite the type of girl, too, who will make a good political hostess, brains without being brainy, you know. Just the right thing. Of course, it would be premature to make any definite announcement at present——"

"It would hardly be premature for my partner to announce what she means to make trumps," interrupted Lady Caroline, in a voice of such sinister gentleness that St. Michael fled headlong back to his own table.

"Oh, is it me? I beg your pardon. I leave it," said Serena.

"Thank you. No trumps," declared Lady Caroline. The hand was successful, and the rubber ultimately fell to her with a comfortable margin of honours. The same partners cut together again, and this time the cards went distinctly against Francesca and Ada Spelvexit, and a heavily piled-up score confronted them at the close of the rubber. Francesca was conscious that a certain amount of rather erratic play on her part had at least contributed to the result. St. Michael's incursion into the conversation had proved rather a powerful distraction to her ordinarily sound bridge-craft.

Ada Spelvexit emptied her purse of several gold pieces, and infused a corresponding degree of superiority into her manner.

"I must be going now," she announced; "I'm dining early. I have to give an address to some charwomen afterwards."

"Why?" asked Lady Caroline, with a disconcerting directness that was one of her most formidable characteristics.

"Oh, well, I have some things to say to them that I daresay they will like to hear," said Ada, with a thin laugh.

Her statement was received with a silence that betokened profound unbelief in any such probability.

"I go about a good deal among working-class women," she added.

"No one has ever said it," observed Lady Caroline, "but how painfully true it is that the poor have us always with them!"

Ada Spelvexit hastened her departure; the marred impressiveness of her retreat came as a culminating discomfiture on the top of her ill-fortune at the card-table. Possibly, however, the multiplication of her own annoyances enabled her to survey charwomen's troubles with increased cheerfulness. None of them, at any rate, had spent an afternoon with Lady Caroline.

Francesca cut in at another table, and with better fortune attending on her, succeeded in winning back most of her losses. A sense of satisfaction was distinctly dominant as she took leave of her hostess. St. Michael's gossip, or rather the manner in which it had been received, had given her a clue to the real state of affairs, which, however slender and conjectural, at least pointed in the desired direction. At first she had been horribly afraid lest she should be listening to a definite announcement which would have been the death-blow to her hopes, but as the recitation went on without any of those assured little minor details which St. Michael so loved to supply, she had come to the conclusion that it was merely a piece of intelligent guesswork. And if Lady Caroline had really believed in the story of Elaine de Frey's virtual engagement to Courtenay Youghal she would have taken a malicious pleasure in encouraging St. Michael in his confidences, and in watching Francesca's discomfiture under the recital. The irritated manner in which she had cut short the discussion betrayed the fact that, as far as the old woman's information went, it was Comus, and not Courtenay Youghal, who held the field. And in this particular case Lady Caroline's information was likely to be nearer the truth than St. Michael's confident gossip.

Francesca always gave a penny to the first crossing-sweeper or match-seller she chanced across after a successful sitting at bridge. This afternoon she had come out of the fray some fifteen shillings to the bad, but she gave two pennies to a crossing-sweeper at the north-west corner of Berkeley Square as a sort of thank-offering to the gods.

CHAPTER VIII

IT was a fresh rain-repentant afternoon, following a morning that had been sultry and torrentially wet by turns: the sort of afternoon that impels people to talk graciously of the rain as having done a lot of good, its chief merit in their eyes probably having been its recognition of the art of moderation. Also it was an afternoon that invited bodily activity after the convalescent languor of the earlier part of the day. Elaine had instinctively found her way into her riding-habit and sent an order down to the stables—a blessed oasis that still smelt sweetly of horse and hay and cleanliness in a world that reeked of petrol, and now she set her mare at a smart pace through a succession of long-stretching country lanes. She was due some time that afternoon at a garden-party, but she rode with determination in an opposite direction. In the first place, neither Comus nor Courtenay would be at the party, which fact seemed to remove any valid reason that could be thought of for inviting her attendance thereat; in the second place about a hundred human beings would be gathered there, and human gatherings were not her most crying need at the present moment. Since her last encounter with her wooers, under the cedars in her own garden, Elaine realized that she was either very happy or cruelly unhappy, she could not quite determine which. She seemed to have what she most wanted in the world lying at her feet, and she was dreadfully uncertain in her more reflective moments whether she really wanted to stretch out her hand and take it. It was all very like some situation in an *Arabian Nights* tale or a story of Pagan Hellas, and consequently the more puzzling and disconcerting to a girl brought up on the methodical lines of Victorian Christianity. Her appeal court was in permanent session these last few days, but it gave no decisions, at least none that she would listen to. And the ride on her fast light-stepping little mare, alone and unattended, through the fresh-smelling leafy lanes into unexplored country, seemed just what she wanted at the moment. The mare made some small delicate pretence of being road-shy, not the staring dolt-like kind of nervousness that shows itself in an irritating hanging-back as each conspicuous wayside object presents itself, but the nerve-flutter of an imaginative animal that merely results in a quick whisk of the head and a swifter bound forward. She might have paraphrased the mental attitude of the immortalized Peter Bell into

> A basket underneath a tree
> A yellow tiger is to me,
> If it is nothing more.

The more really alarming episodes of the road, the hoot and whir of a passing motor-car or the loud vibrating hum of a wayside threshing-machine, were treated with indifference.

On turning a corner out of a narrow coppice-bordered lane into a wider road that sloped steadily upward in a long stretch of hill, Elaine saw, coming toward her at no great distance, a string of yellow-painted vans, drawn for the most part by skewbald or speckled horses. A certain rakish air about these oncoming road-craft proclaimed them as belonging to a travelling wild-beast show, decked out in the rich primitive colouring that one's taste in childhood would have insisted on before it had been schooled in the artistic value of dulness. It was an unlooked-for and distinctly unwelcome encounter. The mare had already commenced a sixfold scrutiny with nostrils, eyes, and daintily-pricked ears; one ear made hurried little backward movements to hear what Elaine was saying about the eminent niceness and respectability of the approaching caravan, but even Elaine felt that she would be unable satisfactorily to explain the elephants and camels that could certainly form part of the procession. To turn back would seem rather craven, and the mare might take fright at the manœuvre and try to bolt; a gate standing ajar at the entrance to a farmyard lane provided a convenient way out of the difficulty.

As Elaine pushed her way through she became aware of a man standing just inside the lane, who made a movement forward to open the gate for her.

"Thank you. I'm just getting out of the way of a wildbeast show," she explained; "my mare is tolerant of motors and traction-engines, but I expect camels—hallo!" she broke off, recognizing the man as an old acquaintance, "I heard you had taken rooms in a farm-house somewhere. Fancy meeting you in this way!"

In the not very distant days of her little-girlhood, Tom Keriway had been a man to be looked upon with a certain awe and envy; indeed the glamour of his roving career would have fired the imagination, and wistful desire to do likewise, of many young Englishmen. It seemed to be the grown-up realization of the games played in dark rooms in winter firelit evenings, and the dreams dreamed over favourite books of adventure. Making Vienna his headquarters, almost his home, he had rambled where he listed through the lands of the Near and Middle East as leisurely and thoroughly as tamer souls might explore Paris. He had wandered through Hungarian horse-fairs, hunted shy crafty beasts on lonely Balkan hillsides, dropped himself pebble-wise into the stagnant human pool of some Bulgarian monastery, threaded his way through the strange racial mosaic of Salonika, listened with amused politeness to the shallow ultra-modern opinions of a voluble editor or lawyer in some wayside Russian town, or learned wisdom from a chance tavern companion, one of the atoms of the busy ant-stream of men and merchandise that moves untiringly round the shores of the Black Sea. And far and wide as he might roam, he always managed to turn up at frequent intervals, at ball and supper and theatre, in the gay Hauptstadt of the Habsburgs, haunting his favourite cafés and wine-vaults, skimming through his favourite news-sheets, greeting old acquaintances and friends, from ambassadors down to cobblers in the social scale. He seldom talked of his travels, but it might be said that his travels talked of him; there was an air about him that a German diplomat once summed up in a phrase: "a man that wolves have sniffed at."

And then two things happened, which he had not mapped out in his route; a severe illness shook half the life and all the energy out of him, and a heavy money loss brought him almost to the door of destitution. With something, perhaps, of the impulse which drives a stricken animal away from its kind, Tom Keriway left the haunts where he had known so much happiness, and withdrew into the shelter of a secluded farm-house lodging; more than ever he became to Elaine a hearsay personality. And now the chance meeting with the caravan had flung her across the threshold of his retreat.

"What a charming little nook you've got hold of!" she exclaimed with instinctive politeness, and then looked searchingly round, and discovered that she had spoken the truth; it really was charming. The farm-house had that intensely English look that one seldom sees out of Normandy. Over the whole scene of rickyard, garden, outbuildings, horsepond and orchard, brooded that air which seems rightfully to belong to out-of-the-way farm-yards, an air of wakeful dreaminess which suggests that here man and beast and bird have got up so early that the rest of the world has never caught them up and never will.

Elaine dismounted, and Keriway led the mare round to a little paddock by the side of a great grey barn. At the end of the lane they could see the show go past, a string of lumbering vans and great striding beasts that seemed to link the vast silences of the desert with the noises and sights and smells, the naphtha-flares and advertisement hoardings and trampled orange-peel, of an endless succession of towns.

"You had better let the caravan pass well on its way before you get on the road again," said Keriway; "the smell of the beasts may make your mare nervous and restive going home."

Then he called to a boy, who was busy with a hoe among some defiantly prosperous weeds, to fetch the lady a glass of milk and a piece of currant loaf.

"I don't know when I've seen anything so utterly charming and peaceful," said Elaine, propping herself on a seat that a pear-tree had obligingly designed in the fantastic curve of its trunk.

"Charming, certainly," said Keriway, "but too full of the stress of its own little life struggle to be peaceful. Since I have lived here I've learnt, what I've always suspected, that a country farm-house, set away in a world of its own, is one of the most wonderful studies of interwoven happenings and tragedies that can be imagined. It is like the old chronicles of mediæval Europe in the days when there was a sort of ordered anarchy between feudal lords and overlords, and burg-grafs, and mitred abbots, and prince-bishops, robber barons and merchant guilds, and Electors and so forth, all striving and contending and counter-plotting, and interfering with each other under some vague code of loosely-applied rules. Here one sees it reproduced under one's eyes, like a musty page of black-letter come to life. Look at one little section of it, the poultry-life on the farm. Villa poultry, dull egg-machines, with records kept of how many ounces of food they eat, and how many penny-worths of eggs they lay, give you no idea of the wonder-life of these farm-birds; their feuds and jealousies, and carefully maintained prerogatives, their unsparing tyrannies and persecutions, their calculated courage and bravado or sedulously hidden cowardice, it might all be some human chapter from the annals of the old Rhineland or mediæval Italy. And then, outside their own bickering wars and hates, the grim enemies that come up against them from the woodlands; the hawk that dashes among the coops like a moss-trooper raiding the border, knowing well that a charge of shot may tear him to bits at any moment. And the stoat, a creeping slip of brown fur a few inches long, intently and unstayably out for blood.

And the hunger-taught master of craft, the red fox, who has waited perhaps half the afternoon for his chance while the fowls were dusting themselves under the hedge, and just as they were turning supper-ward to the yard one has stopped a moment to give her feathers a final shake and found death springing upon her. Do you know," he continued, as Elaine fed herself and the mare with morsels of currant-loaf, "I don't think any tragedy in literature that I have ever come across impressed me so much as the first one that I spelled out slowly for myself in words of three letters: the bad fox has got the red hen. There was something so dramatically complete about it; the badness of the fox, added to all the traditional guile of his race, seemed to heighten the horror of the hen's fate, and there was such a suggestion of masterful malice about the word 'got.' One felt that a countryside in arms would not get that hen away from the bad fox. They used to think me a slow dull reader for not getting on with my lesson, but I used to sit and picture to myself the red hen, with its wings beating helplessly, screeching in terrified protest, or perhaps, if he had got it by the neck, with beak wide agape and silent, and eyes staring, as it left the farmyard for ever. I have seen blood-spilling and down-crushings and abject defeat here and there in my time, but the red hen has remained in my mind as the type of helpless tragedy." He was silent for a moment as if he were again musing over the three-letter drama that had so dwelt in his childhood's imagination.

"Tell me some of the things you have seen in your time," was the request that was nearly on Elaine's lips, but she hastily checked herself and substituted another.

"Tell me more about the farm, please."

And he told her of a whole world, or rather of several intermingled worlds, set apart in this sleepy hollow in the hills, of beast lore and wood lore and farm craft, at times touching almost the border of witchcraft—passing lightly here, not with the probing eagerness of those who know nothing, but with the averted glance of those who fear to see too much. He told her of those things that slept and those that prowled when the dusk fell, of strange hunting cats, of the yard swine and the stalled cattle, of the farm folk themselves, as curious and remote in their way, in their ideas and fears and wants and tragedies, as the brutes and feathered stock that they tended. It seemed to Elaine as if a musty store of old-world children's books had been fetched down from some cobwebbed lumber-room and brought to life. Sitting there in the little paddock, grown thickly with tall weeds and rank grasses, and shadowed by the weather-beaten old grey barn, listening to this chronicle of wonderful things, half fanciful, half very real, she could scarcely believe that a few miles away there was a garden-party in full swing, with smart frocks and smart conversation, fashionable refreshments and fashionable music, and a fevered undercurrent of social strivings and snubbings. Did Vienna and the Balkan Mountains and the Black Sea seem as remote and hard to believe in, she wondered, to the man sitting by her side, who had discovered or invented this wonderful fairy-land? Was it a true and merciful arrangement of fate and life that the things of the moment thrust out the after-taste of the things that had been? Here was one who had held much that was priceless in the hollow of his hand and lost it all, and he was happy and absorbed and well content with the little way-side corner of the world into which he had crept. And Elaine, who held so many desirable things in the hollow of her hand, could not make up her mind to be even moderately happy. She did not even know whether to take this hero of her child-hood down from his pedestal, or to place him on a higher one; on the whole she was inclined to resent rather than approve the idea that ill-health and misfortune could so completely subdue and tame an erstwhile bold and roving spirit.

The mare was showing signs of delicately-hinted impatience; the paddock, with its teasing insects and very indifferent grazing, had not thrust out the image of her own comfortable well-foddered loose-box. Elaine divested her habit of some remaining crumbs of bun-loaf and jumped lightly on to her saddle. As she rode slowly down the lane, with Keriway escorting her as far as its gate, she looked round at what had seemed to her, a short while ago, just a picturesque old farm-stead, a place of bee-hives and hollyhocks and gabled cart-sheds; now it was in her eyes a magic city, with an under-current of reality beneath its magic.

"You are a person to be envied," she said to Keriway; "you have created a fairyland, and you are living in it yourself."

"Envied?"

He shot the question out with sudden bitterness. She looked down and saw the wistful misery that had come into his face.

"Once," he said to her, "in a German paper I read a short story about a tame crippled crane that lived in the park of some small town. I forget what happened in the story, but there was one line that I shall always remember: 'it was lame, that is why it was tame.'"

He had created a fairyland, but assuredly he was not living in it.

CHAPTER IX

IN the warmth of a late June morning the long shaded stretch of raked earth, gravel-walk and rhododendron bush that is known affectionately as the Row was alive with the monotonous movement and alert stagnation appropriate to the time and place. The seekers after health, the seekers after notoriety and recognition, and the lovers of good exercise were all well represented on the galloping ground; the gravel-walk and chairs and long seats held a population whose varied instincts and motives would have baffled a social catalogue-maker. The children, handled or in perambulators, might be excused from instinct or motive; they were brought.

Pleasingly conspicuous among a bunch of indifferent riders pacing along by the rails where the onlookers were thickest was Courtenay Youghal, on his handsome plum-roan gelding Anne de Joyeuse. That delicately stepping animal had taken a prize at Islington and nearly taken the life of a stable-boy of whom he disapproved, but his strongest claims to distinction were his good looks and his high opinion of himself. Youghal evidently believed in thorough accord between horse and rider.

"Please stop and talk to me," said a quiet beckoning voice from the other side of the rails, and Youghal drew rein and greeted Lady Veula Croot. Lady Veula had married into a family of commercial solidity and enterprising political nonentity. She had a devoted husband, some blond teachable children, and a look of unutterable weariness in her eyes. To see her standing at the top of an expensively horticultured staircase receiving her husband's guests was rather like watching an animal performing on a music-hall stage. One always tells oneself that the animal likes it, and one always knows that it doesn't.

"Lady Veula is an ardent Free Trader, isn't she?" some one once remarked to Lady Caroline.

"I wonder," said Lady Caroline, in her gently questioning voice; "a woman whose dresses are made in Paris and whose marriage has been made in heaven might be equally biased for and against free imports."

Lady Veula looked at Youghal and his mount with slow critical appraisement, and there was a note of blended raillery and wistfulness in her voice.

"You two dear things, I should love to stroke you both, but I'm not sure how Joyeuse would take it. So I'll stroke you down verbally instead. I admired your attack on Sir Edward immensely, though of course I don't agree with a word of it. Your description of him building a hedge round the German cuckoo and hoping he was isolating it was rather sweet. Seriously though, I regard him as one of the pillars of the Administration."

"So do I," said Youghal; "the misfortune is that he is merely propping up a canvas roof. It's just his regrettable solidity and integrity that makes him so expensively dangerous. The average Briton arrives at the same judgment about Roan's handling of foreign affairs as Omar does of the Supreme Being in his dealings with the world: 'He's a good fellow and 'twill all be well.' "

Lady Veula laughed lightly. "My Party is in power, so I may exercise the privilege of being optimistic. Who is that who bowed to you?" she continued, as a dark young man with an inclination to stoutness passed by them on foot; "I've seen him about a good deal lately. He's been to one or two of my dances."

"Andrei Drakoloff," said Youghal; "he's just produced a play that has had a big success in Moscow and is certain to be extremely popular all over Russia. In the first three acts the heroine is supposed to by dying of consumption; in the last act they find she is really dying of cancer."

"Are the Russians really such a gloomy people?"

"Gloom-loving, but not in the least gloomy. They merely take their sadness pleasurably, just as we are accused of taking our pleasures sadly. Have you noticed that dreadful Klopstock youth has been pounding past us at shortening intervals? He'll come up and talk if he half catches your eye."

"I only just know him. Isn't he at an agricultural college or something of the sort?"

"Yes, studying to be a gentleman farmer, he told me. I didn't ask if both subjects were compulsory."

"You're really rather dreadful," said Lady Veula, trying to look as if she thought so; "remember, we are all equal in the sight of Heaven."

For a preacher of wholesome truths her voice rather lacked conviction.

"If I and Ernest Klopstock are really equal in the sight of Heaven," said Youghal, with intense complacency, "I should recommend Heaven to consult an eye specialist."

There was a heavy spattering of loose earth, and a squelching of saddle-leather, as the Klopstock youth lumbered up to the rails and delivered himself of loud, cheerful greetings. Joyeuse laid his ears well back as the ungainly bay cob and his appropriately matched rider drew up beside him; his verdict was reflected and endorsed by the cold stare of Youghal's eyes.

"I've been having a nailing fine time," recounted the newcomer with clamorous enthusiasm; "I was over in Paris last month and had lots of strawberries there, then I had a lot more in London, and now I've been having a late crop of them in

Herefordshire, so I've had quite a lot this year." And he laughed as one who had deserved well and received well of Fate.

"The charm of that story," said Youghal, "is that it can be told in any drawing-room." And with a sweep of his wide-brimmed hat to Lady Veula he turned the impatient Joyeuse into the moving stream of horses and horsemen.

"That woman reminds me of some verse I've read and liked," thought Youghal, as Joyeuse sprang into a light showy canter that gave full recognition to the existence of observant human beings along the side-walk. "Ah, I have it."

And he quoted almost aloud, as one does in the exhilaration of a canter:

> "How much I loved that way you had
> Of smiling most, when very sad,
> A smile which carried tender hints
> Of sun and spring,
> And yet, more than all other thing,
> Of weariness beyond all words."

And having satisfactorily fitted Lady Veula on to a quotation he dismissed her from his mind. With the constancy of her sex she thought about him, his good looks and his youth and his railing tongue, till late in the afternoon.

While Youghal was putting Joyeuse through his paces under the elm trees of the Row a little drama in which he was directly interested was being played out not many hundred yards away. Elaine and Comus were indulging themselves in two pennyworths of Park chair, drawn aside just a little from the serried rows of sitters who were set out like bedded plants over an acre or so of turf. Comus was, for the moment, in a mood of pugnacious gaiety, disbursing a fund of pointed criticism and unsparing anecdote concerning those of the promenaders or loungers whom he knew personally or by sight. Elaine was rather quieter than usual, and the grave serenity of the Leonardo da Vinci portrait seemed intensified in her face this morning. In his leisurely courtship Comus had relied almost exclusively on his physical attraction and the fitful drollery of his wit and high spirits, and these graces had gone far to make him seem a very desirable and rather lovable thing in Elaine's eyes. But he had left out of account the disfavour which he constantly risked and sometimes incurred from his frank and undisguised indifference to other people's interests and wishes, including, at times, Elaine's. And the more that she felt that she liked him the more she was irritated by his lack of consideration for her. Without expecting that her every wish should become a law to him, she would at least have liked it to reach the formality of a Second Reading. Another important factor he had also left out of his reckoning, namely the presence on the scene of another suitor, who also had youth and wit to recommend him, and who certainly did not lack physical attractions. Comus, marching carelessly through unknown country to effect what seemed already an assured victory, made the mistake of disregarding the existence of an unbeaten army on his flank.

Today Elaine felt that, without having actually quarrelled, she and Comus had drifted a little bit out of sympathy with one another. The fault she knew was scarcely hers, in fact from the most good-natured point of view it could hardly be denied that it was almost entirely his. The incident of the silver dish had lacked even the attraction of novelty; it had been one of a series, all bearing a strong connecting likeness. There had been small unrepaid loans which Elaine would not have grudged in themselves, though the application for them brought a certain qualm of distaste; with the perversity which seemed inseparable from his doings, Comus had always flung away a portion of his borrowings in some ostentatious piece of glaring and utterly profitless extravagance, which outraged all the canons of her upbringing without bringing him an atom of understandable satisfaction. Under these repeated discouragements it was not surprising that some small part of her affection should have slipped away, but she had come to the Park that morning with an unconfessed expectation of being gently wooed back to the mood of gracious forgetfulness that she was only too eager to assume. It was almost worth while being angry with Comus for the sake of experiencing the pleasure of being coaxed into friendliness again with the charm which he knew so well how to exert. It was delicious here under the trees on this perfect June morning, and Elaine had the blessed assurance that most of the women within range were envying her the companionship of the handsome merry-hearted youth who sat by her side. With special complacence she contemplated her cousin Suzette, who was self-consciously but not very elatedly basking in the attentions of her fiancé, an earnest-looking young man who was superintendent of a People's something-or-other on the south side of the river, and whose clothes Comus had described as having been made in Southwark rather than in anger.

Most of the pleasures in life must be paid for, and the chair-ticket vendor in due time made his appearance in quest of pennies. Comus paid him from out of a varied assortment of coins and then balanced the remainder in the palm of his hand. Elaine felt a sudden foreknowledge of something disagreeable about to happen, and a red spot deepened in her cheeks.

"Four shillings and fivepence and a halfpenny," said Comus reflectively. "It's a ridiculous sum to last me for the next three days, and I owe a card debt of over two pounds."

"Yes?" commented Elaine dryly and with an apparent lack of interest in his exchequer statement. Surely, she was thinking hurriedly to herself, he could not be foolish enough to broach the matter of another loan.

"The card debt is rather a nuisance," pursued Comus, with fatalistic persistency.

"You won seven pounds last week, didn't you?" asked Elaine; "don't you put any of your winnings to balance losses?"

"The four shillings and the fivepence and the halfpenny represent the rearguard of the seven pounds," said Comus; "the rest have fallen by the way. If I can pay the two pounds today I daresay I shall win something more to go on with; I'm holding rather good cards just now. But if I can't pay it, of course I shan't show up at the club. So you see the fix I am in."

Elaine took no notice of this indirect application. The Appeal Court was assembling in haste to consider new evidence, and this time there was the rapidity of sudden determination about its movement.

The conversation strayed away from the fateful topic for a few moments, and then Comus brought it deliberately back to the danger zone.

"It would be awfully nice if you would let me have a fiver for a few days, Elaine," he said quickly; "if you don't I really don't know what I shall do."

"If you are really bothered about your card debt I will send you the two pounds by messenger boy early this afternoon." She spoke quietly and with great decision. "And I shall not be at the Connors' dance tonight," she continued; "it's too hot for dancing. I'm going home now; please don't bother to accompany me, I particularly wish to go alone."

Comus saw that he had overstepped the mark of her good nature. Wisely he made no immediate attempt to force himself back into her good graces. He would wait till her indignation had cooled.

His tactics would have been excellent if he had not forgotten that unbeaten army on his flank.

Elaine de Frey had known very clearly what qualities she had wanted in Comus, and she had known, against all efforts at self-deception, that he fell far short of those qualities. She had been willing to lower her standard of moral requirements in proportion as she was fond of the boy, but there was a point beyond which she would not go. He had hurt her pride, besides alarming her sense of caution. Suzette, on whom she felt a thoroughly justified tendency to look down, had at any rate an attentive and considerate lover. Elaine walked towards the Park gates feeling that in one essential Suzette possessed something that had been denied to her, and at the gates she met Joyeuse and his spruce young rider preparing to turn homeward.

"Get rid of Joyeuse and come and take me out to lunch somewhere," demanded Elaine.

"How jolly!" said Youghal. "Let's go to the Corridor Restaurant. The head-waiter there is an old Viennese friend of mine and looks after me beautifully. I've never been there with a lady before, and he's sure to ask me afterwards, in his fatherly way, if we're engaged."

The lunch was a success in every way. There was just enough orchestral effort to immerse the conversation without drowning it, and Youghal was an attentive and inspired host. Through an open doorway Elaine could see the café reading-room, with its imposing array of *Neue Freie Presse, Berliner Tageblatt,* and other exotic newspapers hanging on the wall. She looked across at the young man seated opposite her, who gave one the impression of having centred the most serious efforts of his brain on his toilet and his food, and recalled some of the flattering remarks that the Press had bestowed on his recent speeches.

"Doesn't it make you conceited, Courtenay," she asked, "to look at all those foreign newspapers hanging there and know that most of them have got paragraphs and articles about your Persian speech?"

Youghal laughed.

"There's always a chastening corrective in the thought that some of them may have printed your portrait. When once you've seen your features hurriedly reproduced in the *Matin,* for instance, you feel you would like to be a veiled Turkish woman for the rest of your life."

And Youghal gazed long and lovingly at his reflection in the nearest mirror, as an antidote against possible incitements to humility in the portrait gallery of fame.

Elaine felt a certain soothed satisfaction in the fact that this young man, whose knowledge of the Middle East was an embarrassment to Ministers at question time and in debate, was showing himself equally well informed on the subject of her culinary likes and dislikes. If Suzette could have been forced to attend as a witness at a neighbouring table she would have felt even happier.

"Did the head-waiter ask if we were engaged?" asked Elaine, when Courtenay had settled the bill, and she had finished collecting her sunshade and gloves and other impedimenta from the hands of obsequious attendants.

"Yes," said Youghal, "and he seemed quite crestfallen when I had to say 'No.'"

"It would be horrid to disappoint him when he's looked after us so charmingly," said Elaine; "tell him that we are."

CHAPTER X

THE Rutland Galleries were crowded, especially in the neighbourhood of the tea-buffet, by a fashionable throng of art-patrons which had gathered to inspect Mervyn Quentock's collection of Society portraits. Quentock was a young artist whose abilities were just receiving due recognition from the critics; that the recognition was not overdue he owed largely to his perception of the fact that if one hides one's talent under a bushel one must be careful to point out to every one the exact bushel under which it is hidden. There are two manners of receiving recognition: one is to be discovered so long after one's death that one's grandchildren have to write to the papers to establish their relationship; the other is to be discovered, like the infant Moses, at the very outset of one's career. Mervyn Quentock had chosen the latter and happier manner. In an age when many aspiring young men strive to advertise their wares by imparting to them a freakish imbecility, Quentock turned out work that was characterized by a pleasing delicate restraint, but he contrived to herald his output with a certain fanfare of personal eccentricity, thereby compelling an attention which might otherwise have strayed past his studio. In appearance he was the ordinary cleanly young Englishman, except, perhaps, that his eyes rather suggested a library edition of the *Arabian Nights;* his clothes matched his appearance and showed no taint of the sartorial disorder by which the bourgeois of the garden-city and the Latin Quarter anxiously seeks to proclaim his kinship with art and thought. His eccentricity took the form of flying in the face of some of the prevailing social currents of the day, but as a reactionary, never as a reformer. He produced a gasp of admiring astonishment in fashionable circles by refusing to

paint actresses—except, of course, those who had left the legitimate drama to appear between the boards of Debrett. He absolutely declined to execute portraits of Americans unless they
hailed from certain favoured States. His "water-colour line,"
as a New York paper phrased it, earned for him a crop of
angry criticism and a shoal of Transatlantic commissions, and
criticism and commissions were the things that Quentock most
wanted.

"Of course he is perfectly right," said Lady Caroline
Benaresq, calmly rescuing a piled-up plate of caviare sandwiches from the neighbourhood of a trio of young ladies who
had established themselves hopefully within easy reach of it.
"Art," she continued, addressing herself to the Rev. Poltimore
Vardon, "has always been geographically exclusive. London
may be more important from most points of view than Venice,
but the art of portrait painting, which would never concern
itself with a Lord Mayor, simply grovels at the feet of the
Doges. As a Socialist I'm bound to recognize the right of
Ealing to compare itself with Avignon, but one cannot expect
the Muses to put the two on a level."

"Exclusiveness," said the Reverend Poltimore, "has been the
salvation of Art, just as the lack of it is proving the downfall
of religion. My colleagues of the cloth go about zealously proclaiming the fact that Christianity, in some form or other, is
attracting shoals of converts among all sorts of races and tribes
that one had scarcely ever heard of, except in reviews of books
of travel that one never read. That sort of thing was all very
well when the world was more sparsely populated, but nowadays, when it simply teems with human beings, no one is particularly impressed by the fact that a few million, more or less,
of converts, of a low stage of mental development, have accepted the teachings of some particular religion. It not only
chills one's enthusiasm, it positively shakes one's convictions
when one hears that the things one has been brought up to believe as true are being very favourably spoken of by Buriats and
Samoyeds and Kanakas."

The Rev. Poltimore Vardon had once seen a resemblance in

himself to Voltaire, and had lived alongside the comparison ever
since.

"No modern cult or fashion," he continued, "would be favourably influenced by considerations based on statistics; fancy
adopting a certain style of hat or cut of coat, because it was
being largely worn in Lancashire and the Midlands; fancy favouring a certain brand of champagne because it was being extensively patronized in German summer resorts! No wonder
that religion is falling into disuse in this country under such ill-
directed methods."

"You can't prevent the heathen being converted if they
choose to be," said Lady Caroline; "this is an age of tol-
eration."

"You could always deny it," said the Reverend Poltimore,
"like the Belgians do with regrettable occurrences in the Congo.
But I would go further than that. I would stimulate the waning enthusiasm for Christianity in this country by labelling it
as the exclusive possession of a privileged few. If one could induce the Duchess of Pelm, for instance, to assert that the Kingdom of Heaven, as far as the British Isles are concerned, is
strictly limited to herself, two of the under-gardeners at Pelmby,
and, possibly, but not certainly, the Dean of Dunster, there
would be an instant reshaping of the popular attitude towards
religious convictions and observances. Once let the idea get
about that the Christian Church is rather more exclusive than
the Lawn at Ascot, and you would have a quickening of religious life such as this generation has never witnessed. But as
long as the clergy and the religious organizations advertise their
creed on the lines of 'Everybody ought to believe in us: millions do,' one can expect nothing but indifference and waning
faith."

"Time is just as exclusive in its way as Art," said Lady
Caroline.

"In what way?" said the Reverend Poltimore.

"Your pleasantries about religion would have sounded quite
clever and advanced in the early 'nineties. Today they have a
dreadfully warmed-up flavour. That is the great delusion of

you would-be advanced satirists; you imagine you can sit down comfortably for a couple of decades saying daring and startling things about the age you live in, which, whatever other defects it may have, is certainly not standing still. The whole of the Sherard Blaw school of discursive drama suggests, to my mind, Early Victorian furniture in a travelling circus. However, you will always have relays of people from the suburbs to listen to the Mocking Bird of yesterday, and sincerely imagine it is the harbinger of something new and revolutionizing."

"*Would* you mind passing that plate of sandwiches?" asked one of the trio of young ladies, emboldened by famine.

"With pleasure," said Lady Caroline, deftly passing her a nearly empty plate of bread-and-butter.

"I meant the plate of caviare sandwiches. So sorry to trouble you," persisted the young lady.

Her sorrow was misapplied; Lady Caroline had turned her attention to a new-comer.

"A very interesting exhibition," Ada Spelvexit was saying; "faultless technique, as far as I am a judge of technique, and quite a master-touch in the way of poses. But have you noticed how very animal his art is? He seems to shut out the soul from his portraits. I nearly cried when I saw dear Winifred depicted simply as a good-looking healthy blonde."

"I wish you had," said Lady Caroline; "the spectacle of a strong, brave woman weeping at a private view in the Rutland Galleries would have been so sensational. It would certainly have been reproduced in the next Drury Lane drama. And I'm so unlucky; I never see these sensational events. I was ill with appendicitis, you know, when Lulu Braminguard dramatically forgave her husband, after seventeen years of estrangement, during a State luncheon party at Windsor. The old Queen was furious about it. She said it was so disrespectful to the cook to be thinking of such a thing at such a time."

Lady Caroline's recollections of things that hadn't happened at the court of Queen Victoria were notoriously vivid; it was the very widespread fear that she might one day write a book of reminiscences that made her so universally respected.

"As for his full-length picture of Lady Brickfield," contin-

ued Ada, ignoring Lady Caroline's commentary as far as possible, "all the expression seems to have been deliberately concentrated in the feet; beautiful feet, no doubt, but still, hardly
the most distinctive part of a human being."

"To paint the right people at the wrong end may be an eccentricity, but it is scarcely an indiscretion," pronounced Lady
Caroline.

One of the portraits which attracted more than a passing
flutter of attention was a costume study of Francesca Bassington. Francesca had secured some highly desirable patronage for
the young artist, and in return he had enriched her pantheon
of personal possessions with a clever piece of work into which
he had thrown an unusual amount of imaginative detail. He
had painted her in a costume of the Great Louis's brightest
period, seated in front of a tapestry that was so prominent in
the composition that it could scarcely be said to form part of
the background. Flowers and fruit, in exotic profusion, were
its dominant note; quinces, pomegranates, passion-flowers, giant
convolvulus, great mauve-pink roses, and grapes that were already being pressed by gleeful cupids in a riotous Arcadian vin-
tage, stood out on its woven texture. The same note was struck
in the beflowered satin of the lady's kirtle, and in the pome-
granate pattern of the brocade that draped the couch on which
she was seated. The artist had called his picture "Recolte." And
after one had taken in all the details of fruit and flower and
foliage that earned the composition its name, one noted the
landscape that showed through a broad casement in the left-
hand corner. It was a landscape clutched in the grip of winter,
naked, bleak, black-frozen; a winter in which things died and
knew no rewakening. If the picture typified harvest, it was a
harvest of artificial growth.

"It leaves a great deal to the imagination, doesn't it?" said
Ada Spelvexit, who had edged away from the range of Lady
Caroline's tongue.

"At any rate one can tell who it's meant for," said Serena
Golackly.

"Oh, yes, it's a good likeness of dear Francesca," admitted
Ada; "of course, it flatters her."

"That, too, is a fault on the right side in portrait painting," said Serena; "after all, if posterity is going to stare at one for centuries it's only kind and reasonable to be looking just a little better than one's best."

"What a curiously unequal style the artist has!" continued Ada, almost as if she felt a personal grievance against him. "I was just noticing what a lack of soul there was in most of his portraits. Dear Winifred, you know, who speaks so beautifully and feelingly at my gatherings for old women, he's made her look just an ordinary dairy-maidish blonde; and Francesca, who is quite the most soulless woman I've ever met, well, he's given her quite———"

"Hush!" said Serena, "the Bassington boy is just behind you."

Comus stood looking at the portrait of his mother with the feeling of one who comes suddenly across a once-familiar, half-forgotten acquaintance in unfamiliar surroundings. The likeness was undoubtedly a good one, but the artist had caught an expression in Francesca's eyes which few people had ever seen there. It was the expression of a woman who had forgotten for one short moment to be absorbed in the small cares and excitements of her life, the money worries and little social plannings, and had found time to send a look of half-wistful friendliness to some sympathetic companion. Comus could recall that look, fitful and fleeting, in his mother's eyes when she had been a few years younger, before her world had grown to be such a committee-room of ways and means. Almost as a re-discovery, he remembered that she had once figured in his boyish mind as a "rather good sort," more ready to see the laughable side of a piece of mischief than to labour forth a reproof. That the by-gone feeling of good-fellowship had been stamped out was, he knew, probably in great part his own doing, and it was possible that the old friendliness was still there under the surface of things, ready to show itself again if he willed it, and friends were becoming scarcer with him than enemies in these days. Looking at the picture with its wistful hint of a long-ago comradeship, Comus made up his mind that he very much wanted things to be back on their earlier footing, and to see again on his mother's face the look that the artist had caught and perpetuated in its momentary flitting. If the projected Elaine marriage came off, and in spite of recent maladroit behaviour on his part he still counted it an assured thing, much of the immediate cause for estrangement between himself and his mother would be removed, or at any rate easily removable. With the influence of Elaine's money behind him, he promised himself that he would find some occupation that would remove from himself the reproach of being a waster and idler. There were lots of careers, he told himself, that were open to a man with solid financial backing and good connexions. There might yet be jolly times ahead, in which his mother would have her share of the good things that were going, and carking thin-lipped Henry Greech and other of Comus's detractors could take their sour looks and words out of sight and hearing. Thus, staring at the picture as though he were studying its every detail, and seeing really only that wistful friendly smile, Comus made his plans and dispositions for a battle that was already fought and lost.

The crowd grew thicker in the galleries, cheerfully enduring an amount of overcrowding that would have been fiercely resented in a railway carriage. Near the entrance Mervyn Quentock was talking to a Serene Highness, a lady who led a life of obtrusive usefulness, largely imposed on her by a good-natured inability to say "No." "That woman creates a positive draught with the number of bazaars she opens," a frivolously-spoken ex-Cabinet Minister had once remarked. At the present moment she was being whimsically apologetic.

"When I think of the legions of well-meaning young men and women to whom I've given away prizes for proficiency in art-school curriculum, I feel that I ought not to show my face inside a picture gallery. I always imagine that my punishment in another world will be perpetually sharpening pencils and cleaning palettes for unending relays of misguided young people whom I deliberately encouraged in their artistic delusions."

"Do you suppose we shall all get appropriate punishments in another world for our sins in this?" asked Quentock.

"Not so much for our sins as for our indiscretions; they are the things which do the most harm and cause the greatest trouble. I feel certain that Christopher Columbus will undergo the endless torment of being discovered by parties of American tourists. You see I am quite old-fashioned in my ideas about the terrors and inconveniences of the next world. And now I must be running away; I've got to open a Free Library somewhere. You know the sort of thing that happens—one unveils a bust of Carlyle and makes a speech about Ruskin, and then people come in their thousands and read *Rabid Ralph, or Should He Have Bitten Her?* Don't forget, please, I'm going to have the medallion with the fat cupid sitting on a sundial. And just one thing more—perhaps I ought not to ask you, but you have such nice kind eyes, you embolden one to make daring requests, *would* you send me the recipe for those lovely chestnut-and-chicken-liver sandwiches? I know the ingredients, of course, but it's the proportions that make such a difference— just how much liver to how much chestnut, and what amount of red pepper and other things. Thank you so much. I really am going now."

Staring round with a vague half-smile at everybody within nodding distance, Her Serene Highness made one of her characteristic exits, which Lady Caroline declared always reminded her of a scrambled egg slipping off a piece of toast. At the entrance she stopped for a moment to exchange a word or two with a young man who had just arrived. From a corner where he was momentarily hemmed in by a group of tea-consuming dowagers, Comus recognized the new-comer as Courtenay Youghal, and began slowly to labour his way towards him. Youghal was not at the moment the person whose society he most craved for in the world, but there was at least the possibility that he might provide an opportunity for a game of bridge, which was the dominant desire of the moment. The young politician was already surrounded by a group of friends and acquaintances, and was evidently being made the recipient of a salvo of congratulation—presumably on his recent performances in the Foreign Office debate, Comus concluded. But Youghal himself seemed to be announcing the event with which the congratulations were connected. Had some dramatic catastrophe overtaken the Government? Comus wondered. And then, as he pressed nearer, a chance word, the coupling of two names, told him the news.

CHAPTER XI

AFTER the momentous lunch at the Corridor Restaurant, Elaine had returned to Manchester Square (where she was staying with one of her numerous aunts) in a frame of mind that embraced a tangle of competing emotions. In the first place she was conscious of a dominant feeling of relief; in a moment of impetuosity, not wholly uninfluenced by pique, she had settled the problem which hours of hard thinking and serious heart-searching had brought no nearer to solution, and, although she felt just a little inclined to be scared at the head-long manner of her final decision, she had now very little doubt in her own mind that the decision had been the right one. In fact, the wonder seemed rather that she should have been so long in doubt as to which of her wooers really enjoyed her honest approval. She had been in love these many weeks past with an imaginary Comus, but now that she had definitely walked out of her dreamland she saw that nearly all the qualities that had appealed to her on his behalf had been absent from, or only fitfully present in, the character of the real Comus. And now that she had installed Youghal in the first place of her affections he had rapidly acquired in her eyes some of the qualities which ranked highest in her estimation. Like the proverbial buyer she had the happy feminine tendency of magnifying the worth of her possession as soon as she had ac-quired it. And Courtenay Youghal gave Elaine some justifica-tion for her sense of having chosen wisely. Above all other things, selfish and cynical though he might appear at times, he was unfailingly courteous and considerate towards her. That was a circumstance which would always have carried weight with her in judging any man; in this case its value was enor-mously heightened by contrast with the behaviour of her other wooer. And Youghal had in her eyes the advantage which the glamour of combat, even the combat of words and wire-pulling, throws over the fighter. He stood well in the forefront of a battle which however carefully stage-managed, however honeycombed with personal insincerities and overlaid with cal-culated mock-heroics, really meant something, really counted for good or wrong in the nation's development and the world's history. Shrewd parliamentary observers might have warned her that Youghal would never stand much higher in the political world than he did at present, as a brilliant Opposition free-lance, leading lively and rather meaningless forays against the dull and rather purposeless foreign policy of a Government that was scarcely either to be blamed for or congratulated on its handling of foreign affairs. The young politician had not the strength of character or convictions that keeps a man natu-rally in the forefront of affairs and gives his counsels a sterling value, and on the other hand his insincerity was not deep enough to allow him to pose artificially and successfully as a leader of men and shaper of movements. For the moment, how-ever, his place in public life was sufficiently marked out to give him a secure footing in that world where people are counted individually and not in herds. The woman whom he would make his wife would have the chance, too, if she had the will and the skill, to become an individual who counted.

There was balm to Elaine in this reflection, yet it did not wholly suffice to drive out the feeling of pique which Comus had called into being by his slighting view of her as a conven-ient cash supply in moments of emergency. She found a certain satisfaction in scrupulously observing her promise, made earlier on that eventful day, and sent off a messenger with the stipu-lated loan. Then a reaction of compunction set in, and she re-minded herself that in fairness she ought to write and tell her news in as friendly a fashion as possible to her dismissed suitor before it burst upon him from some other quarter. They parted on more or less quarrelling terms, it was true, but neither of them had foreseen the finality of the parting nor the perma-nence of the breach between them; Comus might even now be thinking himself half-forgiven, and the awakening would be rather cruel. The letter, however, did not prove an easy one to write; not only did it present difficulties of its own, but it suffered from the competing urgency of a desire to be doing something far pleasanter than writing explanatory and valedictory phrases. Elaine was possessed with an unusual but quite overmastering hankering to visit her cousin Suzette Brankley. They met but rarely at each other's houses and very seldom anywhere else, and Elaine for her part was never conscious of feeling that their opportunities for intercourse lacked anything in the way of adequacy. Suzette accorded her just that touch of patronage which a moderately well-off and immoderately dull girl will usually try to mete out to an acquaintance who is known to be wealthy and suspected of possessing brains. In return Elaine armed herself with that particular brand of mock humility which can be so terribly disconcerting if properly wielded. No quarrel of any description stood between them and one could not legitimately have described them as enemies, but they never disarmed in one another's presence. A misfortune of any magnitude falling on one of them would have been sincerely regretted by the other, but any minor discomfiture would have produced a feeling very much akin to satisfaction. Human nature knows millions of these inconsequent little feuds, springing up and flourishing apart from any basis of racial, political, religious or economic causes, as a hint perhaps to crass unseeing altruists that enmity has its place and purpose in the world as well as benevolence.

Elaine had not personally congratulated Suzette since the formal announcement of her engagement to the young man with the dissentient tailoring effects. The impulse to go and do so now overmastered her sense of what was due to Comus in the way of explanation. The letter was still in its blank unwritten stage, an unmarshalled sequence of sentences forming in her brain, when she ordered her car and made a hurried but well-thought-out change into her most sumptuously sober afternoon toilette. Suzette, she felt tolerably sure, would still be in the costume that she had worn in the Park that morning, a costume that aimed at elaboration of detail, and was damned with overmuch success.

Suzette's mother welcomed her unexpected visitor with obvious satisfaction. Her daughter's engagement, she explained, was not so brilliant from the social point of view as a girl of Suzette's attractions and advantages might have legitimately aspired to, but Egbert was a thoroughly commendable and dependable young man, who would very probably win his way before long to membership of the County Council.

"From there, of course, the road would be open to him to higher things."

"Yes," said Elaine, "he might become an alderman."

"Have you seen their photographs, taken together?" asked Mrs. Brankley, abandoning the subject of Egbert's prospective career.

"No; do show me," said Elaine, with a flattering show of interest; "I've never seen that sort of thing before. It used to be the fashion once for engaged couples to be photographed together, didn't it?"

"It's *very* much the fashion now," said Mrs. Brankley assertively, but some of the complacency had filtered out of her voice.

Suzette came into the room, wearing the dress that she had worn in the Park that morning.

"Of course, you've been hearing all about *the* engagement from mother," she cried, and then set to work conscientiously to cover the same ground.

"We met at Grindelwald, you know. He always calls me his Ice Maiden because we first got to know each other on the skating-rink. Quite romantic, wasn't it? Then we asked him to tea one day, and we got to be quite friendly. Then he proposed."

"He wasn't the only one who was smitten with Suzette," Mrs. Brankley hastened to put in, fearful lest Elaine might suppose that Egbert had had things all his own way. "There was an American millionaire who was quite taken with her, and a Polish count of a very old family. I assure you I felt quite nervous at some of our tea-parties."

Mrs. Brankley had given Grindelwald a sinister but rather alluring reputation among a large circle of untravelled friends as a place where the insolence of birth and wealth was held in precarious check from breaking forth into scenes of savage violence.

"My marriage with Egbert will, of course, enlarge the sphere of my life enormously," pursued Suzette.

"Yes," said Elaine; her eyes were rather remorselessly taking in the details of her cousin's toilette. It is said that nothing is sadder than victory except defeat. Suzette began to feel that the tragedy of both was concentrated in the creation which had given her such unalloyed gratification till Elaine had come on the scene.

"A woman can be so immensely helpful in the social way to a man who is making a career for himself. And I'm so glad to find that we've a great many ideas in common. We each made out a list of our idea of the hundred best books, and quite a number of them were the same."

"He looks bookish," said Elaine, with a critical glance at the photograph.

"Oh, he's not at all a bookworm," said Suzette quickly, "though he's tremendously well-read. He's quite the man of action."

"Does he hunt?" asked Elaine.

"No, he doesn't get much time or opportunity for riding."

"What a pity!" commented Elaine. "I don't think I could marry a man who wasn't fond of riding."

"Of course that's a matter of taste," said Suzette stiffly; "horsey men are not usually gifted with overmuch brains, are they?"

"There is as much difference between a horseman and a horsey man as there is between a well-dressed man and a dressy one," said Elaine judicially; "and you may have noticed how seldom a dressy woman really knows how to dress. As an old lady of my acquaintance observed the other day, some people are born with a sense of how to clothe themselves, others acquire it, others look as if their clothes had been thrust upon them."

She gave Lady Caroline her due quotation marks, but the sudden tactfulness with which she looked away from her cousin's frock was entirely her own idea.

A young man entering the room at this moment caused a diversion that was rather welcome to Suzette.

"Here comes Egbert," she announced, with an air of subdued triumph; it was at least a satisfaction to be able to produce the captive of her charms, alive and in good condition, on the scene. Elaine might be as critical as she pleased, but a live lover outweighed any number of well-dressed straight-riding cavaliers who existed only as a distant vision of the delectable husband.

Egbert was one of those men who have no small talk, but possess an inexhaustible supply of the larger variety. In whatever society he happened to be, and particularly in the immediate neighbourhood of an afternoon-tea table, with a limited audience of womenfolk, he gave the impression of some one who was addressing a public meeting, and would be happy to answer questions afterwards. A suggestion of gaslit mission-halls, wet umbrellas, and discreet applause seemed to accompany him everywhere. He was an exponent, among other things, of what he called New Thought, which seemed to lend itself conveniently to the employment of a good deal of rather stale phraseology. Probably in the course of some thirty odd years of existence he had never been of any notable use to man, woman, child, or animal, but it was his firmly-announced intention to leave the world a better, happier, purer place than he had found it; against the danger of any relapse to earlier conditions after his disappearance from the scene, he was, of course, powerless to guard. 'Tis not in mortals to ensure succession, and Egbert was admittedly mortal.

Elaine found him immensely entertaining, and would certainly have exerted herself to draw him out if such a proceeding had been at all necessary. She listened to his conversation with the complacent appreciation that one bestows on a stage tragedy, from whose calamities one can escape at any moment by the simple process of leaving one's seat. When at last he checked the flow of his opinions by a hurried reference to his watch, and declared that he must be moving on elsewhere, Elaine almost expected a vote of thanks to be accorded him, or to be asked to signify herself in favour of some resolution by holding up her hand.

When the young man had bidden the company a rapid business-like farewell, tempered in Suzette's case by the exact degree of tender intimacy that it would have been considered improper to omit or overstep, Elaine turned to her expectant cousin with an air of cordial congratulation.

"He is exactly the husband I should have chosen for you, Suzette."

For the second time that afternoon Suzette felt a sense of waning enthusiasm for one of her possessions.

Mrs. Brankley detected the note of ironical congratulation in her visitor's verdict.

"I suppose she means he's not her idea of a husband, but he's good enough for Suzette," she observed to herself, with a snort that expressed itself somewhere in the nostrils of the brain. Then with a smiling air of heavy patronage she delivered herself of her one idea of a damaging counterstroke.

"And when are we to hear of your engagement, my dear?"

"Now," said Elaine quietly, but with electrical effect; "I came to announce it to you but I wanted to hear all about Suzette first. It will be formally announced in the papers in a day or two."

"But who is it? Is it the young man who was with you in the Park this morning?" asked Suzette.

"Let me see, who was I with in the Park this morning? A very good-looking dark boy? Oh, no, not Comus Bassington. Some one you know by name, anyway, and I expect you've seen his portrait in the papers."

"A flying-man?" asked Mrs. Brankley.

"Courtenay Youghal," said Elaine.

Mrs. Brankley and Suzette had often rehearsed in the privacy of their minds the occasion when Elaine should come to pay her personal congratulations to her engaged cousin. It had never been in the least like this.

On her return from her enjoyable afternoon visit Elaine

found an express messenger letter waiting for her. It was from Comus, thanking her for her loan—and returning it.

"I suppose I ought never to have asked you for it," he wrote, "but you are always so deliciously solemn about money matters that I couldn't resist. Just heard the news of your engagement to Courtenay. Congrats. to you both. I'm far too stony broke to buy you a wedding present so I'm going to give you back the bread-and-butter dish. Luckily it still has your crest on it. I shall love to think of you and Courtenay eating bread-and-butter out of it for the rest of your lives."

That was all he had to say on the matter about which Elaine had been preparing to write a long and kindly-expressed letter, closing a rather momentous chapter in her life and his. There was not a trace of regret or upbraiding in his note; he had walked out of their mutual fairyland as abruptly as she had, and to all appearances far more unconcernedly. Reading the letter again and again, Elaine could come to no decision as to whether this was merely a courageous gibe at defeat, or whether it represented the real value that Comus set on the thing that he had lost.

And she would never know. If Comus possessed one useless gift to perfection it was the gift of laughing at Fate even when it had struck him hardest. One day, perhaps, the laughter and mockery would be silent on his lips, and Fate would have the advantage of laughing last.

CHAPTER XII

A DOOR closed and Francesca Bassington sat alone in her well-beloved drawing-room. The visitor who had been enjoying the hospitality of her afternoon-tea table had just taken his departure. The *tête-à-tête* had not been a pleasant one, at any rate as far as Francesca was concerned, but at least it had brought her the information for which she had been seeking. Her rôle of looker-on from a tactful distance had necessarily left her much in the dark concerning the progress of the all-important wooing, but during the last few hours she had, on slender though significant evidence, exchanged her complacent expectancy for a conviction that something had gone wrong. She had spent the previous evening at her brother's house, and had naturally seen nothing of Comus in that uncongenial quarter; neither had he put in an appearance at the breakfast table the following morning. She had met him in the hall at eleven o'clock, and he had hurried past her, merely imparting the information that he would not be in till dinner that evening. He spoke in his sulkiest tone, and his face wore a look of defeat, thinly masked by an air of defiance; it was not the defiance of a man who is losing, but of one who has already lost.

Francesca's conviction that things had gone wrong between Comus and Elaine de Frey grew in strength as the day wore on. She lunched at a friend's house, but it was not a quarter where special social information of any importance was likely to come early to hand. Instead of the news she was hankering for, she had to listen to trivial gossip and speculation on the flirtations and "cases" and "affairs" of a string of acquaintances whose matrimonial projects interested her about as much as the nesting arrangements of the wildfowl in St. James's Park.

"Of course," said her hostess, with the duly impressive emphasis of a privileged chronicler, "we've always regarded Claire as the marrying one of the family, so when Emily came to us and said, 'I've got some news for you,' we all said, 'Claire's engaged!' 'Oh, no,' said Emily, 'it's not Claire this time, it's me.' So then we had to guess who the lucky man was. 'It can't be Captain Parminter,' we all said, 'because he's always been sweet on Joan.' And then Emily said——"

The recording voice reeled off the catalogue of inane remarks with a comfortable purring complacency that held out no hope of an early abandoning of the topic. Francesca sat and wondered why the innocent acceptance of a cutlet and a glass of indifferent claret should lay one open to such unsparing punishment.

A stroll homeward through the Park after lunch brought no further enlightenment on the subject that was uppermost in her mind; what was worse, it brought her, without possibility of escape, within hailing distance of Merla Blathlington, who fastened on to her with the enthusiasm of a lonely tsetse fly encountering an outpost of civilization.

"Just think," she buzzed inconsequently, "my sister in Cambridgeshire has hatched out thirty-three White Orpington chickens in her incubator!"

"What eggs did she put in it?" asked Francesca.

"Oh, some very special strain of White Orpington."

"Then I don't see anything remarkable in the result. If she had put in crocodiles' eggs and hatched out White Orpingtons, there might have been something to write to *Country Life* about."

"What funny fascinating things these little green park-chairs are," said Merla, starting off on a fresh topic; "they always look so quaint and knowing when they're stuck away in pairs by themselves under the trees, as if they were having a heart-to-heart talk or discussing a piece of very private scandal. If they could only speak, what tragedies and comedies they could tell us of, what flirtations and proposals!"

"Let us be devoutly thankful that they can't," said Francesca, with a shuddering recollection of the luncheon-table conversation.

"Of course, it would make one very careful what one said before them—or above them rather," Merla rattled on, and then, to Francesca's infinite relief, she espied another acquaintance sitting in unprotected solitude, who promised to supply a more durable audience than her present rapidly moving companion. Francesca was free to return to her drawing-room in Blue Street to await with such patience as she could command the coming of some visitor who might be able to throw light on the subject that was puzzling and disquieting her. The arrival of George St. Michael boded bad news, but at any rate news, and she gave him an almost cordial welcome.

"Well, you see I wasn't far wrong about Miss de Frey and Courtenay Youghal, was I?" he chirruped, almost before he had seated himself. Francesca was to be spared any further spinning-out of her period of uncertainty. "Yes, it's officially given out," he went on, "and it's to appear in the *Morning Post* tomorrow. I heard it from Colonel Deel this morning, and he had it direct from Youghal himself. Yes, please, one lump; I'm not fashionable, you see." He had made the same remark about the sugar in his tea with unfailing regularity for at least thirty years. Fashions in sugar are apparently stationary. "They say," he continued hurriedly, "that he proposed to her on the Terrace of the House, and a division bell rang and he had to hurry off before she had time to give her answer, and when he got back she simply said, 'The Ayes have it.'" St. Michael paused in his narrative to give an appreciative giggle.

"Just the sort of inanity that would go the rounds," remarked Francesca, with the satisfaction of knowing that she was making the criticism direct to the author and begetter of the inanity in question. Now that the blow had fallen and she knew the full extent of its weight, her feeling towards the bringer of bad news, who sat complacently nibbling at her tea-cakes and scattering crumbs of tiresome small-talk at her feet, was one of whole-hearted dislike. She could sympathize with, or at any rate understand, the tendency of Oriental despots to inflict death or ignominious chastisement on messengers bearing tidings of misfortune and defeat, and St. Michael, she perfectly well knew, was thoroughly aware of the fact that her hopes and wishes had been centred on the possibility of having Elaine for a daughter-in-law; every purring remark that his mean little soul prompted him to contribute to the conversation had an easily recognizable undercurrent of malice. Fortunately for her powers of polite endurance, which had been put to such searching and repeated tests that day, St. Michael had planned out for himself a busy little time-table of afternoon visits, at each of which his self-appointed task of forestalling and embellishing the newspaper announcements of the Youghal-de Frey engagement would be hurriedly but thoroughly performed.

"They'll be quite one of the best-looking and most interesting couples of the season, won't they?" he cried, by way of farewell. The door closed, and Francesca Bassington sat alone in her drawing-room.

Before she could give way to the bitter luxury of reflection on the downfall of her hopes, it was prudent to take precautionary measures against unwelcome intrusion. Summoning the maid who had just speeded the departing St. Michael, she gave the order: "I am not at home this afternoon to Lady Caroline Benaresq." On second thoughts she extended the taboo to all possible callers, and sent a telephone message to catch Comus at his club, asking him to come and see her as soon as he could manage before it was time to dress for dinner. Then she sat down to think, and her thinking was beyond the relief of tears.

She had built herself a castle of hopes, and it had not been a castle in Spain, but a structure well on the probable side of the Pyrenees. There had been a solid foundation on which to build. Miss de Frey's fortune was an assured and unhampered one, her liking for Comus had been an obvious fact; his courtship of her a serious reality. The young people had been much together in public, and their names had naturally been coupled in the match-making gossip of the day. The only serious shadow cast over the scene had been the persistent presence, in foreground or background, of Courtenay Youghal. And now the shadow suddenly stood forth as the reality, and the castle of hopes was a ruin, a hideous mortification of dust and debris, with the skeleton outlines of its chambers still standing to make mockery of its discomfited architect. The daily anxiety about Comus and his extravagant ways and intractable disposition had been gradually lulled by the prospect of his making an advantageous marriage, which would have transformed him from a ne'er-do-well and adventurer into a wealthy idler. He might even have been moulded, by the resourceful influence of an ambitious wife, into a man with some definite purpose in life. The prospect had vanished with cruel suddenness, and the anxieties were crowding back again, more insistent than ever. The boy had had his one good chance in the matrimonial market and missed it; if he were to transfer his attentions to some other well-dowered girl he would be marked down at once as a fortune-hunter, and that would constitute a heavy handicap to the most plausible of wooers. His liking for Elaine had

evidently been genuine in its way, though perhaps it would
have been rash to read any deeper sentiment into it, but even
with the spur of his own inclination to assist him he had failed
to win the prize that had seemed so temptingly within his reach.
And in the dashing of his prospects, Francesca saw the threatening of her own. The old anxiety as to her precarious tenure
of her present quarters put on again all its familiar terrors.
One day, she foresaw, in the horribly near future, George St.
Michael would come pattering up her stairs with the breathless
intelligence that Emmeline Chetrof was going to marry somebody or other in the Guards or the Record Office, as the case
might be, and then there would be an uprooting of her life
from its home and haven in Blue Street and a wandering forth
to some cheap unhappy far-off dwelling, where the stately Van
der Meulen and its companion host of beautiful and desirable
things would be stuffed and stowed away in soulless surroundings, like courtly *émigrés* fallen on evil days. It was unthink-
able, but the trouble was that it had to be thought about. And
if Comus had played his cards well and transformed himself
from an encumbrance into a son with wealth at his command,
the tragedy which she saw looming in front of her might have
been avoided, or at the worst whittled down to easily bearable
proportions. With money behind one, the problem of where to
live approaches more nearly to the simple question of where do
you wish to live, and a rich daughter-in-law would have surely
seen to it that she did not have to leave her square mile of
Mecca and go out into the wilderness of bricks and mortar. If
the house in Blue Street could not have been compounded for
there were other desirable residences which would have been
capable of consoling Francesca for her lost Eden. And now the
detested Courtenay Youghal, with his mocking eyes and air of
youthful cynicism, had stepped in and overthrown those golden
hopes and plans whose non-fulfilment would make such a world
of change in her future. Assuredly she had reason to feel bitter
against that young man, and she was not disposed to take a
very lenient view of Comus's own mismanagement of the affair; her greeting when he at last arrived was not couched in
a sympathetic strain.

"So you have lost your chance with the heiress," she remarked abruptly.

"Yes," said Comus coolly; "Courtenay Youghal has added her to his other successes."

"And you have added her to your other failures," pursued Francesca relentlessly; her temper had been tried that day beyond ordinary limits.

"I thought you seemed getting along so well with her," she continued, as Comus remained uncommunicative.

"We hit it off rather well together," said Comus, and added with deliberate bluntness, "I suppose she got rather sick at my borrowing money from her. She thought it was all I was after."

"You borrowed money from her!" said Francesca; "you were fool enough to borrow money from a girl who was favourably disposed towards you, and with Courtenay Youghal in the background waiting to step in and oust you!"

Francesca's voice trembled with misery and rage. This great stroke of good luck that had seemed about to fall into their laps had been thrust aside by an act or series of acts of wanton paltry folly. The good ship had been lost for the sake of the traditional ha'p'orth of tar. Comus had paid some pressing tailor's or tobacconist's bill with a loan unwillingly put at his disposal by the girl he was courting, and had flung away his chances of securing a wealthy and in every way desirable bride. Elaine de Frey and her fortune might have been the making of Comus, but he had hurried in as usual to effect his own undoing. Calmness did not in this case come with reflection; the more Francesca thought about the matter, the more exasperated she grew. Comus threw himself down in a low chair and watched her without a trace of embarrassment or concern at her mortification. He had come to her feeling rather sorry for himself, and bitterly conscious of his defeat, and she had met him with a taunt and without the least hint of sympathy; he determined that she should be tantalized with the knowledge of how small and stupid a thing had stood between the realization and ruin of her hopes for him.

"And to think she should be captured by Courtenay Youghal," said Francesca bitterly; "I've always deplored your intimacy with that young man."

"It's hardly my intimacy with him that's made Elaine accept him," said Comus.

Francesca realized the futility of further upbraiding. Through the tears of vexation that stood in her eyes she looked across at the handsome boy who sat opposite her, mocking at his own misfortune, perversely indifferent to his folly, seemingly almost indifferent to its consequences.

"Comus," she said quietly and wearily, "you are an exact reversal of the legend of Pandora's Box. You have all the charm and advantages that a boy could want to help him on in the world, and behind it all there is the fatal damning gift of utter hopelessness."

"I think," said Comus, "that is the best description that any one has ever given of me."

For the moment there was a flush of sympathy and something like outspoken affection between mother and son. They seemed very much alone in the world just now, and in the general overturn of hopes and plans there flickered a chance that each might stretch out a hand to the other, and summon back to their lives an old dead love that was the best and strongest feeling either of them had known. But the sting of disappointment was too keen, and the flood of resentment mounted too high on either side to allow the chance more than a moment in which to flicker away into nothingness. The old fatal topic of estrangement came to the fore, the question of immediate ways and means, and mother and son faced themselves again as antagonists on a well-disputed field.

"What is done is done," said Francesca, with a movement of tragic impatience that belied the philosophy of her words; "there is nothing to be gained by crying over spilt milk. There is the present and the future to be thought about, though. One can't go on indefinitely as a tenant-for-life in a fools' paradise." Then she pulled herself together and proceeded to deliver an ultimatum which the force of circumstances no longer permitted her to hold in reserve.

"It's not much use talking to you about money, as I know

from long experience, but I can only tell you this, that in the middle of the season I'm already obliged to be thinking of leaving town. And you, I'm afraid, will have to be thinking of leaving England at equally short notice. Henry told me the other day that he can get you something out in West Africa. You've had your chance of doing something better for yourself from the financial point of view, and you've thrown it away for the sake of borrowing a little ready money for your luxuries, so now you must take what you can get. The pay won't be very good at first, but living is not dear out there."

"West Africa," said Comus reflectively; "it's a sort of modern substitute for the old-fashioned *oubliette*, a convenient depository for tiresome people. Dear Uncle Henry may talk lugubriously about the burden of Empire, but he evidently recognizes its uses as a refuse consumer."

"My dear Comus, you are talking of the West Africa of yesterday. While you have been wasting your time at school, and worse than wasting your time in the West End, other people have been grappling with the study of tropical diseases, and the West African coast country is being rapidly transformed from a lethal chamber into a sanatorium."

Comus laughed mockingly.

"What a beautiful bit of persuasive prose! It reminds one of the Psalms, and even more of a company prospectus. If you were honest you'd confess that you lifted it straight out of a rubber or railway promotion scheme. Seriously, mother, if I must grub about for a living, why can't I do it in England? I could go into a brewery, for instance."

Francesca shook her head decisively; she could foresee the sort of steady work Comus was likely to accomplish, with the lodestone of town and the minor attractions of race-meetings and similar festivities always beckoning to him from a conveniently attainable distance, but apart from that aspect of the case there was a financial obstacle in the way of his obtaining any employment at home.

"Breweries and all those sort of things necessitate money to start with; one has to pay premiums or invest capital in the undertaking and so forth. And as we have no money available, and can scarcely pay our debts as it is, it's no use thinking about it."

"Can't we sell something?" asked Comus.

He made no actual suggestion as to what should be sacrificed, but he was looking straight at the Van der Meulen.

For a moment Francesca felt a stifling sensation of weakness, as though her heart was going to stop beating. Then she sat forward in her chair and spoke with energy, almost fierceness.

"When I am dead my things can be sold and dispersed. As long as I am alive I prefer to keep them by me."

In her holy place, with all her treasured possessions around her, this dreadful suggestion had been made. Some of her cherished household gods, souvenirs and keepsakes from past days, would, perhaps, not have fetched a very considerable sum in the auction-room, others had a distinct value of their own, but to her they were all precious. And the Van der Meulen, at which Comus had looked with impious appraising eyes, was the most sacred of them all. When Francesca had been away from her town residence or had been confined to her bedroom through illness, the great picture with its stately solemn representation of a long-ago battle-scene, painted to flatter the flattery-loving soul of a warrior-king who was dignified even in his campaigns—this was the first thing she visited on her return to town or convalescence. If an alarm of fire had been raised it would have been the first thing for whose safety she would have troubled. And Comus had almost suggested that it should be parted with, as one sold railway shares and other soulless things.

Scolding, she had long ago realized, was a useless waste of time and energy where Comus was concerned, but this evening she unloosed her tongue for the mere relief that it gave to her surcharged feelings. He sat listening without comment, though she purposely let fall remarks that she hoped might sting him into self-defence or protest. It was an unsparing indictment, the more damaging in that it was so irrefutably true, the more tragic in that it came from perhaps the one person in the world whose opinion he had ever cared for. And he sat through it as silent and seemingly unmoved as though she had been rehearsing a speech for some drawing-room comedy. When she had had her say his method of retort was not the soft answer that turneth away wrath, but the inconsequent one that shelves it.

"Let's go and dress for dinner."

The meal, like so many that Francesca and Comus had eaten in each other's company of late, was a silent one. Now that the full bearings of the disaster had been discussed in all its aspects, there was nothing more to be said. Any attempt at ignoring the situation and passing on to less controversial topics would have been a mockery and pretence which neither of them would have troubled to sustain. So the meal went forward with its dragged-out dreary intimacy of two people who were separated by a gulf of bitterness, and whose hearts were hard with resentment against one another.

Francesca felt a sense of relief when she was able to give the maid the order to serve her coffee upstairs. Comus had a sullen scowl on his face, but he looked up as she rose to leave the room, and gave his half-mocking little laugh.

"You needn't look so tragic," he said. "You're going to have your own way. I'll go out to that West African hole."

CHAPTER XIII

COMUS found his way to his seat in the stalls of the Straw Exchange Theatre, and turned to watch the stream of distinguished and distinguishable people who made their appearance as a matter of course at a First Night in the height of the season. Pit and gallery were already packed with a throng, tense, expectant and alert, that waited for the rise of the curtain with the eager patience of a terrier watching a dilatory human prepare for outdoor exercises. Stalls and boxes filled slowly and hesitatingly with a crowd whose component units seemed for the most part to recognize the probability that they were quite as interesting as any play they were likely to see. Those who bore no particular face-value themselves derived a certain amount of social dignity from the near neighbourhood of obvious notabilities; if one could not obtain recognition oneself there was some vague pleasure in being able to recognize notoriety at intimately close quarters.

"Who is that woman with the auburn hair and a rather effective belligerent gleam in her eyes?" asked a man sitting just behind Comus. "She looks as if she might have created the world in six days and destroyed it on the seventh."

"I forget her name," said his neighbour; "she writes. She's the author of that book, *The Woman Who Wished it was Wednesday*, you know. It used to be the convention that women writers should be plain and dowdy; now we have gone to the other extreme and build them on extravagantly decorative lines."

A buzz of recognition came from the front rows of the pit, together with a craning of necks on the part of those in less favoured seats. It heralded the arrival of Sherard Blaw, the dramatist who had discovered himself, and who had given so ungrudgingly of his discovery to the world. Lady Caroline, who was already directing little conversational onslaughts from her box, gazed gently for a moment at the new arrival, and then turned to the silver-haired Archdeacon sitting beside her.

"They say the poor man is haunted by the fear that he will die during a general election, and that his obituary notices will be seriously curtailed by the space taken up by the election results. The curse of our party system, from his point of view, is that it takes up so much room in the Press."

The Archdeacon smiled indulgently. As a man he was so exquisitely worldly that he fully merited the name of the Heavenly Worldling bestowed on him by an admiring duchess, and withal his texture was shot with a pattern of such genuine saintliness that one felt that whoever else might hold the keys of Paradise he, at least, possessed a private latchkey to that abode.

"Is it not significant of the altered grouping of things," he observed, "that the Church, as represented by me, sympathizes with the message of Sherard Blaw, while neither the man nor his message find acceptance with unbelievers like you, Lady Caroline?"

Lady Caroline blinked her eyes. "My dear Archdeacon," she said, "no one can be an unbeliever nowadays. The Christian Apologists have left one nothing to disbelieve."

The Archdeacon rose with a delighted chuckle. "I must go and tell that to De la Poulett," he said, indicating a clerical figure sitting in the third row of the stalls; "he spends his life explaining from his pulpit that the glory of Christianity consists in the fact that though it is not true it has been found necessary to invent it."

The door of the box opened and Courtenay Youghal entered, bringing with him a subtle suggestion of chaminade and an atmosphere of political tension. The Government had fallen out of the good graces of a section of its supporters, and those who were not in the know were busy predicting a serious crisis over a forthcoming division in the Committee stage of an important Bill. This was Saturday night, and unless some successful cajolery were effected between now and Monday afternoon, Ministers would be, seemingly, in danger of defeat.

"Ah, here is Youghal," said the Archdeacon; "he will be able to tell us what is going to happen in the next forty-eight hours. I hear the Prime Minister says it is a matter of conscience, and they will stand or fall by it."

His hopes and sympathies were notoriously on the Ministerial side.

Youghal greeted Lady Caroline and subsided gracefully into a chair well in the front of the box. A buzz of recognition rippled slowly across the house.

"For the Government to fall on a matter of conscience," he said, "would be like a man cutting himself with a safety razor."

Lady Caroline purred a gentle approval.

"I'm afraid it's true, Archdeacon," she said.

No one can effectively defend a Government when it's been in office several years. The Archdeacon took refuge in light skirmishing.

"I believe Lady Caroline sees the makings of a great Socialist statesman in you, Youghal," he observed.

"Great Socialist statesmen aren't made, they're stillborn," replied Youghal.

"What is the play about tonight?" asked a pale young woman who had taken no part in the talk.

"I don't know," said Lady Caroline, "but I hope it's dull. If there is any brilliant conversation in it I shall burst into tears."

In the front row of the upper circle a woman with a restless starling-voice was discussing the work of a temporarily fashionable composer, chiefly in relation to her own emotions, which she seemed to think might prove generally interesting to those around her.

"Whenever I hear his music I feel that I want to go up into a mountain and pray. Can you understand that feeling?"

The girl to whom she was unburdening herself shook her head.

"You see, I've heard his music chiefly in Switzerland, and we were up among the mountains all the time, so it wouldn't have made any difference."

"In that case," said the woman, who seemed to have emergency emotions to suit all geographical conditions, "I should have wanted to be in a great silent plain by the side of a rushing river."

"What I think is so splendid about his music——" commenced another starling-voice on the farther side of the girl. Like sheep that feed greedily before the coming of a storm, the starling-voices seemed impelled to extra effort by the knowledge of four imminent intervals of acting during which they would be hushed into constrained silence.

In the back row of the dress circle a late-comer, after a cursory glance at the programme, had settled down into a comfortable narrative, which was evidently the resumed thread of an unfinished taxi-drive monologue.

"We all said, 'It can't be Captain Parminter, because he's always been sweet on Joan,' and then Emily said——"

The curtain went up, and Emily's contribution to the discussion had to be held over till the entr'acte.

The play promised to be a success. The author, avoiding the pitfall of brilliancy, had aimed at being interesting; and as far as possible, bearing in mind that his play was a comedy, he had striven to be amusing. Above all he had remembered that in the laws of stage proportions it is permissible and generally desirable that the part should be greater than the whole; hence he had been careful to give the leading lady such a clear and commanding lead over the other characters of the play that it was impossible for any of them ever to get on level terms with her. The action of the piece was now and then delayed thereby, but the duration of its run would be materially prolonged.

The curtain came down on the first act amid an encouraging instalment of applause, and the audience turned its back on the stage and began to take a renewed interest in itself. The authoress of *The Woman Who Wished it was Wednesday* had swept like a convalescent whirlwind, subdued but potentially tempestuous, into Lady Caroline's box.

"I've just trodden with all my weight on the foot of an eminent publisher as I was leaving my seat," she cried, with a peal of delighted laughter. "He was such a dear about it; I said I hoped I hadn't hurt him, and he said, 'I suppose you think, who drives hard bargains should himself be hard.' Wasn't it pet lamb of him?"

"I've never trodden on a pet lamb," said Lady Caroline, "so I've no idea what its behaviour would be under the circumstances."

"Tell me," said the authoress, coming to the front of the box, the better to survey the house, and perhaps also with a charitable desire to make things easy for those who might pardonably wish to survey her, "tell me, please, where is the girl sitting whom Courtenay Youghal is engaged to?"

Elaine was pointed out to her, sitting in the fourth row of the stalls, on the opposite side of the house to where Comus had his seat. Once during the interval she had turned to give him a friendly nod of recognition as he stood in one of the side gangways, but he was absorbed at the moment in looking at himself in the glass panel. The grave brown eyes and the mocking green-grey ones had looked their last into each other's depths.

For Comus this first-night performance, with its brilliant gathering of spectators, its groups and coteries of lively talkers, even its counterfoil of dull chatterers, its pervading atmosphere of stage and social movement, and its intruding undercurrent of political flutter, all this composed a tragedy in which he was the chief character. It was the life he knew and loved and basked in, and it was the life he was leaving. It would go on reproducing itself again and again, with its stage interest and social interest and intruding outside interests, with the same lively chattering crowd, the people who had done things being pointed out by people who recognized them to people who didn't—it would all go on with unflagging animation and sparkle and enjoyment, and for him it would have stopped utterly. He would be in some unheard-of sun-blistered wilderness, where natives and pariah dogs and raucous-throated crows fringed round mockingly on one's loneliness, where one rode for sweltering miles for the chance of meeting a collector or police officer, with whom most likely on closer acquaintance one had hardly two ideas in common, where female society was represented at long intervals by some climate-withered woman missionary or official's wife, where food and sickness and veterinary lore became at last the three outstanding subjects on which the mind settled, or rather sank. That was the the life he foresaw and dreaded, and that was the life he was going to. For a boy who went out to it from the dulness of some country rectory, from a neighbourhood where a flower show and a cricket march formed the social landmarks of the year, the feeling of exile might not be very crushing, might indeed be lost in the sense of change and adventure. But Comus had lived too thoroughly in the centre of things to regard life in a backwater as anything else than stagnation, and stagnation while one is young he justly regarded as an offence against nature and reason, in keeping with the perverted mockery that sends decrepit invalids touring painfully about the world and shuts panthers up in narrow cages. He was being put aside, as a wine is put aside, but to deteriorate instead of gaining in the process, to lose the best time of his youth and health and good looks in a world where youth and health and good looks count for much and where time never returns lost possessions. And thus, as the curtain swept down on the close of each act, Comus felt a sense of depression and deprivation sweep down on himself; bitterly he watched his last evening of social gaiety slipping away to its end. In less than an hour it would be over; in a few months' time it would be an unreal memory.

In the third interval, as he gazed round at the chattering house, some one touched him on the arm. It was Lady Veula Croot.

"I suppose in a week's time you'll be on the high seas?" she said. "I'm coming to your farewell dinner, you know; your mother has just asked me. I'm not going to talk the usual rot to you about how much you will like it and so on. I sometimes think that one of the advantages of hell will be that no one will have the impertinence to point out to you that you're really better off than you would be anywhere else. What do you think of the play? Of course one can foresee the end; she will come to her husband with the announcement that their longed-for child is going to be born, and that will smooth over everything. So conveniently effective to wind up a comedy with the commencement of some one else's tragedy. And every one will go away saying, 'I'm glad it had a happy ending.' "

Lady Veula moved back to her seat, with her pleasant smile on her lips and the look of infinite weariness in her eyes.

The interval, the last interval, was drawing to a close, and the house began to turn with fidgety attention towards the stage for the unfolding of the final phase of the play. Francesca sat in Serena Golackly's box listening to Colonel Springfield's story of what happened to a pigeon-cote in his compound at Poona. Every one who knew the Colonel had to listen to that story a good many times, but Lady Caroline had mitigated the boredom of the infliction, and in fact invested it with a certain sporting interest, by offering a prize to the person who heard it oftenest in the course of the season, the competitors being under an honourable understanding not to lead up to the subject. Ada Spelvexit and a boy in the Foreign Office were at present at the top of the list with five recitals each to their score, but the former was suspected of doubtful adherence to the rules and spirit of the competition.

"And there, dear lady," concluded the Colonel, "were the eleven dead pigeons. What had become of the bandicoot no one ever knew."

Francesca thanked him for his story, and complacently inscribed the figure 4 on the margin of her theatre programme. Almost at the same moment she heard George St. Michael's voice pattering out a breathless piece of intelligence for the edification of Serena Golackly and any one else who might care to listen. Francesca galvanized into sudden attention.

"Emmeline Chetrof to a fellow in the Indian Forest Department. He's got nothing but his pay, and they can't be married for four or five years: an absurdly long engagement, don't you think so? All very well to wait seven years for a wife in patriarchal times when you probably had others to go on with, and you lived long enough to celebrate your own tercentenary, but under modern conditions it seems a foolish arrangement."

St. Michael spoke almost with a sense of grievance. A marriage project that tied up all the small pleasant nuptial gossip-items about bridesmaids and honeymoon and recalcitrant aunts and so forth for an indefinite number of years seemed scarcely decent in his eyes, and there was little satisfaction or importance to be derived from early and special knowledge of an event which loomed as far distant as a Presidential Election or a change of Viceroy. But to Francesca, who had listened with startled apprehension at the mention of Emmeline Chetrof's name, the news came in a flood of relief and thankfulness. Short of entering a nunnery and taking celibate vows, Emmeline could hardly have behaved more conveniently than in tying herself up to a lover whose circumstances made it necessary to relegate marriage to the distant future. For four or five years Francesca was assured of undisturbed possession of the house in Blue Street, and after that period who knew what might happen? The engagement might stretch on indefinitely, it might even come to nothing under the weight of its accumulated years, as sometimes happened with these protracted affairs. Emmeline might lose her fancy for her absentee lover, and might never replace him with another. A golden possibility of perpetual tenancy of her present home began to float once more through Francesca's mind. As long as Emmeline had been unbespoken in the marriage market there had always been the haunting likelihood of seeing the dreaded announcement, "A marriage has been arranged and will shortly take place," in connexion with her name. And now a marriage had been arranged and would *not* shortly take place, might indeed never take place. St. Michael's information was likely to be correct in this instance; he would never have invented a piece of matrimonial intelligence which gave such little scope for supplementary detail of the kind he loved to supply. As Francesca turned to watch the fourth act of the play, her mind was singing a pæan of thankfulness and exultation. It was as though some artificer sent by the gods had reinforced with a substantial cord the horsehair thread that held up the sword of Damocles over her head. Her love for her home, for her treasured household possessions and her pleasant social life, was able to expand once more in present security, and feed on future hope. She was still young enough to count four or five years as a long time, and tonight she was optimistic enough to prophesy smooth things of the future that lay beyond that span. Of the fourth act, with its carefully held back but obviously imminent reconciliation between the leading characters, she took in but little, except that she vaguely understood it to have a happy ending. As the lights went up she looked round on the dispersing audience with a feeling of friendliness uppermost in her mind; even the sight of Elaine de Frey and Courtenay Youghal leaving the theatre together did not inspire her with a tenth part of the annoyance that their entrance had caused her. Serena's invitation to go on to the Savoy for supper fitted in exactly with her mood of exhilaration. It would be a fit and appropriate wind-up to an auspicious evening. The cold chicken and modest brand of Chablis waiting for her at home should give way to a banquet of more festive nature.

In the crush of the vestibule, friends and enemies, personal and political, were jostled and locked together in the general effort to rejoin temporarily estranged garments and secure the attendance of elusive vehicles. Lady Caroline found herself at close quarters with the estimable Henry Greech, and experienced some of the joy which comes to the homeward wending sportsman when a chance shot presents itself on which he may expend his remaining cartridges.

"So the Government is going to climb down, after all," she said, with a provocative assumption of private information on the subject.

"I assure you the Government will do nothing of the kind," replied the Member of Parliament with befitting dignity; "the Prime Minister told me last night that under no circumstances——"

"My dear Mr. Greech," said Lady Caroline, "we all know that Prime Ministers are wedded to the truth, but like other wedded couples they sometimes live apart."

For her, at any rate, the comedy had had a happy ending.

Comus made his way slowly and lingeringly from the stalls, so slowly that the lights were already being turned down and great shroud-like dustcloths were being swathed over the ornamental gilt-work. The laughing, chattering, yawning throng had filtered out of the vestibule, and was melting away in final groups from the steps of the theatre. An impatient attendant gave him his coat and locked up the cloak-room. Comus stepped out under the portico; he looked at the posters announcing the play, and in anticipation he could see other posters announcing its 200th performance. Two hundred performances; by that time the Straw Exchange Theatre would be to him something so remote and unreal that it would hardly seem to exist or to have ever existed except in his fancy. And to the laughing, chattering throng that would pass in under that portico to the 200th performance, he would be, to those that had known him, something equally remote and nonexistent. "The good-looking Bassington boy? Oh, dead, or rubber-growing or sheep-farming, or something of that sort."

CHAPTER XIV

THE farewell dinner which Francesca had hurriedly or-ganized in honour of her son's departure threatened from the outset to be a doubtfully successful function. In the first place, as he observed privately, there was very little of Comus and a good deal of farewell in it. His own particular friends were unrepresented. Courtenay Youghal was out of the ques-tion; and though Francesca would have stretched a point and welcomed some of his other male associates of whom she scarcely approved, he himself had been opposed to including any of them in the invitations. On the other hand, as Henry Greech had provided Comus with this job that he was going out to, and was, moreover, finding part of the money for the necessary outfit, Francesca had felt it her duty to ask him and his wife to the dinner; the obtuseness that seems to cling to some people like a garment throughout their life had caused Mr. Greech to accept the invitation. When Comus heard of the circumstance he laughed long and boisterously; his spirits, Francesca noted, seemed to be rising fast as the hour for de-parture drew near.

The other guests included Serena Golackly and Lady Veula, the latter having been asked on the inspiration of the moment at the theatrical first night. In the height of the season it was not easy to get together a goodly selection of guests at short no-tice, and Francesca had gladly fallen in with Serena's sug-gestion of bringing with her Stephen Thorle, who was alleged, in loose feminine phrasing, to "know all about" tropical Africa. His travels and experiences in those regions probably did not cover much ground or stretch over any great length of time, but he was one of those individuals who can describe a conti-nent on the strength of a few days' stay in a coast town as intimately and dogmatically as a palæontologist will recon-

THE UNBEARABLE BASSINGTON 117

struct an extinct mammal from the evidence of a stray shin-bone. He had the loud penetrating voice and the prominent penetrating eyes of a man who can do no listening in the ordinary way and whose eyes have to perform the function of listening for him. His vanity did not necessarily make him unbearable, unless one had to spend much time in his society, and his need for a wide field of audience and admiration was mercifully calculated to spread his operations over a considerable human area. Moreover, his craving for attentive listeners forced him to interest himself in a wonderful variety of subjects on which he was able to discourse fluently and with a certain semblance of special knowledge. Politics he avoided; the ground was too well known, and there was a definite No to every definite Yes that could be put forward. Moreover, argument was not congenial to his disposition, which preferred an unchallenged flow of dissertation modified by occasional helpful questions which formed the starting-point for new offshoots of word-spinning. The promotion of cottage industries, the prevention of juvenile street trading, the extension of the Borstal prison system, the furtherance of vague talkative religious movements, the fostering of inter-racial *ententes*, all found in him a tireless exponent, a fluent and entertaining, though perhaps not very convincing, advocate. With the real motive power behind these various causes he was not very closely identified; to the spade-workers who carried on the actual labours of each particular movement he bore the relation of a trowel-worker, delving superficially at the surface, but able to devote a proportionately far greater amount of time to the advertisement of his progress and achievements. Such was Stephen Thorle, a governess in the nursery of Chelsea-bred religions, a skilled window-dresser in the emporium of his own personality, and needless to say, evanescently popular amid a wide but shifting circle of acquaintances. He improved on the record of a socially much-travelled individual whose experience has become classical, and went to most of the best houses—twice.

His inclusion as a guest at this particular dinner-party was

not a very happy inspiration. He was inclined to patronize
Comus, as well as the African continent, and on even slighter
acquaintance. With the exception of Henry Greech, whose
feelings towards his nephew had been soured by many years
of overt antagonism, there was an uncomfortable feeling
among those present that the topic of the black-sheep export
trade, as Comus would have himself expressed it, was being
given undue prominence in what should have been a festive
farewell banquet. And Comus, in whose honour the feast was
given, did not contribute much towards its success; though
his spirits seemed strung up to a high pitch, his merriment was
more the merriment of a cynical and amused onlooker than of
one who responds to the gaiety of his companions. Sometimes
he laughed quietly to himself at some chance remark of a
scarcely mirth-provoking nature, and Lady Veula, watching
him narrowly, came to the conclusion that an element of fear
was blended with his seemingly buoyant spirits. Once or twice
he caught her eye across the table, and a certain sympathy
seemed to grow up between them, as though they were both
consciously watching some lugubrious comedy that was being
played out before them.

An untoward little incident had marked the commencement
of the meal. A small still-life picture that hung over the side-
board had snapped its cord and slid down with an alarming
clatter on to the crowded board beneath it. The picture itself
was scarcely damaged, but its fall had been accompanied by
a tinkle of broken glass, and it was found that a liqueur glass,
one out of a set of seven that would be impossible to match,
had been shivered into fragments. Francesca's almost motherly
love for her possessions made her peculiarly sensible to a feeling of annoyance and depression at the accident, but she turned
politely to listen to Mrs. Greech's account of a misfortune in
which four soup-plates were involved. Mrs. Henry was not a
brilliant conversationalist, and her flank was speedily turned by
Stephen Thorle, who recounted a slum experience in which
two entire families did all their feeding out of one damaged
soup-plate.

"The gratitude of those poor creatures when I presented

them with a set of table crockery apiece, the tears in their eyes
and in their voices when they thanked me, would be impossible to describe."

"Thank you all the same for describing it," said Comus.

The listening eyes went swiftly round the table to gather
evidence as to how this rather disconcerting remark had been
received, but Thòrle's voice continued uninterruptedly to retail stories of East End gratitude, never failing to mention
the particular deeds of disinterested charity on his part which
had evoked and justified the gratitude. Mrs. Greech had to
suppress the interesting sequel to her broken crockery narrative,
to wit, how she subsequently matched the shattered soup-plates
at Harrod's. Like an imported plant species that sometimes
flourishes exceedingly, and makes itself at home to the dwarf-
ing and overshadowing of all native species, Thorle dominated
the dinner-party and thrust its original purport somewhat into
the background. Serena began to look helplessly apologetic.
It was altogether rather a relief when the filling of champagne
glasses gave Francesca an excuse for bringing matters back
to their intended footing.

"We must all drink a health," she said. "Comus, my own
dear boy, a safe and happy voyage to you, much prosperity in
the life you are going out to, and in due time a safe and happy
return——"

Her hand gave an involuntary jerk in the act of raising the
glass, and the wine went streaming across the tablecloth in a
froth of yellow bubbles. It certainly was not turning out a
comfortable or auspicious dinner-party.

"My dear mother," cried Comus, "you must have been
drinking healths all the afternoon to make your hand so un-
steady."

He laughed gaily and with apparent carelessness, but again
Lady Veula caught the frightened note in his laughter. Mrs.
Henry, with practical sympathy, was telling Francesca two
good ways for getting wine-stains out of tablecloths. The
smaller economies of life were an unnecessary branch of learning for Mrs. Greech, but she studied them as carefully and
conscientiously as a stay-at-home plain-dwelling English child

commits to memory the measurements and altitudes of the world's principal peaks. Some women of her temperament and mentality know by heart the favourite colours, flowers, and hymn-tunes of all the members of the Royal Family; Mrs. Greech would possibly have failed in an examination of that nature, but she knew what to do with carrots that have been over-long in storage.

Francesca did not renew her speech-making; a chill seemed to have fallen over all efforts at festivity, and she contented herself with refilling her glass and simply drinking to her boy's good health. The others followed her example, and Comus drained his glass with a brief "Thank you all very much." The sense of constraint which hung over the company was not, however, marked by any uncomfortable pause in the conversation. Henry Greech was a fluent thinker, of the kind that prefer to do their thinking aloud; the silence that descended on him as a mantle in the House of Commons was an official livery of which he divested himself as thoroughly as possible in private life. He did not propose to sit through dinner as a mere listener to Mr. Thorle's personal narrative of philanthropic movements and experiences, and took the first opportunity of launching himself into a flow of satirical observations on current political affairs. Lady Veula was inured to this sort of thing in her own home circle, and sat listening with the stoical indifference with which an Eskimo might accept the occurrence of one snowstorm the more, in the course of an Arctic winter. Serena Golackly felt a certain relief at the fact that her imported guest was not, after all, monopolizing the conversation. But the latter was too determined a personality to allow himself to be thrust aside for many minutes by the talkative M.P. Henry Greech paused for an instant to chuckle at one of his own shafts of satire, and immediately Thorle's penetrating voice swept across the table.

"Oh, you politicians!" he exclaimed, with pleasant superiority; "you are always fighting about how things should be done, and the consequence is you are never able to do anything. Would you like me to tell you what a Unitarian horse-dealer said to me at Brindisi about politicians?"

A Unitarian horse-dealer at Brindisi had all the allurement of the unexpected. Henry Greech's witticisms at the expense of the Front Opposition bench were destined to remain as unfinished as his wife's history of the broken soup-plates. Thorle was primed with an ample succession of stories and themes, chiefly concerning poverty, thriftlessness, reclamation, reformed characters, and so forth, which carried him in an almost uninterrupted sequence through the remainder of the dinner.

"What I want to do is to make people think," he said, turning his prominent eyes on to his hostess; "it's so hard to make people think."

"At any rate you give them the opportunity," said Comus cryptically.

As the ladies rose to leave the table Comus crossed over to pick up one of Lady Veula's gloves that had fallen to the floor.

"I did not know you kept a dog," said Lady Veula.

"We don't," said Comus, "there isn't one in the house."

"I could have sworn I saw one follow you across the hall this evening," she said.

"A small black dog, something like a schipperke?" asked Comus in a low voice.

"Yes, that was it."

"I saw it myself tonight; it ran from behind my chair just as I was sitting down. Don't say anything to the others about it; it would frighten my mother."

"Have you ever seen it before?" Lady Veula asked quickly.

"Once, when I was six years old. It followed my father downstairs."

Lady Veula said nothing. She knew that Comus had lost his father at the age of six.

In the drawing-room Serena made nervous excuses for her talkative friend.

"Really, rather an interesting man, you know, and up to the eyes in all sorts of movements. Just the sort of person to turn loose at a drawing-room meeting, or to send down to a mission-hall in some unheard-of neighbourhood. Given a sounding-board and a harmonium, and a titled woman of some sort in the chair, and he'll be perfectly happy; I must say I hadn't realized how overpowering he might be at a small dinner-party."

"I should say he was a very good man," said Mrs. Greech; she had forgiven the mutilation of her soup-plate story.

The party broke up early, as most of the guests had other engagements to keep. With a belated recognition of the farewell nature of the occasion they made pleasant little good-bye remarks to Comus, with the usual predictions of prosperity and anticipations of an ultimate auspicious return. Even Henry Greech sank his personal dislike of the boy for the moment, and made hearty jocular allusions to a home-coming, which, in the elder man's eyes, seemed possibly pleasantly remote. Lady Veula alone made no reference to the future; she simply said, "Good-bye, Comus," but her voice was the kindest of all, and he responded with a look of gratitude. The weariness in her eyes was more marked than ever as she lay back against the cushions of her carriage.

"What a tragedy life is!" she said aloud to herself.

Serena and Stephen Thorle were the last to leave, and Francesca stood alone for a moment at the head of the stairway watching Comus laughing and chatting as he escorted the departing guests to the door. The ice-wall was melting under the influence of coming separation, and never had he looked more adorably handsome in her eyes, never had his merry laugh and mischief-loving gaiety seemed more infectious than on this night of his farewell banquet. She was glad enough that he was going away from a life of idleness and extravagance and temptation, but she began to suspect that she would miss, for a little while at any rate, the high-spirited boy who could be so attractive in his better moods. Her impulse, after the guests had gone, was to call him to her and hold him once more in her arms, and repeat her wishes for his happiness and good-luck in the land he was going to, and her promise of his welcome back, some not too distant day, to the land he was leaving. She wanted to forget, and to make him forget, the months of irritable jangling and sharp discussions, the months of cold aloofness and indifference, and to remember only that he was her own dear Comus as in the days of yore, before he had grown from an unmanageable pickle into a weariful problem. But she feared lest she should break down, and she did not wish to cloud his light-hearted gaiety on the very eve of his departure. She watched him for a moment as he stood in the hall, settling his tie before a mirror, and then went quietly back to her drawing-room. It had not been a very successful dinner-party, and the general effect it had left on her was one of depression.

Comus, with a lively musical-comedy air on his lips, and a look of wretchedness in his eyes, went out to visit the haunts that he was leaving so soon.

CHAPTER XV

ELAINE YOUGHAL sat at lunch in the Speise Saal of one of Vienna's costlier hotels. The double-headed eagle, with its "K.u.K." legend, everywhere met the eye and announced the imperial favour in which the establishment basked. Some several square yards of yellow bunting, charged with the image of another double-headed eagle, floating from the highest flagstaff above the building, betrayed to the initiated the fact that a Russian Grand Duke was concealed somewhere on the premises. Unannounced by heraldic symbolism, but unconcealable by reason of nature's own blazonry, were several citizens and citizenesses of the great republic of the Western world. One or two Cobdenite members of the British Parliament, engaged in the useful task of proving that the cost of living in Vienna was on an exorbitant scale, flitted with restrained importance through a land whose fatness they had come to spy out; every fancied overcharge in their bills was welcome as providing another nail in the coffin of their fiscal opponents. It is the glory of democracies that they may be misled, but never driven. Here and there, like brave deeds in a dust-patterned world, flashed and glittered the sumptuous uniforms of representatives of the Austrian military caste. Also in evidence, at discreet intervals, were stray units of the Semitic tribe that nineteen centuries of European neglect had been unable to mislay.

Elaine, sitting with Courtenay at an elaborately appointed luncheon table, gay with high goblets of Bohemian glassware, was mistress of three discoveries. First, to her disappointment, that if you frequent the more expensive hotels of Europe you must be prepared to find, in whatever country you may chance to be staying, a depressing international likeness between them all. Secondly, to her relief, that one is not expected to be sentimentally amorous during a modern honeymoon. Thirdly, rather to her dismay, that Courtenay Youghal did not necessarily expect her to be markedly affectionate in private. Some one had described him, after their marriage, as one of Nature's bachelors, and she began to see how aptly the description fitted him.

"Will those Germans on our left never stop talking?" she asked, as an undying flow of Teutonic small-talk rattled and jangled across the intervening stretch of carpet. "Not one of those three women has ceased talking for an instant since we've been sitting here."

"They will presently, if only for a moment," said Courtenay; "when the dish you have ordered comes in there will be a deathly silence at the next table. No German can see a *plat* brought in for some one else without being possessed with a great fear that it represents a more toothsome morsel or a better money's worth than what he has ordered for himself."

The exuberant Teutonic chatter was balanced on the other side of the room by an even more penetrating conversation unflaggingly maintained by a party of Americans, who were sitting in judgment on the cuisine of the country they were passing through, and finding few extenuating circumstances.

"What Mr. Lonkins wants is a real *deep* cherry pie," announced a lady in a tone of dramatic and honest conviction.

"Why, yes, that is so," corroborated a gentleman who was apparently the Mr. Lonkins in question; "a real *deep* cherry pie."

"We had the same trouble way back in Paris," proclaimed

another lady; "little Jerome and the girls don't want to eat any more *crème renversée*. I'd give anything if they could get some real cherry pie."

"Real *deep* cherry pie," assented Mr. Lonkins.

"Way down in Ohio we used to have peach pie that was real good," said Mrs. Lonkins, turning on a tap of reminiscence that presently flowed to a cascade. The subject of pies seemed to lend itself to indefinite expansion.

"So those people think of nothing but their food?" asked Elaine, as the virtues of roasted mutton suddenly came to the fore and received emphatic recognition, even the absent and youthful Jerome being quoted in its favour.

"On the contrary," said Courtenay, "they are a widely-travelled set, and the man has had a notably interesting career. It is a form of homesickness with them to discuss and lament the cookery and foods that they've never had the leisure to stay at home and digest. The Wandering Jew probably babbled unremittingly about some breakfast dish that took so long to prepare that he had never time to eat it."

A waiter deposited a dish of Wiener Nierenbraten in front of Elaine. At the same moment a magic hush fell upon the three German ladies at the adjoining table, and the flicker of a great fear passed across their eyes. Then they burst forth again into tumultuous chatter. Courtenay had proved a reliable prophet.

Almost at the same moment as the luncheon-dish appeared on the scene, two ladies arrived at a neighbouring table, and bowed with dignified cordiality to Elaine and Courtenay. They were two of the more worldly and travelled of Elaine's extensive stock of aunts, and they happened to be making a short stay at the same hotel as the young couple. They were far too correct and rationally minded to intrude themselves on their niece, but it was significant of Elaine's altered view as to the sanctity of honeymoon life that she secretly rather welcomed the presence of her two relatives in the hotel, and had found time and occasion to give them more of her society than she would have considered necessary or desirable a few weeks ago. The younger of the two she rather liked, in a restrained

fashion, as one likes an unpretentious watering-place or a restaurant that does not try to give one a musical education in
addition to one's dinner. One felt instinctively about her that
she would never wear rather more valuable diamonds than any
other woman in the room, and would never be the only person
to be saved in a steamboat disaster or hotel fire. As a child she
might have been perfectly well able to recite "On Linden
when the sun was low," but one felt certain that nothing ever
induced her to do so. The elder aunt, Mrs. Goldbrook, did not
share her sister's character as a human rest-cure; most people
found her rather disturbing, chiefly, perhaps, from her habit of
asking unimportant questions with enormous solemnity. Her
manner of inquiring after a trifling ailment gave one the impression that she was more concerned with the fortunes of the
malady than with oneself, and when one got rid of a cold one
felt that she almost expected to be given its postal address.
Probably her manner was merely the defensive outwork of an
innate shyness, but she was not a woman who commanded
confidences.

"A telephone call for Courtenay," commented the younger
of the two women as Youghal hurriedly flashed through the
room; "the telephone system seems to enter very largely into
the young man's life."

"The telephone has robbed matrimony of most of its sting,"
said the elder; "so much more discreet than pen and ink com-
munications which get read by the wrong people."

Elaine's aunts were conscientiously worldly; they were the
natural outcome of a stock that had been conscientiously strait-
laced for many generations.

Elaine had progressed to the pancake stage before Courtenay returned.

"Sorry to be away so long," he said, "but I've arranged
something rather nice for tonight. There's rather a jolly masquerade ball on. I've 'phoned about getting a costume for you,
and it's all right. It will suit you beautifully, and I've got my
harlequin dress with me. Madame Kelnicort, excellent soul,
is going to chaperon you, and she'll take you back any time
you like; I'm quite unreliable when I get into fancy dress. I

shall probably keep going till some unearthly hour of the morning."

A masquerade ball in a strange city hardly represented Elaine's idea of enjoyment. Carefully to disguise one's identity in a neighbourhood where one was entirely unknown seemed to her rather meaningless. With Courtenay, of course, it was different; he seemed to have friends and acquaintances everywhere. However, the matter had progressed to a point which would have made a refusal to go seem rather ungracious. Elaine finished her pancake and began to take a polite interest in her costume.

"What is your character?" asked Madame Kelnicort that evening, as they uncloaked, preparatory to entering the already crowded ball-room.

"I believe I'm supposed to represent Marjolaine de Montfort, whoever she may have been," said Elaine. "Courtenay declares he only wanted to marry me because I'm his ideal of her."

"But what a mistake to go as a character you know nothing about. To enjoy a masquerade ball you ought to throw away your own self and be the character you represent. Now Courtenay has been Harlequin since half-way through dinner; I could see it dancing in his eyes. At about six o'clock tomorrow morning he will fall asleep and wake up a member of the British House of Parliament on his honeymoon, but tonight he is unrestrainedly Harlequin."

Elaine stood in the ball-room surrounded by a laughing, jostling throng of pierrots, jockeys, Dresden-china shepherdesses, Rumanian peasant-girls, and all the lively make-believe creatures that form the ingredients of a fancy-dress ball. As she stood watching them she experienced a growing feeling of annoyance, chiefly with herself. She was assisting, as the French say, at one of the gayest scenes of Europe's gayest capital, and she was conscious of being absolutely unaffected by the gaiety around her. The costumes were certainly interesting to look at, and the music good to listen to, and to that extent she was amused, but the *abandon* of the scene made no appeal to her. It was like watching a game of which you did not know the rules, and in the issue of which you were not interested. Elaine began to wonder what was the earliest moment at which she could drag Madame Kelnicort away from the revel without being guilty of sheer cruelty. Then Courtenay wriggled out of the crush and came towards her, a joyous, laughing Courtenay, looking younger and handsomer than she had ever seen him. She could scarcely recognize in him tonight the rising young debater who made embarrassing onslaughts on the Government's foreign policy before a crowded House of Commons. He claimed her for the dance that was just starting, and steered her dexterously into the heart of the waltzing crowd.

"You look more like Marjolaine than I should have thought a mortal woman of these days could look," he declared, "only Marjolaine did smile sometimes. You have rather the air of wondering if you'd left out enough tea for the servants' breakfast. Don't mind my teasing; I love you to look like that, and besides, it makes a splendid foil to my Harlequin—my selfishness coming to the fore again, you see. But you really are to go home the moment you're bored; the excellent Kelnicort gets heaps of dances throughout the winter, so don't mind sacrificing her."

A little later in the evening Elaine found herself standing out a dance with a grave young gentleman from the Russian Embassy.

"Monsieur Courtenay enjoys himself, doesn't he?" he observed, as the youthful-looking harlequin flashed past them, looking like some restless gorgeous-hued dragon-fly. "Why is it that the good God has given your countrymen the boon of eternal youth? Some of your countrywomen, too, but all of the men."

Elaine could think of many of her countrymen who were not and never could have been youthful, but as far as Courtenay was concerned she recognized the fitness of the remark. And the recognition carried with it a sense of depression. Would he always remain youthful and keen on gaiety and revelling, while she grew staid and retiring? She had thrust the lively intractable Comus out of her mind, as by his perverseness he had thrust himself out of her heart, and she had chosen the brilliant young man of affairs as her husband. He had honestly let her see the selfish side of his character while he was courting her, but she had been prepared to make due sacrifices to the selfishness of a public man who had his career to consider above all other things. Would she also have to make sacrifices to the harlequin spirit which was now revealing itself as an undercurrent in his nature? When one has inured oneself to the idea of a particular form of victimization it is disconcerting to be confronted with another. Many a man who would patiently undergo martyrdom for religion's sake would be furiously unwilling to be a martyr to neuralgia.

"I think that is why you English love animals so much," pursued the young diplomat; "you are such splendid animals yourselves. You are lively because you want to be lively, not because people are looking on at you. Monsieur Courtenay is certainly an animal. I mean it as a high compliment."

"Am I an animal?" asked Elaine.

"I was going to say you are an angel," said the Russian, in some embarrassment, "but I do not think that would do; angels and animals would never get on together. To get on with animals you must have a sense of humour, and I don't suppose angels have any sense of humour; you see it would be no use to them as they never hear any jokes."

"Perhaps," said Elaine, with a tinge of bitterness in her voice, "perhaps I am a vegetable."

"I think you most remind me of a picture," said the Russian.

It was not the first time Elaine had heard the simile.

"I know," she said, "the Narrow Gallery at the Louvre: attributed to Leonardo da Vinci."

Evidently the impression she made on people was solely one of externals.

Was that how Courtenay regarded her? Was that to be her function and place in life, a painted background, a decorative setting to other people's triumphs and tragedies? Somehow tonight she had the feeling that a general might have who brought imposing forces into the field and could do nothing with them. She possessed youth and good looks, considerable wealth, and had just made what would be thought by most people a very satisfactory marriage. And already she seemed to be standing aside as an onlooker where she had expected herself to be taking a leading part.

"Does this sort of thing appeal to you?" she asked the young Russian, nodding towards the gay scrimmage of masqueraders and rather prepared to hear an amused negative.

"But yes, of course," he answered; "costume balls, fancy fairs, café chantant, casino, anything that is not real life appeals to us Russians. Real life with us is the sort of thing that Maxim Gorki deals in. It interests us immensely, but we like to get away from it sometimes."

Madame Kelnicort came up with another prospective partner, and Elaine delivered her ukase: one more dance and then back to the hotel. Without any special regret she made her retreat from the revel which Courtenay was enjoying under the impression that it was life and the young Russian under the firm conviction that it was not.

Elaine breakfasted at her aunts' table the next morning at much her usual hour. Courtenay was sleeping the sleep of a happy tired animal. He had given instructions to be called at eleven o'clock, from which time onward the *Neue Freie Presse*, the *Zeit*, and his toilet would occupy his attention till he appeared at the luncheon table. There were not many people breakfasting when Elaine arrived on the scene, but the room seemed to be fuller than it really was by reason of a penetrating voice that was engaged in recounting how far the standard of Viennese breakfast fare fell below the expectations and desires of little Jerome and the girls.

"If ever little Jerome becomes President of the United States," said Elaine, "I shall be able to contribute quite an informing article on his gastronomic likes and dislikes to the papers."

The aunts were discreetly inquisitive as to the previous evening's entertainment.

"If Elaine would flirt mildly with somebody it would be such a good thing," said Mrs. Goldbrook; "it would remind

Courtenay that he's not the only attractive young man in the world."

Elaine, however, did not gratify their hopes; she referred to the ball with the detachment she would have shown in describing a drawing-room show of cottage industries. It was not difficult to discern in her description of the affair the confession that she had been slightly bored. From Courtenay, later in the day, the aunts received a much livelier impression of the festivities, from which it was abundantly clear that he, at any rate, had managed to amuse himself. Neither did it appear that his good opinion of his own attractions had suffered any serious shock. He was distinctly in a very good temper.

"The secret of enjoying a honeymoon," said Mrs. Goldbrook afterwards to her sister, "is not to attempt too much."

"You mean——?"

"Courtenay is content to try and keep one person amused and happy, and he thoroughly succeeds."

"I certainly don't think Elaine is going to be very happy," said her sister, "but at least Courtenay saved her from making the greatest mistake she could have made—marrying that young Bassington."

"He has also," said Mrs. Goldbrook, "helped her to make the next biggest mistake of her life—marrying Courtenay Youghal."

CHAPTER XVI

IT was late afternoon by the banks of a swiftly rushing river, a river that gave back a haze of heat from its waters as though it were some stagnant steaming lagoon, and yet seemed to be whirling onward with the determination of a living thing, perpetually eager and remorseless, leaping savagely at any obstacle that attempted to stay its course; an unfriendly river, to whose waters you committed yourself at your peril. Under the hot breathless shade of the trees on its shore arose that acrid all-pervading smell that seems to hang everywhere about the tropics, a smell as of some monstrous musty still-room where herbs and spices have been crushed and distilled and stored for hundreds of years, and where the windows have seldom been opened. In the dazzling heat that still held undisputed sway over the scene, insects and birds seemed preposterously alive and active, flitting their gay colours through the sunbeams, and crawling over the baked dust in the full swing and pursuit of their several businesses; the flies engaged in Heaven knows what, and the fly-catchers busy with the flies. Beasts and humans showed no such indifference to the temperature; the sun would have to slant yet farther downward before the earth would become a fit arena for their revived activities. In the sheltered basement of a wayside rest-house a gang of native hammock-bearers slept or chattered drowsily through the last hours of the long midday halt; wide awake, yet almost motionless in the thrall of a heavy lassitude, their European master sat alone in an upper chamber, staring out through a narrow window-opening at the native village, spreading away in thick clusters of huts girt around with cultivated vegetation. It seemed a vast human ant-hill, which would presently be astir with its teeming human life, as though the Sun God in his last departing stride had roused it with a careless kick. Even as Comus watched he could see the beginnings of the evening's awakening. Women, squatting in front of their huts, began to pound away at the rice or maize that would form the evening meal, girls were collecting their water-pots preparatory to a walk down to the river, and enterprising goats made tentative forays through gaps in the ill-kept fences of neighbouring garden-plots; their hurried retreats showed that here at least some one was keeping alert and wakeful vigil. Behind a hut perched on a steep hill-side, just opposite to the rest-house, two boys were splitting wood with a certain languid industry; farther down the road a group of dogs were leisurely working themselves up to quarrelling pitch. Here and there, bands of evil-looking pigs roamed about, busy with foraging excursions that came unpleasantly athwart the border-line of scavenging. And from the trees that bounded and intersected the village rose the horrible, tireless, spiteful-sounding squawking of the iron-throated crows.

Comus sat and watched it all with a sense of growing ach-

ing depression. It was so utterly trivial to his eyes, so devoid
of interest, and yet it was so real, so serious, so implacable in
its continuity. The brain grew tired with the thought of its
unceasing reproduction. It had all gone on, as it was going on
now, by the side of the great rushing, swirling river, this tilling
and planting and harvesting, marketing and store-keeping,
feast-making and fetish-worship and love-making, burying
and giving in marriage, child-bearing and child-rearing, all
this had been going on, in the shimmering, blistering heat and
the warm nights, while he had been a youngster at school,
dimly recognizing Africa as a division of the earth's surface
that it was advisable to have a certain nodding acquaintance
with. It had been going on in all its trifling detail, all its serious intensity, when his father and his grandfather in their day
had been little boys at school, it would go on just as intently as
ever long after Comus and his generation had passed away,
just as the shadows would lengthen and fade under the mulberry trees in that far-away English garden, round the old
stone fountain where a leaden otter for ever preyed on a leaden
salmon.

Comus rose impatiently from his seat, and walked wearily
across the hut to another window-opening which commanded
a broad view of the river. There was something which fasci-
nated and then depressed one in its ceaseless hurrying onward
sweep, its tons of water rushing on for all time, as long as the
face of the earth should remain unchanged. On its farther
shore could be seen spread out at intervals other teeming villages, with their cultivated plots and pasture clearings, their
moving dots which meant cattle and goats and dogs and children. And far up its course, lost in the forest growth that
fringed its banks, were hidden away yet more villages, human
herding-grounds where men dwelt and worked and bartered,
squabbled and worshipped, sickened and perished, while the
river went by with its endless swirl and rush of gleaming
waters. One could well understand primitive early races making propitiatory sacrifices to the spirit of a great river on
whose shores they dwelt. Time and the river were the two
great forces that seemed to matter here.

It was almost a relief to turn back to that other outlook and watch the village life that was now beginning to wake in earnest. The procession of water-fetchers had formed itself in a long chattering line that stretched riverwards. Comus wondered how many tens of thousands of times that procession had been formed since first the village came into existence. They had been doing it while he was playing in the cricket-fields at school, while he was spending Christmas holidays in Paris, while he was going his careless round of theatres, dances, suppers and card-parties, just as they were doing it now; they would be doing it when there was no one alive who remembered Comus Bassington. This thought recurred again and again with painful persistence, a morbid growth arising in part from his loneliness.

Staring dumbly out at the toiling, sweltering human ant-hill, Comus marvelled how missionary enthusiasts could labour hopefully at the work of transplanting their religion, with its home-grown accretions of fatherly parochial benevolence, in this heat-blistered, fever-scourged wilderness, where men lived like groundbait and died like flies. Demons one might believe in, if one did not hold one's imagination in healthy check, but a kindly all-managing God, never. Somewhere in the west country of England Comus had an uncle who lived in a rose-smothered rectory and taught a wholesome gentle-hearted creed that expressed itself in the spirit of "Little lamb, Who made thee?" and faithfully reflected the beautiful homely Christ-child sentiment of Saxon Europe. What a far-away, unreal fairy-story it all seemed here in this West African land, where the bodies of men were of as little account as the bubbles that floated on the oily froth of the great flowing river, and where it required a stretch of wild profitless imagination to credit them with undying souls! In the life he had come from Comus had been accustomed to think of individuals as definite masterful personalities, making their several marks on the circumstances that revolved around them; they did well or ill, or in most cases indifferently, and were criticized, praised, blamed, thwarted, or tolerated, or given way to. In any case, humdrum or outstanding, they had their spheres of importance, little or big. They dominated a breakfast table or harassed a Government, according to their capabilities or opportunities, or perhaps they merely had irritating mannerisms. At any rate it seemed highly probable that they had souls. Here a man simply made a unit in an unnumbered population, an inconsequent dot in a loosely-compiled death-roll. Even his own position as a white man exalted conspicuously above a horde of black natives did not save Comus from the depressing sense of nothingness which his first experience of fever had thrown over him. He was a lost, soulless body in this great uncaring land; if he died another would take his place, his few effects would be inventoried and sent down to the coast, some one else would finish off any tea or whisky that he left behind —that would be all.

It was nearly time to be starting towards the next halting-place where he would dine, or at any rate eat something. But the lassitude which the fever had bequeathed him made the tedium of travelling through interminable forest-tracks a weariness to be deferred as long as possible. The bearers were nothing loath to let another half-hour or so slip by, and Comus dragged a battered paper-covered novel from the pocket of his coat. It was a story dealing with the elaborately tangled love affairs of a surpassingly uninteresting couple, and even in his almost bookless state Comus had not been able to plough his way through more than two-thirds of its dull length; bound up with the cover, however, were some pages of advertisement, and these the exile scanned with a hungry intentness that the romance itself could never have commanded. The name of a shop, of a street, the address of a restaurant, came to him as a bitter reminder of the world he had lost, a world that ate and drank and flirted, gambled and made merry, a world that debated and intrigued and wire-pulled, fought or compromised political battles—and recked nothing of its outcasts wandering through forest paths and steamy swamps or lying in the grip of fever. Comus read and re-read those few lines of advertisement, just as he treasured a much-crumpled programme of a first-night performance at the Straw Exchange Theatre; they seemed to make a little more real the past that was already so shadowy and so utterly remote. For a moment he could almost capture the sensation of being once again in those haunts that he loved; then he looked round and pushed the book wearily from him. The steaming heat, the forest, the rushing river hemmed him in on all sides.

The two boys who had been splitting wood ceased from their labours and straightened their backs; suddenly the smaller of the two gave the other a resounding whack with a split lath that he still held in his hand, and flew up the hillside with a scream of laughter and simulated terror, the bigger lad following in hot pursuit. Up and down the steep bush-grown slope they raced and twisted and dodged, coming sometimes to close quarters in a hurricane of squeals and smacks, rolling over and over like fighting kittens, and breaking away again to start fresh provocation and fresh pursuit. Now and again they would lie for a time panting in what seemed the last stage of exhaustion, and then they would be off in another wild scamper, their dusky bodies flitting through the bushes, disappearing and reappearing with equal sudden-ness. Presently two girls of their own age, who had returned from the water-fetching, sprang out on them from ambush, and the four joined in one joyous gambol that lit up the hill-side with shrill echoes and glimpses of flying limbs. Comus sat and watched, at first with an amused interest, then with a re-turning flood of depression and heartache. Those wild young human kittens represented the joy of life, he was the outsider, the lonely alien, watching something in which he could not join, a happiness in which he had no part or lot. He would pass presently out of the village and his bearers' feet would leave their indentations in the dust: that would be his most permanent memorial in this little oasis of teeming life. And that other life, in which he once moved with such confident sense of his own necessary participation in it, how completely he had passed out of it! Amid all its laughing throngs, its card-parties and race-meetings and country-house gatherings, he was just a mere name, remembered or forgotten, Comus Bassington, the boy who went away. He had loved himself very well and never troubled greatly whether any one else really loved him, and now he realized what he had made of his life. And at the same time he knew that if his chance were to come again he would throw it away just as surely, just as perversely. Fate played with him with loaded dice; he would lose always.

One person in the whole world had cared for him, for longer than he could remember, cared for him perhaps more than he knew, cared for him perhaps now. But a wall of ice had mounted up between him and her, and across it there blew that cold breath that chills or kills affection.

The words of a well-known old song, the wistful cry of a lost cause, rang with insistent mockery through his brain:

> Better loved you canna be,
> Will ye ne'er come back again?

If it was love that was to bring him back he must be an exile for ever. His epitaph in the mouths of those that remembered him would be: Comus Bassington, the boy who never came back.

And in his unutterable loneliness he bowed his head on his arms, that he might not see the joyous scrambling frolic on yonder hillside.

CHAPTER XVII

THE bleak rawness of a grey December day held sway over St. James's Park, that sanctuary of lawn and tree and pool, into which the bourgeois innovator has rushed ambitiously time and again, to find that he must take the patent leather from off his feet, for the ground on which he stands is hallowed ground.

In the lonely hour of early afternoon, when the workers had gone back to their work, and the loiterers were scarcely yet gathered again, Francesca Bassington made her way restlessly along the stretches of gravelled walk that bordered the ornamental water. The overmastering unhappiness that filled her heart and stifled her thinking powers found answering echo in her surroundings. There is a sorrow that lingers in old parks and gardens that the busy streets have no leisure to keep by them; the dead must bury their dead in Whitehall or the Place de la Concorde, but there are quieter spots where they may still keep tryst with the living and intrude the memory of their bygone selves on generations that have almost forgotten them. Even in tourist-trampled Versailles the desolation of a tragedy that cannot die haunts the terraces and fountains like a blood-stain that will not wash out; in the Saxon Garden at Warsaw there broods the memory of long-dead things, coeval with the stately trees that shade its walks, and with the carp that swim today in its ponds as they doubtless swam there when "Lieber Augustin" was a living person and not as yet an immortal couplet. And St. James's Park, with its lawns and walks and water-fowl, harbours still its associations with a bygone order of men and women, whose happiness and sadness are woven into its history, dim and grey as they were once bright and glowing, like the faded pattern worked into the fabric of an old tapestry. It was here that Francesca had made her way when the intolerable inaction of waiting had driven her forth from her home. She was waiting for that worst news of all, the news which does not kill hope, because there has been none to kill, but merely ends suspense. An early message had said that Comus was ill, which might have meant much or little; then there had come that morning a cablegram which only meant one thing; in a few hours she would get a final message, of which this was the preparatory forerunner. She already knew as much as that awaited message would tell her. She knew that she would never see Comus again, and she knew now that she loved him beyond all things that the world could hold for her. It was no sudden rush of pity or compunction that clouded her judgment or gilded her recollection of him; she saw him as he was, the beautiful wayward laughing boy, with his naughtiness, his exasperating selfishness, his insurmountable folly and perverseness, his cruelty that spared not even himself, and as he was, as he always had been, she knew that he was the one thing that the Fates had willed that she should love. She did not

stop to accuse or excuse herself for having sent him forth to
what was to prove his death. It was, doubtless, right and reasonable that he should have gone out there, as hundreds of
other men went out, in pursuit of careers; the terrible thing
was that he would never come back. The old cruel hopelessness
that had always chequered her pride and pleasure in his good
looks and high spirits and fitfully charming ways had dealt
her a last crushing blow; he was dying somewhere thousands
of miles away without hope of recovery, without a word of love
to comfort him, and without hope or shred of consolation she
was waiting to hear of the end. The end; that last dreadful
piece of news which would write "Nevermore" across his life
and hers.

The lively bustle in the streets had been a torture that she
could not bear. It wanted but two days to Christmas, and the
gaiety of the season, forced or genuine, rang out everywhere.
Christmas shopping, with its anxious solicitude or self-centred
absorption, overspread the West End and made the pavements
scarcely passable at certain favoured points. Proud parents,
parcel-laden and surrounded by escorts of their young people,
compared notes with one another on the looks and qualities
of their offspring and exchanged loud hurried confidences on
the difficulty or success which each had experienced in getting
the right presents for one and all. Shouted directions where to
find this or that article at its best mingled with salvos of Christmas good wishes. To Francesca, making her way frantically
through the carnival of happiness with that lonely deathbed
in her eyes, it had seemed a callous mockery of her pain; could
not people remember that there were crucifixions as well as
joyous birthdays in the world? Every mother that she passed
happy in the company of a fresh-looking, clean-limbed schoolboy son sent a fresh stab at her heart, and the very shops had
their bitter memories. There was the tea-shop where he and
she had often taken tea together, or, in the days of their estrangement, sat with their separate friends at separate tables.
There were other shops where extravagantly-incurred bills
had furnished material for those frequently recurring scenes
of recrimination, and the Colonial outfitters, where, as he had

phrased it in whimsical mockery, he had bought grave-clothes for his burying-alive. The "oubliette"! She remembered the bitter petulant name he had flung at his destined exile. There at least he had been harder on himself than the Fates were pleased to will; never, as long as Francesca lived and had a brain that served her, would she be able to forget. That narcotic would never be given to her. Unrelenting, unsparing memory would be with her always to remind her of those last days of tragedy. Already her mind was dwelling on the details of that ghastly farewell dinner-party and recalling one by one the incidents of ill-omen that had marked it; how they had sat down seven to table and how one liqueur glass in the set of seven had been shivered into fragments; how her glass had slipped from her hand as she raised it to her lips to wish Comus a safe return; and the strange, quiet hopelessness of Lady Veula's "Good-bye"; she remembered now how it had chilled and frightened her at the moment.

The park was filling again with its floating population of loiterers, and Francesca's footsteps began to take a homeward direction. Something seemed to tell her that the message for which she waited had arrived and was lying there on the hall table. Her brother, who had announced his intention of visiting her early in the afternoon, would have gone by now; he knew nothing of this morning's bad news—the instinct of a wounded animal to creep away by itself had prompted her to keep her sorrow from him as long as possible. His visit did not necessitate her presence; he was bringing an Austrian friend, who was compiling a work on the Franco-Flemish school of painting, to inspect the Van der Meulen, which Henry Greech hoped might perhaps figure as an illustration in the book. They were due to arrive shortly after lunch, and Francesca had left a note of apology, pleading an urgent engagement elsewhere. As she turned to make her way across the Mall into the Green Park a gentle voice hailed her from a carriage that was just drawing up by the sidewalk. Lady Caroline Benaresq had been favouring the Victoria Memorial with a long unfriendly stare.

"In primitive days," she remarked, "I believe it was the fashion for great chiefs and rulers to have large numbers of their relatives and dependents killed and buried with them; in these more enlightened times we have invented quite another way of making a great sovereign universally regretted. My dear Francesca," she broke off suddenly, catching the misery that had settled in the other's eyes, "what is the matter? Have you had bad news from out there?"

"I am waiting for very bad news," said Francesca, and Lady Caroline knew what had happened.

"I wish I could say something; I can't." Lady Caroline spoke in a harsh, grunting voice that few people had ever heard her use.

Francesca crossed the Mall, and the carriage drove on.

"Heaven help that poor woman," said Lady Caroline, which was, for her, startlingly like a prayer.

As Francesca entered the hall she gave a quick look at the table; several packages, evidently an early batch of Christmas presents, were there, and two or three letters. On a salver by itself was the cablegram for which she had waited. A maid, who had evidently been on the look-out for her, brought her the salver. The servants were well aware of the dreadful thing that was happening, and there was pity on the girl's face and in her voice.

"This came for you ten minutes ago, ma'am, and Mr. Greech has been here, ma'am, with another gentleman, and was sorry you weren't at home. Mr. Greech said he would call again in about half an hour."

Francesca carried the cablegram unopened into the drawing-room and sat down for a moment to think. There was no need to read it yet, for she knew what she would find written there. For a few pitiful moments Comus would seem less hopelessly lost to her if she put off the reading of that last terrible message. She rose and crossed over to the windows and pulled down the blinds, shutting out the waning December day, and then re-seated herself. Perhaps in the shadowy half-light her boy would come and sit with her again for awhile and let her look her last upon his loved face; she could never touch him again or hear his laughing petulant voice, but surely she might look on her dead. And her starving eyes saw only the hateful soulless things of bronze and silver and porcelain that she had set up and worshipped as gods; look where she would they were there around her, the cold ruling deities of the home that held no place for her dead boy. He had moved in and out among them, the warm, living, breathing thing that had been hers to love, and she had turned her eyes from that youthful comely figure to adore a few feet of painted canvas, a musty relic of a long-departed craftsman. And now he was gone from her sight, from her touch, from her hearing for ever, without even a thought to flash between them for all the dreary years that she should live, and these things of canvas and pigment and wrought metal would stay with her. They were her soul. And what shall it profit a man if he save his soul and slay his heart in torment?

On a small table by her side was Mervyn Quentock's portrait of her—the prophetic symbol of her tragedy; the rich dead harvest of unreal things that had never known life, and the bleak thrall of black unending Winter, a Winter in which things died and knew no re-awakening.

Francesca turned to the small envelope lying in her lap; very slowly she opened it and read the short message. Then she sat numb and silent for a long, long time, or perhaps only for minutes. The voice of Henry Greech in the hall, inquiring for her, called her to herself. Hurriedly she crushed the piece of paper out of sight; he would have to be told, of course, but just yet her pain seemed too dreadful to be laid bare. "Comus is dead" was a sentence beyond her power to speak.

"I have bad news for you, Francesca, I'm sorry to say," Henry announced. Had he heard, too?

"Henneberg has been here and looked at the picture," he continued, seating himself by her side, "and though he admired it immensely as a work of art, he gave me a disagreeable surprise by assuring me that it's not a genuine Van der Meulen. It's a splendid copy, but still, unfortunately, only a copy."

Henry paused and glanced at his sister to see how she had taken the unwelcome announcement. Even in the dim light he caught some of the anguish in her eyes.

"My dear Francesca," he said soothingly, laying his hand

affectionately on her arm, "I know that this must be a great disappointment to you, you've always set such store by this picture, but you mustn't take it too much to heart. These disagreeable discoveries come at times to most picture fanciers and owners. Why, about twenty per cent. of the alleged Old Masters in the Louvre are supposed to be wrongly attributed. And there are heaps of similar cases in this country. Lady Dovecourt was telling me the other day that they simply daren't have an expert in to examine the Van Dykes at Columbey for fear of unwelcome disclosures. And, besides, your picture is such an excellent copy that it's by no means without a value of its own. You must get over the disappointment you naturally feel, and take a philosophical view of the matter. . . ."

Francesca sat in stricken silence, crushing the folded morsel of paper tightly in her hand and wondering if the thin, cheerful voice with its pitiless, ghastly mockery of consolation would never stop.

When William Came

A STORY OF LONDON UNDER
THE HOHENZOLLERNS

First published, 1913

INTRODUCTION

by Lord Charnwood

WHEN *William Came* stands almost alone among works of fiction for the directness and timeliness of its prophetic purpose. The Great War was in a sense a great surprise; for it came upon us, as tremendous things often do, at the moment when many people least expected it; and of course it is not possible or desirable for most of us to be looking forward perpetually to what may happen—and may not. Yet those who forewarned the British people did not labour in vain. Numberless Englishmen had turned their minds to coming events often enough and seriously enough, to respond to the sudden emergency more calmly and vigorously than they could otherwise have done. For this mental preparedness, more pervasive than appeared on the surface, we have to thank first and foremost the Territorial movement and the reviled Minister who rejuvenated the old Volunteers as the Territorials; and to thank hardly less his critic, Lord Roberts, who, whether his own scheme was well thought out or not, strove devotedly to make us see what would happen, and, when it happened, never said "I told you so." But the same warning was sounded in less solemn ways. We may remember Colonel Guy du Maurier's popular melodrama, *The Englishman's Home,* and the ill-advised contempt with which our superior friends treated that genuine and effective piece of work. Hector Munro, and one man less happily remembered, Erskine Childers, embodied the warning in works of imaginative art, which, different as they are, may both hold their place amid abiding English literature.

So long as its author's friends live *When William Came* will be dear to them, because it expresses freely and strongly a beloved personality which his other works might easily conceal. Hector Munro was a Highlander; and that light-footed fancy, gay or sad, in which men of Gaelic race are apt to excel, is seldom (to tell the truth) quite pleasant to mere Anglo-Saxons—the dull compatriots of Shakespeare. Charming it is; but the irresponsibility, to which it owes its charm, grates upon us—if we dared say so—by its seeming heartlessness and its actual remoteness from this warm-blooded world of reality. If I am wrong in this hinted dispraise of much by which our author amused and astonished us, it matters little; my point is that such dispraise, right or wrong, becomes impossible when we turn to this, Munro's maturest work. The art for which critics had praised him has not suffered. Surely the light touch is as light, the wit as flashing, the satire—here restricted to its proper use—as keen of edge as before. And the dialogue has become real dialogue; the characters are real too; while—a lesser matter perhaps—an uncommon gift of scenery painting, true and relevant to the story, here displays itself. Here, anyway, is the real Hector, whom his friends knew, tender-hearted, caring for things lovely and of good report, caring for them passionately, and every inch a man. Nor is it the least achievement of a literary man, who gave his life before (it may be) his gifts had fully unfolded, that his most deadly earnest could vent itself in what remains light literature of his accustomed kind, welcome in our tired hours.

With some reluctance I tread heavily where he trod lightly, and say one word about the man and a few about his message.

Of many who offered and lost their lives in the War—(many too, be it remembered, who offered but did not lose them)—we, their elders, recall that their military service was more than an adventure of gallant youth, or the cheerful acceptance of an inexorable duty; that they did indeed "there offer and present themselves, their souls and bodies, to be a reasonable, holy and lively sacrifice." In no one was this consecration more plain than in Hector Munro, as some few comrades remember him in his too short fighting days, and as some friends at home last saw him while he was still impatiently waiting under training in England. In him, as in others, it shone the more brightly because it in no way impaired the simplicity of his demeanour as a normal, ordinary young man. Yet in one way his conduct was singular, as of a man with a special call and that a humble one. He had seen much of the world; the fighting blood in him was hotter than in most men; and he was certainly not lacking in common all-round capacity and self-reliance. In short, his fitness for a commission and its responsibilities was obvious; while he was no longer quite so young as to be callous to hardship and fatigue or at all unappreciative of any of the comparative amenities in an officer's life. But it was of his own choice that he died a Corporal. In the ranks, among youths and boys who did not share his advantages of talent and upbringing, he found himself the possessor of an influence which could nerve and calm and uplift them; and with them, well knowing what it cost him, he determined to stay. I do not say that it was a decision to which he could rightly have adhered had he lived; but this glimpse of our author, as he was when "William" did so nearly "come," may make the reader appreciate even better the mind which reveals itself so clearly in this book.

How does Munro's prophecy look, now that searching experience has tested it? It is of course no reflection upon any one's foresight that the thing, which he did a man's part towards preventing, was in fact by some means prevented; and it would be absurd to scrutinize, as a grave essay in statecraft, a book whose whole worth depended upon remaining in the realm of fancy. The most salient difference between this forecast and the event is that the Navy was ready for its task—(that "contemptible little Army," which spent itself in parrying the first, all but deadly, thrust, was ready too.) Yet in some essential respects, as Lord Jellicoe has shown, the margin of safety in our naval preparation was very slight, and the shocking fact should be remembered that just before that time political leaders, who have since earned fame as patriots, intrigued and agitated for parsimony in this matter at all costs. But, again, it is not so plain a proposition as Munro probably thought that our nation ought to have been trained to arms (as one of those few who used then to speak for Lord Roberts' policy, I ought to admit my own conviction now that there was a fatal miscalculation in the idea). Be these things as they may, what matters in the book is the writer's infectious love of his country for what is best in it, and the just humour of his discernment between tendencies good and evil which still conflict or mingle in our national life.

That life suffers yet the inevitable reaction from the high tension of the War; the causes that work to enfeeble it are more apparent than before; they do not necessarily go deeper. "Society," as hugely pleased with its own inanity as Munro described it, flourishes; but it concerns fewer people than the writers whom it applauds and provides with copy suppose. In the thought of wider circles the same enervating influences which he hated have revived, and popular religion has renewed its complaisance towards them. We are taught with truth that peace has greater glories than war; and the peacemakers indeed are blessed. It seems the temptation of Churches today to offer us that blessedness cheap. Now another fight for the very life of our country may be a remote danger; and it is a sane and honourable hope that the world may yet be guided into ways of lasting peace. But—not to labour what conscience plainly tells—it is chiefly upon a strong, a united, and a rightly proud England that that hope depends. The "militarism" still denounced in pulpits is a palpably "extinct Satan"; there is a greater spiritual danger of forgetting that—

> "In our halls is hung
> Armoury of the invincible knights of old."

But enough. The tale in our hands is the memorial of a knight like them. It comes from the heart of one who most gladly "gave his life that our nation might live."

CONTENTS FOR
WHEN WILLIAM CAME

WHEN WILLIAM CAME

CHAPTER I

THE SINGING-BIRD AND THE BAROMETER

CICELY YEOVIL sat in a low swing chair, alternately looking at herself in a mirror and at the other occupant of the room in the flesh. Both prospects gave her undisguised satisfaction. Without being vain she was duly appreciative of good looks, whether in herself or in another, and the reflection that she saw in the mirror, and the young man whom she saw seated at the piano, would have come with credit out of a more severely critical inspection. Probably she looked longer and with greater appreciation at the piano-player than at her own image; her good looks were an inherited possession, that had been with her more or less all her life, while Ronnie Storre was a comparatively new acquisition, discovered and achieved, so to speak, by her own enterprise, selected by her own good taste. Fate had given her adorable eyelashes and an excellent profile. Ronnie was an indulgence she had bestowed on herself.

Cicely had long ago planned out for herself a complete philosophy of life, and had resolutely set to work to carry her philosophy into practice. "When love is over how little of love even the lover understands," she quoted to herself from one of her favourite poets, and transposed the saying into "While life is with us how little of life even the materialist understands." Most people that she knew took endless pains and precautions to preserve and prolong their lives and keep their powers of enjoyment unimpaired; few, very few, seemed to make any intelligent effort at understanding what they really wanted in the way of enjoying their lives, or to ascertain what were the best means for satisfying those wants. Fewer still bent their whole energies to the one paramount aim of getting what they wanted in the fullest possible measure. Her scheme of life was not a wholly selfish one; no one could understand what she wanted as well as she did herself, therefore she felt that she was the best person to pursue her own ends and cater for her own wants. To have others thinking and acting for one merely meant that one had to be perpetually grateful for a lot of well-meant and usually unsatisfactory services. It was like the case of a rich man giving a community a free library, when probably the community only wanted free fishing or reduced tram-fares. Cicely studied her own whims and wishes, experimented in the best method of carrying them into effect, compared the accumulated results of her experiments, and gradually arrived at a very clear idea of what she wanted in life, and how best to achieve it. She was not by disposition a self-centred soul, therefore she did not make the mistake of supposing that one can live successfully and gracefully in a crowded world without taking due notice of the other human elements around one. She was instinctively far more thoughtful for others than many a person who is genuinely but unseeingly addicted to unselfishness. Also she kept in her armoury the weapon which can be so mightily effective if used sparingly by a really sincere individual—the knowledge of when to be a humbug.

Ambition entered to a certain extent into her life, and governed it perhaps rather more than she knew. She desired to escape from the doom of being a nonentity, but the escape would have to be effected in her own way and in her own time; to be governed by ambition was only a shade or two better than being governed by convention.

The drawing-room in which she and Ronnie were sitting was of such proportions that one hardly knew whether it was intended to be one room or several, and it had the merit of being moderately cool at two o'clock on a particularly hot July afternoon. In the coolest of its many alcoves servants had noiselessly set out an improvised luncheon table: a tempting array of caviare, crab and mushroom salads, cold asparagus, slender hock bottles and high-stemmed wine goblets peeped out from amid a sitting of Charlotte Klemm roses.

Cicely rose from her seat and went over to the piano.

"Come," she said, touching the young man lightly with a finger-tip on the top of his very sleek, copper-hued head, "we're going to have picnic-lunch today up here; it's so much cooler than any of the downstairs rooms, and we shan't be bothered with the servants trotting in and out all the time. Rather a good idea of mine, wasn't it?"

Ronnie, after looking anxiously to see that the word "picnic" did not portend tongue sandwiches and biscuits, gave the idea his blessing.

"What is young Storre's profession?" some one had once asked concerning him.

"He has a great many friends who have independent incomes," had been the answer.

The meal was begun in an appreciative silence; a picnic in which three kinds of red pepper were available, for the caviare demanded a certain amount of respectful attention.

"My heart ought to be like a singing-bird today, I suppose," said Cicely presently.

"Because your good man is coming home?" asked Ronnie.

Cicely nodded.

"He's expected some time this afternoon, though I'm rather vague as to which train he arrives by. Rather a stifling day for railway travelling."

"And *is* your heart doing the singing-bird business?" asked Ronnie.

"That depends," said Cicely, "if I may choose the bird. A missel-thrush would do, perhaps; it sings loudest in stormy weather, I believe."

Ronnie disposed of two or three stems of asparagus before making any comment on this remark.

"Is there going to be stormy weather?" he asked.

"The domestic barometer is set rather that way," said Cicely. "You see, Murrey has been away for ever so long, and, of course, there will be lots of things he won't be used to, and I'm afraid matters may be rather strained and uncomfortable for a time."

"Do you mean that he will object to me?" asked Ronnie.

"Not in the least," said Cicely, "he's quite broad-minded on most subjects, and he realizes that this is an age in which sensible people know thoroughly well what they want, and are determined to get what they want. It pleases me to see a lot of you, and to spoil you and pay you extravagant compliments about your good looks and your music, and to imagine at times that I'm in danger of getting fond of you; I don't see any harm in it, and I don't suppose Murrey will either—in fact, I shouldn't be surprised if he takes rather a liking to you. No, it's the general situation that will trouble and exasperate him; he's not had time to get accustomed to the *fait accompli* like we have. It will break on him with horrible suddenness."

"He was somewhere in Russia when the war broke out, wasn't he?" said Ronnie.

"Somewhere in the wilds of Eastern Siberia, shooting and bird collecting, miles away from a railway or telegraph line, and it was all over before he knew anything about it; it didn't last very long, when you come to think of it. He was due home somewhere about that time, and when the weeks slipped by without my hearing from him, I quite thought he'd been captured in the Baltic or somewhere on the way back. It turned out that he was down with marsh fever in some out-of-the-way spot, and everything was over and finished with before he got back to civilization and newspapers."

"It must have been a bit of a shock," said Ronnie, busy with a well-devised salad; "still, I don't see why there should be domestic storms when he comes back. You are hardly responsible for the catastrophe that has happened."

"No," said Cicely, "but he'll come back naturally feeling sore and savage with everything he sees around him, and he won't realize just at once that we've been through all that ourselves, and have reached the stage of sullen acquiescence in what can't be helped. He won't understand, for instance, how we can be enthusiastic and excited over Gorla Mustelford's début, and things of that sort; he'll think we are a set of callous revellers, fiddling while Rome is burning."

"In this case," said Ronnie, "Rome isn't burning, it's burnt. All that remains to be done is to rebuild it—when possible."

"Exactly, and he'll say we're not doing much towards helping at that."

"But," protested Ronnie, "the whole thing has only just happened. 'Rome wasn't built in a day,' and we can't rebuild our Rome in a day."

"I know," said Cicely, "but so many of our friends, and especially Murrey's friends, have taken the thing in a tragical fashion, and cleared off to the Colonies, or shut themselves up in their country houses, as though there was a sort of moral leprosy infecting London."

"I don't see what good that does," said Ronnie.

"It doesn't do any good, but it's what a lot of them have done because they felt like doing it, and Murrey will feel like doing it too. That is where I foresee trouble and disagreement."

Ronnie shrugged his shoulders.

"I would take things tragically if I saw the good of it," he said; "as matters stand it's too late in the day and too early to be anything but philosophical about what one can't help. For the present we've just got to make the best of things. Besides, you can't very well turn down Gorla at the last moment."

"I'm not going to turn down Gorla, or anybody," said Cicely with decision. "I think it would be silly, and silliness doesn't appeal to me. That is why I foresee storms on the domestic horizon. After all, Gorla has her career to think of. Do you know," she added, with a change of tone, "I rather wish you would fall in love with Gorla; it would make me horribly jealous, and a little jealousy is such a good tonic for any woman who knows how to dress well. Also, Ronnie, it would prove that you are capable of falling in love with some one, of which I've grave doubts up to the present."

"Love is one of the few things in which the make-believe is superior to the genuine," said Ronnie, "it lasts longer, and you get more fun out of it, and it's easier to replace when you've done with it."

"Still, it's rather like playing with coloured paper instead of playing with fire," objected Cicely.

A footman came round the corner with the trained silence that tactfully contrives to make itself felt.

"Mr. Luton to see you, madam," he announced. "Shall I say you are in?"

"Mr. Luton? Oh, yes," said Cicely, "he'll probably have something to tell us about Gorla's concert," she added, turning to Ronnie.

Tony Luton was a young man who had sprung from the people, and had taken care that there should be no recoil. He was scarcely twenty years of age, but a tightly packed chronicle of vicissitudes lay behind his sprightly insouciant appearance. Since his fifteenth year he had lived, Heaven knew how, getting sometimes a minor engagement at some minor music-hall, sometimes a temporary job as secretary-valet-companion to a roving invalid, dining now and then on plovers' eggs and asparagus at one of the smarter West End restaurants, at other times devouring a kipper or a sausage in some stuffy Edgwara Road eating-house; always seemingly amused by life, and always amusing. It is possible that somewhere in such heart as he possessed there lurked a rankling bitterness against the hard things of life, or a scrap of gratitude towards the one or two friends who had helped him disinterestedly, but his most intimate associates could not have guessed at the existence of such feelings. Tony Luton was just a merry-eyed dancing faun, whom Fate had surrounded with streets instead of woods, and it would have been in the highest degree inartistic to have sounded him for a heart or a heartache.

The dancing of the faun took one day a livelier and more assured turn, the joyousness became more real, and the worst of the vicissitudes seemed suddenly over. A musical friend, gifted with mediocre but marketable abilities, supplied Tony with a song, for which he obtained a trial performance at an East End hall. Dressed as a jockey, for no particular reason except that the costume suited him, he sang, "They quaff the gay bubbly in Eccleston Square" to an appreciative audience, which included the manager of a famous West End theatre of varieties. Tony and his song won the managerial favour, and were immediately transplanted to the West End house, where they scored a success of which the drooping music-hall industry was at the moment badly in need.

It was just after the great catastrophe, and men of the London world were in no humour to think; they had witnessed the inconceivable befall them, they had nothing but political ruin to stare at, and they were anxious to look the other way. The words of Tony's song were more or less meaningless, though he sang them remarkably well, but the tune, with its air of slyness and furtive joyousness, appealed in some unaccountable manner to people who were furtively unhappy, and who were trying to appear stoically cheerful.

"What must be, must be," and "It's a poor heart that never rejoices," were the popular expressions of the London public at that moment, and the men who had to cater for that public were thankful when they were able to stumble across anything that fitted in with the prevailing mood. For the first time in his life Tony Luton discovered that agents and managers were a leisured class, and that office boys had manners.

He entered Cicely's drawing-room with the air of one to whom assurance of manner has become a sheathed weapon, a court accessory rather than a trade implement. He was more quietly dressed than the usual run of music-hall successes; he had looked critically at life from too many angles not to know that though clothes cannot make a man they can certainly damn him.

"Thank you, I have lunched already," he said in answer to a question from Cicely. "Thank you," he said again in a cheerful affirmative, as the question of hock in a tall ice-cold goblet was propounded to him.

"I've come to tell you the latest about the Gorla Mustelford evening," he continued. "Old Laurent is putting his back into it, and it's really going to be rather a big affair. She's going to out-Russian the Russians. Of course, she hasn't their technique nor a tenth of their training, but she's having tons of advertisement. The name Gorla is almost an advertisement in itself, and then there's the fact that she's the daughter of a peer."

"She has temperament," said Cicely, with the decision of one who makes a vague statement in a good cause.

"So Laurent says," observed Tony. "He discovers temperament in every one that he intends to boom. He told me that I had temperament to the finger-tips, and I was too polite to contradict him. But I haven't told you the really important thing about the Mustelford début. It is a profound secret, more or less, so you must promise not to breathe a word about it till half-past four, when it will appear in all the six o'clock newspapers."

Tony paused for dramatic effect, while he drained his goblet, and then made his announcement.

"Majesty is going to be present. Informally and unofficially, but still present in the flesh. A sort of casual dropping in, carefully heralded by unconfirmed rumour a week ahead."

"Heavens!" exclaimed Cicely, in genuine excitement, "what a bold stroke. Lady Shalem has worked that, I bet. I suppose it will go down all right."

"Trust Laurent to see to that," said Tony, "he knows how to fill his house with the right sort of people, and he's not the one to risk a fiasco. He knows what he's about. I tell you, it's going to be a big evening."

"I say!" exclaimed Ronnie suddenly, "give a supper party here for Gorla on the night, and ask the Shalem woman and all her crowd. It will be awful fun."

Cicely caught at the suggestion with some enthusiasm. She did not particularly care for Lady Shalem, but she thought it would be just as well to care for her as far as outward appearances went.

Grace, Lady Shalem, was a woman who had blossomed into sudden importance by constituting herself a sort of foster-mother to the *fait accompli*. At a moment when London was denuded of most of its aforetime social leaders she had seen her opportunity, and made the most of it. She had not contented herself with bowing to the inevitable, she had stretched out her hand to it, and forced herself to smile graciously at it, and her polite attentions had been reciprocated. Lady Shalem, without being a beauty or a wit, or a grand lady in the traditional sense of the word, was in a fair way to becoming a power in the land; others, more capable and with stronger claims to social recognition, would doubtless overshadow her and displace her in due course, but for the moment she was a person whose good graces counted for something, and Cicely was quite alive to the advantage of being in those good graces.

"It would be rather fun," she said, running over in her mind the possibilities of the suggested supper-party.

"It would be jolly useful," put in Ronnie eagerly; "you could get all sorts of interesting people together, and it would be an excellent advertisement for Gorla."

Ronnie approved of supper-parties on principle, but he was also thinking of the advantage which might accrue to the drawing-room concert which Cicely had projected (with himself as the chief performer), if he could be brought into contact with a wider circle of music patrons.

"I know it would be useful," said Cicely, "it would be almost historical; there's no knowing who might not come to it—and things are dreadfully slack in the entertaining line just now."

The ambitious note in her character was making itself felt at that moment.

"Let's go down to the library, and work out a list of people to invite," said Ronnie.

A servant entered the room and made a brief announcement.

"Mr. Yeovil has arrived, madam."

"Bother," said Ronnie sulkily. "Now you'll cool off about that supper party, and turn down Gorla and the rest of us."

It was certainly true that the supper already seemed a more difficult proposition in Cicely's eye than it had a moment or two ago.

" 'You'll not forget my only daughter,
E'en though Saphia has crossed the sea,' "

quoted Tony, with mocking laughter in his voice and eyes.

Cicely went down to greet her husband. She felt that she was probably very glad that he was home once more; she was angry with herself for not feeling greater certainty on the point. Even the well-beloved, however, can select the wrong moment for return. If Cicely Yeovil's heart was like a singing-bird, it was of a kind that has frequent lapses into silence.

CHAPTER II

THE HOMECOMING

MURREY YEOVIL got out of the boat-train at Victoria Station, and stood waiting, in an attitude something between listlessness and impatience, while a porter dragged his light travelling kit out of the railway carriage and went in search of his heavier baggage with a hand-truck. Yeovil was a grey-faced young man, with restless eyes, and a rather wistful mouth, and an air of lassitude that was evidently only a temporary characteristic. The hot dusty station, with its blended crowds of dawdling and scurrying people, its little streams of suburban passengers pouring out every now and then from this or that platform, like ants swarming across a garden path, made a wearisome climax to what had been a rather wearisome journey. Yeovil glanced quickly, almost furtively, around him in all directions, with the air of a man who is constrained by morbid curiosity to look for things that he would rather not see. The announcements placed in German alternatively with English over the booking office, left-luggage office, refreshment buffets, and so forth, the crowned eagle and monogram displayed on the post boxes, caught his eye in quick succession.

He turned to help the porter to shepherd his belongings on to the truck, and followed him to the outer yard of the station, where a string of taxicabs was being slowly absorbed by an outpouring crowd of travellers.

Portmanteaux, wraps, and a trunk or two, much be-labelled

and travel-worn, were stowed into a taxi, and Yeovil turned to give the direction to the driver.

"Twenty-eight, Berkshire Street."

"Berkschirestrasse, acht-und-zwanzig," echoed the man, a bulky spectacled individual of unmistakable Teuton type.

"Twenty-eight, Berkshire Street," repeated Yeovil, and got into the cab, leaving the driver to re-translate the direction into his own language.

A succession of cabs leaving the station blocked the roadway for a moment or two, and Yeovil had leisure to observe the fact that Viktoria Strasse was lettered side by side with the familiar English name of the street. A notice directing the public to the neighbouring swimming baths was also written up in both languages. London had become a bilingual city, even as Warsaw.

The cab threaded its way swiftly along Buckingham Palace Road towards the Mall. As they passed the long front of the Palace the traveller turned his head resolutely away, that he might not see the alien uniforms at the gates and the eagle standard flapping in the sunlight. The taxi driver, who seemed to have combative instincts, slowed down as he was turning into the Mall, and pointed to the white pile of memorial statuary in front of the palace gates.

"Grossmutter Denkmal, yes," he announced, and resumed his journey.

Arrived at his destination, Yeovil stood on the steps of his house and pressed the bell with an odd sense of forlornness, as though he were a stranger drifting from nowhere into a land that had no cognizance of him; a moment later he was standing in his own hall, the object of respectful solicitude and attention. Sprucely garbed and groomed lackeys busied themselves with his battered travel-soiled baggage; the door closed on the guttural-voiced taxi driver, and the glaring July sunshine. The wearisome journey was over.

"Poor dear, how dreadfully pulled-down you look," said Cicely, when the first greetings had been exchanged.

"It's been a slow business, getting well," said Yeovil. "I'm only three-quarter way there yet."

He looked at his reflection in a mirror and laughed ruefully.

"You should have seen what I looked like five or six weeks ago," he added.

"You ought to have let me come out and nurse you," said Cicely; "you know I wanted to."

"Oh, they nursed me well enough," said Yeovil, "and it would have been a shame dragging you out there; a small Finnish health resort, out of the season, is not a very amusing place, and it would have been worse for any one who didn't talk Russian."

"You must have been buried alive there," said Cicely, with commiseration in her voice.

"I wanted to be buried alive," said Yeovil. "The news from the outer world was not of a kind that helped a despondent invalid towards convalescence. They spoke to me as little as possible about what was happening, and I was grateful for your letters because they also told me very little. When one is abroad, among foreigners, one's country's misfortunes cause one an acuter, more personal distress, than they would at home even."

"Well, you are at home now, anyway," said Cicely, "and you can jog along the road to complete recovery at your own pace. A little quiet shooting this autumn and a little hunting, just enough to keep you fit and not to overtire you; you mustn't overtax your strength."

"I'm getting my strength back all right," said Yeovil. "This journey hasnt tired me half as much as one might have expected. It's the awful drag of listlessness, mental and physical, that is the worst after-effect of these marsh fevers; they drain the energy out of you in bucketfuls, and it trickles back again in teaspoonfuls. And just now untiring energy is what I shall need, even more than strength; I don't want to degenerate into a slacker."

"Look here, Murrey," said Cicely, "after we've had dinner together tonight, I'm going to do a seemingly unwifely thing. I'm going to go out and leave you alone with an old friend. Doctor Holham is coming in to drink coffee and smoke with you. I arranged this because I knew it was what you would like. Men can talk these things over best by themselves, and Holham can tell you everything that happened—since you went away. It will be a dreary story, I'm afraid, but you will want to hear it all. It was a nightmare time, but now one sees it in a calmer perspective."

"I feel in a nightmare still," said Yeovil.

"We all felt like that," said Cicely, rather with the air of an elder person who tells a child that it will understand things better when it grows up; "time is always something of a nar-cotic, you know. Things seem absolutely unbearable, and then bit by bit we find out that we are bearing them. And now, dear, I'll fill up your notification paper and leave you to super-intend your unpacking. Robert will give you any help you want."

"What is the notification paper?" asked Yeovil.

"Oh, a stupid form to be filled up when any one arrives, to say where they come from, and their business and nationality and religion, and all that sort of thing. We're rather more bureaucratic than we used to be, you know."

Yeovil said nothing, but into the sallow greyness of his face there crept a dark flush, that faded presently and left his col-our more grey and bloodless than before.

The journey seemed suddenly to have recommenced; he was under his own roof, his servants were waiting on him, his familiar possessions were in evidence around him, but the sense of being at home had vanished. It was as though he had arrived at some wayside hotel, and been asked to regis-ter his name and status and destination. Other things of dis-gust and irritation he had foreseen in the London he was coming to—the alterations on stamps and coinage, the intru-sive Teuton element, the alien uniforms cropping up every-where, the new orientation of social life; such things he was prepared for, but this personal evidence of his subject state came on him unawares, at a moment when he had, so to speak, laid his armour aside. Cicely spoke lightly of the hateful for-mality that had been forced on them; would he, too, come to regard things in the same acquiescent spirit?

CHAPTER III

"THE METSKIE TSAR"

"I WAS in the early stages of my fever when I got the first inkling of what was going on," said Yeovil to the doctor, as they sat over their coffee in a recess of the big smoking-room; "just able to potter about a bit in the daytime, fighting against depression and inertia, feverish as evening came on, and delirious in the night. My game tracker and my attendant were both Buriats, and spoke very little Russian, and that was the only language we had in common to converse in. In matters concerning food and sport we soon got to understand each other, but on other subjects we were not easily able to exchange ideas. One day my tracker had been to a distant trading-store to get some things of which we were in need; the store was eighty miles from the nearest point of railroad, eighty miles of terribly bad roads, but it was in its way a centre and transmitter of news from the outside world. The tracker brought back with him vague tidings of a conflict of some sort between the 'Metskie Tsar' and the 'Angliskie Tsar,' and kept repeating the Russian word for defeat. The 'Angliskie Tsar' I recognized, of course, as the King of England, but my brain was too sick and dull to read any further meaning into the man's reiterated gabble. I grew so ill just then that I had to give up the struggle against fever, and make my way as best I could towards the nearest point where nursing and doctoring could be had. It was one evening, in a lonely rest-hut on the edge of a huge forest, as I was waiting for my boy to bring the meal for which I was feverishly impatient, and which I knew I should loathe as soon as it was brought, that the explanation of the word 'Metskie' flashed on me. I had thought of it as referring to some Oriental potentate, some rebellious rajah perhaps, who was giving trouble, and whose followers had possibly discomfited an isolated British force in some out-of-the-way corner of our Empire. And all of a sudden I knew that 'Nemetskie Tsar,' German Emperor, had been the name that the man had been trying to convey to me. I shouted for the tracker, and put him through a breathless cross-examination; he confirmed what my fears had told me. The 'Metskie Tsar' was a big European ruler, he had been in conflict with the 'Angliskie Tsar,' and the latter had been defeated, swept away; the man spoke the word that he used for ships, and made energetic pantomime to express the sinking of a fleet. Holham, there was nothing for it but to hope that this was a false, groundless rumour, that had somehow crept to the confines of civilization. In my saner balanced moments it was possible to disbelieve it, but if you have ever suffered from delirium you will know what raging torments of agony I went through in the nights, how my brain fought and refought that rumoured disaster."

The doctor gave a murmur of sympathetic understanding.

"Then," continued Yeovil, "I reached the small Siberian town towards which I had been struggling. There was a little colony of Russians there, traders, officials, a doctor or two, and some army officers. I put up at the primitive hotel-restaurant, which was the general gathering-place of the community. I knew quickly that the news was true. Russians are the most tactful of any European race that I have ever met; they did not stare with insolent or pitying curiosity, but there was something changed in their attitude which told me that the travelling Briton was no longer in their eyes the interesting respect-commanding personality that he had been in past days. I went to my own room, where the samovar was bubbling its familiar tune and a smiling red-shirted Russian boy was helping my Buriat servant to unpack my wardrobe, and I asked for any back numbers of newspapers that could be supplied at a moment's notice. I was given a bundle of well-thumbed sheets, odd pieces of the *Novoe Vremya*, the *Moskovskie Viedomosti*, one or two complete numbers of local papers published at Perm and Tobolsk. I do not read Russian well, though I speak it fairly readily, but from the fragments of disconnected telegrams that I pieced together I gathered enough information to acquaint me with the extent of the tragedy that had been worked out in a few crowded hours in a corner of

North-Western Europe. I searched frantically for telegrams of later dates that would put a better complexion on the matter, that would retrieve something from the ruin; presently I came across a page of the illustrated supplement that the *Novoe Vremya* publishes once a week. There was a photograph of a long-fronted building with a flag flying over it, labelled 'The new standard floating over Buckingham Palace.' The picture was not much more than a smudge, but the flag, possibly touched up, was unmistakable. It was the eagle of the Nemetskie Tsar. I have a vivid recollection of that plainly-furnished little room, with the inevitable gilt ikon in one corner, and the samovar hissing and gurgling on the table, and the thrumming music of a balalaika orchestra coming up from the restaurant below; the next coherent thing I can remember was weeks and weeks later, discussing in an impersonal detached manner whether I was strong enough to stand the fatigue of the long railway journey to Finland.

"Since then, Holham, I have been encouraged to keep my mind as much off the war and public affairs as possible, and I have been glad to do so. I knew the worst and there was no particular use in deepening my despondency by dragging out the details. But now I am more or less a live man again, and I want to fill in the gaps in my knowledge of what happened. You know how much I know, and how little; those fragments of Russian newspapers were about all the information that I had. I don't even know clearly how the whole thing started."

Yeovil settled himself back in his chair with the air of a man who has done some necessary talking, and now assumes the rôle of listener.

"It started," said the doctor, "with a wholly unimportant disagreement about some frontier business in East Africa; there was a slight attack of nerves in the stock markets, and then the whole thing seemed in a fair way towards being settled. Then the negotiations over the affair began to drag unduly, and there was a further flutter of nervousness in the money world. And then one morning the papers reported a highly menacing speech by one of the German Ministers, and the situation began to look black indeed. 'He will be disavowed,' every one said over here, but in less than twenty-four hours those who knew anything knew that the crisis was on us—only their knowledge came too late. 'War between two such civilized and enlightened nations is an impossibility,' one of our leaders of public opinion had declared on the Saturday; by the following Friday the war had indeed become an impossibility, because we could no longer carry it on. It burst on us with calculated suddenness, and we were just not enough, everywhere where the pressure came. Our ships were good against their ships, our seamen were better than their seamen, but our ships were not able to cope with their ships plus their superiority in aircraft. Our trained men were good against their trained men, but they could not be in several places at once, and the enemy could. Our half-trained men and our untrained men could not master the science of war at a moment's notice, and a moment's notice was all they got. The enemy were a nation apprenticed in arms, we were not even the idle apprentice: we had not deemed apprenticeship worth our while. There was courage enough running loose in the land, but it was like unharnessed electricity, it controlled no forces, it struck no blows. There was no time for the heroism and the devotion which a drawn-out struggle, however hopeless, can produce; the war was over almost as soon as it had begun. After the reverses which happened with lightning rapidity in the first three days of warfare, the newspapers made no effort to pretend that the situation could be retrieved; editors and public alike recognized that these were blows over the heart, and that it was a matter of moments before we were counted out. One might liken the whole affair to a snap checkmate early in a game of chess; one side had thought out the moves, and brought the requisite pieces into play, the other side was hampered and helpless, with its resources unavailable, its strategy discounted in advance. That, in a nutshell, is the history of the war."

Yeovil was silent for a moment or two, then he asked:

"And the sequel the peace?"

"The collapse was so complete that I fancy even the enemy were hardly prepared for the consequences of their victory. No one had quite realized what one disastrous campaign would mean for an island nation with a closely packed population. The conquerors were in a position to dictate what terms they pleased, and it was not wonderful that their ideas of aggrandizement expanded in the hour of intoxication. There was no European combination ready to say them nay, and certainly no one Power was going to be rash enough to step in to contest the terms of the treaty that they imposed on the conquered. Annexation had probably never been a dream before the war; after the war it suddenly became temptingly practical. *Warum nicht?* became the theme of leader-writers in the German Press; they pointed out that Britain, defeated and humiliated, but with enormous powers of recuperation, would be a dangerous and inevitable enemy for the Germany of tomorrow, while Britain incorporated within the Hohenzollern Empire would merely be a disaffected province, without a navy to make its disaffection a serious menace, and with great tax-paying capabilities, which would be available for relieving the burdens of the other Imperial States. Wherefore, why not annex? The *warum nicht?* party prevailed. Our King, as you know, retired with his Court to Delhi, as Emperor in the East, with most of his overseas dominions still subject to his sway. The British Isles came under the German Crown as a *Reichsland*, a sort of Alsace-Lorraine washed by the North Sea instead of the Rhine. We still retain our Parliament, but it is a clipped and pruned-down shadow of its former self, with most of its functions in abeyance; when the elections were held it was difficult to get decent candidates to come forward or to get people to vote. It makes one smile bitterly to think that a year or two ago we were seriously squabbling as to who should have votes. And, of course, the old party divisions have more or less crumbled away. The Liberals naturally are under the blackest of clouds, for having steered the country to disaster, though to do them justice it was no more their fault than the fault of any other party. In a democracy such as ours was the Government of the day must more or less reflect the ideas and temperament of the nation in all vital matters, and the British nation in those days could not have been persuaded of the urgent need for military apprenticeship or of the deadly nature of its danger. It was willing now and then to be half-frightened and to have half-measures, or, one might better say, quarter-measures taken to reassure it, and the governments of the day were willing to take them, but any political party or group of statesmen that had said 'the danger is enormous and immediate, the sacrifices and burdens must be enormous and immediate,' would have met with certain defeat at the polls. Still, of course, the Liberals, as the party that had held office for nearly a decade, incurred the odium of a people maddened by defeat and humiliation; one Minister, who had had less responsibility for military organization than perhaps any of them, was attacked and nearly killed at Newcastle, another was hiding for three days on Exmoor, and escaped in disguise."

"And the Conservatives?"

"They are also under eclipse, but it is more or less voluntary in their case. For generations they had taken their stand as supporters of Throne and Constitution, and when they suddenly found the Constitution gone and the Throne filled by an alien dynasty, their political orientation had vanished. They are in much the same position as the Jacobites occupied after the Hanoverian accession. Many of the leading Tory families have emigrated to the British lands beyond the seas, others are shut up in their country houses, retrenching their expenses, selling their acres, and investing their money abroad. The Labour faction, again, are almost in as bad odour as the Liberals, because of having hob-nobbed too effusively and ostentatiously with the German democratic parties on the eve of the war, exploiting an evangel of universal brotherhood which did not blunt a single Teuton bayonet when the hour came. I suppose in time party divisions will reassert themselves in some form or other; there will be a Socialist Party, and the mercantile and manufacturing interests will evolve a sort of bourgeoisie party, and the different religious bodies will try to get themselves represented——"

Yeovil made a movement of impatience.

"All these things that you forecast," he said, "must take time, considerable time; is this nightmare, then, to go on for ever?"

"It is not a nightmare, unfortunately," said the doctor, "it is a reality."

"But, surely—a nation such as ours, a virile, highly-civilized nation with an age-long tradition of mastery behind it, cannot be held under for ever by a few thousand bayonets and machine guns. We must surely rise up one day and drive them out."

"Dear man," said the doctor, "we might, of course, at some given moment overpower the garrison that is maintained here, and seize the forts, and perhaps we might be able to mine the harbours; what then? In a fortnight or so we could be starved into unconditional submission. Remember, all the advantages of isolated position that told in our favour while we had the sea dominion, tell against us now that the sea dominion is in other hands. The enemy would not need to mobilize a single army corps or to bring a single battleship into action; a fleet of nimble cruisers and destroyers circling round our coasts would be sufficient to shut out our food supplies."

"Are you trying to tell me that this is a final overthrow?" said Yeovil in a shaking voice; "are we to remain a subject race like the Poles?"

"Let us hope for a better fate," said the doctor. "Our opportunity may come if the Master Power is ever involved in an unsuccessful naval war with some other nation, or perhaps in some time of European crisis, when everything hung in the balance, our latent hostility might have to be squared by a concession of independence. That is what we have to hope for and watch for. On the other hand, the conquerors have to count on time and tact to weaken and finally obliterate the old feelings of nationality; the middle-aged of today will grow old and acquiescent in the changed state of things; the young generations will grow up never having known anything different. It's a far cry to Delhi, as the old Indian proverb says, and the strange half-European, half-Asiatic Court out there will seem more and more a thing exotic and unreal. 'The King across the water' was a rallying-cry once upon a time in our history, but a king on the farther side of the Indian Ocean is a shadowy competitor for one who alternates between Potsdam and Windsor."

"I want you to tell me everything," said Yeovil, after another pause; "tell me, Holham, how far has this obliterating process of 'time and tact' gone? It seems to be pretty fairly started already. I bought a newspaper as soon as I landed, and I read it in the train coming up. I read things that puzzled and disgusted me. There were announcements of concerts and plays and first-nights and private views; there were even small dances. There were advertisements of house-boats and week-end cottages and string bands for garden parties. It struck me that it was rather like merry-making with a dead body lying in the house."

"Yeovil," said the doctor, "you must bear in mind two things. First, the necessity for the life of the country going on as if nothing had happened. It is true that many thousands of our working men and women have emigrated and thousands of our upper and middle class too; they were the people who were not tied down by business, or who could afford to cut those ties. But those represent comparatively a few out of the many. The great businesses and the small businesses must go on, people must be fed and clothed and housed and medically treated, and their thousand-and-one wants and necessities supplied. Look at me, for instance; however much I loathe coming under a foreign domination and paying taxes to an alien government, I can't abandon my practice and my patients, and set up anew in Toronto or Allahabad, and if I could, some other doctor would have to take my place here. I or that other doctor must have our servants and motors and food and furniture and newspapers, even our sport. The golf links and the hunting field have been wellnigh deserted since the war, but they are beginning to get back their votaries because outdoor sport has become a necessity, and a very rational necessity, with numbers of men who have to work otherwise under unnatural and exacting conditions. That is one factor of the situation. The other affects London more especially, but through London it influences the rest of the country to a certain extent. You will see around you here much that will strike you as indications of heartless indifference to the calamity that has befallen our nation. Well, you must remember that many things in modern life, especially in the big cities, are not national but international. In the world of music and art and the drama, for instance, the foreign names are legion, they confront you at every turn, and some of our British devotees of such arts are more acclimatized to the ways of Munich or Moscow than they are familiar with the life, say, of Stirling or York. For years they have lived and thought and spoken in an atmosphere and jargon of denationalized culture—even those of them who have never left our shores. They would take pains to be intimately familiar with the domestic affairs and views of life of some Galician gipsy dramatist, and gravely quote and discuss his opinions on debts and mistresses and cookery, while they would shudder at 'D'ye ken John Peel?' as a piece of uncouth barbarity. You cannot expect a world of that sort to be permanently concerned or downcast because the Crown of Charlemagne takes its place now on the top of the Royal box in the theatres, or at the head of programmes at State concerts. And then there are the Jews."

"There are many in the land, or at least in London," said Yeovil.

"There are even more of them now than there used to be," said Holham. "I am to a great extent a disliker of Jews myself, but I will be fair to them, and admit that those of them who were in any genuine sense British have remained British and have stuck by us loyally in our misfortune; all honour to them. But of the others, the men who by temperament and everything else were far more Teuton or Polish or Latin than they were British, it was not to be expected that they would be heartbroken because London had suddenly lost its place among the political capitals of the world, and became a cosmopolitan city. They had appreciated the free and easy liberty of the old days, under British rule, but there was a stiff insularity in the ruling race that they chafed against. Now, putting aside some petty Government restrictions that Teutonic bureaucracy has brought in, there is really, in their eyes, more licence and social adaptability in London than before. It has taken on some of the aspects of a No-Man's-Land, and the Jew, if he likes, may almost consider himself as of the dominant race; at any rate he is ubiquitous. Pleasure, of the café and cabaret and boulevard kind, the sort of thing that gave Berlin the aspect of the gayest capital in Europe within the last decade, that is the insidious leaven that will help to denationalize London. Berlin will probably climb back to some of its old austerity and simplicity, a world-ruling city with a great sense of its position and its responsibilities, while London will become more and more the centre of what these people understand by life."

Yeovil made a movement of impatience and disgust.

"I know, I know," said the doctor, sympathetically; "life and enjoyment mean to you the howl of a wolf in a forest, the call of a wild swan on the frozen tundras, the smell of a wood fire in some little inn among the mountains. There is more music to you in the quick thud, thud of hoofs on desert mud as a free-stepping horse is led up to your tent door than in all the dronings and flourishes that a highly-paid orchestra can reel out to an expensively fed audience. But the tastes of modern London, as we see them crystallized around us, lie in a very different direction. People of the world that I am speaking of, our dominant world at the present moment, herd together as closely packed to the square yard as possible, doing nothing worth doing, and saying nothing worth saying, but doing it and saying it over and over again, listening to the same melodies, watching the same artistes, echoing the same catchwords, ordering the same dishes in the same restaurants, suffering each other's cigarette smoke and perfumes and conversation, feverishly, anxiously making arrangements to meet each other again tomorrow, next week, and the week after next, and repeat the same gregarious experience. If they were not herded together in a corner of western London, watching each other with restless intelligent eyes, they would be herded together at Brighton or Dieppe, doing the same thing. Well, you will find that life of that sort goes forward just as usual, only it is even more prominent and noticeable now because there is less public life of other kinds."

Yeovil said something which was possibly the Buriat word for the nether world.

Outside in the neighbouring square a band had been playing at intervals during the evening. Now it struck up an air that Yeovil had already heard whistled several times since his landing, an air with a captivating suggestion of slyness and furtive joyousness running through it.

He rose and walked across to the window, opening it a little wider. He listened till the last notes had died away.

"What is that tune they have just played?" he asked.

"You'll hear it often enough," said the doctor. "A Frenchman writing in the *Matin* the other day called it the 'National Anthem of the *fait accompli*.'"

CHAPTER IV

"Es ist Verboten"

YEOVIL wakened next morning to the pleasant sensation of being in a household where elaborate machinery for the smooth achievement of one's daily life was noiselessly and unceasingly at work. Fever and the long weariness of convalescence in indifferently comfortable surroundings had given luxury a new value in his eyes. Money had not always been plentiful with him in his younger days; in his twenty-eighth year he had inherited a fairly substantial fortune, and he had married a wealthy woman a few months later. It was characteristic of the man and his breed that the chief use to which he had put his newly-acquired wealth had been in seizing the opportunity which it gave him for indulging in unlimited travel in wild, out-of-the-way regions, where the comforts of life were meagrely represented. Cicely occasionally accompanied him to the threshold of his expeditions, such as Cairo or St. Petersburg or Constantinople, but her own tastes in the matter of roving were more or less condensed within an area that comprised Cannes, Homburg, the Scottish Highlands, and the Norwegian Fiords. Things outlandish and barbaric appealed to her chiefly when presented under artistic but highly civilized stage management on the boards of Covent Garden, and if she wanted to look at wolves or sand grouse, she preferred doing so in the company of an intelligent Fellow of the Zoological Society on some fine Sunday afternoon in Regent's Park. It was one of the bonds of union and good-fellowship between her husband and herself that each understood and sympathized with the other's tastes without in the least wanting to share them; they went their own ways and were pleased and comrade-like when the ways happened to run together for a span, without self-reproach or heart-searching when the ways diverged. Moreover, they had separate and adequate banking accounts, which constitute, if not the keys of the matrimonial Heaven, at least the oil that lubricates them.

Yeovil found Cicely and breakfast waiting for him in the cool breakfast-room, and enjoyed, with the appreciation of a recent invalid, the comfort and resources of a meal that had not to be ordered or thought about in advance, but seemed as though it were there, foreordained from the beginning of time in its smallest detail. Each desire of the breakfasting mind seemed to have its realization in some dish, lurking unobtrusively in hidden corners until asked for. Did one want grilled mushrooms, English fashion, they were there, black and moist and sizzling, and extremely edible; did one desire mushrooms *à la Russe*, they appeared, blanched and cool and toothsome under their white blanketing of sauce. At one's bidding was a service of coffee, prepared with rather more forethought and circumspection than would go to the preparation of a revolution in a South American Republic.

The exotic blooms that reigned in profusion over the other parts of the house were scrupulously banished from the breakfast-room; bowls of wild thyme and other flowering weeds of the meadow and hedgerow gave it an atmosphere of country freshness that was in keeping with the morning meal.

"You look dreadfully tired still," said Cicely critically, "otherwise I would recommend a ride in the Park, before it gets too hot. There is a new cob in the stable that you will just love, but he is rather lively, and you had better content yourself for the present with some more sedate exercise than he is likely to give you. He is apt to try and jump out of his skin when the flies tease him. The Park is rather jolly for a walk just now."

"I think that will be about my form after my long journey," said Yeovil, "an hour's stroll before lunch under the trees. That ought not to fatigue me unduly. In the afternoon I'll look up one or two people."

"Don't count on finding too many of your old set," said Cicely rather hurriedly. "I dare say some of them will find their way back some time, but at present there's been rather an exodus."

"The Bredes," said Yeovil, "are they here?"

"No, the Bredes are in Scotland, at their place in Sutherlandshire; they don't come south now, and the Ricardes are farming somewhere in East Africa, the whole lot of them. Valham has got an appointment of some sort in the Straits Settlement, and has taken his family with him. The Collards are down at their mother's place in Norfolk; a German banker has bought their house in Manchester Square."

"And the Hebways?" asked Yeovil.

"Dick Hebway is in India," said Cicely, "but his mother lives in Paris; poor Hugo, you know, was killed in the war. My friends the Allinsons are in Paris too. It's rather a clearance, isn't it? However, there are some left, and I expect others will come back in time. Pitherby is here; he's one of those who are trying to make the best of things under the new *régime*."

"He would be," said Yeovil, shortly.

"It's a difficult question," said Cicely, "whether one should stay at home and face the music or go away and live a transplanted life under the British flag. Either attitude might be dictated by patriotism."

"It is one thing to face the music, it is another thing to dance to it," said Yeovil.

Cicely poured out some more coffee for herself and changed the conversation.

"You'll be in to lunch, I suppose? The Clubs are not very.

attractive just now, I believe, and the restaurants are mostly hot in the middle of the day. Ronnie Storre is coming in; he's here pretty often these days. A rather good-looking young animal with something midway between talent and genius in the piano-playing line."

"Not long-haired and Semitic or Tcheque or anything of that sort, I suppose?" asked Yeovil.

Cicely laughed at the vision of Ronnie conjured up by her husband's words.

"No, beautifully groomed and clipped and Anglo-Saxon. I expect you'll like him. He plays bridge almost as well as he plays the piano. I suppose you wonder at any one who can play bridge well wanting to play the piano."

"I'm not quite so intolerant as all that," said Yeovil; "anyhow I promise to like Ronnie. Is any one else coming to lunch?"

"Joan Mardle will probably drop in, in fact I'm afraid she's a certainty. She invited herself in that way of hers that brooks of no refusal. On the other hand, as a mitigating circumstance, there will be a *point d'asperge* omelette such as few kitchens could turn out, so don't be late."

Yeovil set out for his morning walk with the curious sensation of one who starts on a voyage of discovery in a land that is well known to him. He turned into the Park at Hyde Park Corner and made his way along the familiar paths and alleys that bordered the Row. The familiarity vanished when he left the region of fenced-in lawns and rhododendron bushes and came to the open space that stretched away beyond the bandstand. The bandstand was still there, and a military band, in sky-blue Saxon uniform, was executing the first item in the forenoon programme of music. Around it, instead of the serried rows of green chairs that Yeovil remembered, was spread out an acre or so of small round tables, most of which had their quota of customers, engaged in a steady consumption of lager beer, coffee, lemonade and syrups. Farther in the background, but well within earshot of the band, a gaily painted pagoda-restaurant sheltered a number of more commodious tables under its awnings, and gave a hint of convenient indoor accommodation for wet or windy weather. Movable screens of trellis-trained foliage and climbing roses formed little hedges by means of which any particular table could be shut off from its neighbours if semi-privacy were desired. One or two decorative advertisements of popularized brands of champagne and Rhine wines adorned the outside walls of the building, and under the central gable of its upper story was a flamboyant portrait of a stern-faced man, whose image and superscription might also be found on the newer coinage of the land. A mass of bunting hung in folds round the flagpole on the gable, and blew out now and then on a favouring breeze, a long three-coloured strip, black, white, and scarlet, and over the whole scene the elm trees towered with an absurd sardonic air of nothing having changed around their roots.

Yeovil stood for a minute or two, taking in every detail of the unfamiliar spectacle.

"They have certainly accomplished something that we never attempted," he muttered to himself. Then he turned on his heel and made his way back to the shady walk that ran alongside the Row. At first sight little was changed in the aspect of the well-known exercising ground. One or two riding masters cantered up and down as of yore, with their attendant broods of anxious-faced young girls and awkwardly bumping women pupils, while horsey-looking men put marketable animals through their paces or drew up to the rails for long conversations with horsey-looking friends on foot. Sportingly attired young women, sitting astride of their horses, careered by at intervals as though an extremely game fox were leading hounds a merry chase a short way ahead of them; it all seemed much as usual.

Presently, from the middle distance a bright patch of colour set in a whirl of dust drew rapidly nearer and resolved itself into a group of cavalry officers extending their chargers in a smart gallop. They were well mounted and sat their horses to perfection, and they made a brave show as they raced past Yeovil with a clink and clatter and rhythmic thud, thud of hoofs, and became once more a patch of colour in a whirl of dust. An answering glow of colour seemed to have burned itself into the grey face of the young man, who had seen them pass without appearing to look at them, a stinging rush of blood, accompanied by a choking catch in the throat and a hot white blindness across the eyes. The weakness of fever broke down at times the rampart of outward indifference that a man of Yeovil's temperament builds coldly round his heartstrings.

The Row and its riders had become suddenly detestable to the wanderer; he would not run the risk of seeing that insolently joyous cavalcade come galloping past again. Beyond a narrow stretch of tree-shaded grass lay the placid sunlit water of the Serpentine, and Yeovil made a short cut across the turf to reach its gravelled bank.

"Can't you read either English or German?" asked a policeman who confronted him as he stepped off the turf.

Yeovil stared at the man and then turned to look at the small neatly-printed notice to which the official was imperiously pointing; in two languages it was made known that it was forbidden and *verboten*, punishable and *straffbar*, to walk on the grass.

"Three shilling fine," said the policeman, extending his hand for the money.

"Do I pay you?" asked Yeovil, feeling almost inclined to laugh; "I'm rather a stranger to the new order of things."

"You pay me," said the policeman, "and you receive a quittance for the sum paid," and he proceeded to tear a counterfoil receipt for a three shilling fine from a small pocket book.

"May I ask," said Yeovil, as he handed over the sum demanded and received his quittance, "what the red and white band on your sleeve stands for?"

"Bi-lingual," said the constable, with an air of importance. "Preference is given to members of the Force who qualify in both languages. Nearly all the police engaged on Park duty are bi-lingual. About as many foreigners as English use the parks nowadays; in fact, on a fine Sunday afternoon, you'll find three foreigners to every two English. The park habit is more Continental than British, I take it."

"And are there many Germans in the Police Force?" asked Yeovil.

"Well, yes, a good few; there had to be," said the constable; "there were such a lot of resignations when the change came, and they had to be filled up somehow. Lots of men what used to be in the Force emigrated or found work of some other kind, but everybody couldn't take that line; wives and children had to be thought of. 'Tisn't every head of a family that can chuck up a job on the chance of finding another. Starvation's been the lot of a good many what went out. Those of us that stayed on got better pay than we did before, but then of course the duties are much more multitudinous."

"They must be," said Yeovil, fingering his three shilling State document; "by the way," he asked, "are all the grass plots in the Park out of bounds for human feet?"

"Everywhere where you see the notices," said the policeman, "and that's about three-fourths of the whole grass space; there's been a lot of new gravel walks opened up in all directions. People don't want to walk on the grass when they've got clean paths to walk on."

And with this parting reproof the bi-lingual constable strode heavily away, his loss of consideration and self-esteem as a unit of a sometime ruling race evidently compensated for to some extent by his enhanced importance as an official.

"The women and children," thought Yeovil, as he looked after the retreating figure; "yes, that is one side of the problem. The children that have to be fed and schooled, the women folk that have to be cared for, an old mother, perhaps, in the home that cannot be broken up. The old case of giving hostages."

He followed the path alongside the Serpentine, passing under the archway of the bridge and continuing his walk into Kensington Gardens. In another moment he was within view of the Peter Pan statue and at once observed that it had companions. On one side was a group representing a scene from one of the Grimm fairy stories, on the other was Alice in conversation with Gryphon and Mockturtle, the episode looking distressingly stiff and meaningless in its sculptured form. Two other spaces had been cleared in the neighbouring turf, evidently for the reception of further statue groups, which Yeovil mentally assigned to Struwelpeter and Little Lord Fauntleroy.

"German middle-class taste," he commented, "but in this matter we certainly gave them a lead. I suppose the idea is that childish fancy is dead and that it is only decent to erect some sort of memorial to it."

The day was growing hotter, and the Park had ceased to seem a desirable place to loiter in. Yeovil turned his steps homeward, passing on his way the bandstand with its surrounding acreage of tables. It was now nearly one o'clock, and luncheon parties were beginning to assemble under the awnings of the restaurant. Lighter refreshments, in the shape of sausages and potato salads, were being carried out by scurrying waiters to the drinkers of lager beer at the small tables. A park orchestra, in brilliant trappings, had taken the place of the military band. As Yeovil passed the musicians launched out into the tune which the doctor had truly predicted he would hear to repletion before he had been many days in London; the "National Anthem of the *fait accompli*."

CHAPTER V

L'ART D'ETRE COUSINE

JOAN MARDLE had reached forty in the leisurely untroubled fashion of a woman who intends to be comely and attractive at fifty. She cultivated a jovial, almost joyous manner, with a top-dressing of hearty good will and good nature which disarmed strangers and recent acquaintances; on getting to know her better they hastily re-armed themselves. Some one had once aptly described her as a hedgehog with the protective mimicry of a puffball. If there was an awkward remark to be made at an inconvenient moment before undesired listeners, Joan invariably made it, and when the occasion did not present itself she was usually capable of creating it. She was not without a certain popularity, the sort of popularity that a dashing highwayman sometimes achieved among those who were not in the habit of travelling on his particular highway. A great-aunt on her mother's side of the family had married so often that Joan imagined herself justified in claiming cousinship with a large circle of disconnected houses, and treating them all on a relationship footing, which theoretical kinship enabled her to exact luncheons and other accommodations under the plea of keeping the lamp of family life aglow.

"I felt I simply had to come today," she chuckled at Yeovil; "I was just dying to see the returned traveller. Of course, I know perfectly well that neither of you want me, when you haven't seen each other for so long and must have heaps and heaps to say to one another, but I thought I would risk the odium of being the third person on an occasion when two are company and three are a nuisance. Wasn't it brave of me?"

She spoke in full knowledge of the fact that the luncheon party would not in any case have been restricted to Yeovil and his wife, having seen Ronnie arrive in the hall as she was being shown upstairs.

"Ronnie Storre is coming, I believe," said Cicely, "so you're not breaking into a tête-à-tête."

"Ronnie, oh, I don't count him," said Joan gaily; "he's just a boy who looks nice and eats asparagus. I hear he's getting to play the piano really well. Such a pity. He will grow fat; musicians always do, and it will ruin him. I speak feelingly because I'm gravitating towards plumpness myself. The Divine Architect turns us out fearfully and wonderfully built, and the result is charming to the eye, and then He adds another chin and two or three extra inches round the waist, and the effect is ruined. Fortunately you can always find another Ronnie when this one grows fat and uninteresting; the supply of boys who look nice and eat asparagus is unlimited. Hullo, Mr. Storre, we were all talking about you."

"Nothing very damaging, I hope?" said Ronnie, who had just entered the room.

"No, we were merely deciding that, whatever you may do with your life, your chin must remain single. When one's chin begins to lead a double life one's own opportunities for depravity are insensibly narrowed. You needn't tell me that you haven't any hankerings after depravity; people with your coloured eyes and hair are always depraved."

"Let me introduce you to my husband, Ronnie," said Cicely, "and then let's go and begin lunch."

"You two must almost feel as if you were honeymooning again," said Joan as they sat down; "you must have quite forgotten each other's tastes and peculiarities since you last met. Old Emily Fronding was talking about you yesterday, when I mentioned that Murrey was expected home; 'curious sort of marriage tie,' she said, in that stupid staring way of hers, 'when husband and wife spend most of their time in different continents. I don't call it marriage at all.' 'Nonsense,' I said, 'it's the best way of doing things. The Yeovils will be a united and devoted couple long after heaps of their married contemporaries have trundled through the Divorce Court.' I forgot at the moment that her youngest girl had divorced her husband last year, and that her second girl is rumoured to be contemplating a similar step. One can't remember everything."

Joan Mardle was remarkable for being able to remember the smallest details in the family lives of two or three hundred acquaintances.

From personal matters she went with a bound to the political small talk of the moment.

"The Official Declaration as to the House of Lords is out at last," she said; "I bought a paper just before coming here, but I left it in the Tube. All existing titles are to lapse if three successive holders, including the present ones, fail to take the oath of allegiance."

"Have any taken it up to the present?" asked Yeovil.

"Only about nineteen, so far, and none of them representing very leading families; of course others will come in gradually, as the change of Dynasty becomes more and more an accepted fact, and of course there will be lots of new creations to fill up the gaps. I hear for certain that Pitherby is to get a title of some sort, in recognition of his literary labours. He has written a short history of the House of Hohenzollern, for use in schools you know, and he's bringing out a popular Life of Frederick the Great—at least he hopes it will be popular."

"I didn't know that writing was much in his line," said Yeovil, "beyond the occasional editing of a company prospectus."

"I understand his historical researches have given every satisfaction in exalted quarters," said Joan; "something may be lacking in the style, perhaps, but the august approval can make good that defect with the style of Baron. Pitherby has such a kind heart; 'kind hearts are more than coronets,' we all know, but the two go quite well together. And the dear man is not content with his services to literature, he's blossoming forth as a liberal patron of the arts. He's taken quite a lot of tickets for dear Gorla's début; half the second row of the dress-circle."

"Do you mean Gorla Mustelford?" asked Yeovil, catching at the name; "what on earth is she having a début about?"

"What?" cried Joan, in loud-voiced amazement; "haven't you heard? Hasn't Cicely told you? How funny that you shouldn't have heard. Why, it's going to be one of the events of the season. Everybody's talking about it. She's going to do suggestion dancing at the Caravansery Theatre."

"Good Heavens, what is suggestion dancing?" asked Yeovil.

"Oh, something quite new," explained Joan; "at any rate the name is quite new and Gorla is new as far as the public are concerned, and that is enough to establish the novelty of the thing. Among other things she does a dance suggesting the life of a fern; I saw one of the rehearsals, and to me it would have equally well suggested the life of John Wesley. However, that is probably the fault of my imagination—I've either got too much or too little. Anyhow it is an understood thing that she is to take London by storm."

"When I last saw Gorla Mustelford," observed Yeovil, "she was a rather serious flapper who thought the world was in urgent need of regeneration and was not certain whether she would regenerate it or take up miniature painting. I forget which she attempted ultimately."

"She is quite serious about her art," put in Cicely; "she's studied a good deal abroad and worked hard at mastering the technique of her profession. She's not a mere amateur with a hankering after the footlights. I fancy she will do well."

"But what do her people say about it?" asked Yeovil.

"Oh, they're simply furious about it," answered Joan; "the idea of a daughter of the house of Mustelford prancing and twisting about the stage for Prussian officers and Hamburg Jews to gaze at is a dreadful cup of humiliation for them. It's unfortunate, of course, that they should feel so acutely about it, but still one can understand their point of view."

"I don't see what other point of view they could possibly take," said Yeovil sharply; "if Gorla thinks that the necessities of art, or her own inclinations, demand that she should dance in public, why can't she do it in Paris or even Vienna? Anywhere would be better, one would think, than in London under present conditions."

He had given Joan the indication that she was looking for as to his attitude towards the *fait accompli*. Without asking a question she had discovered that husband and wife were divided on the fundamental issue that underlay all others at the present moment. Cicely was weaving social schemes for the future, Yeovil had come home in a frame of mind that threatened the destruction of those schemes, or at any rate a serious hindrance to their execution. The situation presented itself to Joan's mind with an alluring piquancy.

"You are giving a grand supper-party for Gorla on the night of her début, aren't you?" she asked Cicely; "several people spoke to me about it, so I suppose it must be true."

Tony Luton and young Storre had taken care to spread the news of the projected supper function, in order to ensure against a change of plans on Cicely's part.

"Gorla is a great friend of mine," said Cicely, trying to talk as if the conversation had taken a perfectly indifferent turn; "also I think she deserves a little encouragement after the hard work she has been through. I thought it would be doing her a kindness to arrange a supper party for her on her first night."

There was a moment's silence. Yeovil said nothing, and Joan understood the value of being occasionally tongue-tied.

"The whole question is," continued Cicely as the silence became oppressive, "whether one is to mope and hold aloof from the national life, or take our share in it; the life has got to go on whether we participate in it or not. It seems to me to be more patriotic to come down into the dust of the market-place than to withdraw oneself behind walls or beyond the seas."

"Of course the industrial life of the country has to go on," said Yeovil; "no one could criticize Gorla if she interested herself in organizing cottage industries or anything of that sort, in which she would be helping her own people. That one could understand, but I don't think a cosmopolitan concern like the music-hall business calls for personal sacrifices from young women of good family at a moment like the present."

"It is just at a moment like the present that the people want something to interest them and take them out of themselves," said Cicely argumentatively; "what has happened, has happened, and we can't undo it or escape the consequences. What we can do, or attempt to do, is to make things less dreary, and make people less unhappy."

"In a word, more contented," said Yeovil; "if I were a German statesman, that is the end I would labour for and encourage others to labour for, to make the people forget that they were discontented. All this work of regalvanizing the social side of London life may be summed up in the phrase 'travailler pour le roi de Prusse.' "

"I don't think there is any use in discussing the matter further," said Cicely.

"I can see that grand supper-party not coming off," said Joan provocatively.

Ronnie looked anxiously at Cicely.

"You can see it coming on, if you're gifted with prophetic vision of a reliable kind," said Cicely; "of course as Murrey doesn't take kindly to the idea of Gorla's enterprise I won't have the party here. I'll give it at a restaurant, that's all. I can see Murrey's point of view, and sympathize with it, but I'm not going to throw Gorla over."

There was another pause of uncomfortably protracted duration.

"I say, this is a top-hole omelette," said Ronnie.

It was his only contribution to the conversation, but it was a valuable one.

CHAPTER VI

HERR VON KWARL

HERR VON KWARL sat at his favourite table in the Brandenburg Café, the new building that made such an imposing show (and did such thriving business) at the lower end of what most of its patrons called the Regentstrasse. Though the establishment was new it had already achieved its unwritten code of customs, and the sanctity of Herr von Kwarl's specially reserved table had acquired the authority of a tradition. A set of chess-men, a copy of the *Kreuz Zeitung* and the *Times*, and a slim-necked bottle of Rhenish wine, ice-cool from the cellar, were always to be found there early in the forenoon, and the honoured guest for whom these preparations were made usually arrived on the scene shortly after eleven o'clock. For an hour or so he would read and silently digest the contents of his two newspapers, and then at the first sign of flagging interest on his part, another of the café's regular customers would march across the floor, exchange a word or two on the affairs of the day, and be bidden with a wave of the hand into the opposite seat. A waiter would instantly place the chess-board with its marshalled ranks of combatants in the required position, and the contest would begin.

Herr von Kwarl was a heavily built man of mature middle-age, of the blond North-German type, with a facial aspect that suggested stupidity and brutality. The stupidity of his mien masked an ability and shrewdness that was distinctly above the average and the suggestion of brutality was belied by the fact that von Kwarl was as kind-hearted a man as one could meet with in a day's journey. Early in life, almost before he was in his teens, Fritz von Kwarl had made up his mind to accept the world as it was, and to that philosophical resolution, steadfastly adhered to, he attributed his excellent digestion and his unruffled happiness. Perhaps he confused cause and effect; the excellent digestion may have been responsible for at least some of the philosophical serenity.

He was a bachelor of the type that is called confirmed, and which might better be labelled consecrated; from his early youth onward to his present age he had never had the faintest flickering intention of marriage. Children and animals he adored, women and plants he accounted somewhat of a nuisance. A world without women and roses and asparagus would, he admitted, be robbed of much of its charm, but with all their charm these things were tiresome and thorny and capricious, always wanting to climb or creep in places where they were not wanted, and resolutely drooping and fading away when they were desired to flourish. Animals, on the other hand, accepted the world as it was and made the best of it, and children, at least nice children, uncontaminated by grown-up influences, lived in worlds of their own making.

Von Kwarl held no acknowledged official position in the country of his residence, but it was an open secret that those responsible for the real direction of affairs sought his counsel on nearly every step that they meditated, and that his counsel was very rarely disregarded. Some of the shrewdest and most successful enactments of the ruling power were believed to have originated in the brain-cells of the bovine-fronted *Stammgast* of the Brandenburg Café.

Around the wood-panelled walls of the Café were set at intervals well-mounted heads of boar, elk, stag, roebuck, and other game-beasts of a northern forest, while in between were carved armorial escutcheons of the principal cities of the lately expanded realm, Magdeburg, Manchester, Hamburg, Bremen, Bristol and so forth. Below these came shelves on which stood a wonderful array of stone beer-mugs, each decorated with some fantastic device or motto, and most of them pertaining individually and sacredly to some regular and unfailing customer. In one particular corner of the highest shelf, greatly at his ease and in nowise to be disturbed, slept Wotan, the huge grey house-cat, dreaming doubtless of certain nimble and audacious mice down in the cellar three floors below, whose nim-

bleness and audacity were as precious to him as the forward-
ness of the birds is to a skilled gun on a grouse moor. Once
every day Wotan came marching in stately fashion across the
polished floor, halted midway to resume an unfinished toilet
operation, and then proceeded to pay his leisurely respects to
his friend von Kwarl. The latter was said to be prouder of
this daily demonstration of esteem than of his many coveted
orders of merit. Several of his friends and acquaintances shared
with him the distinction of having achieved the Black Eagle,
but not one of them had ever succeeded in obtaining the slightest recognition of their existence from Wotan.

The daily greeting had been exchanged and the proud grey
beast had marched away to the music of a slumberous purr.
The *Kreuz Zeitung* and the *Times* underwent a final scrutiny
and were pushed aside, and von Kwarl glanced aimlessly out
at the July sunshine bathing the walls and windows of the
Piccadilly Hotel. Herr Rebinok, the plump little Pomeranian
banker, stepped across the floor, almost as noiselessly as Wotan
had done, though with considerably less grace, and some half-
minute later was engaged in sliding pawns and knights and
bishops to and fro on the chess-board in a series of lightning
moves bewildering to look on. Neither he nor his opponent
played with the skill that they severally brought to bear on
banking and statecraft, nor did they conduct their game with
the politeness that they punctiliously observed in other affairs
of life. A running fire of contemptuous remarks and aggressive
satire accompanied each move, and the mere record of the conversation would have given an uninitiated onlooker the puzzling impression that an easy and crushing victory was assured
to both the players.

"Aha, he is puzzled. Poor man, he doesn't know what to
do. . . . Oho, he thinks he will move there, does he? Much
good that will do him. . . . Never have I seen such a mess as
he is in . . . he cannot do anything, he is absolutely helpless,
helpless."

"Ah, you take my bishop, do you? Much I care for that.
Nothing. See, I give you check. Ah, now he is in a fright! He
doesn't know where to go. What a mess he is in. . . ."

So the game proceeded, with a brisk exchange of pieces and incivilities and a fluctuation of fortunes, till the little banker lost his queen as the result of an incautious move, and, after several woebegone contortions of his shoulders and hands, declined further contest. A sleek-headed piccolo rushed forward to remove the board, and the erstwhile combatants resumed the courteous dignity that they discarded in their chess-playing moments.

"Have you see the *Germania* today?" asked Herr Rebinok, as soon as the boy had receded to a respectful distance.

"No," said von Kwarl, "I never see the *Germania*. I count on you to tell me if there is anything noteworthy in it."

"It has an article today headed, 'Occupation or Assimilation,'" said the banker. "It is of some importance, and well written. It is very pessimistic."

"Catholic papers are always pessimistic about the things of this world," said von Kwarl, "just as they are unduly optimistic about the things of the next world. What line does it take?"

"It says that our conquest of Britain can only result in a temporary occupation, with a 'notice to quit' always hanging over our heads; that we can never hope to assimilate the people of these islands in our Empire as a sort of maritime Saxony or Bavaria, all the teaching of history is against it; Saxony and Bavaria are part of the Empire because of their past history. England is being bound into the Empire in spite of her past history; and so forth."

"The writer of the article has not studied history very deeply," said von Kwarl. "The impossible thing that he speaks of has been done before, and done in these very islands, too. The Norman Conquest became an assimilation in comparatively few generations."

"Ah, in those days, yes," said the banker, "but the conditions were altogether different. There was not the rapid transmission of news and the means of keeping the public mind instructed in what was happening; in fact, one can scarcely say that the public mind was there to instruct. There was not the same strong bond of brotherhood between men of the same nation that exists now. Northumberland was almost as foreign to Devon or Kent as Normandy was. And the Church in those days was a great international factor, and the Crusades bound men together fighting under one leader for a common cause. Also there was not a great national past to be forgotten as there is in this case."

"There are many factors, certainly, that are against us," conceded the statesman, "but you must also take into account those that will help us. In most cases in recent history where the conquered have stood out against all attempts at assimilation, there has been a religious difference to add to the racial one—take Poland, for instance, and the Catholic parts of Ireland. If the Bretons ever seriously begin to assert their nationality as against the French, it will be because they have remained more Catholic in practice and sentiment than their neighbours. Here there is no such complication; we are in the bulk a Protestant nation with a Catholic minority, and the same may be said of the British. Then in modern days there is the alchemy of Sport and the Drama to bring men of different races amicably together. One or two sportsmanlike Germans in a London football team will do more to break down racial antagonism than anything that Governments or Councils can effect. As for the Stage, it has long been international in its tendencies. You can see that every day."

The banker nodded his head.

"London is not our greatest difficulty," continued von Kwarl. "You must remember the steady influx of Germans since the war; whole districts are changing the complexion of their inhabitants, and in some streets you might almost fancy yourself in a German town. We can scarcely hope to make much impression on the country districts and the provincial towns at present, but you must remember that thousands and thousands of the more virile and restless-souled men have emigrated, and thousands more will follow their example. We shall fill up their places with our own surplus population, as the Teuton races colonized England in the old pre-Christian days. That is better, is it not, to people the fat meadows of the Thames valley and the healthy downs and uplands of Sussex and Berkshire than to go hunting for elbow-room among the flies and fevers of the tropics? We have somewhere to go to, now, better than the scrub and the veldt and the thorn-jungles."

"Of course, of course," assented Herr Rebinok, "but while this desirable process of infiltration and assimilation goes on, how are you going to provide against the hostility of the conquered nation? A people with a great tradition behind them and the ruling instinct strongly developed, won't sit with their eyes closed and their hands folded while you carry on the process of Germanization. What will keep them quiet?"

"The hopelessness of the situation. For centuries Britain has ruled the seas, and been able to dictate to half the world in consequence; then she let slip the mastery of the seas, as something too costly and onerous to keep up, something which aroused too much jealousy and uneasiness in others, and now the seas rule her. Every wave that breaks on her shore rattles the keys of her prison. I am no fire-eater, Herr Rebinok, but I confess that when I am at Dover, say, or Southampton, and see those dark blots on the sea and those grey specks in the sky, our battleships and cruisers and aircraft, and realize what they mean to us, my heart beats just a little quicker. If every German was flung out of England tomorrow, in three weeks' time we should be coming in again on our own terms. With our sea scouts and air scouts spread in organized network around, not a shipload of food-stuff could reach the country. They know that; they can calculate how many days of independence and starvation they could endure, and they will make no attempt to bring about such a certain fiasco. Brave men fight for a forlorn hope, but the bravest do not fight for an issue they know to be hopeless."

"That is so," said Herr Rebinok; "as things are at present they can do nothing from within, absolutely nothing. We have weighed all that beforehand. But, as the *Germania* points out, there is another Britain beyond the seas. Supposing the Court at Delhi were to engineer a league——"

"A league? A league with whom?" interrupted the statesman. "Russia we can watch and hold. We are rather nearer to its western frontier than Delhi is, and we could throttle its Baltic trade at five hours' notice. France and Holland are not inclined to provoke our hostility; they would have everything to lose by such a course."

"There are other forces in the world that might be arrayed against as," argued the banker; "the United States, Japan, Italy, they all have navies."

"Does the teaching of history show you that it is the strong Power, armed and ready, that has to suffer from the hostility of the world?" asked von Kwarl. "As far as sentiment goes, perhaps, but not in practice. The danger has always been for the weak, dismembered nation. Think you a moment, has the enfeebled scattered British Empire overseas no undefended territories that are a temptation to her neighbours? Has Japan nothing to glean where we have harvested? Are there no North American possessions which might slip into other keeping? Has Russia herself no traditional temptations beyond the Oxus? Mind you, we are not making the mistake Napoleon made, when he forced all Europe to be for him or against him. We threaten no world aggressions, we are satiated where he was insatiable. We have cast down one overshadowing Power from the face of the world, because it stood in our way, but we have made no attempt to spread our branches over all the space that it covered. We have not tried to set up a tributary Canadian republic or to partition South Africa; we have dreamed no dream of making ourselves Lords of Hindostan. On the contrary, we have given proof of our friendly intentions towards our neighbours. We backed France up the other day in her squabble with Spain over the Moroccan boundaries, and proclaimed our opinion that the Republic had as indisputable a mission on the North Africa coast as we have in the North Sea. That is not the action or the language of aggression. No," continued von Kwarl, after a moment's silence, "the world may fear us and dislike us, but, for the present at any rate, there will be no leagues against us. No, there is one rock on which our attempt at assimilation will founder or find firm anchorage."

"And that is—?"

"The youth of the country, the generation that is at the threshold now. It is them that we must capture. We must teach them to learn, and coax them to forget. In course of time Anglo-Saxon may blend with German, as the Elbe Saxons and the Bavarians and Swabians have blended with the Prussians into a loyal united people under the sceptre of the Hohenzollerns. Then we should be doubly strong, Rome and Carthage rolled into one, an Empire of the West greater than Charlemagne ever knew. Then we could look Slav and Latin and Asiatic in the face and keep our place as the central dominant force of the civilized world."

The speaker paused for a moment and drank a deep draught of wine, as though he were invoking the prosperity of that future world-power. Then he resumed in a more level tone:

"On the other hand, the younger generation of Britons may grow up in hereditary hatred, repulsing all our overtures, forgetting nothing and forgiving nothing, waiting and watching for the time when some weakness assails us, when some crisis entangles us, when we cannot be everywhere at once. Then our work will be imperilled, perhaps undone. There lies the danger, there lies the hope, the younger generation."

"There is another danger," said the banker, after he had pondered over von Kwarl's remarks for a moment or two amid the incense-clouds of a fat cigar; "a danger that I foresee in the immediate future; perhaps not so much a danger as an element of exasperation which may ultimately defeat your plans. The law as to military service will have to be promulgated shortly, and that cannot fail to be bitterly unpopular. The people of these islands will have to be brought into line with the rest of the Empire in the matter of military training and military service, and how will they like that? Will not the enforcing of such a measure infuriate them against us? Remember, they have made great sacrifices to avoid the burden of military service."

"Dear God," exclaimed Herr von Kwarl, "as you say, they have made sacrifices on that altar!"

CHAPTER VII

THE LURE

CICELY had successfully insisted on having her own way concerning the projected supper-party; Yeovil had said nothing further in opposition to it, whatever his feelings on the subject might be. Having gained her point, however, she was anxious to give her husband the impression of having been consulted, and to put her victory as far as possible on the footing of a compromise. It was also rather a relief to be able to discuss the matter out of range of Joan's disconcerting tongue and observant eyes.

"I hope you are not really annoyed about this silly supper-party," she said on the morning before the much-talked-of first night. "I had pledged myself to give it, so I couldn't back out without seeming mean to Gorla, and in any case it would have been impolitic to cry off."

"Why impolitic?" asked Yeovil coldly.

"It would give offence in quarters where I don't want to give offence," said Cicely.

"In quarters were the *fait accompli* is an object of solicitude," said Yeovil.

"Look here," said Cicely in her most disarming manner, "it's just as well to be perfectly frank about the whole matter. If one wants to live in the London of the present day one must make up one's mind to accept the *fait accompli* with as good a grace as possible. I do want to live in London, and I don't want to change my way of living and start under different conditions in some other place. I can't face the prospect of tearing up my life by the roots; I feel certain that I shouldn't bear transplanting. I can't imagine myself re-creating my circle of interests in some foreign town or colonial centre or even in a country town in England. India I couldn't stand. London is not merely a home to me, it is a world, and it happens to be just the world that suits me and that I am suited to. The German occupation, or whatever one likes to call it, is a calamity, but it's not like a molten deluge from Vesuvius that need send us all scuttling away from another Pompeii. Of course," she added, "there are things that jar horribly on one, even when one has got more or less accustomed to them, but one must just learn to be philosophical and bear them."

"Supposing they are not bearable?" said Yeovil; "during the few days that I've been in the land I've seen things that I cannot imagine will ever be bearable."

"That is because they're new to you," said Cicely.

"I don't wish that they should ever come to seem bearable," retorted Yeovil. "I've been bred and reared as a unit of a ruling race; I don't want to find myself settling down resignedly as a member of an enslaved one."

"There's no need to make things out worse than they are," protested Cicely. "We've had a military disaster on a big scale, and there's been a great political dislocation in consequence. But there's no reason why everything shouldn't right itself in time, as it has done after other similar disasters in the history of nations. We are not scattered to the winds or wiped off the face of the earth, we are still an important racial unit."

"A racial unit in a foreign Empire," commented Yeovil.

"We may arrive at the position of being the dominant factor in that Empire," said Cicely, "impressing our national characteristics on it, and perhaps dictating its dynastic future and the whole trend of its policy. Such things have happened in history. Or we may become strong enough to throw off the foreign connexion at a moment when it can be done effectually and advantageously. But meanwhile it is necessary to preserve our industrial life and our social life, and for that reason we must accommodate ourselves to present circumstances, however distasteful they may be. Emigration to some colonial wilderness, or holding ourselves rigidly aloof from the life of the capital, won't help matters. Really, Murrey, if you will think things over a bit, you will see that the course I am following is the one dictated by sane patriotism."

"Whom the gods wish to render harmless they first afflict with sanity," said Yeovil bitterly. "You may be content to wait for a hundred years or so, for this national revival to creep and crawl us back into a semblance of independence and world-importance. I'm afraid I haven't the patience or the philosophy to sit down comfortably and wait for a change of fortune that won't come in my time—if it comes at all."

Cicely changed the drift of the conversation; she had only introduced the argument for the purpose of defining her point of view and accustoming Yeovil to it, as one leads a nervous horse up to an unfamiliar barrier that he is required eventually to jump.

"In any case," she said, "from the immediately practical standpoint England is the best place for you till you have shaken off all traces of that fever. Pass the time away somehow till the hunting begins, and then go down to the East Wessex country; they are looking out for a new master after this season, and if you were strong enough you might take it on for a while. You could go to Norway for fishing in the summer and hunt the East Wessex in the winter. I'll come down and do a bit of hunting too, and we'll have house-parties, and get a little golf in between whiles. It will be like old times."

Yeovil looked at his wife and laughed.

"Who was that old fellow who used to hunt his hounds regularly through the fiercest times of the great Civil War? There is a picture of him, by Caton Woodville, I think, leading his pack between King Charles's army and the Parliament forces just as some battle was going to begin. I have often thought that the King must have disliked him rather more than he disliked the men who were in arms against him; they at least cared, one way or the other. I fancy that old chap would have a great many imitators nowadays, though, when it came to be a question of sport against soldiering. I don't know whether any one has said it, but one might almost assert that the German victory was won on the golf-links of Britain."

"I don't see why you should saddle one particular form of sport with a special responsibility," protested Cicely.

"Of course not," said Yeovil, "except that it absorbed perhaps more of the energy and attention of the leisured class than other sports did, and in this country the leisured class was the only bulwark we had against official indifference. The

200 THE NOVELS AND PLAYS OF SAKI

working classes had a big share of the apathy, and, indirectly, a greater share of the responsibility, because the voting power was in their hands. They had not the leisure, however, to sit down and think clearly what the danger was; their own industrial warfare was more real to them than anything that was threatening from the nation that they only knew from samples of German clerks and German waiters."

"In any case," said Cicely, "as regards the hunting, there is no Civil War or national war raging just now, and there is no immediate likelihood of one. A good many hunting seasons will have to come and go before we can think of a war of independence as even a distant possibility, and in the meantime hunting and horse-breeding and country sports generally are the things most likely to keep Englishmen together on the land. That is why so many men who hate the German occupation are trying to keep field sports alive, and in the right hands. However, I won't go on arguing. You and I always think things out for ourselves and decide for ourselves, which is much the best way in the long run."

Cicely slipped away to her writing-room to make final arrangements over the telephone for the all-important supper-party, leaving Yeovil to turn over in his mind the suggestion that she had thrown out. It was an obvious lure, a lure to draw him away from the fret and fury that possessed him so inconveniently, but its obvious nature did not detract from its effectiveness. Yeovil had pleasant recollections of the East Wessex, a cheery little hunt that afforded good sport in an unpretentious manner, a joyous thread of life running through a rather sleepy countryside, like a merry brook careering through a placid valley. For a man coming slowly and yet eagerly back to the activities of life from the weariness of a long fever, the prospect of a leisurely season with the East Wessex was singularly attractive, and side by side with its attractiveness there was a tempting argument in favour of yielding to its attractions. Among the small squires and yeoman farmers, doctors, country tradesmen, auctioneers and so forth who would gather at the covert-side and at the hunt breakfasts, there might be a local nucleus of revolt against the enslavement of the land, a dis-

couraged and leaderless band waiting for some one to mould
their resistance into effective shape and keep their loyalty to
the old dynasty and the old national cause steadily burning.
Yeovil could see himself taking up that position, stimulating
the spirit of hostility to the *fait accompli*, organizing stubborn
opposition to every Germanizing influence that was brought
into play, schooling the youth of the countryside to look steadily Delhiward. That was the bait that Yeovil threw out to his
conscience, while slowly considering the other bait that was ap-
pealing so strongly to his senses. The dry warm scent of the
stable, the nip of the morning air, the pleasant squelch-squelch
of the saddle leather, the moist earthy fragrance of the autumn
woods and wet fallows, the cold white mists of winter days,
the whimper of hounds and the hot restless pushing of the
pack through ditch and hedgerow and undergrowth, the birds
that flew up and clucked and chattered as you passed, the
hearty greeting and pleasant gossip in farmhouse kitchens and
market-day bar-parlours—all these remembered delights of the
chase marshalled themselves in the brain, and made a cumulative appeal that came with special intensity to a man who
was a little tired of his wanderings, more than a little drawn
away from the jarring centres of life. The hot London sunshine baking the soot-grimed walls and the ugly incessant hoot
and grunt of the motor traffic gave an added charm to the
vision of hill and hollow and copse that flickered in Yeovil's
mind. Slowly, with a sensuous lingering over detail, his imagination carried him down to a small, sleepy, yet withal pleasantly bustling market town, and placed him unerringly in a
wide straw-littered yard, half-full of men and quarter-full of
horses, with a bob-tailed sheep-dog or two trying not to get in
everybody's way, but insisting on being in the thick of things.
The horses gradually detached themselves from the crowd of
unimportant men and came one by one into momentary prominence, to be discussed and appraised for their good points and
bad points, and finally to be bid for. And always there was one
horse that detached itself conspicuously from the rest, the ideal
hunter, or at any rate, Yeovil's ideal of the ideal hunter. Mentally it was put through its paces before him, its pedigree and

brief history recounted to him; mentally he saw a stable lad put it over a jump or two, with credit to all concerned, and inevitably he saw himself outbidding less discerning rivals and securing the desired piece of horseflesh, to be the chief glory and mainstay of his hunting stable, to carry him well and truly and cleverly through many a joyous long-to-be-remembered run. That scene had been one of the recurring half-waking dreams of his long days of weakness in the far-away Finnish nursing-home, a dream sometimes of tantalizing mockery, sometimes of pleasure in the foretaste of a joy to come. And now it need scarcely be a dream any longer, he had only to go down at the right moment and take an actual part in his oft-rehearsed vision. Everything would be there, exactly as his imagination had placed it, even down to the bob-tailed sheep-dogs; the horse of his imagining would be there waiting for him, or if not absolutely the ideal animal, something very like it. He might even go beyond the limits of his dream and pick up a couple of desirable animals—there would probably be fewer purchasers for good class hunters in these days than of yore. And with the coming of this reflection his dream faded suddenly and his mind came back with a throb of pain to the things he had for the moment forgotten, the weary, hateful things that were symbolized for him by the standard that floated yellow and black over the frontage of Buckingham Palace.

Yeovil wandered down to his snuggery, a mood of listless dejection possessing him. He fidgeted aimlessly with one or two books and papers, filled a pipe, and half filled a waste-paper basket with torn circulars and accumulated writing-table litter. Then he lit the pipe and settled down in his most comfortable arm-chair with an old notebook in his hand. It was a sort of disjointed diary, running fitfully through the winter months of some past years, and recording noteworthy days with the East Wessex.

And over the telephone Cicely talked and arranged and consulted with men and women to whom the joys of a good gallop or the love of a stricken fatherland were as letters in an unknown alphabet.

CHAPTER VIII

THE FIRST NIGHT

HUGE posters outside the Caravansery Theatre of Varieties announced the first performance of the uniquely interesting Suggestion Dances, interpreted by the Hon. Gorla Mustelford. An impressionist portrait of a rather severe-looking young woman gave the public some idea of what the *danseuse* might be like in appearance, and the further information was added that her performance was the greatest dramatic event of the season. Yet another piece of information was conveyed to the public a few minutes after the doors had opened, in the shape of large notices bearing the brief announcement, "House full." For the first-night function most of the seats had been reserved for specially invited guests or else bespoken by those who considered it due to their own importance to be visible on such an occasion.

Even at the commencement of the ordinary programme of the evening (Gorla was not due to appear till late in the list) the theatre was crowded with a throng of chattering, expectant human beings; it seemed as though every one had come early to see every one else arrive. As a matter of fact it was the rumour-heralded arrival of one personage in particular that had drawn people early to their seats and given a double edge to the expectancy of the moment.

At first sight and first hearing the bulk of the audience seemed to comprise representatives of the chief European races in well-distributed proportions, but if one gave it closer consideration it could be seen that the distribution was geographically rather than ethnographically diversified. Men and women there were from Paris, Munich, Rome, Moscow and Vienna, from Sweden and Holland and divers other cities and countries, but in the majority of cases the Jordan Valley had supplied their forefathers with a common cradle-ground. The lack of a fire burning on a national altar seemed to have drawn them by universal impulse to the congenial flare of the footlights, whether as artists, producers, impresarios, critics, agents, go-betweens, or merely as highly intelligent and fearsomely well-informed spectators. They were prominent in the chief seats, they were represented, more sparsely but still in fair numbers, in the cheaper places, and everywhere they were voluble, emphatic, sanguine or sceptical, prodigal of word and gesture, with eyes that seemed to miss nothing and acknowledge nothing, and a general restless dread of not being seen and noticed. Of the theatre-going London public there was also a fair muster, more particularly centred in the less expensive parts of the house, while in boxes, stalls and circles a sprinkling of military uniforms gave an unfamiliar tone to the scene in the eyes of those who had not previously witnessed a first-night performance under the new conditions.

Yeovil, while standing aloof from his wife's participation in this social event, had made private arrangements for being a personal spectator of the scene; as one of the ticket-buying public he had secured a seat in the back row of a low-priced gallery, whence he might watch, observant and unobserved, the much-talked-of début of Gorla Mustelford, and the writing of a new chapter in the history of the *fait accompli*. Around him he noticed an incessant undercurrent of jangling laughter, an unending give-and-take of meaningless mirthless jest and catchword. He had noticed the same thing in streets and public places since his arrival in London, a noisy, empty interchange of chaff and laughter that he had been at a loss to account for. The Londoner is not well adapted for the irresponsible noisiness of jesting tongue that bubbles up naturally in a Southern race, and the effort to be volatile was the more noticeable because it so obviously was an effort. Turning over the pages of a book that told the story of Bulgarian social life in the days of Turkish rule, Yeovil had that morning come across a passage that seemed to throw some light on the thing that had puzzled him:

"Bondage has this one advantage: it makes a nation merry. Where far-reaching ambition has no scope for its development the community squanders its energy on the trivial and personal cares of its daily life, and seeks relief and recreation in simple and easily obtained material enjoyment." The writer was a man who had known bondage, so he spoke at any rate with authority. Of the London of the moment it could not, however, be said with any truth that it was merry, but merely that its inhabitants made desperate endeavour not to appear crushed under their catastrophe. Surrounded as he was now with a babble of tongues and shrill mechanical repartee, Yeovil's mind went back to the book and its account of a theatre audience in the Turkish days of Bulgaria, with its light and laughing crowd of critics and spectators. Bulgaria! The thought of that determined little nation came to him with a sharp sense of irony. There was a people who had not thought it beneath the dignity of their manhood to learn the trade and discipline of arms. They had their reward; torn and exhausted and debt-encumbered from their campaigns, they were masters in their own house, the Bulgarian flag flew over the Bulgarian mountains. And Yeovil stole a glance at the crown of Charlemagne set over the Royal box.

In a capacious box immediately opposite the one set aside for royalty the Lady Shalem sat in well-considered prominence, confident that every Press critic and reporter would note her presence, and that one or two of them would describe, or mis-describe, her toilet. Already quite a considerable section of the audience knew her by name, and the frequency with which she graciously nodded towards various quarters of the house suggested the presence of a great many personal acquaintances. She had attained to that desirable feminine altitude of purse and position when people who go about everywhere know you well by sight and have never met your dress before.

Lady Shalem was a woman of commanding presence, of that type which suggests a consciousness that the command may not necessarily be obeyed; she had observant eyes and a well-managed voice. Her successes in life had been worked for, but they were also to some considerable extent the result of accident. Her public history went back to the time when, in the person of her husband, Mr. Conrad Dort, she had contested two hopeless and very expensive Parliamentary elections on behalf of her party; on each occasion the declaration of the poll had shown a heavy though reduced majority on the wrong side, but she might have perpetrated an apt misquotation of the French monarch's traditional message after the defeat of Pavia, and assured the world "all is lost save honours." The forthcoming Honours List had duly proclaimed the fact that Conrad Dort, Esquire, had entered Parliament by another door as Baron Shalem of Wireskiln, in the county of Suffolk. Success had crowned the lady's efforts as far as the achievement of the title went, but her social ambitions seemed unlikely to make further headway. The new Baron and his wife, their title and money notwithstanding, did not "go down" in their particular segment of county society, and in London there were other titles and incomes to compete with. People were willing to worship the Golden Calf, but allowed themselves a choice of altars. No one could justly say that the Shalems were either oppressively vulgar or insufferably bumptious; probably the chief reason for their lack of popularity was their intense and obvious desire to be popular. They kept open house in such an insistently open manner that they created a social draught. The people who accepted their invitations for the second or third time were not the sort of people whose names gave importance to a dinner party or a house gathering. Failure, in a thinly-disguised form, attended the assiduous efforts of the Shalems to play a leading rôle in the world that they had climbed into. The Baron began to observe to his acquaintances that "gadding about" and entertaining on a big scale was not much in his line; a quiet after-dinner pipe and talk with some brother legislator was his ideal way of spending an evening.

Then came the great catastrophe, involving the old order of society in the national overthrow. Lady Shalem, after a decent interval of patriotic mourning, began to look around her and take stock of her chances and opportunities under the new régime. It was easier to achieve distinction as a titled oasis in the social desert that London had become than it had been to obtain recognition as a new growth in a rather overcrowded field. The observant eyes and agile brain quickly noted this circumstance, and her ladyship set to work to adapt herself to the altered conditions that governed her world. Lord Shalem was

one of the few Peers who kissed the hand of the new Sovereign,
his wife was one of the few hostesses who attempted to throw
a semblance of gaiety and lavish elegance over the travesty of
a London season following the year of disaster. The world of
tradesmen and purveyors and caterers, and the thousands who
were dependent on them for employment, privately blessed the
example set by Shalem House, whatever their feelings might
be towards the *fait accompli*, and the august new-comer who
had added an old Saxon kingdom and some of its accretions to
the Teutonic realm of Charlemagne was duly beholden to an ac-
quired subject who was willing to forget the bitterness of defeat and to help others to forget it also. Among other acts of
Imperial recognition an earldom was being held in readiness
for the Baron who had known how to accept accomplished
facts with a good grace. One of the wits of the Cockatrice
Club had asserted that the new earl would take as supporters
for his coat of arms a lion and a unicorn oublié.

In the box with Lady Shalem was the Gräfin von Tolb, a
well-dressed woman of some fifty-six years, comfortable and
placid in appearance, yet alert withal, rather suggesting a thoroughly wide-awake dormouse. Rich, amiable and intelligent
were the adjectives which would best have described her character and her life-story. In her own rather difficult social circle
at Paderborn she had earned for herself the reputation of being
one of the most tactful and discerning hostesses in Germany,
and it was generally suspected that she had come over and
taken up her residence in London in response to a wish expressed in high quarters; the lavish hospitality which she dis-
pensed at her house in Berkeley Square was a considerable re-
inforcement to the stricken social life of the metropolis.

In a neighbouring box Cicely Yeovil presided over a large
and lively party, which of course included Ronnie Storre, who
was for once in a way in a chattering mood, and also included
an American dowager, who had never been known to be in
anything else. A tone of literary distinction was imparted to
the group by the presence of Augusta Smith, better known
under her pen-name of Rhapsodie Pantril, author of a play that
had had a limited but well-advertised success in Sheffield and

the United States of America, author also of a book of reminiscences, entitled *Things I Cannot Forget*. She had beautiful eyes, a knowledge of how to dress, and a pleasant disposition, cankered just a little by a perpetual dread of the non-recognition of her genius. As the woman, Augusta Smith, she probably would have been unreservedly happy; as the superwoman, Rhapsodie Pantril, she lived within the border-line of discontent. Her most ordinary remarks were framed with the view of arresting attention; some one once said of her that she ordered a sack of potatoes with the air of one who is making inquiry for a love-philtre.

"Do you see what colour the curtain is?" she asked Cicely, throwing a note of intense meaning into her question.

Cicely turned quickly and looked at the drop-curtain.

"Rather a nice blue," she said.

"Alexandrine blue—*my* colour—the colour of hope," said Rhapsodie impressively.

"It goes well with the general colour-scheme," said Cicely, feeling that she was hardly rising to the occasion.

"Say, is it really true that His Majesty is coming?" asked the lively American dowager. "I've put on my nooest frock and my best diamonds on purpose, and I shall be mortified to death if he doesn't see them."

"There!" pouted Ronnie, "I felt certain you'd put them on for me."

"Why no, I should have put on rubies and orange opals for you. People with our colour of hair always like barbaric display——"

"They don't," said Ronnie, "they have chaste cold tastes. You are absolutely mistaken."

"Well, I think I ought to know!" protested the dowager; "I've lived longer in the world than you have, anyway."

"Yes," said Ronnie with devastating truthfulness, "but my hair has been this colour longer than yours has."

Peace was restored by the opportune arrival of a middle-aged man of blond North-German type, with an expression of brutality on his rather stupid face, who sat in the front of the box for a few minutes on a visit of ceremony to Cicely. His appearance caused a slight buzz of recognition among the audience, and if Yeovil had cared to make enquiry of his neighbours he might have learned that this decorated and obviously important personage was the redoubtable von Kwarl, artificer and shaper of much of the statecraft for which other men got the public credit.

The orchestra played a selection from the "Gondola Girl," which was the leading musical-comedy of the moment. Most of the audience, those in the more expensive seats at any rate, heard the same airs two or three times daily, at restaurant lunches, teas, dinners and suppers, and occasionally in the Park; they were justified therefore in treating the music as a background to slightly louder conversation than they had hitherto indulged in. The music came to an end, episode number two in the evening's entertainment was signalled, the curtain of Alexandrine blue rolled heavily upward, and a troupe of performing wolves was presented to the public. Yeovil had encountered wolves in North Africa deserts and in Siberian forest and wold, he had seen them at twilight stealing like dark shadows across the snow, and heard their long whimpering howl in the darkness amid the pines; he could well understand how a magic lore had grown up round them through the ages among the peoples of four continents, how their name had passed into a hundred strange sayings and inspired a hundred traditions. And now he saw them ride round the stage on tricycles, with grotesque ruffles round their necks and clown caps on their heads, their eyes blinking miserably in the blaze of the footlights. In response to the applause of the house a stout, atrociously smiling man in evening dress came forward and bowed; he had had nothing to do either with the capture or the training of the animals, having bought them ready for use from a continental emporium where wild beasts were prepared for the music-hall market, but he continued bowing and smiling till the curtain fell.

Two American musicians with comic tendencies (denoted by the elaborate rags and tatters of their costumes) succeeded the wolves. Their musical performance was not without merit, but their comic "business" seemed to have been invented long ago by some man who had patented a monopoly of all music-hall humour and forthwith retired from the trade. Some day, Yeovil reflected, the rights of the monopoly might expire and new "business" become available for the knockabout profession.

The audience brightened considerably when item number five of the programme was signalled. The orchestra struck up a rollicking measure and Tony Luton made his entrance amid a rousing storm of applause. He was dressed as an errand-boy of some West End shop, with a livery and box-tricycle, as spruce and decorative as the most ambitious errand-boy could see himself in his most ambitious dreams. His song was a lively and very audacious chronicle of life behind the scenes of a big retail establishment, and sparkled with allusions which might fitly have been described as suggestive—at any rate they appeared to suggest meanings to the audience quite as clearly as Gorla Mustelford's dances were likely to do, even with the aid, in her case, of long explanations on the programmes. When the final verse seemed about to reach an unpardonable climax a stage policeman opportunely appeared and moved the lively songster on for obstructing the imaginary traffic of an imaginary Bond Street. The house received the new number with genial enthusiasm, and mingled its applause with demands for an earlier favourite. The orchestra struck up the familiar air, and in a few moments the smart errand-boy, transformed now into a smart jockey, was singing "They quaff the gay bubbly in Eccleston Square" to an audience that hummed and nodded its unstinted approval.

The next number but one was the Gorla Mustelford début, and the house settled itself down to yawn and fidget and chatter for ten or twelve minutes while a troupe of talented Japanese jugglers performed some artistic and quite uninteresting marvels with fans and butterflies and lacquer boxes. The interval of waiting was not destined, however, to be without its interest; in its way it provided the one really important and dramatic moment of the evening. One or two uniforms and evening toilettes had already made their appearance in the Imperial box; now there was observable in that quarter a slight commotion, an unobtrusive reshuffling and reseating, and then every eye in the suddenly quiet semi-darkened house focused itself on one figure. There was no public demonstration from the newly-loyal, it had been particularly wished that there should be none, but a ripple of whisper went through the vast audience from end to end. Majesty had arrived. The Japanese marvel-workers went through their display with even less attention than before. Lady Shalem, sitting well in the front of her box, lowered her observant eyes to her programme and her massive bangles. The evidence of her triumph did not need staring at.

CHAPTER IX

AN EVENING "TO BE REMEMBERED"

TO the uninitiated or unappreciative the dancing of Gorla Mustelford did not seem widely different from much that had been exhibited aforetime by exponents of the posturing school. She was not naturally graceful of movement, she had not undergone years of arduous tutelage, she had not the instinct for sheer joyous energy of action that is stored in some natures; out of these unpromising negative qualities she had produced a style of dancing that might best be labelled a conscientious departure from accepted methods. The highly imaginative titles that she had bestowed on her dances, the "Life of a fern," the "Soul-dream of a topaz," and so forth, at least gave her audience and her critics something to talk about. In themselves they meant absolutely nothing, but they induced discussion, and that to Gorla meant a great deal. It was a season of dearth and emptiness in the footlights and box-office world, and her performance received a welcome that would scarcely have befallen it in a more crowded and prosperous day. Her success, indeed, had been waiting for her, ready-made, as far as the managerial profession was concerned, and nothing had been left undone in the way of advertisement to secure for it the appearance, at any rate, of popular favour. And loud above the interested applause of those who had personal or business motives for acclaiming a success swelled the exaggerated enthusiasm of the fairly numerous art-satellites who are unstinted in their praise of anything that they are certain they cannot understand. Whatever might be the subsequent verdict of the theatre-filling public the majority of the favoured first-night audience was determined to set the seal of its approval on the suggestion dances, and a steady roll of applause greeted the conclusion of each item. The dancer gravely bowed her thanks; in marked contradistinction to the gentleman who had "presented" the performing wolves she did not permit herself the luxury of a smile.

"It teaches us a great deal," said Rhapsodie Pantril vaguely, but impressively, after the Fern dance had been given and applauded.

"At any rate we know now that a fern takes life very seriously," broke in Joan Mardle, who had somehow wriggled herself into Cicely's box.

As Yeovil, from the back of his gallery, watched Gorla running and ricochetting about the stage, looking rather like a wagtail in energetic pursuit of invisible gnats and midges, he wondered how many of the middle-aged women who were eagerly applauding her would have taken the least notice of similar gymnastics on the part of their offspring in nursery or garden, beyond perhaps asking them not to make so much noise. And a bitterer tinge came to his thoughts as he saw the bouquets being handed up, thoughts of the brave old dowager down at Torywood, the woman who had worked and wrought so hard and so unsparingly in her day for the well-being of the State—the State that had fallen helpless into alien hands before her tired eyes. Her eldest son lived invalid-wise in the South of France, her second son lay fathoms deep in the North Sea, with the hulk of a broken battleship for a burial-vault; and now the granddaughter was standing here in the limelight, bowing her thanks for the patronage and favour meted out to her by this cosmopolitan company, with its lavish sprinkling of the uniforms of an alien army.

Prominent among the flowers at her feet was one large golden-petalled bouquet of gorgeous blooms, tied with a broad streamer of golden riband, the tribute rendered by Cæsar to the things that were Cæsar's. The new chapter of the *fait accompli* had been written that night and written well. The audience poured slowly out with the triumphant music of Jancovius's *Kaiser Wilhelm* march, played by the orchestra as a happy inspiration, pealing in its ears.

"It has been a great evening, a most successful evening," said Lady Shalem to Herr von Kwarl, whom she was conveying in her electric brougham to Cicely Yeovil's supper party; "an important evening," she added, choosing her adjectives with deliberation. "It should give pleasure in high quarters, should it not?"

And she turned her observant eyes on the impassive face of her companion.

"Gracious lady," he replied with deliberation and meaning, "it has given pleasure. It is an evening to be remembered."

The gracious lady suppressed a sigh of satisfaction. Memory in high places was a thing fruitful and precious beyond computation.

Cicely's party at the Porphyry Restaurant had grown to imposing dimensions. Every one whom she had asked had come, and so had Joan Mardle. Lady Shalem had suggested several names at the last moment, and there was quite a strong infusion of the Teutonic military and official world. It was just as well, Cicely reflected, that the supper was being given at a restaurant and not in Berkshire Street.

"Quite like ole times," purred the beaming proprietor in Cicely's ear, as the staircase and cloakrooms filled up with a jostling, laughing throng.

The guests settled themselves at four tables, taking their places where chance or fancy led them, late comers having to fit in wherever they could find room. A babel of tongues in various languages reigned round the tables, amid which the rattle of knives and forks and plates and the popping of corks made a subdued hubbub. Gorla Mustelford, the motive for all this sound and movement, this chatter of guests and scurrying of waiters, sat motionless in the fatigued self-conscious silence of a great artist who has delivered a great message.

"Do sit at Lady Peach's table, like a dear boy," Cicely begged of Tony Luton, who had come in late; "she and Gerald Drowly have got together, in spite of all my efforts, and they are both so dull. Try and liven things up a bit."

A loud barking sound, as of fur-seals calling across Arctic ice, came from another table, where Mrs. Mentieth-Mendlesohnn (one of the Mendlesohnns of Invergordon, as she was wont to describe herself) was proclaiming the glories and subtleties of Gorla's achievement.

"It was a revelation," she shouted; "I sat there and saw a whole new scheme of thought unfold itself before my eyes. One could not define it, it was thought translated into action—the best art cannot be defined. One just sat there and knew that one was seeing something one had never seen before, and yet one felt that one had seen it in one's brain, all one's life. That was what was so wonderful—yes, please," she broke off sharply as a fat quail in aspic was presented to her by a questioning waiter.

The voice of Mr. Mauleverer Morle came across the table, like another seal barking at a greater distance.

"Rostand," he observed with studied emphasis, "has been called *le Prince de l'Adjectif Inopiné*; Miss Mustelford deserves to be described as the Queen of Unexpected Movement."

"Oh, I say, do you hear that?" exclaimed Mrs. Mentieth-Mendlesohnn to as wide an audience as she could achieve; "Rostand has been called—tell them what you said, Mr. Morle," she broke off, suddenly mistrusting her ability to handle a French sentence at the top of her voice.

Mr. Morle repeated his remark.

"Pass it on to the next table," commanded Mrs. Mentieth-Mendlesohnn. "It's too good to be lost."

At the next table, however, a grave impressive voice was dwelling at length on a topic remote from the event of the evening. Lady Peach considered that all social gatherings, of whatever nature, were intended for the recital of minor domestic tragedies. She lost no time in regaling the company around her with the detailed history of an interrupted week-end in a Norfolk cottage.

"The most charming and delightful old-world spot that you could imagine, clean and quite comfortable, just a nice distance from the sea and within an easy walk of the Broads. The very place for the children. We'd brought everything for a four days' stay and meant to have a really delightful time. And then on Sunday morning we found that some one had left the springhead, where our only supply of drinking water came from, uncovered, and a dead bird was floating in it; it had fallen in somehow and got drowned. Of course we couldn't use the water that a dead body had been floating in, and there was no other supply for miles round, so we had to come away then and there. Now what do you say to that?"

" 'Ah, that a linnet should die in the Spring,' " quoted Tony Luton with intense feeling.

There was an immediate outburst of hilarity where Lady Peach had confidently looked for expressions of concern and sympathy.

"Isn't Tony just perfectly cute? Isn't he?" exclaimed a young American woman, with an enthusiasm to which Lady Peach entirely failed to respond. She had intended following up her story with the account of another tragedy of a similar nature that had befallen her three years ago in Argyllshire, and now the opportunity had gone. She turned morosely to the consolations of a tongue salad.

At the centre table the excellent von Tolb led a chorus of congratulation and compliment, to which Gorla listened with an air of polite detachment, much as the Sheikh Ul Islam might receive the homage of a Wesleyan Conference. To a close observer it would have seemed probable that her attitude of fatigued indifference to the flattering remarks that were showered on her had been as carefully studied and rehearsed as any of her postures on the stage.

"It is something that one will appreciate more and more fully every time one sees it. . . . One cannot see it too often. . . . I could have sat and watched it for hours. . . . Do you know, I am just looking forward to tomorrow evening, when

I can see it again. . . . I knew it was going to be good, but I had no idea—" so chimed the chorus, between mouthfuls of quail and bites of asparagus.

"Weren't the performing wolves wonderful?" exclaimed Joan in her fresh joyous voice, that rang round the room like laughter of the woodpecker.

If there is one thing that disturbs the complacency of a great artist of the Halls it is the consciousness of sharing his or her triumphs with performing birds and animals, but of course Joan was not to be expected to know that. She pursued her subject with the assurance of one who has hit on a particularly acceptable topic.

"It must have taken them years of training and concentration to master those tricycles," she continued in high-pitched soliloquy. "The nice thing about them is that they don't realize a bit how clever and educational they are. It would be dreadful to have them putting on airs, wouldn't it? And yet I suppose the knowledge of being able to jump through a hoop better than any other wolf would justify a certain amount of 'side.' "

Fortunately at this moment a young Italian journalist at another table rose from his seat and delivered a two-minute oration in praise of the heroine of the evening. He spoke in rapid nervous French, with a North Italian accent, but much of what he said could be understood by the majority of those present, and the applause was unanimous. At any rate he had been brief and it was permissible to suppose that he had been witty.

It was the opening for which Mr. Gerald Drowly had been watching and waiting. The moment that the Italian enthusiast had dropped back into his seat amid a rattle of hand-clapping and rapping of forks and knives on the tables, Drowly sprang to his feet, pushed his chair well away, as for a long separation, and begged to endorse what had been so very aptly and gracefully, and, might he add, truly said by the previous speaker. This was only the prelude to the real burden of his message; with the dexterity that comes of practice he managed, in a couple of hurried sentences, to divert the course of his remarks to his own personality and career, and to inform his listeners that he was an actor of some note and experience, and had had the honour of acting under——and here followed a string of names of eminent actor managers of the day. He thought he might be pardoned for mentioning the fact that his performance of "Peterkin" in the "Broken Nutshell," had won the unstinted approval of the dramatic critics of the Provincial Press. Towards the end of what was a long speech, and which seemed even longer to its hearers, he reverted to the subject of Gorla's dancing and bestowed on it such laudatory remarks as he had left over. Drawing his chair once again into his immediate neighbourhood he sat down, aglow with the satisfied consciousness of a good work worthily performed.

"I once acted a small part in some theatricals got up for a charity," announced Joan in a ringing, confidential voice; "the *Clapham Courier* said that all the minor parts were very creditably sustained. Those were its very words. I felt I must tell you that, and also say how much I enjoyed Miss Mustelford's dancing."

Tony Luton cheered wildly.

"That's the cleverest speech so far," he proclaimed. He had been asked to liven things up at his table and was doing his best to achieve that result, but Mr. Gerald Drowly joined Lady Peach in the unfavourable opinion she had formed of that irrepressible youth.

Ronnie, on whom Cicely kept a solicitous eye, showed no sign of any intention of falling in love with Gorla. He was more profitably engaged in paying court to the Gräfin von Tolb, whose hospitable mansion in Belgrave Square invested her with a special interest in his eyes. As a professional Prince Charming he had every inducement to encourage the cult of Fairy Godmother.

"Yes, yes, agreed, I will come and hear you play, that is a promise," said the Gräfin, "and you must come and dine with me one night and play to me afterwards, that is a promise, also, yes? That is very nice of you, to come and see a tiresome old woman. I am passionately fond of music; if I were honest I would tell you also that I am very fond of good-looking boys, but this is not the age of honesty, so I must leave you to guess that. Come on Thursday in next week, you can? That is nice. I have a reigning Prince dining with me that night. Poor man, he wants cheering up; the art of being a reigning Prince is not a very pleasing one nowadays. He has made it a boast all his life that he is Liberal and his subjects Conservative; now that is all changed—no, not all; he is still Liberal, but his subjects unfortunately are become Socialists. You must play your best for him."

"Are there many Socialists over there, in Germany I mean?" asked Ronnie, who was rather out of his depth where politics were concerned.

"*Ueberall*," said the Gräfin with emphasis; "everywhere, I don't know what it comes from; better education and worse digestions I suppose. I am sure digestion has a good deal to do with it. In my husband's family for example, his generation had excellent digestions, and there wasn't a case of Socialism or suicide among them; the younger generation have no digestions worth speaking of, and there have been two suicides and three Socialists within the last six years. And now I must really be going. I am not a Berliner and late hours don't suit my way of life."

Ronnie bent low over the Gräfin's hand and kissed it, partly because she was the kind of woman who naturally invoked such homage, but chiefly because he knew that the gesture showed off his smooth burnished head to advantage.

The observant eyes of Lady Shalem had noted the animated conversation between the Gräfin and Ronnie, and she had overheard fragments of the invitation that had been accorded to the latter.

"Take us the little foxes, the little foxes that spoil the vines," she quoted to herself; "not that that music-boy would do much in the destructive line, but the principle is good."

CHAPTER X

SOME REFLECTIONS AND A
"TE DEUM"

CICELY awoke, on the morning after the "memorable evening," with the satisfactory feeling of victory achieved, tempered by a troubled sense of having achieved it in the face of a reasonably grounded opposition. She had burned her boats, and was glad of it, but the reek of their burning drifted rather unpleasantly across the jubilant incense-swinging of her *Te Deum* service.

Last night had marked an immense step forward in her social career; without running after the patronage of influential personages she had seen it quietly and tactfully put at her service. People such as the Gräfin von Tolb were going to be a power in the London world for a very long time to come. Herr von Kwarl, with all his useful qualities of brain and temperament, might conceivably fall out of favour in some unexpected turn of the political wheel, and the Shalems would probably have their little day and then a long afternoon of diminishing social importance; the placid dormouse-like Gräfin would outlast them all. She had the qualities which make either for contented mediocrity or else for very durable success, according as circumstances may dictate. She was one of those characters that can neither thrust themselves to the front, nor have any wish to do so, but being there, no ordinary power can thrust them away.

With the Gräfin as her friend Cicely found herself in altogether a different position from that involved by the mere interested patronage of Lady Shalem. A vista of social success was opened up to her, and she did not mean it to be just the ordinary success of a popular and influential hostess moving in an important circle. That people with naturally bad manners should have to be polite and considerate in their dealings with her, that people who usually held themselves aloof should have to be gracious and amiable, that the self-assured should have to be just a little humble and anxious where she was concerned, these things of course she intended to happen; she was a woman. But, she told herself, she intended a great deal more than that when she traced the pattern for her scheme of social influence. In her heart she detested the German occupation as a hateful necessity, but while her heart registered the hatefulness the brain recognized the necessity. The great fighting-machines that the Germans had built up and maintained, on land, on sea, and in air, were three solid crushing facts that demonstrated the hopelessness of any immediate thought of revolt. Twenty years hence, when the present generation was older and greyer, the chances of armed revolt would probably be equally hopeless, equally remote-seeming. But in the meantime something could have been effected in another way. The conquerors might partially Germanize London, but, on the other hand, if the thing were skilfully managed, the British element within the Empire might impress the mark of its influence on everything German. The fighting men might remain Prussian or Bavarian, but the thinking men, and eventually the ruling men, could gradually come under British influence, or even be of British blood. An English Liberal-Conservative "Centre" might stand as a bulwark against the Junkerdom and Socialism of Continental Germany. So Cicely reasoned with herself, in a fashion induced perhaps by an earlier apprenticeship to the reading of *Ninteenth Century* articles, in which the possible political and racial developments of various countries were examined and discussed and put away in the pigeon-holes of probable happenings. She had sufficient knowledge of political history to know that such a development might possibly come to pass, she had not sufficient insight into actual conditions to know that the possibility was as remote as that of armed resistance. And the rôle which she saw herself playing was that of a deft and courtly political intriguer, rallying the British element and making herself agreeable to the German element, a political inspiration to the one and a social distraction to the other. At the back of her mind there lurked an honest confession that she was probably overrating her powers of statecraft and personality, that she was more likely to be carried along by the current of events than to control or divert its direction; the political day-dream remained, however, as day-dreams will, in spite of the clear light of probability shining through them. At any rate she knew, as usual, what she wanted to do, and as usual she had taken steps to carry out her intentions. Last night remained in her mind a night of important victory. There also remained the anxious proceeding of finding out if the victory had entailed any serious losses.

Cicely was not one of those ill-regulated people who treat the first meal of the day as a convenient occasion for serving up any differences or contentions that have been left over from the day before or overlooked in the press of other matters. She enjoyed her breakfast and gave Yeovil unhindered opportunity for enjoying his; a discussion as to the right cooking of a dish that he had first tasted among the Orenburg Tartars was the prevailing topic on this particular morning, and blended well with trout and toast and coffee. In the cozy nook of the smoking-room, in participation of the after-breakfast cigarettes, Cicely made her dash into debatable ground.

"You haven't asked me how my supper-party went off," she said.

"There is a notice of it in two of the morning papers, with a list of those present," said Yeovil; "the conquering race seems to have been very well represented."

"Several races were represented," said Cicely; "a function of that sort, celebrating a dramatic first-night, was bound to be cosmopolitan. In fact, blending of races and nationalities is the tendency of the age we live in."

"The blending of races seems to have been consummated already in one of the individuals at your party," said Yeovil drily; "the name Mentieth-Mendlesohnn struck me as a particularly happy obliteration of racial landmarks."

Cicely laughed.

"A noisy and very wearisome sort of woman," she commented; "she reminds one of garlic that's been planted by mistake in a conservatory. Still, she's useful as an advertising agent to any one who rubs her the right way. She'll be invaluable in proclaiming the merits of Gorla's performance to all and sundry; that's why I invited her. She'll probably lunch today at the Hotel Cecil, and every one sitting within a hundred yards of her table will hear what an emotional education they can get by going to see Gorla dance at the Caravansery."

"She seems to be like the Salvation Army," said Yeovil; "her noise reaches a class of people who wouldn't trouble to read Press notices."

"Exactly," said Cicely. "Gorla gets quite good notices on the whole, doesn't she?"

"The one that took my fancy most was the one in the *Standard*," said Yeovil, picking up that paper from a table by his side and searching its columns for the notice in question. " 'The wolves which appeared earlier in the evening's entertainment are, the programme assures us, trained entirely by kindness. It would have been a further kindness, at any rate to the audience, if some of the training, which the wolves doubtless do not appreciate at its proper value, had been expended on Miss Mustelford's efforts at stage dancing. We are assured, again on the authority of the programme, that the much-talked-of Suggestion Dances are the last word in Posture dancing. The last word belongs by immemorial right to the sex which Miss Mustelford adorns, and it would be ungallant to seek to deprive her of her privilege. As far as the educational aspect of her performance is concerned we must admit that the life of the fern remains to us a private life still. Miss Mustelford has abandoned her own private life in an unavailing attempt to draw the fern into the gaze of publicity. And so it was with her other suggestions. They suggested many things, but nothing that was announced on the programme. Chiefly they suggested one outstanding reflection, that stage-dancing is not like those advertised breakfast foods that can be served up after three minutes' preparation. Half a lifetime, or rather half a youth-time is a much more satisfactory allowance.' "

"The *Standard* is prejudiced," said Cicely; "some of the other papers are quite enthusiastic. The *Dawn* gives her a column and a quarter of notice, nearly all of it complimentary. It says the report of her fame as a dancer went before her,

but that her performance last night caught it up and out-
stripped it."

"I should not like to suggest that the *Dawn* is prejudiced,"
said Yeovil, "but Shalem is a managing director on it, and one
of its biggest shareholders. Gorla's dancing is an event of the
social season, and Shalem is one of those most interested in
keeping up the appearance, at any rate, of a London social
season. Besides, her début gave the opportunity for an Imperial
visit to the theatre—the first appearance at a festive public
function of the Conqueror among the conquered. Apparently
the experiment passed off well; Shalem has every reason to feel
pleased with himself and well-disposed towards Gorla. By the
way," added Yeovil, "talking of Gorla, I'm going down to
Torywood one day next week."

"To Torywood?" exclaimed Cicely. The tone of her exclamation gave the impression that the announcement was not
very acceptable to her.

"I promised the old lady that I would go and have a talk
with her when I came back from my Siberian trip; she travelled
in Eastern Russia, you know, long before the Trans-Siberian
railway was built, and she's enormously interested in those
parts. In any case I should like to see her again."

"She does not see many people nowadays," said Cicely; "I
fancy she is breaking up rather. She was very fond of the son
who went down, you know."

"She has seen a great many of the things she cared for go
down," said Yeovil; "it is a sad old life that is left to her,
when one thinks of all that the past has been to her, of the part
she used to play in the world, the work she used to get through.
It used to seem as though she could never grow old, as if she
would die standing up, with some unfinished command on her
lips. And now I suppose her tragedy is that she has grown old,
bitterly old, and cannot die."

Cicely was silent for a moment, and seemed about to leave
the room. Then she turned back and said:

"I don't think I would say anything about Gorla to her if
I were you."

"It would not have occurred to me to drag her name into

our conversation," said Yeovil coldly, "but in any case the accounts of her dancing performance will have reached Torywood through the newspapers—also the record of your racially-blended supper-party."

Cicely said nothing. She knew that by last night's affair she had definitely identified herself in public opinion with the Shalem clique, and that many of her old friends would look on her with distrust and suspicion on that account. It was unfortunate, but she reckoned it a lesser evil than tearing herself away from her London life, its successes and pleasures and possibilities. These social dislocations and severing of friendships were to be looked for after any great and violent change in State affairs. It was Yeovil's attitude that really troubled her; she would not give way to his prejudices and accept his point of view, but she knew that a victory that involved estrangement from him would only bring a mockery of happiness. She still hoped that he would come round to an acceptance of established facts and deaden his political *malaise* in the absorbing distraction of field sports. The visit to Torywood was a misfortune; it might just turn the balance in the undesired direction. Only a few weeks of late summer and early autumn remained before the hunting season, and its preparations would be at hand, and Yeovil might be caught in the meshes of an old enthusiasm; in those few weeks, however, he might be fired by another sort of enthusiasm, an enthusiasm which would sooner or later mean voluntary or enforced exile for his part, and the probable breaking up of her own social plans and ambitions.

But Cicely knew something of the futility of improvising objections where no real obstacle exists. The visit to Torywood was a graceful attention on Yeovil's part to an old friend; there was no decent ground on which it could be opposed. If the influence of that visit came athwart Yeovil's life and hers with disastrous effect, that was "Kismet."

And once again the reek from her burned and smouldering boats mingled threateningly with the incense fumes of her *Te Deum* for victory. She left the room, and Yeovil turned once more to an item of news in the morning's papers that had already arrested his attention. The Imperial *Aufklärung* on the subject of military service was to be made public in the course of the day.

CHAPTER XI

THE TEA SHOP

YEOVIL wandered down Piccadilly that afternoon in a spirit of restlessness and expectancy. The long-awaited *Aufklärung* dealing with the new law of military service had not yet appeared; at any moment he might meet the hoarse-throated newsboys running along with their papers, announcing the special edition which would give the terms of the edict to the public. Every sound or movement that detached itself with isolated significance from the general whir and scurry of the streets seemed to Yeovil to herald the oncoming clamour and rush that he was looking for. But the long endless succession of motors and buses and vans went by, hooting and grunting, and such newsboys as were to be seen hung about listlessly, bearing no more attractive bait on their posters than the announcement of an "earthquake shock in Hungary; feared loss of life."

The Green Park end of Piccadilly was a changed, and in some respects a livelier thoroughfare to that which Yeovil remembered with affectionate regret. A great political club had migrated from its palatial home to a shrunken habitation in a less prosperous quarter; its place was filled by the flamboyant frontage of the Hotel Konstantinopel. Gorgeous Turkey carpets were spread over the wide entrance steps, and boys in Circassian and Anatolian costumes hung around the doors, or dashed forth in un-Oriental haste to carry such messages as the telephone was unable to transmit. Picturesque sellers of Turkish delight, attar-of-roses, and brass-work coffee services, squatted under the portico, on terms of obvious good understanding with the hotel management. A few doors farther down a service club that had long been a Piccadilly landmark was a landmark still, as the home of the Army Aeronaut Club, and there was a constant coming and going of gay-hued uniforms, Saxon, Prussian, Bavarian, Hessian, and so forth, through its portals. The mastering of the air and the creation of a scientific aerial war fleet, second to none in the world, was an achievement of which the conquering race was pardonably proud, and for which it had good reason to be duly thankful. Over the gateways was blazoned the badge of the club, an elephant, whale, and eagle, typifying the three armed forces of the State, by land and sea and air; the eagle bore in its beak a scroll with the proud legend: "The last am I, but not the least."

To the eastward of this gaily-humming hive the long-shuttered front of a deserted ducal mansion struck a note of protest and mourning amid the noise and whirl and colour of a seemingly uncaring city. On the other side of the roadway, on the gravelled paths of the Green Park, small ragged children from the back streets of Westminster looked wistfully at the smooth trim stretches of grass on which it was now forbidden, in two languages, to set foot. Only the pigeons, disregarding the changes of political geography, walked about as usual, wondering perhaps, if they ever wondered at anything, at the sudden change in the distribution of park humans.

Yeovil turned his steps out of the hot sunlight into the shade of the Burlington Arcade, familiarly known to many of its newer frequenters as the Passage. Here the change that new conditions and requirements had wrought was more immediately noticeable than anywhere else in the West End. Most of the shops on the western side had been cleared away, and in their place had been installed an "open-air" café, converting the long alley into a sort of promenade tea-garden, flanked on one side by a line of haberdashers', perfumers', and jewellers' show windows. The patrons of the café could sit at the little round tables, drinking their coffee and syrups and *apéritifs*, and gazing, if they were so minded, at the pyjamas and cravats and Brazilian diamonds spread out for inspection before them. A string orchestra, hidden away somewhere in the gallery, was alternating grand opera with the *Gondola Girl* and the latest gems of Transatlantic melody. From around the tightly-packed tables arose a babble of tongues, made up chiefly of German, a South American rendering of Spanish, and a North American rendering of English, with here and there the sharp shaken-out staccato of Japanese. A sleepy-looking boy, in a nondescript uniform, was wandering to and fro among the customers, offering for sale the *Matin*, *New York Herald*, *Berliner Tageblatt*, and a host of crudely coloured illustrated papers, embodying the hard-worked wit of a world-legion of comic artists. Yeovil hurried through the Arcade; it was not here, in this atmosphere of staring alien eyes and jangling tongues, that he wanted to read the news of the Imperial *Aufklärung*.

By a succession of by-ways he reached Hanover Square, and thence made his way into Oxford Street. There was no commotion of activity to be noticed yet among the newsboys; the posters still concerned themselves with the earthquake in Hungary, varied with references to the health of the King of Roumania, and a motor accident in South London. Yeovil wandered aimlessly along the street for a few dozen yards, and then turned down into the smoking-room of a cheap tea-shop, where he judged that the flourishing foreign element would be less conspicuously represented. Quiet-voiced, smooth-headed youths, from neighbouring shops and wholesale houses, sat drinking tea and munching pastry, some of them reading, others making a fitful rattle with dominoes on the marble-topped tables. A clean, wholesome smell of tea and coffee made itself felt through the clouds of cigarette smoke; cleanliness and listlessness seemed to be the dominant notes of the place, a cleanliness that was commendable, and a listlessness that seemed unnatural and undesirable where so much youth was gathered together for refreshment and recreation. Yeovil seated himself at a table already occupied by a young clergyman who was smoking a cigarette over the remains of a plateful of buttered toast. He had a keen, clever, hard-lined face, the face of a man who, in an earlier stage of European history, might have been a warlike prior, awkward to tackle at the council-board, greatly to be avoided where blows were being exchanged. A pale, silent damsel drifted up to Yeovil and took his order with an air of being mentally some hundreds of miles away, and utterly indifferent to the requirements of those whom she served; if she had brought calf's-foot jelly instead of the pot of China tea he had asked for, Yeovil would hardly have been surprised. However, the tea duly arrived on the table, and the pale damsel scribbled a figure on a slip of paper, put it silently by the side of the teapot, and drifted silently away. Yeovil had seen the same sort of thing done on the musical-comedy stage, and done rather differently.

"Can you tell me, sir, is the Imperial announcement out yet?" asked the young clergyman, after a brief scrutiny of his neighbour.

"No, I have been waiting about for the last half-hour on the look-out for it," said Yeovil; "the special editions ought to be out by now." Then he added: "I have only just lately come from abroad. I know scarcely anything of London as it is now. You may imagine that a good deal of it is very strange to me. Your profession must take you a good deal among all classes of people. I have seen something of what one may call the upper, or, at any rate, the richer classes, since I came back; do tell me something about the poorer classes of the community. How do they take the new order of things?"

"Badly," said the young cleric, "badly, in more senses than one. They are helpless and they are bitter—bitter in the useless kind of way that produces no great resolutions. They look round for some one to blame for what has happened; they blame the politicians, they blame the leisured classes; in an indirect way I believe they blame the Church. Certainly, the national disaster has not drawn them towards religion in any form. One thing you may be sure of, they do not blame themselves. No true Londoner ever admits that fault lies at his door. 'No, I never!' is an exclamation that is on his lips from earliest childhood, whenever he is charged with anything blameworthy or punishable. That is why school discipline was ever a thing repugnant to the schoolboard child and its parents; no schoolboard scholar ever deserved punishment. However obvious the fault might seem to a disciplinarian, 'No, I never' exonerated it as something that had not happened. Public schoolboys and private schoolboys of the upper and middle class had their fling and took their thrashings, when they were found out, as a piece of bad luck, but 'our Bert' and 'our Sid' were of those for whom there is no condemnation; if *they* were punished it was for faults that 'no, they never' committed. Naturally the grown-up generation of Berts and Sids, the voters and householders, do not realize, still less admit, that it was they who called the tune to which the politicians danced. They had to choose between the vote-mongers and the so-called 'scare-mongers,' and their verdict was for the vote-mongers all the time. And now they are bitter; they are being punished, and punishment is not a thing that they have been schooled to bear. The taxes that are falling on them are a grievous source of discontent, and the military service that will be imposed on them, for the first time in their lives, will be another. There is a more lovable side to their character under misfortune, though," added the young clergyman. "Deep down in their hearts there was a very real affection for the old dynasty. Future historians will perhaps be able to explain how and why the Royal Family of Great Britain captured the imaginations of its subjects in so genuine and lasting a fashion. Among the poorest and the most matter-of-fact, for whom the name of no public man, politician or philanthropist, stands out with any especial significance, the old Queen, and the dead King, the dethroned monarch and the young prince live in a sort of domestic Pantheon, a recollection that is a proud and wistful personal possession when so little remains to be proud of or to possess. There is no favour that I am so often asked for among my poor parishioners as the gift of the picture of this or that member of the old dynasty. 'I have got all of them, only except Princess Mary,' an old woman said to me last week, and she nearly cried with pleasure when I brought her an old *Bystander* portrait that filled the gap in her collection. And on Queen Alexandra's day they bring out and wear the faded wild-rose favours that they bought with their pennies in days gone by."

"The tragedy of the enactment that is about to enforce military service on these people is that it comes when they've no longer a country to fight for," said Yeovil.

The young clergyman gave an exclamation of bitter impatience.

"That is the cruel mockery of the whole thing. Every now and then in the course of my work I have come across lads who were really drifting to the bad through the good qualities in them. A clean combative strain in their blood, and a natural turn for adventure, made the ordinary anæmic routine of shop or warehouse or factory almost unbearable for them. What splendid little soldiers they would have made, and how grandly the discipline of a military training would have steadied them in after-life when steadiness was wanted. The only adventure that their surroundings offered them has been the adventure of practising mildly criminal misdeeds without getting landed in reformatories and prisons; those of them that have not been successful in keeping clear of detection are walking round and round prison yards, experiencing the operation of a discipline that breaks and does not build. They were merry-hearted boys once, with nothing of the criminal or ne'er-do-well in their natures, and now—have you ever seen a prison yard, with that walk round and round and round between grey walls under a blue sky?"

Yeovil nodded.

"It's good enough for criminals and imbeciles," said the parson, "but think of it for those boys, who might have been marching along to the tap of the drum, with a laugh on their lips instead of Hell in their hearts. I have had Hell in my heart sometimes, when I have come in touch with cases like those. I suppose you are thinking that I am a strange sort of parson."

"I was just defining you in my mind," said Yeovil, "as a man of God, with an infinite tenderness for little devils."

The clergyman flushed.

"Rather a fine epitaph to have on one's tombstone," he said, "especially if the tombstone were in some crowded city graveyard. I suppose I am a man of God, but I don't think I could be called a man of peace."

Looking at the strong young face, with its suggestion of a fighting prior of bygone days more marked than ever, Yeovil mentally agreed that he could not.

"I have learned one thing in life," continued the young man, "and that is that peace is not for this world. Peace is what God gives us when He takes us into His rest. Beat your sword into a ploughshare if you like, but beat your enemy into smithereens first."

A long-drawn cry, repeated again and again, detached itself from the throb and hoot and whir of the street traffic.

"Speshul! Military service, spesh-ul!"

The young clergyman sprang from his seat and went up the staircase in a succession of bounds, causing the domino players and novelette readers to look up for a moment in mild astonishment. In a few seconds he was back again, with a copy of an afternoon paper. The Imperial Rescript was set forth in heavy type, in parallel columns of English and German. As the young man read a deep burning flush spread over his face, then ebbed away into a chalky whiteness. He read the announcement to the end, then handed the paper to Yeovil, and left without a word.

Beneath the courtly politeness and benignant phraseology of the document ran a trenchant searing irony. The British-born subjects of the Germanic Crown, inhabiting the islands of Great Britain and Ireland, had habituated themselves as a people to the disuse of arms, and resolutely excluded military service and national training from their political system and daily life. Their judgment that they were unsuited as a race to bear arms and conform to military discipline was not to be set aside. Their new Overlord did not propose to do violence to their feelings and customs by requiring from them the personal military sacrifices and services which were rendered by his subjects German-born. The British subjects of the Crown were to remain a people consecrated to peaceful pursuits, to commerce and trade and husbandry. The defence of their coasts and shipping and the maintenance of order and general safety would be guaranteed by a garrison of German troops, with the co-operation of the Imperial war fleet. German-born subjects residing temporarily or permanently in the British Isles would come under the same laws respecting compulsory military service as their fellow-subjects of German blood in the other parts of the Empire, and special enactments would be drawn up to ensure that their interests did not suffer from a periodical withdrawal on training or other military calls. Necessarily a heavily differentiated scale of war taxation would fall on British taxpayers, to provide for the upkeep of the garrison and to equalize the services and sacrifices rendered by the two branches of His Majesty's subjects. As military service was not henceforth open to any subject of British birth no further necessity for any training or exercise of a military nature existed, therefore all rifle clubs, drill associations, cadet corps and similar bodies were henceforth declared to be illegal. No weapons other than guns for specified sporting purposes, duly declared and registered and open to inspection when required, could be owned, purchased, or carried. The science of arms was to be eliminated altogether from the life of a people who had shown such marked repugnance to its study and practice.

The cold irony of the measure struck home with the greater force because its nature was so utterly unexpected. Public anticipation had guessed at various forms of military service, aggressively irksome or tactfully lightened as the case might be, in any event certain to be bitterly unpopular, and now there had come this contemptuous boon, which had removed, at one stroke, the bogey of compulsory military service from the troubled imaginings of the British people, and fastened on them the cruel distinction of being in actual fact what an enemy had called them in splenetic scorn long years ago—a nation of shopkeepers. Aye, something even below that level, a race of shopkeepers who were no longer a nation.

Yeovil crumpled the paper in his hand and went out into the sunlit street. A sudden roll of drums and crash of brass music filled the air. A company of Bavarian infantry went by, in all the pomp and circumstance of martial array and the joyous swing of rapid rhythmic movement. The street echoed and throbbed in the Englishman's ears with the exultant pulse of youth and mastery set to loud Pagan music. A group of lads from the tea-shop clustered on the pavement and watched the troops go by, staring at a phase of life in which they had no share. The martial trappings, the swaggering joy of life, the comradeship of camp and barracks, the hard discipline of drill yard and fatigue duty, the long sentry watches, the trench digging, forced marches, wounds, cold, hunger, makeshift hospitals, and the blood-wet laurels—these were not for them. Such things they might only guess at, or see on a cinema film, darkly; they belonged to the civilian nation.

The function of afternoon tea was still being languidly observed in the big drawing-room when Yeovil returned to Berkshire Street. Cicely was playing the part of hostess to a man of perhaps forty-one years of age, who looked slightly older from his palpable attempts to look very much younger. Percival Plarsey was a plump, pale-faced, short-legged individual, with puffy cheeks, over-prominent nose, and thin colourless hair. His mother, with nothing more than maternal prejudice to excuse her, had discovered some twenty odd years ago that he was a well-favoured young man, and had easily imbued her son with the same opinion. The slipping away of years and the natural transition of the unathletic boy into the podgy unhealthy-looking man did little to weaken the tradition; Plarsey had never been able to relinquish the idea that a youthful charm and comeliness still centred in his person, and laboured daily at his toilet with the devotion that a hopelessly lost cause is so often able to inspire. He babbled incessantly about himself and the accessory futilities of his life in short, neat, complacent sentences, and in a voice that Ronald Storre said reminded one of a fat bishop blessing a butter-making competition. While he babbled he kept his eyes fastened on his listeners to observe the impression which his important little announcements and pronouncements were making. On the present occasion he was pattering forth a detailed description of the upholstery and fittings of his new music-room.

"All the hangings, *violette de Parme*, all the furniture, rosewood. The only ornament in the room is a *replica* of the Mozart statue in Vienna. Nothing but Mozart is to be played in the room. Absolutely, nothing but Mozart."

"You will get rather tired of that, won't you?" said Cicely, feeling that she was expected to comment on this tremendous announcement.

"One gets tired of everything," said Plarsey, with a fat little sigh of resignation. "I can't tell you *how* tired I am of Rubenstein, and one day I suppose I shall be tired of Mozart, and *violette de Parme* and rosewood. I never thought it possible that I could ever tire of jonquils, and now I simply won't have one in the house. Oh, the scene the other day because some one brought some jonquils into the house! I'm afraid I was dreadfully rude, but I really couldn't help it."

He could talk like this through a long summer day or a long winter evening.

Yeovil belonged to a race forbidden to bear arms. At the moment he would gladly have contented himself with the weapons with which nature had endowed him, if he might have kicked and pommelled the abhorrent specimen of male humanity whom he saw before him.

Instead he broke into the conversation with an inspired flash of malicious untruthfulness.

"It is wonderful," he observed carelessly, "how popular that Viennese statue of Mozart has become. A friend who inspects County Council Art Schools tells me you find a copy of it in every class-room you go into."

It was a poor substitute for physical violence, but it was all that civilization allowed him in the way of relieving his feelings; it had, moreover, the effect of making Plarsey profoundly miserable.

CHAPTER XII

THE TRAVELLING COMPANIONS

THE train bearing Yeovil on his visit to Torywood slid and rattled westward through the hazy dreamland of an English summer landscape. Seen from the train windows the stark bare ugliness of the metalled line was forgotten, and the eye rested only on the green solitude that unfolded itself as the miles went slipping by. Tall grasses and meadow-weeds stood in deep shocks, field after field, between the leafy boundaries of hedge or coppice, thrusting themselves higher and higher till they touched the low sweeping branches of the trees that here and there overshadowed them. Broad streams, bordered with a heavy fringe of reed and sedge, went winding away into a green distance where woodland and meadowland seemed indefinitely prolonged; narrow streamlets, lost to view in the growth that they fostered, disclosed their presence merely by the water-weed that showed in a riband of rank verdure threading the mellower green of the fields. On the stream banks moorhens walked with jerky confident steps, in the easy boldness of those who had a couple of other elements at their disposal in an emergency; more timorous partridges raced away from the apparition of the train, looking all leg and neck, like little forest elves fleeing from human encounter. And in the distance, over the tree line, a heron or two flapped with slow measured wing-beats and an air of being bent on an immeasurably longer journey than the train that hurtled so frantically along the rails. Now and then the meadowland changed itself suddenly into orchard, with close-growing trees already showing the measure of their coming harvest, and then straw-yard and farm buildings would slide into view; heavy dairy cattle, roan and skewbald and dappled, stood near the gates, drowsily resentful of insect stings, and bunched-up companies of ducks halted in seeming irresolution between the charms of the horse-pond and the alluring neighbourhood of the farm kitchen. Away by the banks of some rushing mill-stream, in a setting of copse and cornfield, a village might be guessed at, just a hint of red roof, grey wreathed chimney and old church tower as seen from the windows of the passing train, and over it all brooded a happy, settled calm, like the dreaming murmur of a trout-stream and the far-away cawing of rooks.

It was a land where it seemed as if it must be always summer and generally afternoon, a land where bees hummed among the wild thyme and in the flower-beds of cottage gardens, where the harvest-mice rustled amid the corn and nettles, and the mill-race flowed cool and silent through water-weeds and dark tunnelled sluices, and made soft droning music with the wooden mill-wheel. And the music carried with it the wording of old undying rhymes, and sang of the jolly, uncaring, uncared-for miller, of the farmer who went riding upon his grey mare, of the mouse who lived beneath the merry mill-pin, of the sweet music on yonder green hill and the dancers all in yellow —the songs and fancies of a lingering olden time, when men took life as children take a long summer day, and went to bed at last with a simple trust in something they could not have explained.

Yeovil watched the passing landscape with the intent hungry eyes of a man who revisits a scene that holds high place in his affections. His imagination raced even quicker than the train, following winding roads and twisting valleys into unseen distances, picturing farms and hamlets, hills and hollows, clattering inn yards and sleepy woodlands.

"A beautiful country," said his only fellow-traveller, who was also gazing at the fleeting landscape; "surely a country worth fighting for."

He spoke in fairly correct English, but he was unmistakably a foreigner; one could have allotted him with some certainty to the Eastern half of Europe.

"A beautiful country, as you say," replied Yeovil; then he added the question, "Are you German?"

"No, Hungarian," said the other; "and you, you are English?" he asked.

"I have been much in England, but I am from Russia," said Yeovil, purposely misleading his companion on the subject of his nationality in order to induce him to talk with greater freedom on a delicate topic. While living among foreigners in a foreign land he had shrunk from hearing his country's disaster discussed, or even alluded to; now he was anxious to learn what unprejudiced foreigners thought of the catastrophe and the causes which had led up to it.

"It is a strange spectacle, a wonder, is it not so?" resumed the other, "a great nation such as this was, one of the greatest nations in modern times, or of any time, carrying its flag and its language into all parts of the world, and now, after one short campaign, it is——"

And he shrugged his shoulders many times and made clucking noises at the roof of his voice, like a hen calling to a brood of roving chickens.

"They grew soft," he resumed; "great world-commerce brings great luxury, and luxury brings softness. They had everything to warn them, things happening in their own time and before their eyes, and they would not be warned. They had seen, in one generation, the rise of the military and naval power of the Japanese, a brown-skinned race living in some island rice-fields in a tropical sea, a people one thought of in connexion with paper fans and flowers and pretty tea-gardens, who suddenly marched and sailed into the world's gaze as a Great Power; they had seen, too, the rise of the Bulgars, a poor herd of *zaptieh*-ridden peasants, with a few students scattered in exile in Bucharest and Odessa, who shot up in one generation to be an armed and aggressive nation with history in its hands. The English saw these things happening around them, and with a war-cloud growing blacker and bigger and always more threatening on their own threshold, they sat down to grow soft and peaceful. They grew soft and accommodating in all things; in religion——"

"In religion?" sad Yeovil.

"In religion, yes," said his companion emphatically; "they had come to look on the Christ as a sort of amiable elder Brother, whose letters from abroad were worth reading. Then, when they had emptied all the divine mystery and wonder out of their faith naturally they grew tired of it, oh, but dreadfully tired of it. I know many English of the country parts, and always they tell me they go to church once in each week to set the good example to the servants. They were tired of their faith, but they were not virile enough to become real Pagans; their dancing fauns were good young men who tripped Morris dances and ate health foods and believed in a sort of Socialism which made for the greatest dulness of the greatest number. You will find plenty of them still if you go into what remains of social London."

Yeovil gave a grunt of acquiescence.

"They grew soft in their political ideas," continued the unsparing critic; "for the old insular belief that all foreigners were devils and rogues they substituted another belief, equally grounded on insular lack of knowledge, that most foreigners were amiable, good fellows, who only needed to be talked to and patted on the back to become your friends and benefactors. They began to believe that a foreign Minister would relinquish long-cherished schemes of national policy and hostile expansion if he came over on a holiday and was asked down to country houses and shown the tennis court and the rock-garden and the younger children. Listen. I once heard it solemnly stated at an after-dinner debate in some literary club that a certain very prominent German statesman had a daughter at school in England, and that future friendly relations between the two countries were improved in prospect, if not assured, by that circumstance. You think I am laughing; I am recording a fact, and the men present were politicians and statesmen as well as literary dilettanti. It was an insular lack of insight that worked the mischief, or some of the mischief. We, in Hungary, we live too much cheek by jowl with our racial neighbours to have many illusions about them. Austrians, Roumanians, Serbs, Italians, Czechs, we know what they think of us, and we know what to think of them, we know what we want in the world, and we know what they want; that knowledge does not send us flying at each other's throats, but it does keep us from growing soft. Ah, the British lion was in a hurry to inaugurate the Millennium and to lie down gracefully with the lamb. He made two mistakes, only two, but they were very bad ones; the Millennium hadn't arrived, and it was not a lamb that he was lying down with."

"You do not like the English, I gather," said Yeovil, as the Hungarian went off into a short burst of satirical laughter.

"I have always liked them," he answered, "but now I am angry with them for being soft. Here is my station," he added, as the train slowed down, and he commenced to gather his belongings together. "I am angry with them," he continued, as a final word on the subject, "because I *hate* the Germans."

He raised his hat punctiliously in a parting salute and stepped out on to the platform. His place was taken by a large, loose-limbed man, with florid face and big staring eyes, and an immense array of fishing-basket, rod, fly-cases, and so forth. He was of the type that one could instinctively locate as a loud-voiced, self-constituted authority on whatever topic might happen to be discussed in the bars of small hotels.

"Are you English?" he asked, after a preliminary stare at Yeovil.

This time Yeovil did not trouble to disguise his nationality; he nodded curtly to his questioner.

"Glad of that," said the fisherman; "I don't like travelling with Germans."

"Unfortunately," said Yeovil, "we have to travel with them, as partners in the same State concern, and not by any means the predominant partner either."

"Oh, that will soon right itself," said the other with loud assertiveness, "that will right itself damn soon."

"Nothing in politics rights itself," said Yeovil; "things have to be righted, which is a different matter."

"What d'y'mean?" said the fisherman, who did not like to have his assertions taken up and shaken into shape.

"We have given a clever and domineering people a chance to plant themselves down as masters in our land; I don't imagine that they are going to give us an easy chance to push them out. To do that we shall have to be a little cleverer than they are, a little harder, a little fiercer, and a good deal more self-sacrificing than we have been in my lifetime or in yours."

"We'll be that, right enough," said the fisherman; "we mean business this time. The last war wasn't a war, it was a snap. We weren't prepared and they were. That won't happen again, bless you. I know what I'm talking about. I go up and down the country, and I hear what people are saying."

Yeovil privately doubted if he ever heard anything but his own opinions.

"It stands to reason," continued the fisherman, "that a highly civilized race like ours, with the record that we've had for leading the whole world, is not going to be held under for long by a lot of damned sausage-eating Germans. Don't you believe it! I know what I'm talking about. I've travelled about the world a bit."

Yeovil shrewdly suspected that the world travels amounted to nothing more than a trip to the United States and perhaps the Channel Islands, with, possibly, a week or fortnight in Paris.

"It isn't the past we've got to think of, it's the future," said Yeovil. "Other maritime Powers had pasts to look back on; Spain and Holland, for instance. The past didn't help them when they let their sea-sovereignty slip from them. That is a matter of history and not very distant history either."

"Ah, that's where you make a mistake," said the other; "our sea-sovereignty hasn't slipped from us, and won't do, neither. There's the British Empire beyond the seas; Canada, Australia, New Zealand, East Africa."

He rolled the names round his tongue with obvious relish.

"If it was a list of first-class battleships, and armoured cruisers and destroyers and airships that you were reeling off, there would be some comfort and hope in the situation," said Yeovil; "the loyalty of the colonies is a splendid thing, but it is only pathetically splendid because it can do so little to recover for us what we've lost. Against the Zeppelin air fleet, and the Dreadnought sea squadrons and the new Gelberhaus cruisers, the last word in maritime mobility, of what avail is loyal devotion plus half-a-dozen warships, one keel to ten, scattered over one or two ocean coasts?"

"Ah, but they'll build," said the fisherman confidently; "they'll build. They're only waiting to enlarge their dockyard accommodation and get the right class of artificers and engineers and workmen together. The money will be forthcoming somehow, and they'll start in and build."

"And do you suppose," asked Yeovil in slow bitter contempt, "that the victorious nation is going to sit and watch and wait till the defeated foe has created a new war fleet, big enough to drive it from the seas? Do you suppose it is going to watch keel added to keel, gun to gun, airship to airship, till its preponderance has been wiped out or even threatened? That sort of thing is done once in a generation, not twice. Who is going to protect Australia or New Zealand while they enlarge their dockyards and hangars and build their dreadnoughts and their airships?"

"Here's my station and I'm not sorry," said the fisherman, gathering his tackle together and rising to depart; "I've listened to you long enough. You and me wouldn't agree, not if we was to talk all day. Fact is, I'm an out-and-out patriot and you're only a half-hearted one. That's what you are, half-hearted."

And with that parting shot he left the carriage and lounged heavily down the platform, a patriot who had never handled a rifle or mounted a horse or pulled an oar, but who had never flinched from demolishing his country's enemies with his tongue.

"England has never had any lack of patriots of that type," thought Yeovil sadly; "so many patriots and so little patriotism."

CHAPTER XIII

TORYWOOD

YEOVIL got out of the train at a small, clean wayside station, and rapidly formed the conclusion that neatness, abundant leisure, and a devotion to the cultivation of wall-flowers and wyandottes were the prevailing influences of the station-master's life. The train slid away into the hazy distance of trees and meadows, and left the traveller standing in a world that seemed to be made up in equal parts of rock-garden, chicken coops, and whisky advertisements. The station-master, who appeared also to act as emergency porter, took Yeovil's ticket with the gesture of a kind-hearted person brushing away a troublesome wasp, and returned to a study of the *Poultry Chronicle*, which was giving its readers sage counsel concerning the ailments of belated July chickens. Yeovil called to mind the station-master of a tiny railway town in Siberia, who had held him in long and rather intelligent converse on the poetical merits and demerits of Shelley, and he wondered what the result would be if he were to engage the English official in a discussion on Lermontoff—or for the matter of that, on Shelley. The temptation to experiment was, however, removed by the arrival of a young groom, with brown eyes and a friendly smile, who hurried into the station and took Yeovil once more into a world where he was of fleeting importance.

In the roadway outside was a four-wheeled dog-cart with a pair of the famous Torywood blue roans. It was an agreeable variation in modern locomotion to be met at a station with high-class horseflesh instead of the ubiquitous motor, and the landscape was not of such a nature that one wished to be whirled through it in a cloud of dust. After a quick spin of some ten or fifteen minutes through twisting hedge-girt country roads, the roans turned in at a wide gateway, and went with dancing, rhythmic step along the park drive. The screen of oak-crowned upland suddenly fell away and a grey sharp-cornered building came into view in a setting of low growing beeches and dark pines. Torywood was not a stately, reposeful-looking house; it lay amid the sleepy landscape like a couched watched-dog with pricked ears and wakeful eyes. Built somewhere about the last years of Dutch William's reign, it had been a centre, ever since, for the political life of the countryside; a storm centre of discontent or a rallying ground for the well affected, as the circumstances of the day might entail. On the stone-flagged terrace in front of the house, with its quaint leaden figures of Diana pursuing a hound-pressed stag, successive squires and lords of Torywood had walked to and fro with their friends, watching the thunder-clouds on the political horizon or the shifting shadows on the sundial of political favour, tapping the political barometer for indications of change, working out a party campaign or arranging for the support of some national movement. To and fro they had gone in their respective generations, men with the passion for statecraft and political combat strong in their veins, and many oft-recurring names had echoed under those wakeful-looking casements, names spoken in anger or exultation, or murmured in fear and anxiety: Bolingbroke, Charles Edward, Walpole, the Farmer King, Bonaparte, Pitt, Wellington, Peel, Gladstone—echo and Time might have graven those names on the stone flags and grey walls. And now one tired old woman walked there, with names on her lips that she never uttered.

A friendly riot of fox terriers and spaniels greeted the carriage, leaping and rolling and yelping in an exuberance of sociability, as though horses and coachman and groom were comrades who had been absent for long months instead of half an hour. An indiscriminately affectionate puppy lay flat and whimpering at Yeovil's feet, sending up little showers of gravel with its wildly thumping tail, while two of the terriers raced each other madly across lawn and shrubbery, as though to show the blue roans what speed really was. The laughing-eyed young groom disentangled the puppy from between Yeovil's legs, and then he was ushered into the grey silence of the entrance hall, leaving sunlight and noise and the stir of life behind him.

"Her ladyship will see you in her writing-room," he was told, and he followed a servant along the dark passages to the well-remembered room.

There was something tragic in the sudden contrast between the vigour and youth and pride of life that Yeovil had seen crystallized in those dancing, high-stepping horses, scampering dogs, and alert, clean-limbed young men-servants, and the age-frail woman who came forward to meet him.

Eleanor, Dowager Lady Greymarten, had for more than half a century been the ruling spirit at Torywood. The affairs of the county had not sufficed for her untiring activities of mind and body; in the wider field of national and Imperial service she had worked and schemed and fought with an energy and a far-sightedness that came probably from the blend of caution and bold restlessness in her Scottish blood. For many educated minds the arena of politics and public life is a weariness of dust and disgust, to others it is a fascinating study, to be watched from the comfortable seat of a spectator. To her it was a home. In her town house or down at Torywood, with her writing-pad on her knee and the telephone at her elbow, or in personal counsel with some trusted colleague or persuasive argument with a halting adherent or half-convinced opponent, she had laboured on behalf of the poor and the ill-equipped, had fought for her idea of the Right, and above all, for the safety and sanity of her Fatherland. Spadework when necessary and leadership when called for, came alike within the scope of her activities, and not least of her achievements, though perhaps she hardly realized it, was the force of her example, a lone, indomitable fighter calling to the half-caring and the half-discouraged, to the laggard and the slow-moving.

And now she came across the room with "the tired step of a tired king," and that look which the French so expressively called *l'air défait*. The charm which Heaven bestows on old ladies, reserving its highest gift to the end, had always seemed in her case to be lost sight of in the dignity and interest of a great dame who was still in the full prime of her fighting and ruling powers. Now, in Yeovil's eyes, she had suddenly come to be very old, stricken with the forlorn languor of one who knows that death will be weary to wait for. She had spared herself nothing in the long labour, the ceaseless building, the watch and ward, and in one short autumn week she had seen the overthrow of all that she had built, the falling asunder of the world in which she had laboured. Her life's end was like a harvest home when blight and storm have laid waste the fruit of long toil and unsparing outlay. Victory had been her goal, the death or victory of old heroic challenge, for she had always dreamed to die fighting to the last; death or victory—and the gods had given her neither, only the bitterness of a defeat that could not be measured in words, and the weariness of a life that had outlived happiness or hope. Such was Eleanor, Dowager Lady Greymarten, a shadow amid the young red-blooded life at Torywood, but a shadow that was too real to die, a shadow that was stronger than the substance that surrounded it.

Yeovil talked long and hurriedly of his late travels, of the vast Siberian forests and rivers, the desolate tundras, the lakes and marshes where the wild swans rear their broods, the flower carpet of the summer fields and the winter ice-mantle of Russia's northern sea. He talked as a man talks who avoids the subject that is uppermost in his mind, and in the mind of his hearer, as one who looks away from a wound or deformity that is too cruel to be taken notice of.

Tea was served in a long oak-panelled gallery, where generations of Mustelfords had romped and played as children, and remained yet in effigy, in a collection of more or less faithful portraits. After tea Yeovil was taken by his hostess to the aviaries, which constituted the sole claim which Tory-wood possessed to being considered a show place. The third Earl of Greymarten had collected rare and interesting birds, somewhere about the time when Gilbert White was penning the last of his deathless letters, and his successors in the title had perpetuated the hobby. Little lawns and ponds and shrub-beries were partitioned off for the various ground-loving spe-cies, and higher cages with interlacing perches and rockwork shelves accommodated the birds whose natural expression of movement was on the wing. Quails and francolins scurried about under low-growing shrubs, peacock-pheasants strutted and sunned themselves, pugnacious ruffs engaged in perfunc-tory battles, from force of habit now that the rivalry of the mating season was over; choughs, ravens, and loud-throated gulls occupied sections of a vast rockery, and bright-hued Chinese pond-herons and delicately stepping egrets waded among the water-lilies of a marble-terraced tank. One or two dusky shapes seen dimly in the recesses of a large cage built round a hollow tree would be lively owls when evening came on.

In the course of his many wanderings Yeovil had himself contributed three or four inhabitants to this little feathered town, and he went round the enclosures, renewing old ac-quaintances and examining new additions.

"The falcon cage is empty," said Lady Greymarten, point-ing to a large wired dome that towered high above the other enclosures; "I let the lanner fly free one day. The other birds may be reconciled to their comfortable quarters and abundant food and absence of dangers, but I don't think all those things could make up to a falcon for the wild range of cliff and desert. When one has lost one's own liberty one feels a quicker sym-pathy for other caged things, I suppose."

There was silence for a moment, and then the Dowager went on, in a wistful, passionate voice:

"I am an old woman now, Murrey, I must die in my cage. I haven't the strength to fight. Age is a very real and very cruel thing, though we may shut our eyes to it and pretend it is not there. I thought at one time that I should never really know what it meant, what it brought to one. I thought of it as a messenger that one could keep waiting out in the yard till the very last moment. I know now what it means. . . . But you, Murrey, you are young, you can fight. Are you going to be a fighter, or the very humble servant of the *fait accompli?*"

"I shall never be the servant of the *fait accompli*," said Yeovil. "I loathe it. As to fighting, one must first find out what weapon to use, and how to use it effectively. One must watch and wait."

"One must not wait too long," said the old woman. "Time is on their side, not ours. It is the young people we must fight for now, if they are ever to fight for us. A new generation will spring up, a weaker memory of old glories will survive, the *éclat* of the ruling race will capture young imaginations. If I had your youth, Murrey, and your sex, I would become a commercial traveller."

"A commercial traveller!" exclaimed Yeovil.

"Yes, one whose business took him up and down the country, into contact with all classes, into homes and shops and inns and railway carriages. And as I travelled I would work, work on the minds of every boy and girl I came across, every young father and young mother too, every young couple that were going to be man and wife. I would awaken or keep alive in their memory the things that we have been, the grand, brave things that some of our race have done, and I would stir up a longing, a determination for the future that we must win back. I would be a counter-agent to the agents of the *fait accompli.* In course of time the Government would find out what I was doing, and I should be sent out of the country, but I should have accomplished something, and others would carry on the work. That is what I would do. Murrey, even if it is to be a losing battle, fight it, fight it!"

Yeovil knew that the old lady was fighting her last battle, rallying the discouraged, and spurring on the backward.

A footman came to announce that the carriage waited to take him back to the station. His hostess walked with him through the hall, and came out on to the stone-flagged terrace, the terrace from which a former Lady Greymarten had watched the twinkling bonfires that told of Waterloo.

Yeovil said good-bye to her as she stood there, a wan, shrunken shadow, yet with a greater strength and reality in her flickering life than those parrot men and women that fluttered and chattered through London drawing-rooms and theatre foyers.

As the carriage swung round a bend in the drive Yeovil looked back at Torywood, a lone, grey building, couched like a watch-dog with pricked ears and wakeful eyes in the midst of the sleeping landscape. An old pleading voice was still ringing in his ears:

> *Imperious and yet forlorn,*
> *Came through the silence of the trees,*
> *The echoes of a golden horn,*
> *Calling to distances.*

Somehow Yeovil knew that he would never hear that voice again, and he knew, too, that he would hear it always, with its message, "Be a fighter." And he knew now, with a shame-faced consciousness that sprang suddenly into existence, that the summons would sound for him in vain.

The weary brain-torturing months of fever had left their trail behind, a lassitude of spirit and a sluggishness of blood, a quenching of the desire to roam and court adventure and hardship. In the hours of waking and depression between the raging intervals of delirium he had speculated, with a sort of detached, listless indifference, on the chances of his getting back to life and strength and energy. The prospect of filling a corner of some lonely Siberian graveyard or Finnish cemetery had seemed near realization at times, and for a man who was already half dead the other half didn't particularly matter. But when he had allowed himself to dwell on the more hopeful side of the case it had always been a complete recovery that awaited him; the same Yeovil as of yore, a little thinner and more lined about the eyes perhaps, would go through life in the same way, alert, resolute, enterprising, ready to start off at short notice for some desert or upland where the eagles were circling and the wild-fowl were calling. He had not reckoned that Death, evaded and held off by the doctors' skill, might exact a compromise, and that only part of the man would go free to the West.

And now he began to realize how little of mental and physical energy he could count on. His own country had never seemed in his eyes so comfort-yielding and to-be-desired as it did now when it had passed into alien keeping and become a prisonland as much as a homeland. London with its thin mockery of a Season, and its chattering horde of empty-hearted self-seekers, held no attraction for him, but the spell of English country life was weaving itself round him, now that the charm of the desert was receding into a mist of memories. The waning of pleasant autumn days in an English woodland, the whir of game birds in the clean harvested fields, the grey moist mornings in the saddle, with the magical cry of hounds coming up from some misty hollow, and then the delicious abandon of physical weariness in bathroom and bedroom after a long run, and the heavenly snatched hour of luxurious sleep, before stirring back to life and hunger, the coming of the dinner hour and the jollity of a well-chosen house-party.

That was the call which was competing with that other trumpet-call, and Yeovil knew on which side his choice would incline.

CHAPTER XIV

"A PERFECTLY GLORIOUS AFTERNOON"

IT was one of the last days of July, cooled and freshened by a touch of rain and dropping back again to a languorous warmth. London looked at its summer best, rain-washed and sun-lit, with the maximum of coming and going in its more fashionable streets.

Cicely Yeovil sat in a screened alcove of the Anchorage Restaurant, a feeding-ground which had lately sprung into favour. Opposite her sat Ronnie, confronting the ruins of what had been a dish of prawns in aspic. Cool and clean and fresh-coloured, he was good to look on in the eyes of his companion, and yet, perhaps, there was a ruffle in her soul that called for some answering disturbance on the part of that superbly tranquil young man, and certainly called in vain. Cicely had set up for herself a fetish of onyx with eyes of jade, and doubtless hungered at times with an unreasonable but perfectly natural hunger for something of flesh and blood. It was the religion of her life to know exactly what she wanted and to see that she got it, but there was no possible guarantee against her occasionally experiencing a desire for something else. It is the golden rule of all religions that no one should really live up to their precepts; when a man observes the principles of his religion too exactly he is in immediate danger of founding a new sect.

"Today is going to be your day of triumph," said Cicely to the young man, who was wondering at the moment whether he would care to embark on an artichoke; "I believe I'm more nervous than you are," she added, "and yet I rather hate the idea of you scoring a great success."

"Why?" asked Ronnie, diverting his mind for a moment from the artichoke question and its ramifications of *sauce hollandaise* or *vinaigre*.

"I like you as you are," said Cicely, "just a nice-looking boy to flatter and spoil and pretend to be fond of. You've got a charming young body and you've no soul, and that's such a fascinating combination. If you had a soul you would either dislike or worship me, and I'd much rather have things as they are. And now you are going to go a step beyond that, and other people will applaud you and say that you are wonderful, and invite you to eat with them and motor with them and yacht with them. As soon as that begins to happen, Ronnie, a lot of other things will come to an end. Of course I've always known that you don't really care for me, but as soon as the world knows it you are irrevocably damaged as a plaything. That is the great secret that binds us together, the knowledge that we have no real affection for one another. And this afternoon every one will know that you are a great artist, and no great artist was ever a great lover."

"I shan't be difficult to replace, anyway," said Ronnie, with what he imagined was a becoming modesty; "there are lots of boys standing round ready to be fed and flattered and put on an imaginary pedestal, most of them more or less good-looking and well turned out and amusing to talk to."

"Oh, I dare say I could find a successor for your vacated niche," said Cicely lightly; "one thing I'm determined on though, he shan't be a musician. It's so unsatisfactory to have to share a grand passion with a grand piano. He shall be a delightful young barbarian who would think Saint-Saëns was a Derby winner or a claret."

"Don't be in too much of a hurry to replace me," said Ronnie, who did not care to have his successor too seriously discussed. "I may not score the success you expect this afternoon."

"My dear boy, a minor crowned head from across the sea is coming to hear you play, and that alone will count as a success with most of your listeners. Also, I've secured a real Duchess for you, which is rather an achievement in the London of today."

"An English Duchess?" asked Ronnie, who had early in life learned to apply the Merchandise Marks Act to ducal titles.

"English, oh certainly, at least as far as the title goes; she was born under the constellation of the Star-spangled Banner. I don't suppose the Duke approves of her being here, lending her countenance to the *fait accompli*, but when you've got republican blood in your veins a Kaiser is quite as attractive a lodestar as a King, rather more so. And Canon Mousepace is coming," continued Cicely, referring to a closely-written list of guests; "the excellent von Tolb has been attending his church lately, and the Canon is longing to meet her. She is just the sort of person he adores. I fancy he sincerely realizes how difficult it will be for the rich to enter the Kingdom of Heaven, and he tries to make up for it by being as nice as possible to them in this world."

Ronnie held out his hand for the list.

"I think you know most of the others," said Cicely, passing it to him.

"Leutnant von Gabelroth?" read out Ronnie; "who is he?"

"In one of the hussar regiments quartered here; a friend of the Gräfin's. Ugly but amiable, and I'm told a good cross-country rider. I suppose Murrey will be disgusted at meeting the 'outward and visible sign' under his roof, but these encounters are inevitable as long as he is in London."

"I didn't know Murrey was coming," said Ronnie.

"I believe he's going to look in on us," said Cicely; "it's just as well, you know, otherwise we should have Joan asking in her loudest voice when he was going to be back in England again. I haven't asked her, but she overheard the Gräfin arranging to come and hear you play, and I fancy that will be quite enough."

"How about some Turkish coffee?" said Ronnie, who had decided against the artichoke.

"Turkish coffee, certainly, and a cigarette, and a moment's peace before the serious business of the afternoon claims us. Talking about peace, do you know, Ronnie, it has just occurred to me that we have left out one of the most important things in our *affaire*; we have never had a quarrel."

"I hate quarrels," said Ronnie, "they are so domesticated."

"That's the first time I've ever heard you talk about your home," said Cicely.

"I fancy it would apply to most homes," said Ronnie.

"The last boy-friend I had used to quarrel furiously with me at least once a week," said Cicely reflectively; "but then he had dark slumberous eyes that lit up magnificently when he was angry, so it would have been a sheer waste of God's good gifts not to have sent him into a passion now and then."

"With your excursions into the past and the future you are making me feel dreadfully like an instalment of a serial novel," protested Ronnie; "we have now got to 'synopsis of earlier chapters.'"

"It shan't be teased," said Cicely; "we will live in the present and go no further into the future than to make arrangements for Tuesday's dinner-party. I've asked the Duchess;

she would never have forgiven me if she'd found out that I
had a crowned head dining with me and hadn't asked her to
meet him."

*   *   *   *   *   *   *

A sudden hush descended on the company gathered in the
great drawing-room at Berkshire Street as Ronnie took his
seat at the piano; the voice of Canon Mousepace outlasted the
others for a moment or so, and then subsided into a regretful
but gracious silence. For the next nine or ten minutes Ronnie
held possession of the crowded room, a tense slender figure,
with cold green eyes aflame in a sudden fire, and smooth burnished head bent low over the keyboard that yielded a disci-
plined riot of melody under his strong deft fingers. The world-
weary Landgraf forgot for the moment the regrettable trend
of his subjects towards Parliamentary Socialism, the excellent
Gräfin von Tolb forgot all that the Canon had been saying
to her for the last ten minutes, forgot the depressing certainty
that he would have a great deal more than he wanted to say
in the immediate future, over and above the thirty-five minutes
or so of discourse that she would contract to listen to next
Sunday. And Cicely listened with the wistful equivocal triumph of one whose goose has turned out to be a swan and
who realizes with secret concern that she has only planned the
rôle of goosegirl for herself.

The last chords died away, the fire faded out of the jade-
coloured eyes, and Ronnie became once more a well-groomed
youth in a drawing-room full of well-dressed people. But
around him rose an explosive clamour of applause and congratulation, the sincere tribute of appreciation and the equally
hearty expression of imitative homage.

"It is a great gift, a great gift," chanted Canon Mousepace.
"You must put it to a great use. A talent is vouchsafed to us
for a purpose; you must fulfil the purpose. Talent such as yours
is a responsibility; you must meet that responsibility."

The dictionary of the English language was an inexhaustible quarry, from which the Canon had hewn and fashioned for
himself a great reputation.

"You must gom and blay to me at Schlachsenberg," said

the kindly-faced Landgraf, whom the world adored and thwarted in about equal proportions. "At Christmas, yes, that will be a good time. We still keep the Christ-Fest at Schlach-senberg, though the 'Sozi' keep telling our schoolchildren that it is only a Christ myth. Never mind, I will have the Vice-President of our Landtag to listen to you; he is 'Sozi' but we are good friends outside the Parliament House; you shall blay to him, my young friendt, and gonfince him that there is a Got in Heaven. You will gom? Yes?"

"It was beautiful," said the Gräfin simply; "it made me cry. Go back to the piano again, please, at once."

Perhaps the near neighbourhood of the Canon inspired this command, but the Gräfin had been genuinely charmed. She adored good music and she was unaffectedly fond of good-looking boys.

Ronnie went back to the piano and tasted the matured pleasure of a repeated success. Any measure of nervousness that he may have felt at first had completely passed away. He was sure of his audience and he played as though they did not exist. A renewed clamour of excited approval attended the conclusion of his performance.

"It is a triumph, a perfectly *glorious* triumph," exclaimed the Duchess of Dreyshire, turning to Yeovil, who sat silent among his wife's guests; "isn't it just *glorious?*" she demanded, with a heavy insistent intonation of the word.

"Is it?" said Yeovil.

"Well, isn't it?" she cried, with a rising inflection, "isn't it just *perfectly* glorious?"

"I don't know," confessed Yeovil; "you see, glory hasn't come very much my way lately." Then, before he exactly realized what he was doing, he raised his voice and quoted loudly for the benefit of half the room:

> " 'Other Romans shall arise,
> Heedless of a soldier's name,
> Sounds, not deeds, shall win the prize,
> Harmony the path to fame.' "

There was a sort of shiver of surprised silence at Yeovil's end of the room.

"Hell!"

The word rang out in a strong young voice.

"Hell! And it's true, that's the worst of it. It's damned true!"

Yeovil turned, with some dozen others, to see who was responsible for this vigorously expressed statement.

Tony Luton confronted him, an angry scowl on his face, a blaze in his heavy-lidded eyes. The boy was without a conscience, almost without a soul, as priests and parsons reckon souls, but there was a slumbering devil-god within him, and Yeovil's taunting words had broken the slumber. Life had been for Tony a hard school, in which right and wrong, high endeavour and good resolve, were untaught subjects; but there was a sterling something in him, just that something that helped poor street-scavenged men to die brave-fronted deaths in the trenches of Salamanca, that fired a handful of apprentice boys to shut the gates of Derry and stare unflinchingly at grim leaguer and starvation. It was just that nameless something that was lacking in the young musician, who stood at the farther end of the room, bathed in a flood of compliment and congratulation, enjoying the honey-drops of his triumph.

Luton pushed his way through the crowd and left the room, without troubling to take leave of his hostess.

"What a strange young man," exclaimed the Duchess; "now do take me into the next room," she went on almost in the same breath, "I'm just dying for some iced coffee."

Yeovil escorted her through the throng of Ronnie-worshippers to the desired haven of refreshment.

"Marvellous!" Mrs. Menteith-Mendlesohnn was exclaiming in ringing trumpet tones; "of course I always knew he could play, but this is not mere piano playing, it is tone-mastery, it is sound magic. Mrs. Yeovil has introduced us to a new star in the musical firmament. Do you know, I feel this afternoon just like Cortez, in the poem, gazing at the newly discovered sea."

" 'Silent upon a peak in Darien,' " quoted a penetrating voice that could only belong to Joan Mardle; "I say, can any one picture Mrs. Menteith-Mendlesohnn silent on any peak or under any circumstances?"

If any one had that measure of imagination, no one acknowledged the fact.

"A great gift and a great responsibility," Canon Mousepace was assuring the Gräfin; "the power of evoking sublime melody is akin to the power of awakening thought; a musician can appeal to dormant consciousness as the preacher can appeal to dormant conscience. It is a responsibility, an instrument for good or evil. Our young friend here, we may be sure, will use it as an instrument for good. He has, I feel certain, a sense of his responsibility."

"He is a nice boy," said the Gräfin simply; "he has such pretty hair."

In one of the window recesses Rhapsodie Pantril was talking vaguely but beautifully to a small audience on the subject of chromatic chords; she had the advantage of knowing what she was talking about, an advantage that her listeners did not in the least share. "All through his playing there ran a tone-note of malachite green," she declared recklessly, feeling safe from immediate contradiction; "malachite green, *my* colour—the colour of striving."

Having satisfied the ruling passion that demanded gentle and dexterous self-advertisement, she realized that the Augusta Smith in her craved refreshment, and moved with one of her over-awed admirers towards the haven where peaches and iced coffee might be considered a certainty.

The refreshment alcove, which was really a good-sized room, a sort of chapel-of-ease to the larger drawing-room, was already packed with a crowd who felt that they could best discuss Ronnie's triumph between mouthfuls of fruit salad and iced draughts of hock-cup. So brief is human glory that two or three independent souls had even now drifted from the theme of the moment on to other more personally interesting topics.

"Iced mulberry salad, my dear, it's a *spécialité de la maison,* so to speak; they say the roving husband brought the recipe from Astrakhan, or Seville, or some such outlandish place."

"I wish my husband would roam about a bit and bring back strange palatable dishes. No such luck, he's got asthma and has to keep on a gravel soil with a south aspect and all sorts of other restrictions."

"I don't think you're to be pitied in the least; a husband with asthma is like a captive golf-ball, you can always put your hand on him when you want him."

"All the hangings, *violette de Parme*, all the furniture, rose-wood. Nothing is to be played in it except Mozart. Mozart only. Some of my friends wanted me to have a replica of the Mozart statue at Vienna put up in a corner of the room, with flowers always around it, but I really couldn't. I *couldn't*. One is *so* tired of it, one sees it everywhere. I couldn't do it. I'm like that, you know."

"Yes, I've secured the hero of the hour, Ronnie Storre, oh, yes, rather. He's going to join our yachting trip, third week of August. We're going as far afield as Fiume, in the Adriatic—or is it the Ægean? Won't it be jolly? Oh, no, we're not asking Mrs. Yeovil; it's quite a small yacht, you know—at least, it's a small party."

The excellent von Tolb took her departure, bearing off with her the Landgraf, who had already settled the date and duration of Ronnie's Christmas visit.

"It will be dull, you know," he warned the prospective guest; "our Landtag will not be sitting, and what is a bear-garden without the bears? However, we haf some wildt schwein in our woods, we can show you some sport in that way."

Ronnie instantly saw himself in a well-fitting shooting costume, with a Tyrolese hat placed at a very careful angle on his head, but he confessed that the other details of boar-hunting were rather beyond him.

With the departure of the von Tolb party Canon Mouse-pace gravitated decently but persistently towards a corner where the Duchess, still at concert pitch, was alternatively praising Ronnie's performance and the mulberry salad. Joan Mardle, who formed one of the group, was not openly praising any one, but she was paying a silent tribute to the salad.

"We were just talking about Ronnie Storre's music, Canon," said the Duchess; "I consider it just perfectly glorious."

"It's a great talent, isn't it, Canon," put in Joan briskly, "and of course it's a responsibility as well, don't you think? Music can be such an influence, just as eloquence can; don't you agree with me?"

The quarry of the English language was of course a public property, but it was disconcerting to have one's own particular barrow-load of sentence-building material carried off before one's eyes. The Canon's impressive homily on Ronnie's gift and its possibilities had to be hastily whittled down to a weakly acquiescent, "Quite so, quite so."

"Have you tasted this iced mulberry salad, Canon?" asked the Duchess; "it's perfectly luscious. Just hurry along and get some before it's all gone."

And her Grace hurried along in an opposite direction, to thank Cicely for past favours and to express lively gratitude for the Tuesday to come.

The guests departed, with a rather irritating slowness, for which perhaps the excellence of Cicely's buffet arrangements was partly responsible. The great drawing-room seemed to grow larger and more oppressive as the human wave receded, and the hostess fled at last with some relief to the narrower limits of her writing-room and the sedative influences of a cigarette. She was inclined to be sorry for herself; the triumph of the afternoon had turned out much as she had predicted at lunch-time. Her idol of onyx had not been swept from its pedestal, but the pedestal itself had an air of being packed up ready for transport to some other temple. Ronnie would be flattered and spoiled by half a hundred people, just because he could conjure sounds out of a keyboard, and Cicely felt no great incentive to go on flattering and spoiling him herself. And Ronnie would acquiesce in his dismissal with the good grace born of indifference—the surest guarantor of perfect manners. Already he had social engagements for the coming months in which she had no share; the drifting apart would be mutual. He had been an intelligent and amusing companion, and he had played the game as she had wished it to be played, without the fatigue of keeping up pretences which neither of them could have believed in. "Let us have a wonderfully good time together" had been the single stipulation in their unwritten treaty of comradeship, and they had had the good time. Their whole-hearted pursuit of material happiness would go on as keenly as before, but they would hunt in different company, that was all. Yes, that was all. . . .

Cicely found the effect of her cigarette less sedative than she was disposed to exact. It might be necessary to change the brand.

Some ten or eleven days later Yeovil read an announcement in the papers that, in spite of handsome offers of increased salary, Mr. Tony Luton, the original singer of the popular ditty *Eccleston Square*, had terminated his engagement with Messrs. Isaac Grosvenor and Leon Hebhardt of the Caravansery Theatre, and signed on as a deck hand in the Canadian Marine.

Perhaps, after all, there had been some shred of glory amid the trumpet triumph of that July afternoon.

CHAPTER XV

THE INTELLIGENT ANTICIPATOR OF WANTS

TWO of Yeovil's London clubs, the two that he had been accustomed to frequent, had closed their doors after the catastrophe. One of them had perished from off the face of the earth, its fittings had been sold and its papers lay stored in some solicitor's office, a titbit of material for the pen of some future historian. The other had transplanted itself to Delhi, whither it had removed its early Georgian furniture and its traditions, and sought to reproduce its St. James's Street atmosphere as nearly as the conditions of a tropical Asiatic city would permit. There remained the Cartwheel, a considerably newer institution, which had sprung into existence somewhere about the time of Yeovil's last sojourn in England; he had joined it on the solicitation of a friend who was interested in the venture, and his bankers had paid his subscription during his absence. As he had never been inside its doors there could be no depressing comparisons to make between its present state and aforetime glories, and Yeovil turned into its portals one afternoon with the adventurous detachment of a man who breaks new ground and challenges new experiences.

He entered with a diffident sense of intrusion, conscious that his standing as a member might not be recognized by the keepers of the doors; in a moment, however, he realized that a rajah's escort of elephants might almost have marched through the entrance hall and vestibule without challenge. The general atmosphere of the scene suggested a blend of the railway station at Cologne, the Hotel Bristol in any European capital, and the second act in most musical comedies. A score of brilliant and brilliantined pages decorated the foreground, while Hebraic-looking gentlemen, wearing tartan waistcoats of the clans of their adoption, flitted restlessly between the tape machines and telephone boxes. The army of occupation had obviously established a firm footing in the hospitable premises; a kaleidoscopic pattern of uniforms, sky-blue, indigo and bottle-green, relieved the civilian attire of the groups that clustered in lounge and card-rooms and corridors. Yeovil rapidly came to the conclusion that the joys of membership were not for him. He had turned to go, after a very cursory inspection of the premises and their human occupants, when he was hailed by a young man, dressed with strenuous neatness, whom he remembered having met in past days at the houses of one or two common friends.

Hubert Herlton's parents had brought him into the world, and some twenty-one years later had put him into a motor business. Having taken these pardonable liberties they had completely exhausted their ideas of what to do with him, and Hubert seemed unlikely to develop any ideas of his own on the subject. The motor business elected to conduct itself without his connivance; journalism, the stage, tomato culture (without capital), and other professions that could be entered on at short notice were submitted to his consideration by nimble-minded relations and friends. He listened to their suggestions with polite indifference, being rude only to a cousin who demonstrated how he might achieve a settled income of from two hundred to a thousand pounds a year by the propagation of mushrooms in a London basement. While his walk in life was still an undetermined promenade his parents died, leaving him with a carefully-invested income of thirty-seven pounds a year. At that point of his career Yeovil's knowledge of him stopped short; the journey to Siberia had taken him beyond the range of Herlton's domestic vicissitudes.

The young man greeted him in a decidedly friendly manner.

"I didn't know you were a member here," he exclaimed.

"It's the first time I've ever been in the club," said Yeovil, "and I fancy it will be the last. There is rather too much of the fighting-machine in evidence here. One doesn't want a perpetual reminder of what has happened staring one in the face."

"We tried at first to keep the alien element out," said Herlton apologetically, "but we couldn't have carried on the club if we'd stuck to that line. You see we'd lost more than two-thirds of our old members so we couldn't afford to be exclusive. As a matter of fact the whole thing was decided over our heads; a new syndicate took over the concern, and a new committee was installed, with a good many foreigners on it. I know it's horrid having these uniforms flaunting all over the place, but what is one to do?"

Yeovil said nothing, with the air of a man who could have said a great deal.

"I suppose you wonder, why remain a member under those conditions?" continued Herlton. "Well, as far as I am concerned, a place like this is a necessity for me. In fact, it's my profession, my source of income."

"Are you as good at bridge as all that?" asked Yeovil; "I'm a fairly successful player myself, but I should be sorry to have to live on my winnings, year in, year out."

"I don't play cards," said Herlton, "at least not for serious stakes. My winnings or losings wouldn't come to a tenner in an average year. No, I live by commissions, by introducing likely buyers to would-be sellers."

"Sellers of what?" asked Yeovil.

"Anything, everything; horses, yachts, old masters, plate, shootings, poultry-farms, week-end cottages, motor-cars, almost anything you can think of. Look," and he produced from his breast pocket a bulky notebook illusorily inscribed "Engagements."

"Here," he explained, tapping the book, "I've got a double entry of every likely client that I know, with a note of the things he may have to sell and the things he may want to buy. When it is something that he has for sale there are cross-references to likely purchasers of that particular line of article. I don't limit myself to things that I actually know people to be in want of, I go further than that and have theories, carefully indexed theories, as to the things that people might want to buy. At the right moment, if I can get the opportunity, I mention the article that is in my mind's eye to the possible purchaser who has also been in my mind's eye, and I frequently bring off a sale. I started a chance acquaintance on a career of print-buying the other day merely by telling him of a couple of good prints that I knew of, that were to be had at a quite reasonable price; he is a man with more money than he knows what to do with, and he has laid out quite a lot on old prints since his first purchase. Most of his collection he has got through me, and of course I net a commission on each transaction. So you see, old man, how useful, not to say necessary, a club with a large membership is to me. The more mixed and socially chaotic it is, the more serviceable it is."

"Of course," said Yeovil, "and I suppose, as a matter of fact, a good many of your clients belong to the conquering race."

"Well, you see, they are the people who have got the money," said Herlton; "I don't mean to say that the invading Germans are usually people of wealth, but while they live over here they escape the crushing taxation that falls on the British-born subject. They serve their country as soldiers, and we have to serve it in garrison money, ship money and so forth, besides the ordinary taxes of the State. The German shoulders the rifle, the Englishman has to shoulder everything else. That is what will help more than anything towards the gradual Germanizing of our big towns; the comparatively lightly-taxed German workman over here will have a much bigger spending power and purchasing power than his heavily taxed English neighbour. The public-houses, bars, eating-houses, places of amusement and so forth, will come to cater more and more for money-yielding German patronage. The stream of British emigration will swell rather than diminish, and the stream of Teuton immigration will be equally persistent and progressive. Yes, the military-service ordinance was a cunning stroke on the part of that old fox, von Kwarl. As a civilian statesman he is far and away cleverer than Bismarck was; he smothers with a feather-bed where Bismarck would have tried to smash with a sledge-hammer."

"Have you got me down on your list of noteworthy people?" asked Yeovil, turning the drift of the conversation back to the personal topic.

"Certainly I have," said Herlton, turning the pages of his pocket directory to the letter Y. "As soon as I knew you were back in England I made several entries concerning you. In the first place it was possible that you might have a volume on Siberian travel and natural history notes to publish, and I've cross-referenced you to a publisher I know who rather wants books of that sort on his list."

"I may tell you at once that I've no intentions in that direction," said Yeovil, in some amusement.

"Just as well," said Herlton cheerfully, scribbling a hieroglyphic in his book; "that branch of business is rather outside my line—too little in it, and the gratitude of author and publisher for being introduced to one another is usually short-lived. A more serious entry was the item that if you were wintering in England you would be looking out for a hunter or two. You used to hunt with the East Wessex, I remember; I've got just the very animal that will suit that country, ready waiting for you. A beautiful clean jumper. I've put it over a fence or two myself, and you and I ride much the same weight. A stiffish price is being asked for it, but I've got the letters D.O. after your name."

"In Heaven's name," said Yeovil, now openly grinning, "before I die of curiosity tell me what D.O. stands for."

"It means some one who doesn't object to pay a good price for anything that really suits him. There are some people of course who won't consider a thing unless they can get it for about a third of what they imagine to be its market value. I've got another suggestion down against you in my book; you may not be staying in the country at all, you may be clearing out in disgust at existing conditions. In that case you would be selling a lot of things that you wouldn't want to cart away with you. That involves another set of entries and a whole lot of cross-references."

"I'm afraid I've given you a lot of trouble," said Yeovil dryly.

"Not at all," said Herlton, "but it would simplify matters if we take it for granted that you are going to stay here, for this winter anyhow, and are looking out for hunters. Can you lunch with me here on Wednesday, and come and look at the animal afterwards? It's only thirty-five minutes by train. It will take us longer if we motor. There is a two-fifty-three from Charing Cross that we could catch comfortably."

"If you are going to persuade me to hunt in the East Wessex country this season," said Yeovil, "you must find me a convenient hunting-box somewhere down there."

"I *have* found it," said Herlton, whipping out a stylograph, and hastily scribbling an "order to view" on a card; "central as possible for all the meets, grand stabling accommodation, excellent water-supply, big bathroom, game larder, cellarage, a bakehouse if you want to bake your own bread——"

"Any land with it?"

"Not enough to be a nuisance. An acre or two of paddock and about the same of garden. You are fond of wild things; a wood comes down to the edge of the garden, a wood that harbours owls and buzzards and kestrels."

"Have you got all those details in your book?" asked Yeovil; " 'wood adjoining property, O.B.K.' "

"I keep those details in my head," said Herlton, "but they are quite reliable."

"I shall insist on something substantial off the rent if there are no buzzards," said Yeovil; "now that you have mentioned them they seem an indispensable accessory to any decent hunting-box. Look," he exclaimed, catching sight of a plump middle-aged individual crossing the vestibule with an air of restrained importance, "there goes the delectable Pitherby. Does he come on your books at all?"

"I should say!" exclaimed Herlton fervently. "The delectable P. nourishes expectations of a barony or viscounty at an early date. Most of his life has been spent in streets and squares, with occasional migrations to the esplanades of fashionable watering-places or the gravelled walks of country house gardens. Now that *noblesse* is about to impose its obligations on him, quite a new catalogue of wants has sprung into his mind. There are things that a plain esquire may leave undone without causing scandalized remark, but a fiercer light beats on a baron. Trigger-pulling is one of the obligations. Up to the present Pitherby has never hit a partridge in anger, but this year he has commissioned me to rent him a deer forest. Some pedigree Herefords for his 'home farm' was another commission, and a dozen and a half swans for a swannery. The swannery, I may say, was my idea; I said once in his hearing that it gave a baronial air to an estate; you see, I knew a man who had got a lot of surplus swan stock for sale. Now Pitherby wants a heronry as well. I've put him in communication with a client of mine who suffers from superfluous herons, but of course I can't guarantee that the birds' nesting arrangements will fall in with his territorial requirements. I'm getting him some carp, too, of quite respectable age, for a carp pond; I thought it would look so well for his lady-wife to be discovered by interviewers feeding the carp with her own fair hands, and I put the same idea into Pitherby's mind."

"I had no idea that so many things were necessary to endorse a patent of nobility," said Yeovil. "If there should be any miscarriage in the bestowal of the honour at least Pitherby will have absolved himself from any charge of contributory negligence."

"Shall we say Wednesday, here, one o'clock, lunch first, and go down and look at the horse afterwards?" said Herlton, returning to the matter in hand.

Yeovil hesitated, then he nodded his head.

"There is no harm in going to look at the animal," he said.

CHAPTER XVI

SUNRISE

MRS. KERRICK sat at a little teakwood table in the veranda of a low-pitched teak-built house that stood on the steep slope of a brown hill-side. Her youngest child, with the grave natural dignity of nine-year-old girlhood, maintained a correct but observant silence, looking carefully yet unobtrusively after the wants of the one guest, and checking from time to time the incursions of ubiquitous ants that were obstinately disposed to treat the table-cloth as a foraging ground. The wayfaring visitor, who was experiencing a British blend of Eastern hospitality, was a French naturalist, travelling thus far afield in quest of feathered specimens to enrich the aviaries of a bird-collecting Balkan King. On the previous evening, while shrugging his shoulders and unloosing his vocabulary over the meagre accommodation afforded by the native rest-house, he had been enchanted by receiving an invitation to transfer his quarters to the house on the hill-side, where he found not only a pleasant-voiced hostess and some drinkable wine, but three brown-skinned English youngsters who were able to give him a mass of intelligent first-hand information about the bird life of the region. And now, at the early morning breakfast, ere yet the sun was showing over the rim of the brown-baked hills, he was learning something of the life of the little community he had chanced on.

"I was in these parts many years ago," explained the hostess, "when my husband was alive and had an appointment out here. It is a healthy hill district and I had pleasant memories of the place, so when it became necessary, well, desirable let us say, to leave our English home and find a new one, it occurred to me to bring my boys and my little girl here—my eldest girl is at school in Paris. Labour is cheap here and I try my hand at farming in a small way. Of course it is very different work to just superintending the dairy and poultry-yard arrangements of an English country estate. There are so many things, insect ravages, bird depredations, and so on, that one only knows on a small scale in England, that happen here in wholesale fashion, not to mention droughts and torrential rains and other tropical visitations. And then the domestic animals are so disconcertingly different from the ones one has been used to; humped cattle never seem to behave in the way that straight-backed cattle would, and goats and geese and chickens are not a bit the same here that they are in Europe—and of course the farm servants are utterly unlike the same class in England. One has to unlearn a good deal of what one thought one knew about stock-keeping and agriculture, and take note of the native ways of doing things; they are primitive and unenterprising of course, but they have an accumulated store of experience behind them, and one has to tread warily in initiating improvements."

The Frenchman looked round at the brown sun-scorched hills, with the dusty empty road showing here and there in the middle distance and other brown sun-scorched hills rounding off the scene; he looked at the lizards on the veranda walls, at the jars for keeping the water cool, at the numberless little insect-bored holes in the furniture, at the heat-drawn lines on his hostess's comely face. Notwithstanding his present wanderings he had a Frenchman's strong homing instinct, and he marvelled to hear this lady, who should have been a lively and popular figure in the social circle of some English county town, talking serenely of the ways of humped cattle and native servants.

"And your children, how do they like the change?" he asked.

"It is healthy up here among the hills," said the mother, also looking round at the landscape and thinking doubtless of a very different scene; "they have an outdoor life and plenty of liberty. They have their ponies to ride, and there is a lake up above us that is a fine place for them to bathe and boat in; the three boys are there now, having their morning swim. The eldest is sixteen and he is allowed to have a gun, and there is some good wild-fowl shooting to be had in the reed beds at the farther end of the lake. I think that part of the joy of his shooting expeditions lies in the fact that many of the duck and plover that he comes across belong to the same species that frequent our English moors and rivers."

It was the first hint that she had given of a wistful sense of exile, the yearning for other skies, the message that a dead bird's plumage could bring across rolling seas and scorching plains.

"And the education of your boys, how do you manage for that?" asked the visitor.

"There is a young tutor living out in these wilds," said Mrs. Kerrick; "he was assistant master at a private school in Scotland, but it had to be given up when—when things changed; so many of the boys left the country. He came out to an uncle who has a small estate eight miles from here, and three days in the week he rides over to teach my boys, and three days he goes to another family living in the opposite direction. To-day he is due to come here. It is a great boon to have such an opportunity for getting the boys educated, and of course it helps him to earn a living."

"And the society of the place?" asked the Frenchman.

His hostess laughed.

"I must admit it has to be looked for with a strong pair of field-glasses," she said; "it is almost as difficult to get a good bridge four together as it would have been to get up a tennis tournament or a subscription dance in our particular corner of England. One has to ignore distances and forget fatigue if one wants to be gregarious even on a limited scale. There are one or two officials who are our chief social mainstays, but the difficulty is to muster the few available souls under the same roof at the same moment. A road will be impassable in one quarter, a pony will be lame in another, a stress of work will prevent some one else from coming, and another may be down with a touch of fever. When my little girl gave a birthday party here her only little girl guest had come twelve miles to attend it. The Forest officer happened to drop in on us that evening, so we felt quite festive."

The Frenchman's eyes grew round in wonder. He had once thought that the capital city of a Balkan kingdom was the uttermost limit of social desolation, viewed from a Parisian standpoint, and there at any rate one could get *café chantant*, tennis, picnic parties, an occasional theatre performance by a foreign troupe, now and then a travelling circus, not to speak of Court and diplomatic functions of a more or less sociable character. Here, it seemed, one went a day's journey to reach an evening's entertainment, and the chance arrival of a tired official took on the nature of a festivity. He looked round again at the rolling stretches of brown hills; before he had regarded them merely as the background to this little shut-away world, now he saw that they were foreground as well. They were everything, there was nothing else. And again his glance travelled to the face of his hostess, with its bright, pleasant eyes and smiling mouth.

"And you live here with your children," he said, "here in this wilderness? You leave England, you leave everything, for this?"

His hostess rose and took him over to the far side of the veranda. The beginnings of a garden were spread out before them, with young fruit trees and flowering shrubs, and bushes of pale pink roses. Exuberant tropical growths were interspersed with carefully-tended vestiges of plants that had evidently been brought from a more temperate climate, and had not borne the transition well. Bushes and trees and shrubs spread away for some distance, to where the ground rose in a small hillock and then fell away abruptly into bare hill-side.

"In all this garden that you see," said the Englishwoman, "there is one tree that is sacred."

"A tree?" said the Frenchman.

"A tree that we could not grow in England."

The Frenchman followed the direction of her eyes and saw a tall, bare pole at the summit of the hillock. At the same moment the sun came over the hill-tops in a deep, orange glow, and a new light stole like magic over the brown landscape. And, as if they had timed their arrival to that exact moment of sunburst, three brown-faced boys appeared under the straight, bare pole. A cord shivered and flapped, and something ran swiftly up into the air, and swung out in the breeze that blew across the hills—a blue flag with red and white crosses. The three boys bared their heads and the small girl on the veranda steps stood rigidly to attention. Far away down the hill, a young man, cantering into view round a corner of the dusty road, removed his hat in loyal salutation.

"That is why we live out here," said the Englishwoman quietly.

CHAPTER XVII

THE EVENT OF THE SEASON

IN the first swelter room of the new Osmanli Baths in Cork Street four or five recumbent individuals, in a state of moist nudity and self-respecting inertia, were smoking cigarettes or making occasional pretence of reading damp newspapers. A glass wall with a glass door shut them off from the yet more torrid regions of the further swelter chambers; another glass partition disclosed the dimly-lit vault where other patrons of the establishment had arrived at the stage of being pounded and kneaded and sluiced by Oriental-looking attendants. The splashing and trickling of taps, the flip-flap of wet slippers on a wet floor, and the low murmur of conversation, filtered through glass doors, made an appropriately drowsy accompaniment to the scene.

A new-comer fluttered into the room, beamed at one of the occupants, and settled himself with an air of elaborate languor in a long canvas chair. Cornelian Valpy was a fair young man, with perpetual surprise impinged on his countenance, and a chin that seemed to have retired from competition with the rest of his features. The beam of recognition that he had given to his friend or acquaintance subsided into a subdued but lingering simper.

"What is the matter?" drawled his neighbour lazily, dropping the end of a cigarette into a small bowl of water, and helping himself from a silver case on the table at his side.

"Matter?" said Cornelian, opening wide a pair of eyes in which unhealthy intelligence seemed to struggle in undetermined battle with utter vacuity; "why should you suppose that anything is the matter?"

"When you wear a look of idiotic complacency in a Turkish bath," said the other, "it is the more noticeable from the fact that you are wearing nothing else."

"Were you at the Shalem House dance last night?" asked Cornelian, by way of explaining his air of complacent retrospection.

"No," said the other, "but I feel as if I had been; I've been reading columns about it in the *Dawn*."

"The last event of the season," said Cornelian, "and quite one of the most amusing and lively functions that there have been."

"So the *Dawn* said; but then, as Shalem practically owns and controls that paper, its favourable opinion might be taken for granted."

"The whole idea of the Revel was quite original," said Cornelian, who was not going to have his personal narrative of the event forestalled by anything that a newspaper reporter might have given to the public; "a certain number of guests went as famous personages in the world's history, and each one was accompanied by another guest typifying the prevailing characteristic of that personage. One man went as Julius Cæsar, for instance, and had a girl typifying Ambition as his shadow, another went as Louis the Eleventh, and his companion personified Superstition. Your shadow had to be some one of the opposite sex, you see, and every alternate dance throughout the evening you danced with your shadow-partner.

Quite a clever idea; young Graf von Schnatelstein is supposed to have invented it."

"New York will be deeply beholden to him," said the other; "shadow-dances, with all manner of eccentric variations, will be the rage there for the next eighteen months."

"Some of the costumes were really sumptuous," continued Cornelian; "the Duchess of Dreyshire was magnificent as Aholibah, you never saw so many jewels on one person, only of course she didn't look dark enough for the character; she had Billy Carnset for her shadow, representing Unspeakable Depravity."

"How on earth did he manage that?"

"Oh, a blend of Beardsley and Bakst as far as get-up and costume, and of course his own personality counted for a good deal. Quite one of the successes of the evening was Leutnant von Gabelroth, as George Washington, with Joan Mardle as his shadow, typifying Inconvenient Candour. He put her down officially as Truthfulness, but every one had heard the other version."

"Good for the Gabelroth, though he does belong to the invading Horde; it's not often that any one scores off Joan."

"Another blaze of magnificence was the loud-voiced Bessimer woman, as the Goddess Juno, with peacock tails and opals all over her; she had Ronnie Storre to represent Green-eyed Jealousy. Talking of Ronnie Storre *and* of jealousy, you will naturally wonder whom Mrs. Yeovil went with. I forget what her costume was, but she'd got that dark-headed youth with her that she's been trotting round everywhere the last few days."

Cornelian's neighbour kicked him furtively on the shin, and frowned in the direction of a dark-haired youth reclining in an adjacent chair. The youth in question rose from his seat and stalked into the farther swelter room.

"So clever of him to go into the furnace room," said the unabashed Cornelian; "now if he turns scarlet all over we shall never know how much is embarrassment and how much is due to the process of being boiled. La Yeovil hasn't done badly by the exchange; he's better looking than Ronnie."

"I see that Pitherby went as Frederick the Great," said Cornelian's neighbour, fingering a sheet of the *Dawn*.

"Isn't that exactly what one would have expected Pitherby to do?" said Cornelian. "He's so desperately anxious to announce to all whom it may concern that he has written a life of that hero. He had an uninspiring-looking woman with him, supposed to represent Military Genius."

"The Spirit of Advertisement would have been more appropriate," said the other.

"The opening scene of the Revel was rather effective," continued Cornelian; "all the Shadow people reclined in the dimly-lit centre of the ball-room in an indistinguishable mass, and the human characters marched round the illuminated sides of the room to solemn processional music. Every now and then a shadow would detach itself from the mass, hail its partner by name, and glide out to join him or her in the procession. Then, when the last shadows had found their mates and every one was partnered, the lights were turned up in a blaze, the orchestra crashed out a whirl of nondescript dance music, and people just let themselves go. It was Pandemonium. Afterwards every one strutted about for half an hour or so, showing themselves off, and then the legitimate programme of dances began. There were some rather amusing incidents throughout the evening. One set of lancers was danced entirely by the Seven Deadly Sins and their human exemplars; of course seven couples were not sufficient to make up the set, so they had to bring in an eighth sin, I forget what it was."

"The sin of Patriotism would have been rather appropriate, considering who were giving the dance," said the other.

"Hush!" exclaimed Cornelian nervously. "You don't know who may overhear you in a place like this. You'll get yourself into trouble."

"Wasn't there some rather daring new dance of the 'bunny-hug' variety?" asked the indiscreet one.

"The 'Cubby-Cuddle,'" said Cornelian; "three or four adventurous couples danced it towards the end of the evening."

"The *Dawn* says that without being strikingly new it was strikingly modern."

"The best description I can give of it," said Cornelian, "is summed up in the comment of the Gräfin von Tolb when she saw it being danced: 'if they *really* love each other I suppose it doesn't matter.' By the way," he added with apparent indifference, "is there any detailed account of my costume in the *Dawn*?"

His companion laughed cynically.

"As if you hadn't read everything that the *Dawn* and the other morning papers have to say about the ball hours ago."

"The naked truth should be avoided in a Turkish bath," said Cornelian; "kindly assume that I've only had time to glance at the weather forecast and the news from China."

"Oh, very well," said the other; "your costume isn't described; you simply come amid a host of others as 'Mr. Cornelian Valpy, resplendent as the Emperor Nero; with him Miss Kate Lerra, typifying Insensate Vanity.' Many hard things have been said of Nero, but his unkindest critics have never accused him of resembling you in feature. Until some very clear evidence is produced I shall refuse to believe it."

Cornelian was proof against these shafts; leaning back gracefully in his chair he launched forth into that detailed description of his last night's attire which the *Dawn* had so unaccountably failed to supply.

"I wore a tunic of white Nepaulese silk, with a collar of pearls, real pearls. Round my waist I had a girdle of twisted serpents in beaten gold, studded all over with amethysts. My sandals were of gold, laced with scarlet thread, and I had seven bracelets of gold on each arm. Round my head I had a wreath of golden laurel leaves set with scarlet berries, and hanging over my left shoulder was a silk robe of mulberry purple, broidered with the signs of the zodiac in gold and scarlet; I had it made specially for the occasion. At my side I had an ivory-sheathed dagger, with a green jade handle, hung in a green Cordova leather——"

At this point of the recital his companion rose softly, flung his cigarette end into the little water-bowl, and passed into the farther swelter room. Cornelian Valpy was left, still clothed in a look of ineffable complacency, still engaged, in all probability, in reclothing himself in the finery of the previous evening.

CHAPTER XVIII

THE DEAD WHO DO NOT UNDERSTAND

THE pale light of a November afternoon faded rapidly into the dusk of a November evening. Far over the countryside housewives put up their cottage shutters, lit their lamps, and made the customary remark that the days were drawing in. In barnyards and poultry-runs the greediest pullets made a final tour of inspection, picking up the stray remaining morsels of the evening meal, and then, with much scrambling and squawking, sought the places on the roosting-pole that they thought should belong to them. Labourers working in yard and field began to turn their thoughts homeward or tavernward as the case might be. And through the cold squelching slush of a water-logged meadow a weary, bedraggled, but unbeaten fox stiffly picked his way, climbed a high bramble-grown bank, and flung himself into the sheltering labyrinth of a stretching tangle of woods. The pack of fierce-mouthed things that had rattled him from copse and gorse-cover, along fallow and plough, hedgerow and wooded lane, for nigh on an hour, and had pressed hard on his life for the last few minutes, receded suddenly into the background of his experiences. The cold, wet meadow, the thick mask of woods, and the oncoming dusk had stayed the chase—and the fox had outstayed it. In a short time he would fall mechanically to licking off some of the mud that caked on his weary pads; in a shorter time horsemen and hounds would have drawn off kennelward and homeward.

Yeovil rode through the deepening twilight, relying chiefly on his horse to find its way in the network of hedge-bordered lanes that presumably led to a high road or to some human habitation. He was desperately tired after his day's hunting, a legacy of weakness that the fever had bequeathed to him, but even though he could scarcely sit upright in his saddle his mind dwelt complacently on the day's sport and looked forward to the snug cheery comfort that awaited him at his hunting-box. There was a charm, too, even for a tired man, in the eerie stillness of the lone twilight land through which he was passing, a grey shadow-hung land which seemed to have been emptied of all things that belonged to the daytime, and filled with a lurking, moving life of which one knew nothing be-yond the sense that it was there. There, and very near. If there had been wood-gods and wicked-eyed fauns in the sunlit groves and hill-sides of old Hellas, surely there were watchful, living things of kindred mould in this dusk-hidden wilderness of field and hedge and coppice.

It was Yeovil's third or fourth day with the hounds, with-out taking into account a couple of mornings' cub-hunting. Already he felt that he had been doing nothing different from this all his life. His foreign travels, his illness, his recent weeks in London, they were part of a tapestried background that had very slight and distant connexion with his present existence. Of the future he tried to think with greater energy and deter-mination. For this winter, at any rate, he would hunt and do a little shooting, entertain a few of his neighbours and make friends with any congenial fellow-sportsmen who might be within reach. Next year things would be different; he would have had time to look round him, to regain something of his aforetime vigour of mind and body. Next year, when the hunting season was over, he would set about finding out whether there was any nobler game for him to take a hand in. He would enter into correspondence with old friends who had gone out into the tropics and the backwoods—he would do something.

So he told himself, but he knew thoroughly well that he had found his level. He had ceased to struggle against the fasci-nation of his present surroundings. The slow, quiet comfort and interest of country life appealed with enervating force to the man whom death had half conquered. The pleasures of the chase, well-provided for in every detail, and dovetailed in with the assured luxury of a well-ordered, well-staffed establishment, were exactly what he wanted and exactly what his life down here afforded him. He was experiencing, too, that passionate recurring devotion to an old loved scene that comes at times to men who have travelled far and willingly up and down the world. He was very much at home. The alien standard floating over Buckingham Palace, the Crown of Charlemagne on public buildings and official documents, the grey ships of war riding in Plymouth Bay and Southampton Water with a flag at their stern that older generations of Britons had never looked on, these things seemed far away and inconsequent amid the hedgerows and woods and fallows of the East Wessex country. Horse and hound-craft, harvest, game broods, the planting and felling of timber, the rearing and selling of stock, the letting of grasslands, the care of fisheries, the upkeep of markets and fairs, they were the things that immediately mattered. And Yeovil saw himself, in moments of disgust and self-accusation, settling down into this life of rustic littleness, concerned over the late nesting of a partridge or the defective draining of a loose-box, hugely busy over affairs that a gardener's boy might grapple with, ignoring the struggle-cry that went up, low and bitter and wistful, from a dethroned dispossessed race, in whose glories he had gloried, in whose struggle he lent no hand. In what way, he asked himself in such moments, would his life be better than the life of that parody of manhood who upholstered his rooms with art hangings and rosewood furniture and babbled over the effect?

The lanes seemed interminable and without aim or object except to bisect one another; gates and gaps disclosed nothing in the way of a landmark, and the night began to draw down in increasing shades of darkness. Presently, however, the tired horse quickened its pace, swung round a sharp corner into a broader roadway, and stopped with an air of thankful expectancy at the low doorway of a wayside inn. A cheerful glow of light streamed from the windows and door, and a brighter glare came from the other side of the road, where a large motor-car was being got ready for an immediate start. Yeovil tumbled stiffly out of his saddle, and in answer to the loud rattle of his hunting crop on the open door the innkeeper and two or three hangers-on hurried out to attend to the wants of man and beast. Flour and water for the horse and something hot for himself were Yeovil's first concern, and then he began to clamour for geographical information. He was rather dismayed to find that the cumulative opinions of those whom he consulted, and of several others who joined unbidden in the discussion, placed his destination at nothing nearer than nine miles. Nine miles of dark and hilly country road for a tired man on a tired horse assumed enormous, far-stretching proportions, and although he dimly remembered that he had asked a guest to dinner for that evening he began to wonder whether the wayside inn possessed anything endurable in the way of a bedroom. The landlord interrupted his desperate speculations with a really brilliant effort of suggestion. There was a gentleman in the bar, he said, who was going in a motor-car in the direction for which Yeovil was bound, and who would no doubt be willing to drop him at his destination; the gentleman had also been out with the hounds. Yeovil's horse could be stabled at the inn and fetched home by a groom the next morning. A hurried embassy to the bar parlour resulted in the news that the motorist would be delighted to be of assistance to a fellow-sportsman. Yeovil gratefully accepted the chance that had so obligingly come his way, and hastened to superintend the housing of his horse in its night's quarters. When he had duly seen to the tired animal's comfort and foddering he returned to the roadway, where a young man in hunting garb and a liveried chauffeur were standing by the side of the waiting car.

"I am so very pleased to be of some use to you, Mr. Yeovil," said the car-owner, with a polite bow, and Yoevil recognized the young Leutnant von Gabelroth, who had been present at the musical afternoon at Berkshire Street. He had doubtless seen him at the meet that morning, but in his hunting kit he had escaped his observation.

"I, too, have been out with the hounds," the young man continued; "I have left my horse at the 'Crow and Sceptre' at Dolford. You are living at Black Dene, are you not? I can take you right past your door, it is all on my way."

Yeovil hung back for a moment, overwhelmed with vexation and embarrassment, but it was too late to cancel the arrangement he had unwittingly entered into, and he was constrained to put himself under obligation to the young officer with the best grace he could muster. After all, he reflected, he had met him under his own roof as his wife's guest. He paid his reckoning to mine host, tipped the stable lad who had helped him with his horse, and took his place beside von Gabelroth in the car.

As they glided along the dark roadway and the young German reeled off a string of comments on the incidents of the day's sport, Yeovil lay back amid his comfortable wraps and weighed the measure of his humiliation. It was Cicely's gospel that one should know what one wanted in life and take good care that one got what one wanted. Could he apply that test of achievement to his own life? Was this what he really wanted to be doing, pursuing his uneventful way as a country squire, sharing even his sports and pastimes with men of the nation that had conquered and enslaved his Fatherland?

The car slackened its pace somewhat as they went through a small hamlet, past a schoolhouse, past a rural police-station with the new monogram over its notice-board, past a church with a little tree-grown graveyard. There, in a corner, among wild-rose bushes and tall yews, lay some of Yeovil's own kinsfolk, who had lived in these parts and hunted and found life pleasant in the days that were not so very long ago. Whenever he went past that quiet little gathering-place of the dead Yeovil was wont to raise his hat in mute affectionate salutation to those who were now only memories in his family; tonight he somehow omitted the salute and turned his head the other way. It was as though the dead of his race saw and wondered.

Three or four months ago the thing he was doing would have seemed an impossibility, now it was actually happening; he was listening to the gay, courteous, tactful chatter of his young companion, laughing now and then at some joking remark, answering some question of interest, learning something

of hunting ways and traditions in von Gabelroth's own country. And when the car turned in at the gate of the hunting
lodge and drew up at the steps the laws of hospitality demanded
that Yeovil should ask his benefactor of the road to come in
for a few minutes and drink something a little better than the
wayside inn had been able to supply. The young officer spent
the best part of a half-hour in Yeovil's snuggery, examining
and discussing the trophies of rifle and collecting gun that covered the walls. He had a good knowledge of woodcraft, and
the beasts and birds of Siberian forests and North African
deserts were to him new pages in a familiar book. Yeovil
found himself discoursing eagerly with his chance guest on the
European distribution and local variation of such and such
a species, recounting peculiarities in its habits and incidents of
its pursuit and capture. If the cold observant eyes of Lady
Shalem could have rested on the scene she would have hailed
it as another root-fibre thrown out by the *fait accompli*.

Yeovil closed the hall door on his departing visitor, and
closed his mind on the crowd of angry and accusing thoughts
that were waiting to intrude themselves. His valet had already
got his bath in readiness and in a few minutes the tired hunts-
man was forgetting weariness and the consciousness of outside things in the languorous abandonment that steam and hot
water induce. Brain and limbs seemed to lay themselves down
in a contented waking sleep, the world that was beyond the
bathroom walls dropped away into a far unreal distance; only
somewhere through the steam clouds pierced a hazy consciousness that a dinner, well chosen, was being well cooked, and
would presently be well served—and right well appreciated.
That was the lure to drag the bather away from the Nirvana
land of warmth and steam. The stimulating after-effect of the
bath took its due effect, and Yeovil felt that he was now much
less tired and enormously hungry. A cheery fire burned in his
dressing-room and a lively black kitten helped him to dress,
and incidentally helped him to require a new tassel to the cord
of his dressing-gown. As he finished his toilet and the kitten
finished its sixth and most notable attack on the tassel a ring
was heard at the front door, and a moment later a loud,

hearty, and unmistakably hungry voice resounded in the hall. It belonged to the local doctor, who had also taken part in the day's run and had been bidden to enliven the evening meal with the entertainment of his inexhaustible store of sporting and social reminiscences. He knew the countryside and the countryfolk inside out, and he was a living unwritten chronicle of the East Wessex hunt. His conversation seemed exactly the right accompaniment to the meal; his stories brought glimpses of wet hedgerows, stiff ploughlands, leafy spinneys and muddy brooks in among the rich old Worcester and Georgian silver of the dinner service, the glow and crackle of the wood fire, the pleasant succession of well-cooked dishes and mellow wines. The world narrowed itself down again to a warm, drowsy-scented dining-room, with a productive hinterland of kitchen and cellar beyond it, and beyond that an important outer world of loose-box and harness-room and stable-yard; farther again a dark hushed region where pheasants roosted and owls flitted and foxes prowled.

Yeovil sat and listened to story after story of the men and women and horses of the neighbourhood; even the foxes seemed to have a personality, some of them, and a personal history. It was a little like Hans Andersen, he decided, and a little like the *Reminiscences of an Irish R.M.*, and perhaps just a little like some of the more probable adventures of Baron Munchausen. The newer stories were evidently true to the smallest detail, the earlier ones had altered somewhat in repetition, as plants and animals vary under domestication.

And all the time there was one topic that was never touched on. Of half the families mentioned it was necessary to add the qualifying information that they "used to live" at such and such a place; the countryside knew them no longer. Their properties were for sale or had already passed into the hands of strangers. But neither man cared to allude to the grinning shadow that sat at the feast and sent an icy chill now and again through the cheeriest jest and most jovial story. The brisk run with the hounds that day had stirred and warmed their pulses; it was an evening for comfortable forgetting.

Later that night, in the stillness of his bedroom, with the

dwindling noises of a retiring household dropping off one by one into ordered silence, a door shutting here, a fire being raked out there, the thoughts that had been held away came crowding in. The body was tired, but the brain was not, and Yeovil lay awake with his thoughts for company. The world grew suddenly wide again, filled with the significance of things that mattered, held by the actions of men that mattered. Hunting-box and stable and gun-room dwindled to a mere pin-point in the universe, there were other larger, more absorbing things on which the mind dwelt. There was the grey cold sea outside Dover and Portsmouth and Cork, where the great grey ships of war rocked and swung with the tides, where the sailors sang, in doggerel English, that bitter-sounding adaptation, "Germania rules t'e waves," where the flag of a World-Power floated for the world to see. And in oven-like cities of India there were men who looked out at the white sun-glare, the heat-baked dust, the welter of crowded streets, who listened to the unceasing chorus of harsh-throated crows, the strident creaking of cart-wheels, the buzz and drone of insect swarms and the rattle call of the tree lizards; men whose thoughts went hungrily to the cool grey skies and wet turf and moist ploughlands of an English hunting country, men whose memories listened yearningly to the music of a deep-throated hound and the call of a game-bird in the stubble. Yeovil had secured for himself the enjoyment of the things for which these men hungered; he had known what he wanted in life, slowly and with hesitation, yet nevertheless surely, he had arrived at the achievement of his unconfessed desires. Here, installed under his own roof-tree, with as good horse-flesh in his stable as man could desire, with sport lying almost at his door, with his wife ready to come down and help him to entertain his neighbours, Murrey Yeovil had found the life that he wanted—and was accursed in his own eyes. He argued with himself, and palliated and explained, but he knew why he had turned his eyes away that evening from the little graveyard under the trees; one cannot explain things to the dead.

CHAPTER XIX

THE LITTLE FOXES

"Take us the foxes, the little foxes, that spoil the vines"

ON a warm and sunny May afternoon, some ten months since Yeovil's return from his Siberian wanderings and sickness, Cicely sat at a small table in the open-air restaurant in Hyde Park, finishing her after-luncheon coffee and listening to the meritorious performance of the orchestra. Opposite her sat Larry Meadowfield, absorbed for the moment in the slow enjoyment of a cigarette, which also was not without its short-lived merits. Larry was a well-dressed youngster, who was, in Cicely's opinion, distinctly good to look on—an opinion which the boy himself obviously shared. He had the healthy, well-cared-for appearance of a country-dweller who has been turned into a town dandy without suffering in the process. His blue-black hair, growing very low down on a broad forehead, was brushed back in a smoothness that gave his head the appearance of a rain-polished sloe; his eyebrows were two dark smudges and his large violet-grey eyes expressed the restful good temper of an animal whose immediate requirements have been satisfied. The lunch had been an excellent one, and it was jolly to feed out of doors in the warm spring air—the only drawback to the arrangement being the absence of mirrors. However, if he could not look at himself a great many people could look at him.

Cicely listened to the orchestra as it jerked and strutted through a fantastic dance measure, and as she listened she looked appreciatively at the boy on the other side of the table, whose soul for the moment seemed to be in his cigarette. Her scheme of life, knowing just what you wanted and taking good care that you got it, was justifying itself by results. Ronnie, grown tiresome with success, had not been difficult to replace, and no one in her world had had the satisfaction of being able to condole with her on the undesirable experience of a long interregnum. To feminine acquaintances with fewer advantages of purse and brains and looks she might figure as "that Yeovil woman," but never had she given them justification to allude to her as "poor Cicely Yeovil." And Murrey, dear old soul, had cooled down, as she had hoped and wished, from his white heat of disgust at the things that she had prepared herself to accept philosophically. A new chapter of their married life and man-and-woman friendship had opened; many a rare gallop they had had together that winter, many a cheery dinner gathering and long bridge evening in the cozy hunting-lodge. Though he still hated the new London and held himself aloof from most of her Town set, yet he had not shown himself rigidly intolerant of the sprinkling of Teuton sportsmen who hunted and shot down in his part of the country.

The orchestra finished its clicking and caracoling and was accorded a short clatter of applause.

"The *Danse Macabre*," said Cicely to her companion; "one of Saint-Saëns' best known pieces."

"Is it?" said Larry indifferently; "I'll take your word for it. 'Fraid I don't know much about music."

"You dear boy, that's just what I like in you," said Cicely; "you're such a delicious young barbarian."

"Am I?" said Larry. "I dare say. I suppose you know."

Larry's father had been a brilliantly clever man who had married a brilliantly handsome woman; the Fates had not had the least intention that Larry should take after both parents.

"The fashion of having one's lunch in the open air has quite caught on this season," said Cicely; "one sees everybody here on a fine day. There is Lady Bailquist over there. She used to be Lady Shalem, you know, before her husband got the earldom—to be more correct, before she got it for him. I suppose she is all agog to see the great review."

It was in fact precisely the absorbing topic of the forthcoming Boy-Scout march-past that was engaging the Countess of Bailquist's earnest attention at the moment.

"It is going to be an historical occasion," she was saying to Sir Leonard Pitherby (whose services to literature had up to the present received only a half-measure of recognition); "if it miscarries it will be a serious set-back for the *fait accompli*. If it is a success it will be the biggest step forward in the path of reconciliation between the two races that has yet been taken. It will mean that the younger generation is on our side—not all, of course, but some, that is all we can expect at present, and that will be enough to work on."

"Supposing the Scouts hang back and don't turn up in any numbers," said Sir Leonard anxiously.

"That of course is the danger," said Lady Bailquist quietly; "probably two-thirds of the available strength will hold back, but a third or even a sixth would be enough; it would redeem the parade from the calamity of fiasco, and it would be a nucleus to work on for the future. That is what we want, a good start, a preliminary rally. It is the first step that counts, that is why today's event is of such importance."

"Of course, of course, the first step on the road," assented Sir Leonard.

"I can assure you," continued Lady Bailquist, "that nothing has been left undone to rally the Scouts to the new order of things. Special privileges have been showered on them, alone among all the cadet corps they have been allowed to retain their organization, a decoration of merit has been instituted for them, a large hostelry and gymnasium has been provided for them in Westminster, His Majesty's youngest son is to be their Scoutmaster-in-Chief, a great athletic meeting is to be held for them each year, with valuable prizes, three or four hundred of them are to be taken every summer, free of charge, for a holiday in the Bavarian Highlands and the Baltic Seaboard; besides this the parent of every scout who obtains the medal for efficiency is to be exempted from part of the new war taxation that the people are finding so burdensome."

"One certainly cannot say that they have not had attractions held out to them," said Sir Leonard.

"It is a special effort," said Lady Bailquist; "it is worth making an effort for. They are going to be the Janissaries of the Empire; the younger generation knocking at the doors of progress, and thrusting back the bars and bolts of old racial prejudices. I tell you, Sir Leonard, it will be an historic moment when the first corps of those little khaki-clad boys swings through the gates of the Park."

"When do they come?" asked the baronet, catching something of his companion's zeal.

"The first detachment is due to arrive at three," said Lady Bailquist, referring to a small time-table of the afternoon's proceedings; "three, punctually, and the others will follow in rapid succession. The Emperor and Suite will arrive at two-fifty and take up their positions at the saluting base—over there, where the big flag-staff has been set up. The boys will come in by Hyde Park Corner, the Marble Arch, and the Albert Gate, according to their districts, and form in one big column over there, where the little flags are pegged out. Then the young Prince will inspect them and lead them past His Majesty."

"Who will be with the Imperial party?" asked Sir Leonard.

"Oh, it is to be an important affair; everything will be done to emphasize the significance of the occasion," said Lady Bailquist, again consulting her programme. "The King of Württemberg, and two of the Bavarian royal Princes, an Abyssinian Envoy who is over here—he will lend a touch of picturesque barbarism to the scene—the general commanding the London district and a whole lot of other military bigwigs, and the Austrian, Italian and Roumanian military attachés."

She reeled off the imposing list of notables with an air of quiet satisfaction. Sir Leonard made mental notes of personages to whom he might send presentation copies of his new work *Frederick-William, the Great Elector, a Popular Biography*, as a souvenir of today's auspicious event.

"It is nearly a quarter to three now," he said; "let us get a good position before the crowd gets thicker."

"Come along to my car, it is just opposite to the saluting base," said her ladyship; "I have a police pass that will let us through. We'll ask Mrs. Yeovil and her young friend to join us."

Larry excused himself from joining the party; he had a barbarian's reluctance to assisting at an Imperial triumph.

"I think I'll push off to the swimming-bath," he said to Cicely; "see you again about tea-time."

Cicely walked with Lady Bailquist and the literary baronet towards the crowd of spectators, which was steadily growing in dimensions. A newsboy ran in front of them displaying a poster with the intelligence "Essex wickets fall rapidly"—a semblance of county cricket still survived under the new order of things. Near the saluting base some thirty or forty motor-cars were drawn up in line, and Cicely and her companions exchanged greetings with many of the occupants.

"A lovely day for the review, isn't it?" cried the Gräfin von Tolb, breaking off her conversation with Herr Rebinok, the little Pomeranian banker, who was sitting by her side. "Why haven't you brought young Mr. Meadowfield? Such a nice boy. I wanted him to come and sit in my carriage and talk to me."

"He doesn't talk, you know," said Cicely; "he's only brilliant to look at."

"Well, I could have looked at him," said the Gräfin.

"There'll be thousands of other boys to look at presently," said Cicely, laughing at the old woman's frankness.

"Do you think there will be thousands?" asked the Gräfin, with an anxious lowering of the voice; "really, thousands? Hundreds, perhaps; there is some uncertainty. Every one is not sanguine."

"Hundreds, anyway," said Cicely.

The Gräfin turned to the little banker and spoke to him rapidly and earnestly in German.

"It is most important that we should consolidate our position in this country; we must coax the younger generation over by degrees, we must disarm their hostility. We cannot afford to be always on the watch in this quarter; it is a source of weakness, and we cannot afford to be weak. This Slav upheaval in south-eastern Europe is becoming a serious menace. Have you seen today's telegrams from Agram? They are bad reading. There is no computing the extent of this movement."

"It is directed against us," said the banker.

"Agreed," said the Gräfin; "it is in the nature of things that it must be against us. Let us have no illusions. Within the next ten years, sooner perhaps, we shall be faced with a crisis which will be only a beginning. We shall need all our strength; that is why we cannot afford to be weak over here. Today is an important day; I confess I am anxious."

"Hark! The kettledrums!" exclaimed the commanding voice of Lady Bailquist. "His Majesty is coming. Quick, bundle into the car."

The crowd behind the police-kept lines surged expectantly into closer formation; spectators hurried up from side-walks and stood craning their necks above the shoulders of earlier arrivals.

Through the archway at Hyde Park Corner came a resplendent cavalcade with a swirl of colour and rhythmic movement and a crash of exultant music; life-guards with gleaming helmets, a detachment of Württemberg lancers with a flutter of black and yellow pennons, a rich medley of staff uniforms, a prancing array of princely horsemen, the Imperial Standard, and the King of Prussia, Great Britain, and Ireland, Emperor of the West. It was the most imposing display that Londoners had seen since the catastrophe.

Slowly, grandly, with thunder of music and beat of hoofs, the procession passed through the crowd, across the sward towards the saluting base, slowly the eagle standard, charged with the leopards, lion and harp of the conquered kingdoms, rose mast-high on the flag-staff and fluttered in the breeze, slowly and with military precision the troops and Suite took up their position round the central figure of the great pageant. Trumpets and kettledrums suddenly ceased their music, and in a moment there rose in their stead an eager buzz of comment from the nearest spectators.

"How well the young Prince looks in his scout uniform. . . ." "The King of Württemberg is a much younger man than I thought he was. . . ." "Is that a Prussian or Bavarian uniform, there on the right, the man on a black horse? . . ." "Neither, it's Austrian, the Austrian military attaché. . . ." "That is von Stoppel talking to His Majesty; he organized the Boy Scouts in Germany, you know. . . ." "His Majesty is looking very pleased." "He has reason to look pleased; this is a great event in the history of the two countries. It marks a new epoch. . . ." "Oh, do you see the Abyssinian Envoy?

What a picturesque figure he makes. How well he sits his horse. . . ." "That is the Grand Duke of Baden's nephew, talking to the King of Württemberg now."

On the buzz and chatter of the spectators fell suddenly three sound strokes, distant, measured, sinister; the clang of a clock striking three.

"Three o'clock and not a boy scout within sight or hearing!" exclaimed the loud ringing voice of Joan Mardle; "one can usually hear their drums and trumpets a couple of miles away."

"There is the traffic to get through," said Sir Leonard Pitherby in an equally high-pitched voice; "and of course," he added vaguely, "it takes some time to get the various units together. One must give them a few minutes' grace."

Lady Bailquist said nothing, but her restless watchful eyes were turned first to Hyde Park Corner and then in the direction of the Marble Arch, back again to Hyde Park Corner. Only the dark lines of the waiting crowd met her view, with the yellow newspaper placards flitting in and out, announcing to an indifferent public the fate of Essex wickets. As far as her searching eyes could travel the green stretch of tree and sward remained unbroken, save by casual loiterers. No small brown columns appeared, no drum-beat came throbbing up from the distance. The little flags pegged out to mark the positions of the awaited scout-corps fluttered in meaningless isolation on the empty parade ground.

His Majesty was talking unconcernedly with one of his officers, the foreign attachés looked steadily between their chargers' ears, as though nothing in particular was hanging in the balance, the Abyssinian Envoy displayed an untroubled serenity which was probably genuine. Elsewhere among the Suite was a perceptible fidget, the more obvious because it was elaborately cloaked. Among the privileged onlookers drawn up near the saluting point the fidgeting was more unrestrained.

"Six minutes past three, and not a sign of them!" exclaimed Joan Mardle, with the explosive articulation of one who cannot any longer hold back a truth.

"Hark!" said some one; "I hear trumpets!"

There was an instant concentration of listening, a straining of eyes.

It was only the toot of a passing motor-car. Even Sir Leonard Pitherby, with the eye of faith, could not locate as much as a cloud of dust on the Park horizon.

And now another sound was heard, a sound difficult to define, without beginning, without dimension; the growing murmur of a crowd waking to a slowly dawning sensation.

"I wish the band would strike up an air," said the Gräfin von Tolb fretfully; "it is stupid waiting here in silence."

Joan fingered her watch, but she made no further remark; she realized that no amount of malicious comment could be so dramatically effective now as the slow slipping away of the intolerable seconds.

The murmur from the crowd grew in volume. Some satirical wit started whistling an imitation of an advancing fife and drum band; others took it up and the air resounded with the shrill music of a phantom army on the march. The mock throbbing of drum and squealing of fife rose and fell above the packed masses of spectators, but no answering echo came from beyond the distant trees. Like mushrooms in the night a muster of uniformed police and plain clothes detectives sprang into evidence on all sides; whatever happened there must be no disloyal demonstration. The whistlers and mockers were pointedly invited to keep silence, and one or two addresses were taken.

Under the trees, well at the back of the crowd, a young man stood watching the long stretch of road along which the Scouts should come. Something had drawn him there, against his will, to witness the Imperial Triumph, to watch the writing of yet another chapter in the history of his country's submission to an accepted fact. And now a dull flush crept into his grey face; a look that was partly new-born hope and resurrected pride, partly remorse and shame, burned in his eyes. Shame, the choking, searing shame of self-reproach that cannot be reasoned away, was dominant in his heart. *He* had laid down his arms— there were others who had never hoisted the flag of surrender. He had given up the fight and joined the ranks of the hopelessly subservient; in thousands of English homes throughout the land there were young hearts that had not forgotten, had not compounded, would not yield.

The younger generation had barred the door.

And in the pleasant May sunshine the Eagle standard floated and flapped, the black and yellow pennons shifted restlessly, Emperor and Princes, Generals and guards, sat stiffly in their saddles, and waited.

And waited. . . .

The Westminster Alice

Illustrated by F. CARRUTHERS GOULD

*With apologies to Sir John Tenniel and
to everybody else concerned*

First published, 1902

FOREWORD

by J. A. SPENDER

SO far as the *Westminster Gazette* was concerned, "Saki" was the discovery of F. C. G. How they met, I don't know, but I have a clear recollection of Gould's bringing him to my room at the Office somewhere about the year 1900 and starting then and there on a discussion of articles which the one was to write and the other to illustrate. "Saki" left most of the talking to Gould, and at the beginning one had to dig hard to get a word out of him. But the word when it came was pungent and original, and in a few minutes I came to the conclusion that Gould was justified in his "find." The scheme suggested was that of *The Westminster Alice*—dealing with the South African war and politics in general—republished in this volume, and I own that I had misgivings about it. Parodies of the famous original had several times been submitted to me (as I suppose to most editors) and nearly all had been dismal failures. Such things must either succeed perfectly or fail lamentably, and to succeed perfectly meant not merely copying the form but catching the spirit of the inimitable fantastic original.

I cannot imagine any one doubting that "Saki" is one of the few who have succeeded. Political parodies are generally dead within a few months of their first appearance, but *The Westminster Alice* is alive and sparkling after twenty-five years. In several of the sections it seems almost of no importance to recover the political allusions. The White Knight of "Alice in Pall Mall" remains the symbol of all the War-Ministers who never expected war, and it is a mere accident that he wears the face of the honoured veteran who happened to be in the saddle in 1899 when the unexpected came. His astonishing steed swathed in red-tape steps straight out of the old stable in Pall Mall with trappings devised by generations of Royal Dukes and plumed veterans. The Knight has the pensive melancholy broken by sudden happy thoughts that is so endearing in his prototype. There is perhaps one touch which needs a little explanation. The reader who looks close will see hanging from the saddle a book labelled, *Bloch, Is War Impossible?* Emile Bloch, the Belgian strategical writer, had lately written an elaborate book in eleven volumes to prove that modern warfare on any large scale would be extraordinarily different from what most of the General Staffs supposed it would be, and W. T. Stead in his lively way had peptonized the eleven volumes into one and issued it with the title, *Is War Impossible?* The appearance of "Alice in Pall Mall" with Stead's title in the cartoon moved M. Bloch to send me the whole eleven volumes to prove that he had said not that war was impossible, but something extremely different, and, as events proved, something extremely wise and prescient. I was glad that the correction came after and not before the publication of *The Westminster Alice,* for, if injustice was done to M. Bloch, by the same token an opening was given to "Saki" for one of his most brilliant strokes:

> "You see I had read a book written by some one to prove that warfare under modern conditions is impossible. You may imagine how disturbing that was to a man of my profession. Many men would have thrown up the whole thing and gone home. But I grappled with the situation. You will never guess what I did."
>
> Alice pondered. "You went to war, of course———"
>
> "Yes, *but not under modern conditions.*"
>
> The Knight stopped his horse so that he might enjoy the full effect of this announcement.
>
> "Now, for instance," he continued kindly, seeing that Alice had not recovered her breath, "you observe this little short-range gun that I have hanging to my saddle? Why do you suppose that I have sent out guns of that particular kind? Because, if they happened to fall into the hands of the enemy, they'd be very little use to him. That was my own invention."

Of the many political squibs I can remember none had so immediate and complete a success as this. It was quoted everywhere, and the whole town joined in the laugh. The public at this time had long got over its "Mafficking" and was thoroughly annoyed at the mismanagement of the Boer War and its apparently interminable protraction in the guerrilla stage. But the occasion was not so tragic as to forbid the play of this delicate raillery.

If "Alice in Pall Mall" explains itself, the same may be said of "Alice at Lambeth." Mr. Samuel Smith, who is stirring the Protestant pot in Gould's picture, and Archbishop Temple who makes an inimitable Duchess, have indeed passed from the scene—passed, let us hope, to where Protestant and Anglo-Catholic are at rest—but there is the same trouble today in the Lambeth Kitchen as at the beginning of the century. Temple was one of Gould's favourites, and the benevolent Primate of these times is less tempting to the caricaturist, though scarcely less afflicted than his predecessor. "Alice at St. Stephen's" is in the same way perennial. It was addressed to Mr. Gully and meant as a delicate rebuke of certain prim lawyer-like habits which had got on the nerves of the private member, but it will do for any Speaker from any member, and is a model of the subtle tactics which must be employed by critics of that illustrious functionary, if they do not wish to be haled to the bar of the House of Commons. The other sections are more topical, and though I have added a few notes to the text, something may be said here to explain the circumstances in which they were written.

The first section belongs to July, 1900, and reflects the general uneasiness at the continuance of the Boer War after the taking of Pretoria. It had been a moot point since the war broke out whether the public was angrier with the Boers, the pro-Boers or the Government, and, so far as the Government was concerned, much of the irritation fell upon Mr. Arthur Balfour, the "Ineptitude" of "Saki's" satire. Herein, as I think the more intimate records will show, Mr. Balfour suffered some wrong, but he had got labelled as the "philosophic doubter" and the phrase summed up all that the public found most irritating in the attitude of the Government, its air of being the victim of circumstances which no wisdom could have been expected to foresee, its apparently genuine surprise as the enemy proved to possess guns and to be well-mounted and extremely mobile and elusive. The Head of the Government, the illustrious Lord Salisbury, kept himself so entirely to himself during these months that it was easy to present him as fast asleep, and eventually as the somnolent dormouse of the Mad Hatter's tea-party. In the meantime the formidable Red Queen (Mr. Joseph Chamberlain) goes raging and tearing through the wood and her strident voice, demanding that every one shall wear khaki, sends a shiver down the spines of her more sedate and fastidious colleagues.

There follows the "khaki election" of 1900, and the Wonderland creatures, having triumphed over critics and satirists, are more complacent than ever. They are hard put to it to explain why the war, which they said was over with the taking of Pretoria, should still go on, but when Alice grows too inquisitive they fly to Christian Science or fall asleep. But "Saki" now gets a new opportunity with the Liberal Opposition, which all through 1900 and 1901 was in most evil plight between its retired leaders and its actual leaders, its "Lib. Imps" (Liberal Imperialists) and its pro-Boers. Campbell-Bannerman had not yet won the unique authority that he afterwards obtained, and in "Saki's" hands he is the bewildered White King vainly trying to record his emotions, while his followers go streaming after the Red King (Lord Rosebery) who after a long sleep in "rose-coloured armour that had got a little rusty" had woke up with a crash in his famous Chesterfield speech (December 16, 1901). The final picture carries back to the singular controversy which arose over the interpretation of that speech, the various gardeners (Sir William Harcourt, Sir Edward Grey and Mr. Lloyd George) each endeavouring to paint the rose in his own colour. "Saki" was not of our political complexion, and, having had his fling at his own party, I rather think he enjoyed the opportunity of getting a little of his own back with these gentle gibes.

I cannot refrain from adding a word about Gould's part. Gould catches the spirit of Tenniel, though in his own rougher manner, with the same felicity as "Saki" does that of Lewis Carroll. I well remember the pleasure of both in this collaboration and their long consultations before the result was produced.

Gould's frontispiece seems to me still a little masterpiece, and I hardly know where one could find concentrated in a small space so much of the character and flavour of the period dealt with in this satire.

CONTENTS FOR
THE WESTMINSTER ALICE

These sketches were first published
in the *Westminster Gazette* between
July 25, 1900, and January 24, 1902

THE WESTMINSTER ALICE

INTRODUCTION

"ALICE," Child with dreaming eyes,
    Noting things that come to pass
Turvey-wise in Wonderland
    Backwards through a Looking-Glass.

Figures flit across thy dream,
    Muddle through and flicker out
Some in cocksure blessedness,
    Some in Philosophic Doubt.

Some in brackets, some in sulks,
    Some with latchkeys on the ramp,
Living (in a sort of peace)
    In a Concentration Camp.

Party moves on either side,
    Checks and feints that don't deceive,
Knights and Bishops, Pawns and all,
    In a game of Make-Believe.

Things that fall contrariwise,
    Difficult to understand
Darkly through a Looking-Glass
    Turvey-wise in Wonderland.

"HAVE you ever seen an Ineptitude?" [1] asked the Cheshire Cat suddenly; the Cat was nothing if not abrupt.

"Not in real life," said Alice. "Have you any about here?"

"A few," answered the Cat comprehensively. "Over there, for instance," it added, contracting its pupils to the requisite focus, "is the most perfect specimen we have."

Alice followed the direction of its glance and noticed for the first time a figure sitting in a very uncomfortable attitude on nothing in particular. Alice had no time to wonder how it managed to do it, she was busy taking in the appearance of the creature, which was something like a badly-written note of interrogation and something like a guillemot, and seemed to have been trying to preen its rather untidy plumage with white-wash. "What a dreadful mess it's in!" she remarked, after gazing at it for a few moments in silence. "What is it, and why is it here?"

"It hasn't any meaning," said the Cat, "it simply *is*."

"Can it talk?" asked Alice eagerly.

"It has never done anything else," chuckled the Cat.

"Can you tell me what you are doing here?" Alice inquired politely. The Ineptitude shook its head with a deprecatory motion and commenced to drawl, "I haven't an idea."

"It never has, you know," interrupted the Cheshire Cat rudely, "but in its leisure moments" (Alice thought it must have a good many of them) "when it isn't playing with a gutta-percha ball it unravels the groundwork of what people believe—or don't believe, I forget which."

"It really doesn't matter which," said the Ineptitude with languid interest.

"Of course it doesn't," the Cat went on cheerfully, "because the unravelling got so tangled that no one could follow it. Its theory is," he continued, seeing that Alice was waiting for

[1] "The Ineptitude"—Mr. A. J. (later Earl) Balfour, First Lord of the Treasury in Lord Salisbury's third Administration, 1895-1900.

more, "that you mustn't interfere with the Inevitable. Slide and let slide, you know."

"But what do you keep it here for?" asked Alice.

"Oh, somehow you can't help it; it's so perfectly harmless and amiable and says the nastiest things in the nicest manner,

"CAN YOU TELL ME WHAT YOU ARE DOING HERE?" ALICE
INQUIRED POLITELY

and the King just couldn't do without it. The King is only made of pasteboard, you know, with sharp edges; and the Queen"—here the Cat sank its voice to a whisper—"the Queen comes from another pack, made of Brummagem ware, without polish, but absolutely indestructible; always pushing, you know; but you can't push an Ineptitude. Might as well try to hustle a glacier."

"That's why you keep so many of them about," said Alice.

"Of course. But its temper is not what it used to be. Lots of things have happened to worry it."

"What sort of things?"

"Oh, people have been dying off in round numbers, in the most ostentatious manner, and the Ineptitude dislikes fuss—but hush, here's the King coming."

His Majesty was looking doleful and grumpy, Alice thought, as though he had been disturbed in an afternoon nap. "Who is

with apologies to Sir John Tenniel

THE QUEEN [2]

this, and what is that Cat doing here?" he asked, glancing gloomily at Alice and her companion.

"I really must ask you to give me notice of these questions," said the Ineptitude with a yawn.

"There's a dragon loose somewhere in the garden," the King went on peevishly, "and I am expected to help in getting it under control. Do I look as if I could control dragons?"

Alice thought he certainly did not.

[2] The Queen—Mr. Joseph Chamberlain, Secretary of State for the Colonies, 1895-1903.

"What do you propose doing?" drawled the Ineptitude.

"That's just it," said the King. "I say that whatever is done must be done cautiously and deliberately; the Treasurer says that whatever is done must be done cheaply—I am afraid the Treasurer is the weakest member of the pack," he added anxiously.

THE KING WAS FAST ASLEEP [3]

"Only made of Bristol board, you know," explained the Cat aside to Alice.

"What does the Queen say about it?" asked the Ineptitude.

"The Queen says that if something is not done in less than no time there'll be a Dissolution."

Both looked very grave at this, and nothing was said for some minutes. The King was the first to break the silence. "What are you doing with that whitewash?" he demanded. "The Queen said everything was to be painted khaki."

"I know," said the creature pathetically, "but I had run out of khaki; the Unforeseen again, you know; and things needed whitewash so badly."

The Cat had been slowly vanishing during the last few

[3] The King—the Marquess of Salisbury, Prime Minister, 1895-1902.

minutes, till nothing remained of it but an eye. At the last re-mark it gave a wink at Alice and completed its eclipse.

When Alice turned round she found that both the King and the Ineptitude were fast asleep.

"It's no good remaining here," she thought, and as she did not want to meet either the Queen or the dragon, she turned to make her way out of the street.

"At any rate," she said to herself, "I know what an Inepti-tude is like."

ALICE IN PALL MALL

"THE great art in falling off a horse," said the White Knight,[1] "is to have another handy to fall on to."

"But wouldn't that be rather difficult to arrange?" asked Alice.

"Difficult, of course," replied the Knight, "but in my De-partment one has to be provided for emergencies. Now, for instance, have you ever conducted a war in South Africa?"

Alice shook her head.

"I have," said the Knight, with a gentle complacency in his voice.

"And did you bring it to a successful conclusion?" asked Alice.

"Not exactly to a *conclusion*—not a *definite* conclusion, you know—nor entirely successful either. In fact, I believe it's going on still. . . . But you can't think how much fore-thought it took to get it properly started. I dare say, now, you are wondering at my equipment?"

Alice certainly was; the Knight was riding rather uncom-fortably on a sober-paced horse that was prevented from mov-ing any faster by an elaborate housing of red-tape trappings.

[1] The White Knight—The Marquess of Lansdowne, Secretary of State for War, 1895-1900; became Foreign Secretary November, 1900, in succession to Lord Salisbury, who till then had been both Prime Min-ister and Foreign Secretary.

The inscription on the mane of the Foreign Office horse is an allusion to Lord Lansdowne's reputed facility in the French language.

"Of course, I see the reason for that," thought Alice; "if it
were to move any quicker the Knight would come off." But
there were a number of obsolete weapons and appliances hanging about the saddle that didn't seem of the least practical use.

"You see, I had read a book," the Knight went on in a

ALICE AND THE WHITE KNIGHT
(*With apologies to Sir John Tenniel*)

dreamy far-away tone, "written by some one to prove that
warfare under modern conditions was impossible. You may
imagine how disturbing that was to a man of my profession.
Many men would have thrown up the whole thing and gone
home. But I grappled with the situation. You will never guess
what I did."

Alice pondered. "You went to war, of course——"

"Yes; *but not under modern conditions.*"

The Knight stopped his horse so that he might enjoy the full
effect of this announcement.

"Now, for instance," he continued kindly, seeing that Alice

had not recovered her breath, "you observe this little short-range gun that I have hanging to my saddle? Why do you suppose I sent out guns of that particular kind? Because if they happened to fall into the hands of the enemy they'd be very little use to him. That was my own invention."

"I see," said Alice gravely; "but supposing you wanted to use them against the enemy?"

The Knight looked worried. "I know there is that to be thought of, but I didn't choose to be putting dangerous weapons into the enemy's hands. And then, again, supposing the Basutos had risen, those would have been just the sort of guns to drive them off with. Of course they *didn't* rise; but they might have done so, you know."

At this moment the horse suddenly went on again, and the Knight clutched convulsively at its mane to prevent himself from coming off.

"That's the worst of horses," he remarked apologetically; "they are so Unforeseen in their movements. Now, if I had had my way I would have done without them as far as possible— in fact, I began that way, only it didn't answer. And yet," he went on in an aggrieved tone, "at Crécy it was the footmen who did the most damage."

"But," objected Alice, "if your men hadn't got horses how could they get about from place to place?"

"They couldn't. That would be the beauty of it," said the White Knight eagerly; "the fewer places your army moves to, the fewer maps you have to prepare. And we hadn't prepared very many. I'm not very strong at geography, but," he added, brightening, "you should hear me talk French."

"But," persisted Alice, "supposing the enemy went and attacked you at some other place———"

"They did," interrupted the Knight gloomily; "they appeared in strength at places that weren't even marked on the ordinary maps. But how do you think they got there?"

He paused and fixed his gentle eyes upon Alice as she walked beside him, and then continued in a hollow voice:

"They rode. Rode and carried rifles. They were no mortal foes—they were Mounted Infantry."

The Knight swayed about so with the violence of his emo-
ion that it was inevitable that he should lose his seat, and Alice
was relieved to notice that there was another horse with an
mpty saddle ready for him to scramble on to. There was a
rightful dust, of course, but Alice saw him gathering the reins
of his new mount into a bunch, and smiling down upon her
with increased amiability.

ANOTHER HANDY TO FALL ON TO

"It's not an easy animal to manage," he called out to her,
'but if I pat it and speak to it in French it will probably understand where I want it to go. And," he added hopefully, "it
may go there. A knowledge of French and an amiable disposi-
ion will see one out of most things."

"Well," thought Alice as she watched him settling down
uneasily into the saddle, "it ought not to take long to see him
out of that."

ALICE AND THE LIBERAL PARTY

QUITE a number of them were going past, and the noise
was considerable, but they were marching in sixes and
evens and didn't seem to be guided by any fixed word of com-

mand, so that the effect was not so imposing as it might have
been. Some of them, Alice noticed, had the letters "I.L." em-
broidered on their tunics and headpieces and other conspicuou
places ("I wonder," she thought, "if it's marked on thei
underclothing as well"); others simply had a big "L," and
others again were branded with a little "e." They got dread
fully in each other's way, and were always falling over one
another in little heaps, while many of the mounted ones di
not seem at all sure of their seats. "They won't go very far i
they don't fall into better order," thought Alice, and she wa
glad to find herself the next minute in a spacious hall with
large marble staircase at one end of it. The White King [1] wa
sitting on one of the steps, looking rather anxious and just
little uncomfortable under his heavy crown, which needed
good deal of balancing to keep it in its place.

"Did you happen to meet any fighting men?" he asked
Alice.

"A great many—two or three hundred, I should think."

"Not quite two hundred, all told," said the King, referring
to his notebook.

"Told what?" asked Alice.

"Well, they haven't been told anything, exactly—yet. The
fact is," the King went on nervously, "we're rather in wan
of a messenger just now. I don't know how it is, there are
two or three of them about, but lately they have always been
either out of reach or else out of touch. You don't happen to
have passed any one coming from the direction of Berkeley
Square [2]?" he asked eagerly.

Alice shook her head.

"There's the Primrose Courier, [3] for instance," the King
continued reflectively, "the most reliable Messenger we have;
he understands all about Open Doors and Linked Hands and
all that sort of thing, and he's quite as useful at home. But he
frightens some of them nearly out of their wits by his Imperial

[1] The White King—Sir Henry Campbell-Bannerman.
[2] Berkeley Square, Lord Rosebery's residence (No. 38).
[3] The Primrose Courier—Lord Rosebery, leader of the Liberal Imperialists.

nglo-Saxon attitudes. I wouldn't mind his skipping about so
he'd only come back when he's wanted."

"And haven't you got any one else to carry your messages?"
sked Alice sympathetically.

THE PRIMROSE MESSENGER   THE UNKHAKI MESSENGER
"Out of reach"   *"Out of touch"*

"There's the Unkhaki Messenger,[4]" said the King, consulting his pocket-book.

"I beg your pardon," said Alice.

"You know what Khaki means, I suppose?"

[4] The Unkhaki Messenger—Mr. John (afterwards Viscount) Morley,
who had been active as an anti-Imperialist. Mr. Morley had recently
produced his book on Oliver Cromwell, and Lord Rosebery his book
on Napoleon at St. Helena, entitled *Napoleon; The Last Phase*. Lord
Rosebery had resigned the leadership of the Liberal Party in 1896, and
Mr. Morley had retired from the "councils of the party" in 1898.
But both had reappeared on the scene and the allusions are to Sir Henry
Campbell-Bannerman's perplexities at their disappearances and reap-
pearances.

"It's a sort of colour," said Alice promptly; "something like dust."

"Exactly," said the King; "thou dost—he doesn't. That's why he's called the Unkhaki Messenger."

Alice gave it up.

"Such a dear, obliging creature," the King went on, "but so dreadfully unpunctual. He's always half a century in front of his times or half a century behind them, and that puts one out so."

Alice agreed that it would make a difference.

"It's helped to put us out quite six years already," the King went on plaintively; "but you can't cure him of it. You see he will wander about in by-ways and deserts, hunting for Lost Causes, and whenever he comes across a stream he always wades against the current. All that takes him out of his way, you know; he's somewhere up in the Grampian Hills by this time."

"I see," said Alice; "that's what you mean by being out of touch. And the other Messenger is——"

"Out of reach," said the King. "Precisely."

"Then it follows," said Alice——

"I don't know what you mean by 'it,'" interrupted the King sulkily. "No one follows. That is why we stick in the same place. DON'T," he suddenly screamed, jumping up and down in his agitation. "Don't do it, I say."

"Do what?" asked Alice in some alarm.

"Give advice. I know you're going to. They've all been doing it for the last six weeks. I assure you the letters I get——"

"I wasn't going to give you advice," said Alice indignantly, "and as to letters, you've got too much alphabet as it is."

"Why, you're doing it now," said the King angrily. "Goodbye."

As Alice took the hint and walked away towards the door she heard him calling after her in a kinder tone: "If you *should* meet any one coming from the direction of Berkeley Square——"

ALICE AT LAMBETH

THERE was so much noise inside that Alice thought she might as well go in without knocking.

The atmosphere was as noticeable as the noise when Alice got in, and seemed to be heavily charged with pepper. There was a faint whiff of burning incense, and some candles that had just been put out were smouldering unpleasantly. Quite a number of Articles were strewn about on the floor, some of them more or less broken. The Duchess was seated in the middle of the kitchen, holding, as well as she could, a very unmanageable baby that kept wriggling itself into all manner of postures and uncompromising attitudes. At the back of the kitchen a cook was busily engaged in stirring up a large cauldron, pausing every now and then to fling a reredos or half a rubric at the Duchess, who maintained an air of placid unconcern in spite of the combined fractiousness of the baby and cook and the obtrusiveness of the pepper.

"Your cook seems to have a very violent temper," said Alice, as soon as a lull in the discord enabled her to make herself heard.

"Drat her!" said the Duchess.

"I beg your pardon," said Alice, not quite sure whether she had heard aright; "your Grace was remarking——"

" '*Pax vobiscum,*' was what I said," answered the Duchess; "there's nothing like a dead language when you're dealing with a live volcano."

"But aren't you going to do something to set matters straight a bit?" asked Alice, dodging a whole set of Ornaments that went skimming through the air, and watching with some anxiety the contortions of the baby, which was getting more difficult to hold every moment.

"Of course something must be done," said the Duchess, with decision, "but quietly and gradually—the leaden foot within the velvet shoe, you know."

Alice seemed to recognize the quotation, but she did not notice that anything particular was being done. "At the rate you're going, it will be years before you get settled," she remarked.

"Perhaps it will," said the Duchess resignedly. "I'm paid by the year, you know. *Festina lente*, say I."

"But surely you can keep some sort of order in your Establishment?" said Alice. "Why don't you exert your authority?"

THE DUCHESS,[1] THE BABY, AND THE COOK[2]
(*With apologies to Sir John Tenniel*)

"My dear, it takes me all the exertion I can spare to have any authority. I give orders, and it's my endeavour not to see that they're disobeyed. I'm sure I've given this child my Opinion—but there, you might as well opine to a limpet. As to the cook——"

Here the cook sent the pepper-pot straight at the Duchess, who broke off in a violent fit of sneezing. In the midst of the commotion the baby suddenly disappeared, and as the cook had

[1] The Duchess—Dr. Temple, Archbishop of Canterbury.

[2] The cook—Mr. Samuel Smith, M.P. for Liverpool, who was active in the Protestant cause.

taken up a new caster labelled "cayenne" Alice thought she might as well go and see where it had gone to. As she slipped out of the kitchen she heard the Duchess gasping between her sneezes, "Must . . . be done . . . quietly . . . and . . . gradually."

.   .   .   .

"What happened to the baby?" asked the Cheshire Cat, appearing suddenly a few minutes later.

"I ALWAYS SAID IT WOULD," SAID THE CAT

"It went out—to roam, I think," said Alice.
"I always said it would," said the Cat.

ALICE AT ST. STEPHEN'S

"IT'S very provoking," said Alice to herself; she had been trying for the previous quarter of an hour to attract the attention of a large and very solemn caterpillar that was perched on the top of a big mushroom with a Gothic fringe. "I've heard that the only chance of speaking to it is to catch its eye," she continued, but she found out that however perseveringly she thrust herself into the Caterpillar's[1] range of vision its eye persistently looked beyond her, or beneath her, or around her—never at her. Alice had read somewhere that little girls should be seen and not heard; "but," she thought, "I'm not

THE CATERPILLAR

even seen here, and if I'm not to be heard, what am I here at all for?" In any case she determined to make an attempt at conversation.

"If you please——" she began.

"I don't," said the Caterpillar shortly, without seeming to take any further notice of her.

After an uncomfortable pause she commenced again.

"I should like——"

[1] The Caterpillar—Mr. Speaker Gully.

"You shouldn't," said the Caterpillar with decision.

Alice felt discouraged, but it was no use to be shut up in this way, so she started again as amiably as she could.

"You can't think, Mr. Caterpillar——"

"I can, and I often do," he remarked stiffly; adding, "You mustn't make such wild statements. They're not relevant to the discussion."

"But I only said that in order——"

"You didn't," said the Caterpillar angrily. "I tell you it was not in order."

"You are so dreadfully short," exclaimed Alice; the Caterpillar drew itself up.

"In manner, I mean; no—in memory," she added hastily, for it was thoroughly angry by this time.

"I'm sure I didn't mean anything," she continued humbly, for she felt that it was absurd to quarrel with a caterpillar.

The Caterpillar snorted.

"What's the good of talking if you don't mean anything? If you've talked all this time without meaning anything you're not worth listening to."

"But you put a wrong construction——" Alice began.

"You can't discuss Construction now, you know; that comes on the Estimates. Shrivel!"

"I don't understand," said Alice.

"Shrivel. Dry up," explained the Caterpillar, and proceeded to look in another direction, as if it had forgotten her existence.

"Good-bye," said Alice, after waiting a moment; she half hoped that the Caterpillar might say "See you later," but it took not the slightest notice of her remark, so she got up reluctantly and walked away.

"Well, of all the gubernatorial——" said Alice to herself when she got outside. She did not quite know what it meant, but it was an immense relief to be able to come out with a word of six syllables.

ALICE IN DIFFICULTIES[1]

"HOW are you getting on?" asked the Cheshire Cat.
"I'm not," said Alice.
Which was certainly the truth.

"HOW ARE YOU GETTING ON?" ASKED THE CHESHIRE CAT

It was the most provoking and bewildering game of croquet she had ever played in. The other side did not seem to know what they were expected to do, and, for the most part, they

[1] The difficulties are those of the Liberal Party in 1901. The first flamingo (p. 318) is Sir Edward Grey, the second (p. 319) Lord Rosebery.

The "furrow" is an allusion to a speech in which Lord Rosebery had said, "I must plough my furrow alone" (July, 1901). "Cross-currents" was the term usually employed for differences in the Liberal Party.

One of the hedgehogs (p. 318) is labelled "Rattigan," and the other "I.L.P." (Independent Labour Party) on one side and L.I. (Liberal Imperialist) on the other. This is an allusion to the North-East Lanark by-election in September, 1901, when Sir W. H. Rattigan secured the seat through a split in the Liberal and Radical vote, Mr. Cecil Harmsworth standing as a Liberal Imperialist and Mr. R. Smillie as an Independent Labour candidate.

weren't doing anything, so Alice thought she might have a good chance of winning—though she was ever so many hoops behind. But the ground she had to play over was all lumps and furrows, and some of the hoops were three-cornered in shape, which made them difficult to get through, while as for the balls (which were live hedgehogs and very opinionated), it was all

THE OTHER FLAMINGO

she could do to keep them in position for a minute at a time. Then the flamingo which she was using as a mallet kept stiffening itself into uncompromising attitudes, and had to be coaxed back into a good temper.

"I think I can manage *him* now," she said; "since I let him have a latchkey and allowed him to take up the position he wanted he has been quite amiable. The other flamingo I was playing with," she added regretfully, "strayed off into a furrow. The last I saw of it, it was trying to bore a tunnel."

"A tunnel?" said the Cat.

"Yes; under the sea, you know."

"I see; to avoid the cross-current, of course."

Alice waited till the Cat had stopped grinning at its own joke, and then went on:

"As for the hedgehogs, there's no doing anything with them; they've got such prickly tempers. And they're *so* short-sighted; if they don't happen to be looking the same way they invariably run against each other. I should have won that last hoop if both hedgehogs hadn't tried to get through at the same time."

"Both?"

"Yes, the one I was playing with and the one I wasn't. And every one began shouting out all sorts of different directions till I scarcely knew which I *was* playing with. Really," she continued plaintively, "it's the most discouraging croquet-party I was ever at; if we go on like this there soon won't be any party at all."

"It's no use swearing and humping your back," said the Cat sympathetically. (Alice hadn't done either.) "Keep your temper and your flamingo."

"Is that all?"

"No," said the Cat; "keep on playing *with the right ball.*"

"Which *is* the right ball?" asked Alice.

But the Cat had discreetly vanished.

ALICE ANYWHERE BUT IN DOWNING STREET

"I DON'T know what business you have here," the Red Queen [1] was saying, "if you don't belong to the Cabinet; of course," she added more kindly, "you may be one of the outer ring. There are so many of them, and they're mostly so unimportant, that one can't be expected to remember *all* their faces."

"What is *your* business?" asked Alice, by way of evading the question.

"There isn't any business really," said the White Queen.[2]

[1] The Red Queen—Mr. Joseph Chamberlain.

[2] The White Queen—Mr. Balfour whose favourite occupation was supposed to be golf.

"Her Red Majesty sometimes says more than she means. Fancy," she added eagerly, "I went round in 85 yesterday!"

"Round what?" asked Alice.

"The Links, of course."

"Talking about a Lynx," said the Red Queen, "are you any good at Natural History? Take prestige from a Lion, what would remain?"

"TALKING NONSENSE"
(*With apologies to Sir John Tenniel*)

"The prestige wouldn't, of course," said Alice, "and the Lion might not care to be without it. I suppose nothing——"

"*I* should remain, whatever happened," said the Red Queen with decision.

"She's no good at Natural History," observed the White Queen. "Shall I try her with Christian Science? If there was a sort of warfare going on in a kind of a country, and you wanted to stop it, and didn't know how to, what course of inaction would you pursue?"

"Action, you mean. Her White Majesty occasionally muddles things," interposed the Red Queen.

"It amounts to much the same thing with us," said the White Queen.

Alice pondered. "I suppose I should resign," she hazarded.

Both Queens gasped and held up their hands in reprobation.

"A most improper suggestion," said the White Queen severely. "Now I should simply convince my reasoning faculty that the war didn't exist—and there'd be an end of it."

"But," objected Alice, "supposing the war was to assume that your reasoning faculty was wanting, and went on all the same?"

"The child is talking nonsense," said the Red Queen; "she

THE INTERCESSIONAL
(*With apologies to Sir John Tenniel*)

doesn't know anything of Christian Science. Let's try Political Economy. Supposing you were pledged to introduce a scheme for Old Age Pensions,[3] what would be your next step?"

Alice considered. "I should think——"

"Of course you'd think," said the White Queen, "ever so much. You'd go on thinking off and on for years. I can't tell you how much I've thought about it myself; I still think about it a little, just for practice—principally on Tuesdays."

"I should think," continued Alice, without noticing the interruption, "that the first thing would be to find the money."

[3] Old Age Pensions: Mr. Chamberlain had pledged himself to a scheme of Old Age Pensions, and he was much criticized by the Opposition in these years for postponing or evading the fulfilment of this pledge.

"Dear, no," said the Red Queen pityingly, "*that* wouldn't be Political Economy. The first thing would be to find an excuse for dropping the question."

"What a dreadful lot of unnecessary business we're talking!" said the White Queen fretfully. "It makes me quite miserable—carries me back to the days when I was in Opposition. Can't she sing us something?"

"What shall I sing you?" asked Alice.

"Oh, anything soothing; the 'Intercessional,' if you like."

Alice began, but the words didn't come a bit right, and she wasn't at all sure how the Queens would take it:

> *Voice of the People, lately polled,*
>   *Awed by our broad-cast battle scheme,*
> *By virtue of whose vote we hold*
>   *Our licence still to doze and dream,*
> *Still, falt'ring Voice, complaisant shout,*
> *Lest we go out, lest we go out.*

Alice looked anxiously at the Queens when she had finished, but they were both fast asleep.

"It will take a deal of shouting to rouse them," she thought.

ALICE LUNCHES AT
WESTMINSTER

"I THINK I would rather not hear it just now," said Alice politely.

"It is expressly intended for publication," said Humpty Dumpty; [1] "I don't suppose there'll be a paper tomorrow that won't be talking about it."

---

[1] Humpty Dumpty—General Sir Redvers Buller, V.C. On his return from South Africa in 1901, Sir Redvers was appointed to command the first Army Corps at Aldershot in pursuance of a new Army Reorganization Scheme. There was much criticism of the appointment and on October 10 he answered his critics in a singular speech at the Queen's Hall, Westminster, in which he specially defended himself against the charge that he had counselled the surrender of Ladysmith. His defence was that in heliographing instructions to Sir George White, when he was locked up in Ladysmith, he had "spatchcocked" a passage which

"In that case I suppose I may as well hear it," said Alice with resignation.

"The scene," said Humpty Dumpty, "is Before Ladysmith, and the time—well, the time is After Colenso:

> *I sent a message to the White*
> *To tell him—if you* must, *you might.*
> *But then, I said, you p'raps might not*
> *(The weather was* extremely *hot).*
> *This query, too, I spatchcock-slid,*
> *How would you do it, if you did?*
> *I did not know, I rather thought—*
> *And then I wondered if I ought.*"

"It's dreadfully hard to understand," said Alice.

"It gets easier as it goes on," said Humpty Dumpty, and resumed:

> *They tried a most malignant scheme,*
> *They put dead horses in the stream;*
> *(With One at home I saw it bore*
> *On preference for a horseless war).*
> *But though I held the war might cease,*
> *At least I never held my peace.*
> *I held the key; it was a bore*
> *I could not hit upon the door.*
> *Then One suggested, in my ear,*
> *It would be well to persevere.*
> *The papers followed in that strain,*
> *They said it very loud and plain.*
> *I simply answered with a grin,*
> *"Why, what a hurry they are in."*
> *I went and played a waiting game;*
> *Observe, I got there just the same.*
> *And if you* have *a better man,*
> *Well, show him to me, if you can.*

would have relieved Sir George of responsibility in case he had found it necessary to surrender, and that this passage had been ungenerously twisted into an instruction to surrender. The speech was so confused and eccentric that it greatly perplexed the public, and ten days later the Government cancelled his appointment on the ground that he had committed a breach of regulations in making it. Sir Redvers suggested in his speech that the Boers had put dead horses into the river Tugela, in order to poison the water for the besieged garrison.

"Thank you very much," said Alice; "it's very interesting, but I'm afraid it won't help to cool the atmosphere much."

HUMPTY DUMPTY EXPLAINS

(*With apologies to Everybody*)

"I could tell you lots more like that," Humpty Dumpty began, but Alice hastily interrupted him.

"I hear a lot of fighting going on in the wood; don't you think I had better hear the rest some other time?"

ALICE IN A FOG

"THE Duke and Duchess!"[1] said the White Rabbit nervously as it went scurrying past; "they may be here at any moment, and I haven't got it yet."

"Hasn't got what?" wondered Alice.

THE WHITE RABBIT

"A rhyme for Cornwall," said the Rabbit, as if in answer to her thought; "borne well, yawn well"—and he pattered away into the distance, dropping in his hurry a folded paper that he had been carrying.

"What have you got there?" asked the Cheshire Cat as Alice picked up the paper and opened it.

[1] The Duke of York (now King George V) visited Australia accompanied by the Duchess to open the first session of the Australian Commonwealth Parliament on May 7, 1901, and the Poet Laureate (Mr. Alfred Austin) improved the occasion by writing a royal and loyal ode to greet him on his return. Mr. Austin's poems had been frequently the subject of Gould's satire, and "Saki" takes up the theme.

"It seems to be a kind of poetry," said Alice doubtfully; "at least," she added, "some of the words rhyme and none of them appear to have any particular meaning."

"What is it about?" asked the Cat.

"Well, some one seems to be coming somewhere from everywhere else, and to get a mixed reception:

> . . . *Your Father smiles,*
> *Your Mother weeps.*"

"I've heard something like that before," said the Cat; "it went on, if I remember, 'Your aunt has the pen of the gardener.'"

"There's nothing about that here," said Alice; "supposing she didn't weep when the time came?"

"She would if she had to read all that stuff," said the Cat.

"And then it goes on:

> *You went as came the swallow.*"

"That doesn't help us unless we know how the swallow came," observed the Cat. "If he went as the swallow usually travels he would have won the Deutsch Prize." [2]

> "*. . . homeward draw*
> *Now it hath winged its way to winters green.*

"There seems to have been some urgent reason for avoiding the swallow," continued Alice. "Then all sorts of things happened to the Almanac:

> *Twice a hundred dawns, a hundred noons, a hundred*
> *eves.*

"You see there were two dawns to every noon and evening —it must have been dreadfully confusing."

"It would be at first, of course," agreed the Cat.

"I think it must have been that extra dawn that

> *Never swallow or wandering sea-bird saw*

or else it was the Flag."

"What flag?"

"Well, the flag that some one found,

> *Scouring the field or furrowing the sea.*"

"Would you mind explaining," said the Cat, "which was doing the scouring and furrowing?"

[2] A prize given for aviation in its early days.

"The flag," said Alice, "or the some one. It isn't exactly clear, and it doesn't make sense either way. Anyhow, wherever the flag was unfurled it floated o'er the Free."

"WOULD YOU MIND EXPLAINING?" SAID THE CAT

"Come, that tells us something. Whoever it was must have avoided Dartmoor and St. Helena."

"*You, wandering, saw,*
Young Commonwealths you found."

"There's a great deal of wandering in the poem," observed the Cat.

"You sailed from us to them, from them to us," continued Alice.

"That isn't new, either. It *should* go on: 'You all returned from him to them, though they were mine before.'"

"It doesn't go on quite like that," said Alice; "it ends up with a lot of words that I suppose were left over and couldn't be fitted in anywhere else:

Therefore rejoicing mightier hath been made
Imperial Power."

"That," said the Cat, "is the cleverest thing in the whole poem. People see that at the end, and then they read it through to see what on earth it's about."

"I'd give sixpence to any one who can explain it," said Alice.

ALICE HAS TEA AT THE HOTEL CECIL[1]

THE March Hare and the Dormouse and the Hatter were seated at a very neglected-looking tea-table; they were evidently in agonized consideration of something—even the Dormouse, which was asleep, had a note of interrogation in its tail.

"No room!" they shouted, as soon as they caught sight of Alice.

"There's lots of room for improvement," said Alice, as she sat down.

"You've got no business to be here," said the March Hare.

"And if you had any business you wouldn't be here, you know," said the Hatter; "I hope you don't suppose this is a business gathering. What will you have to eat?" he continued.

Alice looked at a long list of dishes with promising names, but nearly all of them seemed to be crossed off.

"That list was made nearly seven years ago, you know," said the March Hare, in explanation.

"But you can always have patience," said the Hatter. "You

[1] Lord Salisbury's Government was frequently spoken of in popular jest as the "Hotel Cecil" in allusion to the supposed predominance of the Cecil family in its composition. The March Hare is Mr. Balfour, the Mad Hatter, Mr. Chamberlain, and the Dormouse, Lord Salisbury. The Boer War, supposed to have been over in September, 1900, is still going on, and the Irish question has again begun to trouble the Government.

begin with patience and we do the rest." And he leaned back
and seemed prepared to do a lot of rest.

"Your manners want mending," said the March Hare suddenly to Alice.

"They don't," she replied indignantly.

"It's very rude to contradict," said the Hatter; "you would
like to hear me sing something."

TEA AT THE HOTEL CECIL

(*With apologies to Everybody Concerned*)

Alice felt that it would be unwise to contradict again, so she
said nothing, and the Hatter began:

> *Dwindle, dwindle, little war,*
> *How I wonder more and more,*
> *As about the veldt you hop*
> *When you really mean to stop.*

"Talking about stopping," interrupted the March Hare
anxiously, "I wonder how my timepiece is behaving."

He took out of his pocket a large chronometer of complicated workmanship, and mournfully regarded it.

"It's dreadfully behind the times," he said, giving it an
experimental shake. "I would take it to pieces at once if I

was at all sure of getting the bits back in their right places."

"What is the matter with it?" asked Alice.

"The wheels seem to get stuck," said the March Hare. "There is too much Irish butter in the works."

"Ruins the thing from a dramatic point of view," said the Hatter; "too many scenes, too few acts."

"DWINDLE, DWINDLE, LITTLE WAR"

"The result is we never have time to get through the day's work. It's never even time for a free breakfast-table; we do what we can for education at odd moments, but we shall all die of old age before we have a moment to spare for social duties."

"You might lose a lot if you run your business in that way," said Alice.

"Not in this country," said the March Hare. "You see, we have a Commission on everything that we don't do."

"The Dormouse must tell us a story," said the Hatter, giving it a sharp pinch.

The Dormouse awoke with a start, and began as though it

had been awake all the time: "There was an old woman who lived in a shoe——"

"I know," said Alice, "she had so many children that she didn't know what to do."

"Nothing of the sort," said the Dormouse, "you lack the gift of imagination. She put most of them into Treasuries and For-

TRYING TO MAKE HIM LOOK LIKE A LION

eign Offices and Boards of Trade, and all sorts of unlikely places where they could learn things."

"What did they learn?" asked Alice.

"Painting in glowing colours, and attrition, and terminology (that's the science of knowing when things are over), and iteration (that's the same thing over again), and drawing——"

"What did they draw?"

"Salaries. And then there were classes for foreign languages. And such language!" (Here the March Hare and the Hatter shut their eyes and took a big gulp from their tea-cups.) "However, I don't think anybody attended to them."

The Dormouse broke off into a chuckle which ended in a

snore, and as no one seemed inclined to wake it up again Alice thought she might as well be going.

When she looked back the Hatter and the March Hare were trying to stiffen the Dormouse out into the attitude of a lion guardant. "But it will never pass for anything but a Dormouse if it will snore so," she remarked to herself.

ALICE GOES TO CHESTERFIELD[1]

ALICE noticed a good deal of excitement going on among the Looking-Glass creatures; some of them were hurrying off expectantly in one direction, as fast as their legs would carry them, while others were trying to look as if nothing in particular was about to happen.

"Those mimsy-looking birds," she said, catching sight of a group that did not look in the best of spirits, "those must be Borogoves. I've read about them somewhere; in some parts of the country they have to be protected. And, I declare, there is the White King coming through the Wood."

Alice went to meet the King, who was struggling with a very unwieldy pencil to write something in a notebook. "It's a memorandum of my feelings, in case I forget them," he explained. "Only," he added, "I'm not quite sure that I meant to put it that way."

Alice peeped over his shoulder and read: "The High Commissioner may tumble off his post; he balances very badly."

"Could you tell me," she asked, "what all the excitement is about just now?"

[1] Lord Rosebery's speech at Chesterfield on December 16 was the chief event in Liberal politics in the winter of 1901. It caused extraordinary interest and commotion both before and after, and though the South African parts of it were hailed equally by both sections of the party, it opened a new line of division in domestic policy, to the great embarrassment of Sir Henry Campbell-Bannerman (the White King). The picture "Spades in Wonderland" (p. 338) represents the efforts of the different party gardeners, Sir William Harcourt, Sir Edward Grey and Mr. Lloyd George, to paint the rose their own colour, i.e. to make the speech mean what they wished it to mean.

"Haven't an idea," said the White King, "unless it's the awakening."

"The what?" said Alice.

"The Red King, you know; he's been asleep for ever so long, and he's going to wake up today. Not that it makes any

THE RED KING IN THE WOOD

difference that I can see—he talks just as loud when he's asleep."

Alice remembered having seen the Red King, in rose-coloured armour that had got a little rusty, sleeping uneasily in the thickest part of the wood.

"The fact is," the White King went on, "some of them think we're only a part of his dream, and that we shall all go 'piff' when he wakes up. That is what makes them so jumpy just now. Oh," he cried, giving a little jump himself, "there go some more!"

"What are they?" asked Alice, as several strange creatures hurtled past, like puff-balls in a gale.

"They're the Slithy Toves," said the King, "Libimps and

Jubjubs and Bandersnatches. They're always gyring and gim-
bling wherever they can find a wabe."

"Where are they all going in such a hurry?" Alice asked.

"They're going to the meeting to hear the Red King," the
White King said in rather a dismal tone. "They've all got
latchkeys," he went on, "but they'd better not stay out too
late."

THE AWAKENING

Here the White King gave another jump. "What's the matter?" asked Alice.

"Why, I've just remembered that I've got a latchkey too,
my very own! I must go and find it." And away went the
White King into the wood.

"How these kings do run about!" thought Alice. "It seems
to be one of the Rules of the Game that when one moves the
other moves also."

The next moment there was a deafening outburst of drums,
and Alice saw the Red King rushing through the wood with a
big roll of paper.

"Dear me!" she heard him say to himself as he passed, "I

hope I shan't be late for the meeting, and I wonder how they'll take my speech."

Alice noticed that the Borogoves made no attempt to follow,

THE WHITE KING

but tried to look as if they didn't care a bit. And away in the distance she heard a sort of derisive booing with a brogue in it. "That must be the Mome Raths outgribing," she thought.

THE AGED MAN

I shook him well from side to side
Until his face was blue.
"Come, tell me where's the Bill," I cried,
"And what you're going to do."
He said, "I hunt for gibes and pins
To prick the Bishops' calves,
I search for Royal Commissions, too,
To use as safety valves."

[*See the Debate on Temperance Legislation in the House of Lords, May 14, 1901.*[1]]

(*With apologies to Sir John Tenniel*)

[1] Lord Salisbury chaffed the Bishops and suggested another Royal Commission as the next step, thereby evoking a spirited reply from Lord Rosebery.

THE RED KING: Harcourt, Grey, and Lloyd George are
all putting their own colours on, I think I'd better paint it
myself.

(See footnote p. 333.)

Plays

NOTE

First published, 1924

CONTENTS FOR
PLAYS

341

INTRODUCTION

by J. C. SQUIRE

THERE are vagrant authors who, with sudden old zig-zags, always elude the butterfly nets of criticism. Nothing much to the point, save in the way of mere unanalytical praise, has ever been said about Peacock's novels or the *Importance of Being Earnest;* and the precise flavour of "Saki" is as easy to recognize and as impossible to define as that of a good Claret or Hock. Those who write about him are always tempted to discuss the latent qualities of the man whom they knew or whom they can deduce: to show that he satirized things that he hated, that he concealed profound affections, and that in spite of his jokes about all manner of catastrophes he was a sensitive and humane man to whom cruelty was repugnant. This no doubt is all true: and occasionally his loves and even his fears peep out in his writing. It is, characteristically, in an appreciative essay on cats that he ends with:

voicing in its death-yell that agony of bitter remonstrance which human animals, too, have flung at the powers that may be; the last protest against a destiny that might have made them happy—and has not.

But generally he was reserved in speech as in writing: it is enough, for those who were not his friends, to know that the jester died, over-age and a lance-sergeant, in the trenches, and that his last words were "Put that bloody cigarette out." To the commentator on his books what most matters is not the man Munro who concealed himself behind them but the artist "Saki" who wrote them. And "Saki" was a unique example of the man who tells lies with a grave face.

Defoe told lies with a grave face; but they were grave lies. Swift told lies with a grave face, but the gravity was often interrupted either by guffaws or by the rasp of indignation. "The Jumping Frog" and "The Stolen White Elephant" were inventions as admirable as "Saki's," and as seriously recounted; but the telling was all to Mark Twain and the phraseology nothing. Saki's themes were akin to Mark Twain's, though more extravagant, but his manner was more Max Beerbohm's. He related a fantastic fable with the most matter-of-fact air; but, not content with that, he polished his sentences with a spinsterish passion for neatness and chose his words as the last of the dandies might choose his ties. Writing brief stories and sketches for evening newspapers he was as careful with the shaping of his paragraphs as the most anchorite of æsthetes writing for an elect few with glass-fronted bookcases. He expended the pains of a poet upon modern fairy-tales, in which wizardry was exercised by or upon cats and dogs, house parties, duchesses and men-about-town, instead of giants, dragons, trolls and princesses, and the logic of magic operated with trim perfection against a background in which villas took the place of castles, and tennis-lawns were substituted for unfathomable forests. And in telling these fairy-tales, it must be admitted that his object was purely to amuse, and his incidental achievement to make the human race ridiculous.

"One half of the world believes what the other half invents." Mendacity and credulity were the spectacles in which he chiefly delighted, and when he was not almost persuading us to swallow his own prodigious lies, he regaled us with the sight of our kindred swallowing the lies of his favourite heroes and heroines, the remorseless children and cynical young idlers. To Clovis the world was a forest of legs, all waiting to be pulled unobtrusively and with gentlemanly grace. In the end the reader of "Saki" is pleased in proportion to the magnitude of the lie. *The Wolf*, in which everybody believes that the lady has been turned into a female Siberian wolf, is delightful; but even better is *Tobermory*, in which a cat not only is believed to speak, and (without question) accepted as speaking, but actually does speak, and to devastating purpose, the whole theme being perfectly worked out until the grand culmination when the bold discoverer is killed because he tries to teach an elephant German verbs. In this present book the confirmed admirer of "Saki" is almost sorry that the Square Egg is not actually produced, but is represented as an ingenious myth; the lie is good, but "Saki" could have pushed it farther.

His people have to fit his plots. They are consistent not with life, but with themselves and the queer world of his conception; and he contrives, even if he be realistic only in this limited way, to throw certain truths into a high light and to express some (for to tell the unexpected truth is as much one of the conventions of his world as to tell the mountainously obvious lie— it is a more charming form of lying, to make people tell truths they would not tell) which are seldom expressed. *The Watched Pot*, most considerable of his promising dramatic efforts, may lack "action" and be unduly strewn with elaborate witticisms, but there is a great deal of unaccustomed candour in it. Where it differs from the Slavonic plays in which people naïvely bare their souls is not in any extra remoteness from daily life but in an occasional surprising contact with it. We can conceive of Chekhov, in his gloomier moments, as writing a play like *The Watched Pot* in which a household of women should all be trying to marry a placid young man with a gorgon of a mother, and all continually confessing to each other, egging each other on, scratching each other, or impudently maligning each other. Is "Saki" any more lacking in reality because he makes his dialogue witty, or because he shows cook, butler, and housemaids as having a sweepstake on the event in the servants' hall? And half his jokes depend for their force upon their exaggeration of truth. René remarks: "This suit I've got on was paid for last month, so you may judge how old it is." Here the truth is not important, except to tailors: with no more elaboration or afterthought "Saki" would summarize aspects of "world-problems" as they appeared to him, as in:

Government by democracy means government of the mentally unfit by the mentally mediocre tempered by the saving grace of snobbery.

The form of this reminds one of Wilde. Wilde also might have written:

For all I know to the contrary, he may by this time have joined the majority who are powerless to resent these intrusions.

although it took "Saki" to put it into the mouth of an almost agreeable lady talking about her sick husband. We think of Wilde's plays again when, speaking of harvest festivals and the growth of imports, Clare says:

It shows such a nice spirit for a Somersetshire farmer to be duly thankful for the ripening of the Carlsbad plum

and in

So many people who are described as rough diamonds turn out to be merely rough paste

and in

There are heaps of chorus girls who are willing to marry commoners if you set the right way about it

and in the repartee about Mrs. Vulpy's make-up and the sentence about the father who lived at West Kensington but was "sane on most other subjects," and the comparison of the accessibility of Heaven with that of the House of Commons. "Saki" had all Wilde's cleverness at the substitution of a word in a stock saying or the inversion of a familiar proverb, and was an adept at contradicting our favourite clichés of word or thought, or strangely adapting them to unsuitable contexts. Yet though many of his sentences might be mistaken for Wilde's none of his pages could be attributed to another man. They are all pervaded by a personal manner and attitude. The manner is the grave manner of the humorist who opened a story thus:

In an age when it has become increasingly difficult to accomplish anything new or original, Barton Bidderdale interested his generation by dying of a new disease. "We always knew he would do something remarkable one of these days," observed his aunts; "he has justified our belief in him." But there is a section of humanity ever ready to refuse recognition to meritorious achievement, and a large and influential school of doctors asserted their belief that Bidderdale was not really dead. The funeral arrangements had to be held over until the matter was settled one way or the other, and the aunts went provisionally into half-mourning.

As for the attitude, after our initial disclaimer, no more need be said than that it was the attitude of the man who wrote:

Whenever I feel in the least tempted to be business-like or methodical or even decently industrious I go to Kensal Green and look at the graves of those who died in business.

He had seen half the world and had no doubt about his tastes, which he preferred to state by indirection.

THE DEATH-TRAP

CHARACTERS

DIMITRI. (*Reigning Prince of Kedaria.*)

Dr. STRONETZ

Col. GIRNITZA   *Officers of the Kranitzki*

Major VONTIEFF   *Regiment of Guards.*

Captain SHULTZ

SCENE:—*An Ante-chamber in the Prince's Castle at Tzern.*

TIME:—*The Present Day. The scene opens about ten o'clock in the evening.*

An ante-chamber, rather sparsely furnished. Some rugs of Balkan manufacture on the walls. A narrow table in centre of room, another table set with wine bottles and goblets near window, R. Some high-backed chairs set here and there round room. Tiled stove, L. Door in centre.

GIRNITZA, VONTIEFF *and* SHULTZ *are talking together as curtain rises.*

GIRNITZA. The Prince suspects something: I can see it in his manner.

SHULTZ. Let him suspect. He'll know for certain in half an hour's time.

GIR. The moment the Andrieff Regiment has marched out of the town we are ready for him.

SHULTZ (*drawing revolver from case and aiming it at an imaginary person*). And then—short shift for your Royal Highness! I don't think many of my bullets will go astray.

GIR. The revolver was never a favourite weapon of mine. I shall finish the job with this. (*Half draws his sword and sends it back into its scabbard with a click.*)

VONTIEFF. Oh, we shall do for him right enough. It's a

349

pity he's such a boy, though. I would rather we had a grown man to deal with.

GIR. We must take our chance when we can find it. Grown men marry and breed heirs and then one has to massacre a whole family. When we've killed this boy we've killed the last of the dynasty, and laid the way clear for Prince Karl. As long as there was one of this brood left our good Karl could never win the throne.

VONT. Oh, I know this is our great chance. Still I wish the boy could be cleared out of our path by the finger of Heaven rather than by our hands.

SHULTZ. Hush! Here he comes.

(*Enter, by door, centre,* PRINCE DIMITRI, *in undress cavalry uniform. He comes straight into room, begins taking cigarette out of a case, and looks coldly at the three officers.*)

DIMITRI. You needn't wait.

(*They bow and withdraw,* SHULTZ *going last and staring insolently at the* PRINCE. *He seats himself at table, centre. As door shuts he stares for a moment at it, then suddenly bows his head on his arms in attitude of despair. . . . A knock is heard at the door.* DIMITRI *leaps to his feet. Enter* STRONETZ, *in civilian attire.*)

DIMITRI (*eagerly*). Stronetz! My God, how glad I am to see you!

STRONETZ. One wouldn't have thought so, judging by the difficulty I had in gaining admission. I had to invent a special order to see you on a matter of health. And they made me give up my revolver; they said it was some new regulation.

DIM. (*with a short laugh*). They have taken away every weapon I possess, under some pretext or another. My sword has gone to be reset, my revolver is being cleaned, my hunting-knife has been mislaid.

STRON. (*horrified*). My God, Dimitri! You don't mean—?

DIM. Yes, I do. I am trapped. Since I came to the throne three years ago as a boy of fourteen I have been watched and guarded against this moment, but it has caught me unawares.

STRON. But your guards!

DIM. Did you notice the uniforms? The Kranitzki Regiment. They are heart and soul for Prince Karl; the artillery are equally disaffected. The Andrieff Regiment was the only doubtful factor in their plans, and it marches out to camp tonight. The Lonyadi Regiment comes in to relieve it an hour or so later.

STRON. They are loyal surely?

DIM. Yes, but their loyalty will arrive an hour or so too late.

STRON. Dimitri! You mustn't stay here to be killed! You must get out quick!

DIM. My dear good Stronetz, for more than a generation the Karl faction have been trying to stamp our line out of existence. I am the last of the lot; do you suppose that they are going to let me slip out of their claws now? They're not so damned silly.

STRON. But this is awful! You sit there and talk as if it were a move in a chess game.

DIM. (*rising*). Oh, Stronetz! if you knew how I hate death! I'm not a coward, but I do so want to live. Life is so horribly fascinating when one is young, and I've tasted so little of it yet. (*Goes to window.*) Look out of the window at that fairyland of mountains with the forest running up and down all over it. You can just see Grodvitz where I shot all last autumn, up there on the left, and far away beyond it all is Vienna. Were you ever in Vienna, Stronetz? I've only been there once, and it seemed like a magic city to me. And there are other wonderful cities in the world that I've never seen. Oh, I do so want to live. Think of it, here I am alive and talking to you, as we've talked dozens of times in this grey old room, and tomorrow a fat stupid servant will be washing up a red stain in that corner —I think it will probably be in that corner. (*He points to corner near stove, L.*)

STRON. But you mustn't be butchered in cold blood like this, Dimitri. If they've left you nothing to fight with I can give you a drug from my case that will bring you a speedy death before they can touch you.

DIM. Thanks, no, old chap. You had better leave before it begins; they won't touch you. But I won't drug myself. I've never seen any one killed before, and I shan't get another opportunity.

STRON. Then I won't leave you; you can see two men killed while you are about it.

(*A band is heard in distance playing a march.*)

DIM. The Andrieff Regiment marching out! Now they won't waste much time! (*He draws himself up tense in corner by stove.*) Hush, they are coming!

STRON. (*rushing suddenly towards* DIMITRI). Quick! An idea! Tear open your tunic! (*He unfastens* DIMITRI'S *tunic and appears to be testing his heart. The door swings open and the three officers enter.* STRONETZ *waves a hand commanding silence, and continues his testing. The officers stare at him.*)

GIR. Dr. Stronetz, will you have the goodness to leave the room? We have some business with His Royal Highness. Urgent business, Dr. Stronetz.

STRON. (*facing round*). Gentlemen, I fear my business is more grave. I have the saddest of duties to perform. I know you would all gladly lay down your lives for your Prince, but there are some perils which even your courage cannot avert.

GIR. (*puzzled*). What are you talking of, sir?

STRON. The Prince sent for me to prescribe for some disquieting symptoms that have declared themselves. I have made my examination. My duty is a cruel one. . . . I cannot give him six days to live!

(DIMITRI *sinks into chair near table in pretended collapse. The officers turn to each other, nonplussed.*)

GIR. You are certain? It is a grave thing you are saying. You are not making any mistake?

STRON. (*laying his hand on* DIMITRI'S *shoulder*). Would to God I were!

(*The officers again turn, whispering to each other.*)

GIR. It seems our business can wait.

VONT. (*to* DIMITRI). Sire, this is the finger of Heaven.

DIM. (*brokenly*). Leave me.

(*They salute and slowly withdraw.* DIMITRI *slowly raises his head, then springs to his feet, rushes to door and listens, then turns round jubilantly to* STRONETZ.)

DIM. Spoofed them! Ye gods, that was an idea, Stronetz!

STRON. (*who stands quietly looking at* DIMITRI). It was not altogether an inspiration, Dimitri. A look in your eyes suggested it. I had seen men who were stricken with a mortal disease look like that.

DIM. Never mind what suggested it, you have saved me. The Lonyadi Regiment will be here at any moment and Girnitza's gang daren't risk anything then. You've fooled them, Stronetz, you've fooled them.

STRON. (*sadly*). Boy, I haven't fooled them. . . . (DIMITRI *stares at him for a long moment.*) It was a real examination I made while those brutes were waiting there to kill you. It was a real report I made; the malady *is* there.

DIM. (*slowly*). Was it *all* true, what you told them?

STRON. It was all true. You have not six days to live.

DIM. (*bitterly*). Death has come twice for me in one evening. I'm afraid he must be in earnest. (*Passionately.*) Why didn't you let them kill me? That would have been better than this "to-be-left-till-called-for" business. (*Paces across to window,* R., *and looks out. Turns suddenly.*) Stronetz! You offered me a way of escape from a cruel death just now. Let me escape now from a crueler one. I am a monarch. I won't be kept waiting by death. Give me that little bottle.

(STRONETZ *hesitates, then draws out a small case, extracts bottle and gives it to him.*)

STRON. Four or five drops will do what you ask for.

DIM. Thank you. And now, old friend, good-bye. Go quickly. You've seen me just a little brave—I may not keep it up. I want you to remember me as being brave. Good-bye, best of friends, go.

(STRONETZ *wrings his hand and rushes from the room with his face hidden in his arm. The door shuts.* DIMITRI *looks for a moment after his friend. Then he goes quickly over to side table and uncorks wine bottle. He is about to pour some wine into a goblet when he pauses as if struck by a new idea. He goes to door, throws it open and listens, then calls,* "Girnitz, Vontieff, Shultz!" *Darting back to the table he pours the entire phial of poison into the wine bottle, and thrusts phial into his pocket. Enter the three officers.*)

DIM. (*pouring the wine into four goblets*). The Prince is dead—long live the Prince! (*He seats himself.*) The old feud must be healed now, there is no one left of my family to keep it on, Prince Karl must succeed. Long life to Prince Karl! Gentlemen of the Kranitzki Guards, drink to your future sovereign.

(*The three officers drink after glancing at each other.*)

GIR. Sire, we shall never serve a more gallant Prince than your Royal Highness.

DIM. That is true, because you will never serve another Prince. Observe, I drink fair! (*Drains goblet.*)

GIR. What do you mean, never serve another Prince?

DIM. (*rises*). I mean that I am going to march into the next world at the head of my Kranitzki Guards. You came in here tonight to kill me. (*They all start.*) You found that Death had forestalled you. I thought it a pity that the evening should be wasted, so I've killed *you*, that's all!

SHULTZ. The wine! He's poisoned us!

(VONTIEFF *seizes the bottle, and examines it.* SHULTZ *smells his empty goblet.*)

GIR. Ah! Poisoned! (*He draws his sword and makes a step towards* DIMITRI, *who is sitting on the edge of the centre table.*)

DIM. Oh, certainly, if you wish it. I'm due to die of disease in a few days and of poison in a minute or two, but if you like to take a little extra trouble about my end, please yourself. (GIRNITZA *reels and drops sword on table and falls back into chair groaning.* SHULTZ *falls across table and* VONTIEFF *staggers against wall. At that moment a lively march is heard approaching.* DIMITRI *seizes the sword and waves it.*)

DIM. Aha! the Lonyadi Regiment marching in! My good loyal Kranitzki Guards shall keep me company into the next world. God save the Prince! (*Laughs wildly.*) Colonel Girnitza, I never thought death . . . could be . . . so amusing.

(*He falls dying to the ground.*)

CURTAIN

KARL-LUDWIG'S WINDOW

A DRAMA IN ONE ACT

KURT VON JAGDSTEIN.
THE GRÄFIN VON JAGDSTEIN (*his mother*).
ISADORA (*his betrothed*)
PHILIP (*Isadora's brother*) ⎫   *Guests at*
VIKTORIA (*niece of the Gräfin*) ⎬ *Schloss Jagdstein*
BARON RABEL (*a parvenu*) ⎭
AN OFFICER.

SCENE:—"*Karl-Ludwig's Room*" *in the Schloss Jagdstein, on the outskirts of a town in Eastern Europe.*

TIME:—*An evening in Carnival Week, the present day.*

A room furnished in medieval style. In the centre a massive tiled stove of old-German pattern, over which, on a broad shelf, a large clock. Above the clock a painting of a man in sixteenth-century costume. Immediately to Left, *in a deep embrasure, a window with a high window-seat. Immediately on* Right *of stove an old iron-clamped door, approached by two steps. The* Walls *to* Left *and* Right *are hung with faded tapestry. In the foreground a long oak table, with chairs right, left and centre, and a low armchair on* Left *of stage. On the table are high-stemmed goblets and wine bottles, and a decanter of cognac with some smaller glasses.*

The GRÄFIN, *in an old Court costume, and* BARON RABEL, *also in some Court attire of a bygone age, are discovered. Both wear little black velvet masks. The* BARON *bows low to the lady, who makes him a mock curtsy. They remove their masks.*

GRÄFIN (*seating herself at left of table*). Of course we old birds are the first to be ready. Light a cigar, Baron, and make yourself at your ease while the young folks are completing their costumes.

BARON (*seating himself at table*). At my ease in this room
I could never be. It makes my flesh creep every time I enter it.
I am what the world calls a parvenu (*lights cigar*), a man of
today, or perhaps I should say of this afternoon, while your
family is of the day before yesterday and many yesterdays before that. Naturally I envy you your ancestry, your title, your
position, but there is one thing I do not envy you.

GRÄF. (*helping herself to wine*). And that is—?

BAR. Your horrible creepy traditions.

GRÄF. You mean Karl-Ludwig, I suppose. Yes, this room
is certainly full of his associations. There is his portrait, and
there is the window from which he was flung down. Only it
is more than a tradition: it really happened.

BAR. That makes it all the more horrible. I am a man who
belongs to a milder age, and it sickens me to think of the
brutal deed that was carried through in this room. How his
enemies stole in upon him and took him unawares, and how
they dragged him screaming to that dreadful window.

GRÄF. Not screaming, I hope; cursing and storming, perhaps. I don't think a Von Jagdstein would scream even in a
moment like that.

BAR. The bravest man's courage might be turned to water,
looking down at death from that horrid window. It makes
one's breath go even to look down in safety; one can see the
stones of the courtyard fathoms and fathoms below.

GRÄF. Let us hope he hadn't time to think about it. It
would be the thinking of it that would be so terrible.

BAR. (*with a shudder*). Ah, indeed! I assure you the
glimpse down from that window has haunted me ever since I
looked.

GRÄF. The window is not the only thing in the room that
is haunted. They say that whenever one of the family is going
to die a violent death that door swings open and shuts again of
its own accord. It is supposed to be Karl-Ludwig's ghost coming in.

BAR. (*with apprehensive glance behind him*). What an unpleasant room! Let us forget its associations and talk about
something more cheerful. How charming Fräulein Isadora is

looking tonight. It is a pity her betrothed could not get leave to come to the ball with her. She is going as Elsa, is she not?

GRÄF. Something of the sort, I believe. She's told me so often that I've forgotten.

BAR. You will be fortunate in securing such a daughter-in-law, is it not so?

GRÄF. Yes, Isadora has all the most desirable qualifications: heaps of money, average good looks, and absolutely no brains.

BAR. And are the young people very devoted to each other?

GRÄF. I am a woman of the world, Baron, and I don't put too high a value on the sentimental side of things, but even I have never seen an engaged couple who made less pretence of caring for one another. Kurt has always been the naughty boy of the family, but he made surprisingly little fuss about being betrothed to Isadora. He said he should never marry any one he loved, so it didn't matter whom I married him to.

BAR. That was at least accommodating.

GRÄF. Besides the financial advantages of the match the girl's aunt has a very influential position, so for a younger son Kurt is doing rather well.

BAR. He is a clever boy, is he not?

GRÄF. He has that perverse kind of cleverness that is infinitely more troublesome than any amount of stupidity. I prefer a fool like Isadora. You can tell beforehand exactly what she will say or do under any given circumstances, exactly on what days she will have a headache, and exactly how many garments she will send to the wash on Mondays.

BAR. A most convenient temperament.

GRÄF. With Kurt one never knows where one is. Now, being in the same regiment with the Archduke ought to be of some advantage to him in his career, if he plays his cards well. But of course he'll do nothing of the sort.

BAR. Perhaps the fact of being betrothed will work a change in him.

GRÄF. You are an optimist. Nothing ever changes a perverse disposition. Kurt has always been a jarring element in our family circle, but I don't regard one unsatisfactory son out of three as a bad average. It's usually higher.

(*Enter* ISADORA, *dressed as Elsa, followed by* PHILIP, *a blond loutish youth, in the costume of a page, Henry III period.*)

ISADORA. I hope we haven't kept you waiting. I've been helping Viktoria; she'll be here presently.

(*They sit at table.* PHILIP *helps himself to wine.*)

GRÄF. We mustn't wait much longer; it's nearly half-past eight now.

BAR. I've just been saying, what a pity the young Kurt could not be here this evening for the ball.

ISA. Yes, it is a pity. He is only a few miles away with his regiment, but he can't get leave till the end of the week. It is a pity, isn't it?

GRÄF. It is always the way: when one particularly wants people they can never get away.

ISA. It's always the way, isn't it?

GRÄF. As for Kurt, he has a perfect gift for never being where you want him.

(*Enter* KURT, *in undress Cavalry uniform. He comes rapidly into the room.*)

GRÄF. (*rising with the others*). Kurt! How come you to be here? I thought you couldn't get leave.

(KURT *kisses his mother's hand, then that of* ISADORA, *and bows to the two men.*)

KURT. I came away in a hurry (*pours out a glass of wine*) to avoid arrest. Your health, everybody. (*Drains glass thirstily.*)

GRÄF. To avoid arrest!

BAR. Arrest!

(KURT *throws himself wearily into armchair,* Left of Stage. *The others stand staring at him.*)

GRÄF. What *do* you mean? Arrest for what?

KURT (*quietly*). I have killed the Archduke.

GRÄF. Killed the Archduke! Do you mean you have murdered him?

KURT. Scarcely that: it was a fair duel.

GRÄF. (*wringing her hands*). Killed the Archduke in a duel! What an unheard-of scandal! Oh, we are ruined!

BAR. (*throwing his arms about*). It is unbelievable! What,

in Heaven's name, were the seconds about to let such a thing happen?

KURT (*shortly*). There were no seconds.

GRÄF. No seconds! An irregular duel? Worse and worse! What a scandal! What an appalling scandal!

BAR. But how do you mean—no seconds?

KURT. It was in the highest degree desirable that there should be no seconds, so that if the Archduke fell there would be no witnesses to know the why and wherefore of the duel. Of course there will be a scandal, but it will be a sealed scandal.

GRÄF. Our poor family! We are ruined.

BAR. (*persistently*). But *you* are alive. You will have to give an account of what happened.

KURT. There is only one way in which my account can be rendered.

BAR. (*after staring fixedly at him*). You mean—?

KURT (*quietly*). Yes. I escaped arrest only by giving my *parole* to follow the Archduke into the next world as soon as might be.

GRÄF. A suicide in our family! What an appalling affair. People will never stop talking about it.

ISA. It's very unfortunate, isn't it?

GRÄF. (*crossing over to* ISADORA). My poor child!

(ISADORA *dabs at her eyes.*)

(*Enter* VIKTORIA, *dressed in Italian peasant costume.*)

VIK. I'm so sorry to be late. All these necklaces took such a time to fasten. Hullo, where did Kurt spring from?

(KURT *rises.*)

GRÄF. He has brought some bad news.

VIK. Oh, how dreadful. Anything very bad? It won't prevent us from going to the ball, will it? It's going to be a particularly gay affair.

(*A faint sound of a tolling bell is heard.*)

KURT. I don't fancy there will be a ball tonight. The news has come as quickly as I have. The bells are tolling already.

BAR. (*dramatically*). The scandal is complete!

GRÄF. I shall never forgive you, Kurt.

Vik. But what has happened?

Kurt. I should like to say a few words to Isadora. Perhaps you will give us till nine o'clock to talk things over.

Gräf. I suppose it's the proper thing to do under the circumstances. Oh, why should I be afflicted with such a stupid son!

(*Exit the* Gräfin, *followed by the* Baron, *who waves his arms about dramatically, and by* Philip *and* Viktoria. Philip *is explaining matters in whispers to the bewildered* Viktoria *as they go out.*)

Isa. (*stupidly*). This is very unfortunate, isn't it?

Kurt. (*leaning across table with sudden animation as the door closes on the others*). Isadora, I have come to ask you to do something for me. The search party will arrive to arrest me at nine o'clock and I have given my word that they shall not find me alive. I've got less than twenty minutes left. You *must* promise to do what I ask you.

Isa. What is it?

Kurt. I suppose it's a strange thing to ask of a woman I'm betrothed to, but there's really no one else who can do it for me. I want you to take a message to the woman I love.

Isa. Kurt!

Kurt. Of course it's not very conventional, but I knew her and loved her long before I met you, ever since I was eighteen. That's only three years ago, but it seems the greater part of my life. It was a lonely and unhappy life, I remember, till she befriended me, and then it was like the magic of some old fairy-tale.

Isa. Do I know who she is?

Kurt. You must have guessed that long ago. Your aunt will easily be able to get you an opportunity for speaking to her, and you must mention no name, give no token. Just say "I have a message for you." She will know who it comes from.

Isa. I shall be dreadfully frightened. What is the message?

Kurt. Just one word: "Good-bye."

Isa. It's a very short message, isn't it?

Kurt. It's the longest message one heart ever sent to another. Other messages may fade away in the memory, but Time will keep on repeating that message as long as memory lasts. Every sunset and every night-fall will say good-bye for me.

> (*The door swings open, and then slowly closes of its own accord.* KURT *represses a shiver.*)

ISA. (*in a startled voice*). What was that? Who opened the door?

KURT. Oh, it's nothing. It does that sometimes when— when—under circumstances like the present. They say it's old Karl-Ludwig coming in.

ISA. I shall faint!

KURT (*in an agonized voice*). Don't you do anything of the sort. We haven't time for that. You haven't given me your promise; oh, do make haste. Promise you'll give the message! (*He seizes both her hands.*)

ISA. I promise.

KURT. (*kissing her hands*). Thank you. (*With a change to a lighter tone.*) I say, you haven't got a loaded revolver on you, have you? I came away in such a hurry I forgot to bring one.

ISA. Of course I haven't. One doesn't take loaded revolvers to a masquerade ball.

KURT. It must be Karl-Ludwig's window then. (*He unbuckles his sword and throws it into the armchair.*) Oh, I forgot. This miniature mustn't be found on me. Don't be scandalized if I do a little undressing. (*He picks up an illustrated paper from a stool near stove and gives it to* ISADORA *to hold open in front of her.*) Here you are. (*He proceeds to unbutton his tunic at the neck and breast and removes a miniature which is hung round his neck. He gazes at it for a moment, kisses it, gazes again, then drops it on the floor and grinds it to pieces with his heel. Then he goes to window, opens it and looks down.*) I wish the night were darker; one can see right down to the flagstones of the courtyard. It looks awful, but it will look fifty times more horrible in eight minutes' time. (*He comes back to table and seats himself on its edge.*) As I rode along on the way here it seemed such an easy thing to die, and now it's come so close I feel sick with fear. Fancy a Von Jagdstein turning coward. What a scandal, as my dear mother would say. (*He tries to pour out some brandy, but his hand shakes too much.*) Do you mind pouring me out some brandy? I can't steady my hand. (ISADORA *fills a glass for him.*) Thanks. No (*pushing it away*), I won't take it; if I can't have my own courage I won't have that kind. But I wish I hadn't looked down just now. Don't you know what it feels like to go down too quickly in a lift, as if one was racing one's inside and winning by a neck? That's what it will feel like for the first second, and then— (*He hides his eyes a moment in his hands.* ISADORA *falls back in her chair in a faint.* KURT *looks up suddenly at clock.*)

KURT. Isadora! Say that the clock is a minute fast! (*He looks towards her.*) She's fainted. Just what she would do. She isn't a brilliant conversationalist, but she was some one to talk to. How beastly lonely it feels up here. Not a soul to say, "Buck up, Kurt, old boy!" Nothing but a fainting woman and Karl-Ludwig's ghost. I wonder if his ghost is watching me now. I wonder if I shall haunt this room. What a rum idea. (*Looks again at clock and gives a start.*) I *can't* die in three minutes' time. O God! I can't do it. It isn't the jump that I shrink from now—it's the ending of everything. It's too horrible to think of. To have no more life! Isadora and the Baron and millions of stupid people will go on living, every day will bring them something new, and I shall never have one morsel of life after these three minutes. I *can't* do it. (*Falls heavily into chair, left of table.*) I'll go away somewhere where no one knows me; that will be as good as dying. I told them they should not find me here alive. Well, I can slip away before they come. (*He rises and moves towards door; his foot grinds on a piece of the broken miniature. He stoops and picks it up, looks hard and long at it, then drops it through his fingers. He turns his head slowly towards the clock and stands watching it. He takes handkerchief from his sleeve and wipes his mouth, returns handkerchief to sleeve, still watching the clock. Some seconds pass in silence. . . . The clock strikes the first stroke of nine.* KURT *turns and walks to the window. He mounts the window-seat and stands with one foot on the sill, and looks out and down. He makes the sign of the Cross . . . throws up his arms and jumps into space.*)

(*The door opens and the* GRÄFIN *enters, followed by an* OFFICER. *They look at the swooning* ISADORA, *then round the room for* KURT.)

GRÄF. He is gone!

OFFICER. He gave me his word that I should find him here at nine o'clock, and that I should come too late to arrest him. It seems he has tricked me!

GRÄF. A Von Jagdstein always keeps his word.

(*She stares fixedly at the open window. The* OFFICER *follows the direction of her gaze, goes over to window, looks out and down. He turns back to the room, straightens himself and salutes.*)

CURTAIN

THE WATCHED POT

(*Alternative Title*)

THE MISTRESS OF BRIONY

"THE WATCHED POT" was written in collaboration with Mr. Charles Maude, who has sent me the following account concerning the play:

"The circumstances of our writing 'The Watched Pot' were: Mr. Frederick Harrison was very interested in your brother's original 'Watched Pot,' but found it unsuitable for the stage, and brought Saki and myself together in the hope that our joint efforts would make it suitable. My share was shortening it, giving it incident, and generally adapting it for stage purposes. Saki used to write more as a novelist than a playwright.

"He and I used to have many friendly quarrels, as he was so full of witty remarks that it was a cruel business discarding some of his *bons mots*. We always used to terminate such quarrels by agreeing to use his axed witticisms in our next play. . . . Shortly before the war Saki at last gave in on the question of plot, and we had practically completed an entirely new story, still retaining the characters which he loved so dearly and which were so typical of his brain."

The character of Hortensia Bavvel is from life, but the tyranny of her prototype was confined to her own family. She died many years ago.

E. M. M.

CHARACTERS

TREVOR BAVVEL.
HORTENSIA. (*Mrs. Bavvel, his mother.*)
LUDOVIC BAVVEL. *His uncle.*
RENÉ ST. GALL.
AGATHA CLIFFORD ⎱
CLARE HENESSEY
SYBIL BOMONT   ⎰ *Guests at Briony.*
Mrs. PETER VULPY
STEPHEN SPARROWBY ⎰
Col. MUTSOME.
THE YOUNGEST DRUMMOND BOY.
WILLIAM. *Page-boy at Briony.*
JOHN. *Under Butler at Briony.*

ACT I. *Briony Manor Breakfast Room.*
ACT II. *Briony Manor Hall* (*the next evening*).
ACT III. *Briony Manor Breakfast Room* (*the next morning*).

ACT I

Breakfast Room at Briony Manor.

LUDOVIC *fidgeting with papers at escritoire, L., occasionally writing.* MRS. VULPY *seated in armchair, R., with her back partially turned to him, glancing at illustrated papers.*

MRS. VULPY (*with would-be fashionable drawl*). So sweet of your dear cousin Agatha to bring me down here with her. Such a refreshing change from the dust and glare of Folkestone.

LUD. (*absently*). Yes, I suppose so.

MRS. V. And so unexpected. Her invitation took me quite by surprise.

LUD. Dear Agatha is always taking people by surprise. She was born taking people by surprise; in Goodwood Week, I believe, with an Ambassador staying in the house who hated babies. So thoroughly like her. One feels certain that she'll die one of these days in some surprising and highly inconvenient manner; probably from snake-bite on the Terrace of the House of Commons.

MRS. V. I'm afraid you don't like your cousin.

LUD. Oh, dear, yes. I make it a rule to like my relations. I remember only their good qualities and forget their birthdays. (*With increased animation, rising from his seat and approaching her.*) Excuse the question, Mrs. Vulpy, are you a widow?

MRS. V. I really can't say with any certainty.

LUD. You can't say?

MRS. V. With any certainty. According to latest mail advices from Johannesburg my husband, Mr. Peter Vulpy, was not expected by his medical attendants to last into the next week. On the other hand, a cablegram from the local mining organ to a City newspaper over here congratulates that genuine sportsman, Mr. P. Vulpy, on his recovery from his recent severe illness. There happens to be a Percival Vulpy in Johannesburg, so my present information is not very conclusive in either direction. Doctors and journalists are both so untrustworthy, aren't they?

Lud. Could your Mr. P. Vulpy be correctly described as a genuine sportsman?

Mrs. V. There was nothing genuine about Peter. I've never heard of his hitting even a partridge in anger, but he used to wear a horse-shoe scarf-pin, and I've known him to watch football matches, so I suppose he might be described as a sportsman. For all I know to the contrary, he may by this time have joined the majority, who are powerless to resent these intrusions, but my private impression is that he's sitting up and taking light nourishment in increasing doses.

Lud. How extremely unsatisfactory.

Mrs. V. Really, Mr. Bavvel, I think if any one is to mourn Mr. Vulpy's continued existence I should be allowed that privilege. After all, he's my husband, you know. Perhaps you are one of those who don't believe that the marriage tie gives one any proprietary rights.

Lud. Oh, most certainly I do. I am a prospective candidate for Parliamentary honours, and I believe in all the usual things. My objection to Mr. Vulpy's inconvenient vitality is entirely impersonal. If you were in a state of widowhood there would be no obstacle to your marrying Trevor. (*Resumes seat at escritoire, but sits facing her.*)

Mrs. V. Marrying Trevor! Really, this is interesting. And why, pray, should I be singled out for that destiny?

Lud. My dear Mrs. Vulpy, let me be absolutely frank with you. Honoured as we should be to welcome you into the family circle, I may at once confess that my solicitude is not so much to see you married to my nephew as to see him married to somebody; happily and suitably married of course, but anyhow—married.

Mrs. V. Indeed!

Lud. Briefly, the gist of the business is this. Like most gifted young men, Trevor has a mother.

Mrs. V. Oh, I fancy I know *that* already.

Lud. One could scarcely be at Briony for half an hour without making that discovery.

MRS. V. Hortensia, Mrs. Bavvel, is not exactly one of those things that one can hide under a damask cheek, or whatever the saying is.

LUD. Hortensia is a very estimable woman. Most estimable women are apt to be a little trying. Without pretending to an exhaustive knowledge on the subject, I should say Hortensia was the most trying woman in Somersetshire. Probably without exaggeration one of the most trying women in the West of England. My late brother Edward, Hortensia's husband, who was not given to making original observations if he could find others ready-made to his hand, used to declare that marriage was a lottery. Like most popular sayings, that simile breaks down on application. In a lottery there are prizes and blanks; no one who knew her would think of describing Hortensia as either a prize or a blank.

MRS. V. Well, no: she doesn't come comfortably under either heading.

LUD. My brother was distinguished for what is known as a retiring disposition. Hortensia, on the other hand, was dowered with a commanding personality. Needless to say she became a power in the household, in a very short time the only power— a sort of Governor-General and Mother Superior and political Boss rolled into one. A Catherine the Second of Russia without any of Catherine's redeeming vices.

MRS. V. An uncomfortable sort of person to live with.

LUD. Hortensia did everything that had to be done in the management of a large estate—and a great deal that might have been left undone: she engaged and dismissed gardeners, decided which of the under-gamekeepers might marry and how much gooseberry jam should be made in a given year, regulated the speed at which perambulators might be driven through the village street and the number of candles which might be lighted in church on dark afternoons without suspicion of Popery. Almost the only periodical literature that she allowed in the house was the *Spectator* and the *Exchange and Mart*, neither of which showed any tendency to publish betting news. Halma and chess were forbidden on Sundays for fear of setting a bad example to the servants.

Mrs. V. If servants knew how often the fear of leading them astray by bad example holds us back from desperate wickedness, I'm sure they would ask for double wages. And what was poor Mr. Edward doing all this time?

Lud. Edward was not of a complaining disposition, and for a while he endured Hortensia with a certain philosophic calm. Later, however, he gave way to golf.

Mrs. V. And Hortensia went on bossing things?

Lud. From the lack of any organized opposition her autocracy rapidly developed into a despotism. Her gubernatorial energies overflowed the limits of the estate and parish, and she became a sort of minor power in the moral and political life of the county, not to say the nation. Nothing seemed to escape her vigilance, whether it happened in the Established Church or the servants' hall or the Foreign Office. She quarrelled with the Macedonian policy of every successive Government, exposed the hitherto unsuspected Atheism of the nearest Dean and Chapter, and dismissed a page-boy for parting his hair in the middle. With equal readiness she prescribed rules for the better management of the Young Women's Christian Association and the Devon and Somerset Staghounds. Briony used to be a favourite rendezvous for the scattered members of the family. Under the Hortensia *régime* we began to find the train service less convenient and our opportunities for making prolonged visits recurred at rare intervals.

Mrs. V. Didn't her health wear out under all that strain of activity?

Lud. With the exception of an occasional full-dress headache, Hortensia enjoyed implacable good health. We resigned ourselves to the prospect of the good lady's rule at Briony for the rest of our natural lives. Then something happened which we had left out of our calculations. Edward caught a chill out otter-hunting and in less than a week Hortensia was a widow. We are what is known as a very united family, and poor dear Edward's death affected us acutely.

Mrs. V. Naturally it would, coming so suddenly.

Lud. At the same time, there was a rainbow of consolation irradiating our grief. Edward's otherwise untimely decease seemed to promise the early dethronement of Hortensia. Trevor was twenty years of age and in the natural course of things he would soon be absolute master of Briony, and the relict of Edward Bavvel would be denuded of her despotic terrors and become merely a tiresome old woman. As I have said, we were all much attached to poor Edward, but somehow his funeral was one of the most cheerful functions that had been celebrated at Briony for many years. Then came a discovery that cast a genuine gloom over the whole affair. Edward had left the management of the estate and the control of his entire and very considerable fortune to Hortensia until such time as Trevor should take unto himself a wife. (*Rises from seat and takes short steps up and down.*) That was six long years ago and Trevor is still unmarried, unengaged, not even markedly attracted towards any eligible female. Hortensia, on the other hand, has—well, ripened, without undergoing any process of mellowing; rather the reverse.

Mrs. V. Aha! I begin to spot the nigger in the timber-yard.

Lud. I beg your pardon?

Mrs. V. I begin to twig. Deprived by Trevor's marriage of her control of the money-bags, Hortensia, as a domestic tyrant, would shrink down to bearable limits.

Lud. (*seating himself*). Hortensia under existing circumstances is like a permeating dust-storm, which you can't possibly get away from or pretend that it's not there. Living with a comparatively modest establishment at the dower-house, she would be merely like Town in August or the bite of a camel— a painful experience which may be avoided with a little ordinary prudence.

Mrs. V. I don't wonder that you're keen on the change.

Lud. Keen! There is no one on the estate or in the family who doesn't include it in his or her private litany of daily wants.

Mrs. V. And I suppose Mrs. Bavvel is not at all anxious to see herself put on the shelf and does her best to head Mr. Trevor off from any immediate matrimonial projects?

Lud. Of course Hortensia recognizes the desirability of Trevor ultimately finding a suitable consort, if only for carrying on the family. I've no doubt that one day she'll produce some flabby little nonentity who will be flung into Trevor's arms with a maternal benediction.

MRS. V. Meantime you haven't been able to get him to commit himself in any way. But perhaps his mother would break off any engagement she didn't approve of?

LUD. Oh, no fear of that. With all his inertness, Trevor has a wholesome strain of obstinacy in his composition. If he once gets engaged to a girl, he'll marry her. The trouble is that his obstinacy takes the form of his refusing to be seriously attracted by any particular competitor. If patient, determined effort on the part of others would have availed he would have been married dozens of times, but a touch of real genius is required. That is why I appeal to you to help us.

MRS. V. I suppose Agatha considers herself in the running?

LUD. Poor Agatha has a perfect genius for supporting lost causes. I've no doubt she fancies she has an off chance of becoming Mrs. Trevor Bavvel. I've equally no doubt that she never will. Agatha is one of those unaccountable people who are impelled to keep up an inconsequent flow of conversation if they detect you trying to read a book or write a letter, and if you should be suffering from an acknowledged headache she invariably bangs out something particularly triumphant on the nearest piano by way of showing that she at least is not downhearted. Or if you want to think out some complicated problem she will come and sit by your side and read through an entire bulb catalogue to you, with explanatory comments of her own. No, we are all very fond of Agatha, but strictly as a cheerful inane sort of person to have about the house—some one else's house for preference.

MRS. V. And what about Miss Henessey?

LUD. Oh, Clare; she's a rattling good sort in her way, and at one time I used to hope that she and Trevor might hit it off. I think in his own sleepy way he was rather attracted to her. Unfortunately, she only pays rare visits here, and even that she has to keep dark. You see, she's the favourite grandniece and prospective heiress of old Mrs. Packington—you've heard of Mrs. Packington?

MRS. V. No; who is she?

LUD. She lives near Bath, and she's fabulously old, and fabulously rich, and she's been fabulously ill for longer than any living human being can remember. I believe she caught a chill at Queen Victoria's coronation and never let it go again. The most human thing about her is her dislike for Hortensia, who, I believe, once advised her to take more exercise and less medicine. The old lady has ever since alluded to her as a rattlesnake in dove's plumage, and has more than once, with her dying breath, cautioned Clare against intercourse with Briony and its inhabitants. So, you see, there's not much to be hoped for in that direction.

MRS. V. Awfully provoking, isn't it? What about Sybil Bomont?

LUD. Ah, Sybil is the one ray of hope that I can see on the horizon. Personally, she's rather too prickly in her temperament to suit me. She has a fatal gift for detecting the weak spots in her fellow humans and sticking her spikes into them. Matrimony is not reputed to be an invariable bed of roses, but there is no reason why it should be a cactus-hedge. However, she is clever enough to keep that side of her character to the wall whenever Trevor is alongside.

MRS. V. And you think she's got a good sporting chance with him?

LUD. She isn't losing any opportunities that come along, and I'm naturally trying my best to drive the game up her way, but the daily round at Briony doesn't give us much help. We begin the day with solid breakfast businesses; then there are partridges to be tramped after, and Trevor takes his birds rather solemnly, as though it hurt him more than it does them, you know. In the evening a solid dinner, and then Bridge for such small stakes that even Agatha can't lose enough in a fortnight to convince her that she can't play. Then bed.

MRS. V. Well, that's not a very promising programme for any one who's working a matrimonial movement. Couldn't we get up something that would supply a few more openings? Why not theatricals?

LUD. Theatricals? At Briony! You might as well suggest

a massacre of Christian villagers. Hortensia looks on the stage and everything that pertains to it as a sort of early door to the infernal regions.

MRS. V. What about a gymkhana?

LUD. Infinitely worse. The mention of a gymkhana would suggest to Hortensia's mind the unchastened restlessness of the Anglo-Saxon grafted on to the traditional licentiousness of the purple East. The very word "gymkhana" reeks with an aroma of long drinks, sweepstakes, and betrayed husbands, and the usual things that are supposed to strew the social horizon east of Suez.

MRS. V. Well, I'm afraid it's hopeless. I give it up.

LUD. (*rising hastily from his seat*). Dear Mrs. Vulpy, on no account give it up. I rely so much on your tact and insight and experience. You *must* think of something. I'm not a wealthy man, but if you help me to pull this through I promise you my gratitude shall take concrete shape. A commemorative bracelet, for instance—have you any particular favourite stones?

MRS. V. I love all stones—except garnets or moonstones.

LUD. You think it unlucky to have moonstones?

MRS. V. Oh, distinctly, if you've the chance of getting something more valuable. I adore rubies; they're so sympathetic.

LUD. I'll make a note of it. (*Writes in pocketbook.*)

MRS. V. I gather that we're to concentrate on Sybil?

LUD. Sybil, certainly. And of course if there's anything I can do to back you up— (*Enter* CLARE *and* SYBIL *by door: Left back*) . . . no, I don't know that part of Switzerland; I once spent a winter at St. Moritz.

(CLARE *seats herself on couch*, R. SYBIL *takes chair in centre stage.*)

CLARE. You needn't pretend you're discussing Swiss health resorts, because you're not.

MRS. V. Oh, but we are, Miss Henessey. I was just saying Montreux was so——

CLARE. You were discussing Trevor and possible Mrs. Trevors. My dear Mrs. Vulpy, it's our one subject of discussion here.

SYBIL. It's a frightfully absorbing subject, especially for me.

CLARE. Why for you especially?

SYBIL. Oh, well, dear.

LUD. We did touch on the subject, I admit, and Mrs. Vulpy has very kindly offered to help matters along in that direction if she can find an opportunity.

SYBIL. Have you had bad news from South Africa?

MRS. V. Oh, dear, no. My offer is quite disinterested.

SYBIL. How noble of you. How do you propose to begin?

MRS. V. Well, I was just suggesting a little departure from the usual routine of life here, something that would give an opening for a clever girl to bring a man to the scratch. But it seems that Mrs. Bavvel is rather against any of the more promising forms of entertainment.

SYBIL. We've had the annual harvest thanksgiving, but Trevor was seedy and couldn't help with the decorations.

MRS. V. Harvest thanksgiving?

CLARE. Yes, it's one of our rural institutions. We get our corn and most of our fruit from abroad, but we always assemble the local farmers and tenantry to give thanks for the harvest. So broad-minded of us. It shows such a nice spirit for a Somersetshire farmer to be duly thankful for the ripening of the Carlsbad plum.

MRS. V. Is Mrs. Bavvel never absent at dinner parties or anything of that sort? A little impromptu frolic is sometimes a great success.

LUD. Now if you're going to plot anything illicit I must really leave you. Hortensia is not in very great demand as a dinner guest, but she is taking me tomorrow to a meeting at Panfold in connexion with the opening of a Free Library there, and there will be a reception of some sort in the Town Hall afterwards. I entirely disapprove of anything of a festive nature taking place here behind her back, but—we shan't be home much before midnight. It's a fairly long drive. Understand, I entirely disapprove.

(*Gathers papers and Exits, door* Left *front.*)

SYBIL. This threatens to be rather sporting. What have you got up your sleeve?

MRS. V. Oh, nothing, only why not beat up your men and
girl friends at short notice and have a Cinderella? There's a
lovely floor in the morning room and a good piano, and you
could have a scratch supper.

CLARE. And how about the servants? Are we to beg them
all individually to hold their tongues about the affair?

MRS. V. Oh, of course Mrs. Bavvel would have to know
about it next day.

CLARE. It's very well for you to talk like that, you're a
comparative stranger here, and I dare say you'd find a certain amount of amusement in the situation. Those of us who
know what Hortensia is like when anything displeases her—
well, it would simply be a case of Bradshaw at breakfast and
a tea-basket at Yeovil.

MRS. V. But then we're playing to win; it's a sort of *coup
d'état*. With the fun and excitement of the dancing and the
music, and of course the sitting-out places, and, above all, the
charming sense of doing something wrong, the betting is that
Trevor will be engaged to one of you girls before the night's
out. And then the morrow can be left to take care of itself.

SYBIL. It sounds *lovely*. I'm horribly frightened of Hortensia, but I'm game to get up this dance.

CLARE. A *coup d'état* is a wretchedly messy thing. It's as
bad as cooking with a chafing-dish; it takes such ages to clean
things up afterwards.

(*Enter* AGATHA *door* Right *back, with two large baskets piled with asters, dahlias, etc., and long trails of ivy
and brambles.*)

AGATHA. Hullo, you idle people. I'm just going to arrange
the flowers. (*Puts baskets down on escritoire.*)

SYBIL. Are you? Why?

AGATHA. Oh, I always do when I'm here. (*Begins slopping
flowers and leaves about in inconvenient places.*)

MRS. V. We're plotting to have a little impromptu dance
here tomorrow night.

AGATHA (*spilling a lot of dahlias over* MRS. VULPY). Oh,
you dear things, how delightful! But whatever will Hortensia
say?

SYBIL. Hortensia is opening an Ear Hospital or Free Library or some such horror at Panfold, and won't know about it till it's all over, and then it will be too late to say much.

CLARE. I fancy you'll find that Hortensia's motto will be "better late than never."

AGATHA. Oh, I fancy she'll be rather furious. But what fun, all the same. But who will we get to come?

SYBIL. Oh, we can get nine couples easily. There's all the Abingdon house party, they'll be dead nuts on it. And Evelyn Bray plays dance music like a professional.

AGATHA. What a lovely joke. I say—let's make it a fancy dress affair while we're about it.

SYBIL. Oh, let's have fireworks on the lawn and Salome dances and a looping-the-loop performance.

AGATHA. That's talking nonsense. But fancy dress is so easily managed. I went to a ball in North Devon three years ago as Summer, and it was all done at a moment's notice. Just a dress of some soft creamy material with roses in my hair and a few sprays of flowers round the skirt. I've got the dress with me somewhere, and it wouldn't need very much alteration.

SYBIL. It will only want letting out a bit at the waist, and you can call yourself "St. Martin's Summer."

AGATHA. How dare you say such things! Really, you're the most spiteful tongued person I know. I should think you'd better go as an East Wind.

SYBIL. My dear Agatha, I'm not one of the Babes in the Wood, so I wish you'd stop covering me with leaves. And don't let us start quarrelling. Of course you're as jumpy as a grasshopper at the idea of this dance, and I suppose you flatter yourself that you're going to pull it off with Trevor. Because a man has refused you twice there's no particular reason for supposing that he'll accept you at the third bidding. It's merely a superstition.

AGATHA (*furiously*). You utterly odious fablemonger! I suppose it's considered clever to say ill-natured, untrue things about people you happen to be jealous of.

MRS. V. My dear girls, don't waste time in a sparring

match. There's no sense in quarrelling when we want to get our little scheme started.

SYBIL. *I* don't want to quarrel; I'm only too ready to be accommodating all round. If I *do* chance to land a certain eligible individual in my net I'm quite willing to turn my second-best prospect over to any one that applies for him; quite a darling, with a decent rent roll, and a perfect martyr to asthma; ever so many climates that he can't live in, and you'll have to keep him on a gravel soil. Awfully good arrangement. A husband with asthma has all the advantages of a captive golf-ball; you always know pretty well where to put your hand on him when you want him.

AGATHA. But if I had a really nice man for a husband I should want him to be able to come with me wherever I went.

SYBIL. A woman who takes her husband about with her everywhere is like a cat that goes on playing with a mouse long after she's killed it.

MRS. V. First catch your mouse. Which brings us back to the subject of the dance. I think we agree that fancy dress is out of the question?

CLARE. There wouldn't be time.

MRS. V. Well, why not make it a sheet-and-pillow-case dance? (*They all stare at her.*) Quite simple, every one drapes themselves in sheets, with a folded pillow-case arranged as a head-dress, and a little linen mask completes the domino effect. No trouble, only takes ten minutes to arrange, and at a given time every one sheds their masks and headgear, and the sheets make a most effective sort of Greek costume. Lulu Duchess of Dulverton gave quite a smart sheet-and-pillow-case at Bovery the other day.

AGATHA. Was it respectable?

MRS. V. Absolutely. Oh, do take your blessed bramble-bush somewhere else. (AGATHA, *who has impaled* MRS. VULPY's *skirt on a trail of briars, makes violent efforts to disentangle her.*) No, please leave my skirt where it is. I only want the brambles removed.

AGATHA. That's the worst of briars, they do catch on to one's clothes so.

MRS. V. That is one of the reasons why I never sit down in a bramble patch for choice. Of course, if one has a tame hedge following one about the house, one can't help it.

AGATHA (*gathering up remains of her foliage*). Well, I shall go and do the dining-room vases now and leave you irritable things to work out the dance programme. I'll think out a list of people we can invite.

[*Exit, door* Left *front*.

CLARE. Agatha would be almost tolerable in the Arctic regions where the vegetation is too restricted to be used as house decoration.

SYBIL. Look here, I'll bike over to the Abingdons' and get things in marching order there. I've just time before lunch. You're going to help us, I suppose, Clare?

CLARE. Oh, if you are all bent on having a domestic earthquake, I'll stand in with you. I'll send notes over to Evelyn and the Drummond boys. But I know the whole thing will be a horrid fizzle.

SYBIL. You dear old thing. You always turn up trumps when it comes to the pinch.

CLARE. If you dare to call me a dear old thing I'll allude to you in public as a brave little woman. So there.

MRS. V. Well, if you two are going to start sparring, I shall go and write letters.

[*Exit* MRS. VULPY, *door* R. *back*.

CLARE. There's something I don't like about that woman. She looks at me sometimes in a way that's almost malicious. What on earth did Agatha bring her down here for?

SYBIL. Mrs. Vulpy is somewhat of a rough diamond, no doubt.

CLARE. So many people who are described as rough diamonds turn out to be merely rough paste.

SYBIL. Even paste has its uses.

CLARE. Oh, afflictions of most kinds have their uses, I suppose, but one needn't go out of one's way to import them. (*Exit* SYBIL, R. *back; Enter* TREVOR, L. *back; he is about to sit on couch.*) Be careful where you sit, Trevor. Agatha has been shedding bits of bramble all over the room. (*They both begin picking bits of leaf, etc., off the couch.*) When that parable was being read at prayers this morning about going to the hedges and by-ways to fetch in the halt and the blind, I couldn't help thinking Agatha wouldn't have stopped at that: she'd have brought in the hedges as well.

TREVOR (*seating himself with caution on couch*). I've just had about a wheelbarrow-load of gorse prickles removed from the cozy corner in the smoking-room.

CLARE. Gorse prickles? (*Seats herself on couch.*)

TREVOR. Agatha said it was a Japanese design. If it had been an accident I could have forgiven it. I say, Clare, do you know you have got rather beautiful eyes?

CLARE. How should I know, you've never mentioned it before.

TREVOR. Oh, well, I noticed it long ago, but it takes me ages to put my thoughts into words.

CLARE. That's rather unfortunate where compliments are concerned. By the time it occurs to you to tell me that I've got a nice profile I shall probably have developed a double chin.

TREVOR. And that will be the time when you'll be best pleased at being told you've got a nice profile. So you see there's some sense in holding back a compliment.

CLARE. Well, don't be horrid and sensible, just when you were beginning to be interesting. It's not often one catches you in the mood for paying compliments. Please begin over again.

TREVOR. Item, a pair of beautiful eyes, one rather nice chin, with power to add to its number. Quite a lot of very pretty hair, standing in its own grounds—or is it semi-detached?

CLARE. I don't think your compliments are a bit nice; I don't mind how long you keep them back.

TREVOR. I haven't finished yet. (*Takes her hand.*) Do you know, Clare, you've got the most charming hand in the world, because it's a friendly hand. I think if you were once friends with a fellow you'd always be friends with him, even——

CLARE. Even——?

TREVOR. Even if you married him, and that's saying a great deal.

CLARE. I think if I liked a man well enough to marry him I should always be the best of friends with him.

(*Enter* LUDOVIC, *bustles over to escritoire.*)

LUD. (*as they let go each other's hands*). Hullo, has Trevor been telling you your fortune?

CLARE (*rising*). Nothing so romantic; he's been explaining the finger-print system of criminal investigation. If I ever strangle Agatha in a moment of justifiable irritation Trevor will be a most damaging witness.

(LUDOVIC *rings bell and then seats himself at escritoire.*)

TREVOR. Shall I be disturbing you if I smoke a cigarette here?

LUD. Not in the least. I like seeing people idle when I'm occupied. It gives me the impression that I'm working so much harder than I am.

CLARE. Don't be long over your cigarette, Trevor, you've got to be let into a conspiracy that Mr. Ludovic isn't supposed to know anything about.   [*Exit* CLARE.

TREVOR. Are they plotting to give you a birthday present or something of that sort?

LUD. Nothing so laudable.

(*Enter* WILLIAM, R. *front.*)

WILL. Did you ring, sir?

LUD. Yes, just arrange the flowers.

WILL. Yes, sir. (*Gathers up flowers and foliage from various places where* AGATHA *has stacked and strewn them and proceeds to re-arrange them with considerable taste.*)

LUD. (*to* TREVOR). No, it's your despotic mother who mustn't get wind of the plot. I am merely the innocent bystander.

TREVOR. I'm awfully fond of my mother of course, but I must admit things would be a little more comfortable if she wasn't quite so——so——

LUD. Exactly. But she always has been and she always will be. As regards household affairs, of course I've no right to express an opinion, but her constant supervision of the political affairs of the neighbourhood is extremely embarrassing to the Party. My prospective candidature down here is becoming more and more doubtful under the circumstances. Hortensia is not content with having her finger in the pie, she wants to put the whole dish into her pocket.

WILL. (*who is standing near doorway*). Mrs. Bavvel is crossing the hall, sir.

LUD. (*becomes violently busy at escritoire*). The factory system in East Prussia presents many interesting points of comparison— (*Enter* HORTENSIA, R. LUDOVIC *rises.*) Ah, Hortensia.

HOR. William, what are you doing here?

WILL. Arranging the flowers, ma'am.

HOR. They don't want arranging every day. They were arranged only yesterday. (*Seats herself on chair in centre of stage.* LUDOVIC *resumes seat.*)

WILL. It was brought on prematurely, ma'am.

LUD. Agatha had been trying some new effects in autumnal foliage; I told William to put things straight a bit.

HOR. I see. And where is Adolphus?

WILL. The cockatoo, ma'am? She's drying in the pantry after her bath.

HOR. It's not his day for a bath. He always bathes on Thursday.

WILL. She seemed restless, as if she wanted it, ma'am.

HOR. In future, remember he bathes on Thursdays only. And, William——

WILL. Yes, ma'am.

HOR. I think I've spoken about it before. You always hear me allude to the cockatoo as he, or Adolphus, therefore you are not to speak of him in the feminine gender.

WILL. Yes, ma'am.   [*Exit, L. front.*

HOR. A quiet-mannered boy and always behaves reverently at prayers, but I'm afraid he's inclined to be opinionated. What coverts are you shooting this afternoon, Trevor?

TREVOR. The other side of the long plantation.

HOR. I understand that you are employing one of the Brady

boys as a beater. I do not approve of the selection. Kindly discontinue his services.

TREVOR. But, mother, the Bradys are dreadfully poor.

HOR. Not deservingly poor. Mrs. Brady is the most thriftless woman in the parish. Some people can't help being poor, but Mrs. Brady is poor as if she enjoyed it. I'm not going to have that sort of thing encouraged.

LUD. (*rising from seat*). There is another aspect of the matter which I think you are losing sight of, Hortensia. Mrs. Brady may be poor in this world's goods, but she is rich in relatives. She has a husband and one or two uncles, and at least three brothers, and they all have votes. The non-employment of the Brady boy may lose us all those votes at the next election.

HOR. My dear Ludovic, I am not inattentive to local political needs. I supervise the issue of pamphlets dealing with the questions of the day to all electors, in monthly instalments. When the next election comes you may be sure it won't take me by surprise.

LUD. No, but the result may. (*Resumes his seat.*)

HOR. Trevor, oblige me by taking an amended list of beaters to the head-keeper, with the Brady boy left out. Go now, or you will forget.

TREVOR (*rising unwillingly*). As you will, mother. He made a very good beater, you know.

HOR. But not a suitable one. (*Exit* TREVOR. LUDOVIC *throws up his hands.*) Who is this Mrs. Vulpy that Agatha has brought down? I don't care for the look of her.

LUD. I believe Agatha met her at Folkestone.

HOR. That doesn't make it any better. Agatha says she's seen trouble, but she doesn't explain what sort of trouble. Some women see trouble with their eyes open.

LUD. I believe she has a husband in Johannesburg.

HOR. To have a husband in Johannesburg might be a source of anxiety or inconvenience, but it can hardly be called seeing trouble.

LUD. Agatha is so good-natured that she's very easily imposed on.

Hor. I wish her good nature would occasionally take the form of consulting other people's interests. I suppose this Mrs. Vulpy is married after a fashion, though we really know nothing about her. She may be merely a husband-hunting adventuress, and of course Trevor is sufficiently important as a matrimonial prize to attract that sort of woman. Agatha ought to be more careful.

Lud. Wouldn't it be as well, in view of such dangers, if Trevor were to bestir himself to find a suitable wife?

Hor. Nothing of the sort. I must ask you not to give him any advice of that sort. Trevor is far younger than his years, and there is no need to suggest marriage to him for a long while to come. If I thought he had any present intentions that way I should be far more particular what sort of girls I had staying down here. Sybil Bomont and Miss Henessey, for instance, I've no objections to them as guests, but I should require quite a different type of young woman for a daughter-in-law.

Lud. Trevor may have his own views on the subject.

Hor. Hitherto he has expressed none. I must go and write to the Bishop.

Lud. About Trevor?

Hor. (rising). No. About the Dean of Minehead.

Lud. What has the Dean been doing?

Hor. He has treated me with flippancy. I had written asking if he could give me any material for a lecture I am going to give next week on the Puritan movement in England. He replies on a post-card (reads): "The Puritan movement was a disease, wholesome though irritating, which was only malignant if its after effects were not guarded against." Things have come to a disgraceful pass when a Church dignitary can treat the Puritan movement in that spirit.

Lud. Perhaps the Dean was only exercising a little clerical humour.

Hor. I don't think the subject lends itself to jest, and I certainly don't intend that my lecture shall be regarded in a spirit of frivolity. I've something better to do than provide an outlet for Deanery humour. My letter to the Bishop will contain some pretty plain speaking.

LUD. My dear Hortensia, the Dean of Minehead is one of the few churchmen in these parts who give us political support. It would be rather unfortunate to fall out with him.

HOR. In my opinion, it would be still more unfortunate to tolerate post-card flippancies on serious subjects from men in his position. I shall ask the Bishop, among other things, whether it is not high time that certain clerical clowns ceased their unfair competition with the music-halls.

(*Exit* HORTENSIA, R. *back.* LUDOVIC *goes through pantomime of tragic disgust.*)

(*Enter* BUTLER, L. *back.*)

BUTLER. Mr. St. Gall to see you, sir.

LUD. René! What on earth brings him down here? Show him in.

(*Exit* BUTLER, L. *back. Enter* RENÉ, L. *back, crosses stage without shaking hands, looks at himself in mirror, R.*)

RENÉ. I've lost my mother.

LUD. (*wheeling round in chair*). Do I understand you to mean that your mother is dead?

RENÉ (*who has carefully settled himself in armchair, R.*). Oh, nothing so hackneyed. I don't think my mother will ever die as long as she can get credit. She was a Whortleford, you know, and the Whortlefords never waste anything. No, she's simply disappeared and I was wired for. It was most inconvenient.

LUD. But can't she be found?

RENÉ. The butler says she can't. Personally I haven't tried. Only got down late last night. And I've had to come away with simply nothing to wear. I've been in Town for the last three days having some clothes made, and I was to have had two new lounge suits tried on this morning for the first time. Naturally I'm a bit upset.

LUD. But about your mother's disappearance—aren't you doing anything?

RENÉ. Oh, everything that could be done at short notice.

We've notified the police and the family solicitors and consulted a crystal-gazer, and we've told the dairy to send half a pint less milk every day till further notice. I can't think of anything else to do. It's the first time I've lost a mother, you know.

LUD. But do you mean to say there's absolutely no trace of her? Why, I saw her in church only last Sunday.

RENÉ. I expect they've looked for her there; the butler says they've searched everywhere. The servants have been awfully kind and helpful about it. They say they must put their trust in Christian Science, and go on drawing their wages as if nothing had happened. That's all very well, but no amount of Christian Science will help me to be fitted on when I'm here and my clothes are in Sackville Street, will it?

LUD. I think you might show a little natural anxiety and emotion.

RENÉ. But I am showing emotion in a hundred little ways if you'd only notice them. To begin with, I'm walking about practically naked. This suit I've got on was paid for last month, so you may judge how old it is. And that reminds me, I wish you'd do something for me. Something awfully kind and pet-lamb in my hour of trouble. Lend me that emerald scarf-pin that you hardly ever wear. It would go so well with this tie and I should forget how shabbily I'm dressed.

LUD. It would go so well that it would forget to find its way back again. Things that are lent to you, René, are like a hopeless passion, they're never returned. In the light of past experience I absolutely refuse to lend you a thirty-guinea scarf-pin.

RENÉ. How true it is that when one weeps one weeps alone. Anyway, you might lend me your pearl and turquoise one; the pearl is a very poor one, and it can't be worth anything like thirty guineas.

LUD. I don't see why I should be expected to make you a present of it, even if it only cost five.

RENÉ. Oh, well, after all, I've lost a mother. I make less fuss about that than you do at the prospect of separation from a five-guinea scarf-pin. You might show a little kindness to a poor grass orphan. And, Ludovic, now that you've practically given way on that matter, I want you to turn your attention to something that's been worrying me dreadfully of late.

Lud. Gracious, what have you been doing now?

René. Oh, it isn't now, the mischief was done twenty-three years ago, and then it wasn't exactly my doing. It's just this, that I'm twenty-three years old. If my mother had only held me over for a matter of four years I should be nineteen now, which is the only age worth being. Women always rush things so. I shouldn't mind so much being twenty-three if I had the money to carry it off well. The mater does the best she can for me; she can't afford me an allowance, but she borrows money whenever she can from friends and acquaintances, and sends me haphazard cheques. It's quite exciting getting a letter from home. Of course that sort of thing can't go on indefinitely, and now that my only source of income has disappeared without leaving a postal address things have nearly come to a crisis. One can't treat life indefinitely as a prolonged Saturday-to-Monday. There are always the Tuesdays to be reckoned with.

Lud. I don't like to suggest anything so unbecoming as an occupation, but can't you manage to get entangled with a salary of some sort?

René. It's not so beastly easy. I've tried designing posters, and for three weeks I was assistant editor of a paper devoted to fancy mice. The devotion was all on one side. Now, Ludovic, if you'd only do what you sometimes half promised to do, and make me your personal private secretary, and let me do Parliamentary correspondence for you, and tell female deputations that they can't see you because you're in your bath, and all that sort of thing that a busy man can't do for himself——

Lud. My dear boy, I'm not at the present moment a member of Parliament, I'm not even standing as a candidate.

René. But, Ludo, why aren't you? You know you've had a hankering that way for a long time, and you can easily afford it. And it isn't a difficult job. All one has to do is to boil with indignation at discreet intervals over something—the Jews in Russia or impurity in beer or lawlessness in the Church of

England. It doesn't matter particularly what, as long as you really boil. The public likes a touch of the samovar about its representatives. And, then, if you want to be a Parliamentary wit, *that* isn't difficult nowadays. If the Government is making a mess of Persian affairs just mew like a Persian kitten whenever a Minister gets up to speak. It isn't anything really hard I'm asking of you.

LUD. Thanks very much for coaching me. But an indispensable preliminary to all this brilliance is that I should be elected.

RENÉ. You could easily get a seat down here if you wanted to. They've always wanted one of the Bavvels to stand, and old Spindleham is not likely to last another session, so the ball is practically at your feet.

LUD. My dear René, under present circumstances Briony would be an impossible headquarters from which to conduct an election campaign. Have you considered that Hortensia would have her finger in the pie all the time? She would speak at my meetings and pledge me to the most appalling social and political doctrines. She would get down the most unfortunate specimens of the party to support me—in fact, by the time election day came round I should feel inclined to vote against myself. I should very probably be defeated, and if I got in Hortensia would look on me as her nominee, sent to Westminster to represent her views on every subject under the sun. I shouldn't have half an hour's peace. No, as long as Hortensia remains in the foreground I shan't contest a seat in this part of the country. That's absolutely certain.

RENÉ. Ludovic, this Hortensia business is getting to be absurd. Everything you want to do down here you run up against Hortensia, Mrs. Bavvel. When *are* you going to get Trevor married and the old woman dethroned?

LUD. My dear René, as if we hadn't tried! Talk about bringing a horse to the water, we've brought water to the horse, gallons of it, and put it right under his nose. We've advertised eligible young women as if they had been breakfast foods.

RENÉ. And here am I, twenty-three years old, expected to

wait indefinitely for my secretaryship and my daily bread
until Trevor chooses to suit himself with a wife. It's really
ridiculous. That's the worst of you middle-aged folks, if I may
say so without offence. You're so jolly well content to wait
for things to happen. It's only the old and the quite young
who really know the value of hurry.

LUD. But, bless my soul, we can't compel Trevor to marry.

RENÉ. It's absurd of him to persist in celibacy that he isn't
qualified for. He's decent enough in his way, but he hasn't
got the strength of character to fit him for the graver responsibilities of bachelorhood. Can't he be rushed into marrying
somebody?

LUD. Rushing Trevor is not exactly a hopeful operation.
It's rather suggestive of stampeding a tortoise; at the same
time, I may tell you in confidence that something desperate of
that nature is going to be tried tomorrow night in the absence
of Hortensia and myself at Panfold.

RENÉ. Oh, Ludovic! What?

LUD. You must ask Sybil or some of the others for details.
I know nothing about it and entirely disapprove, but the idea
originated with me. Hush!

(*Enter* HORTENSIA, *door* R. *back*.)

(LUDOVIC *and* RENÉ *rise to their feet*.)

HOR. I want you to read my letter to the Bishop. Oh, Mr.
St. Gall. I didn't know the neighbourhood was honoured with
your presence. I needn't ask if you're on a holiday; that is a
permanent condition with you, I believe.

LUD. Mr. St. Gall has lost his mother—she's disappeared.

HOR. Disappeared! What an extraordinary thing to do.
Had she any reasons for disappearing?

RENÉ. Oh, several, but my mother would never do anything for a reason.

HOR. But was anything troubling her? (*Sits chair centre
of stage*.)

RENÉ. Oh, nothing of that kind. She's one of those people with a conscience silk-lined throughout.

LUD. Has she any relatives that she might have gone to?

RENÉ. Relatives? None that she's on speaking terms with. She was a Whortleford, you know, and the Whortlefords don't speak. There is a cousin of hers, a Canon, somewhere in the Midlands; he's got peculiar views—he believes in a future life, or else he doesn't, I forget which. The mater and he used to be rather chummy, but a hen came in between them.

HOR. A hen?

RENÉ. Yes, a bronze Orpington or some such exotic breed; the mater sold it to him at a rather exotic price. It turned out afterwards that the bird was an abstainer from the egg habit, and the Canon wanted his money back. I read some of the letters that passed between them. I don't think the mater is likely to have gone *there*.

HOR. But there is an alarming side to this disappearance which you don't seem to appreciate. Something dreadful may have happened.

RENÉ. It has. I had been measured for two lounge suits, one of them in a rather taking shade of copper beech, and they were to have been tried on for the first time this morning——

LUD. (*hurriedly*). As everything is naturally rather at sixes and sevens at the Oaks, I have asked St. Gall to stay to lunch. I suppose we can give him a bite of something?

HOR. (*coldly*). I am always glad to show hospitality to your friends, Ludovic. I'll read you my letter to the Bishop at a more convenient moment. I'm just going to see Laura Gubbings; she's going out to Afghanistan as a missionary, you know. That country has been scandalously neglected in the way of missionary effort.

LUD. There are considerable political and geographical difficulties in the way.

HOR. Not insuperable, however.

LUD. Perhaps not, but extremely likely to expand. We usually set out on these affairs with the intention of devoting a certain amount of patient effort in making the natives reasonably glad at the introduction of mission work; then we find ourselves involved in a much bigger effort to make them reasonably sorry for having killed the missionaries.

HOR. Really, Ludovic, your reasoning is preposterous. I

should be the first to oppose anything in the shape of armed aggression in Central Asia.

LUD. If you would oppose Miss Gubbings' missionary designs on that region I should feel more comfortable.

RENÉ. I say, can't she take me with her?

HOR. I don't really see in what capacity you could be included in a mission party.

RENÉ. I could give my famous imitation of a nautch-girl. That would fetch the Afghans in shoals, and then Miss Gubbings could hold overflow meetings and convert them.

HOR. A nautch-girl?

RENÉ. Yes, I did it for some friends at St. Petersburg and they just loved it. They said I got as far East as any one could be expected to go. If I wasn't suffering under a domestic bereavement I'd do it for you now.

HOR. Not at Briony, thank you! St. Petersburg may applaud such performances if it pleases. From the things I've heard from there——

RENÉ. Oh, for the matter of that, the things one hears about the Afghans—there is a proverb in that country——

LUD. (hurriedly). In any case Miss Gubbings is hardly likely to accept your collaboration in her labours.

HOR. Miss Gubbings is going out with a religious mission, not with a *café chantant*. From your description of your performance and from what I can guess of its nature, I don't think it would be likely to enhance either our moral or national reputation in the eyes of the Ameer's subjects. (*Rises from chair.*) A boy masquerading as a nautch-girl!

[*Exit* HORTENSIA, *door* L. *front.*

RENÉ. Another avenue of employment closed to me. By the way, where is Trevor? I want to ask him to lend me some sleeve-links. These ones won't go at all with the scarf-pin you're lending me.

LUD. You'll probably find him at the headkeeper's lodge. Lunch is at one sharp.

[*Exit* RENÉ, *door* L. *back.*

Now perhaps I can have a few moments to myself and the Prussian Factory Acts.

(*Enter* SPARROWBY, R. *back.*)

SPAR. (*seating himself astride of chair, centre*). I say, I wish you'd do something to help me.

LUD. (*looks over shoulder and then back to pamphlet*). If it's anything in the way of sleeve-links or scarf-pins you're too late.

SPAR. Oh, nothing of that sort——

LUD. Or are you looking for a strayed relative? I can get you the address of a crystal-gazer.

SPAR. Oh, no, I haven't lost any one; quite the reverse, dear old chap, I've *found* her.

LUD. (*half turning round*). Not Mrs. St. Gall?

SPAR. Mrs. St. Gall! Dear, no. I've found the one woman I could ever want to make my wife, and I want you to help me to pull it off.

LUD. (*returning to the perusal of his pamphlet*). Oh, I see. Delighted to be of any use to you. I don't quite know how you pull these things off, and I'm rather occupied these days, but on Wednesday next, in the early part of the afternoon, I can spare you an hour or two. (*Cuts page of pamphlet and continues reading.*)

SPAR. Oh, but one can't fix a precise time for that sort of thing. The trouble I'm in is that she won't be serious about it. She——

LUD. What does "Bewegungslosigkeit" mean in English?

SPAR. Oh, I don't know, it's a German word, isn't it? I don't know any German. (LUDOVIC *consults dictionary.*) She treats it as a sort of temporary infatuation on my part. She won't realize how hopelessly I'm in love with her.

LUD. (*yawning*). I thought it was the hopelessness of your suit that she did realize. Who is the lady?

SPAR. Sybil Bomont.

LUD. (*leaping round in his seat and letting dictionary fall*). Impossible! Out of the question. You mustn't think of marrying Sybil Bomont.

SPAR. But I can think of nothing else. Why mustn't I marry her?

LUD. You must dismiss the matter completely from your

mind. Go fishing in Norway or fall in love with a chorus girl. There are heaps of chorus girls who are willing to marry commoners if you set the right way about it. But you mustn't think of Sybil Bomont.

SPAR. But what is the objection? Surely there's no madness in her family?

LUD. (*contemplatively*). Madness, no. Oh, no. At least not that one knows of. Certainly her father lives at West Kensington, but he is sane on most other subjects.

SPAR. Then what is this mysterious obstacle? There is nothing against me, I suppose? I am fairly well off as far as income is concerned.

LUD. Ah! And to what sort of environment are you proposing to take this young girl, who has been carefully brought up and kept shielded from the coarser realities of life?

SPAR. Well, I live very quietly in the country and farm a few acres of my own.

LUD. Precisely: I had heard stories to that effect. Now, my dear Sparrowby, the moral atmosphere of a farm, however amateur and non-paying the farm may be, is most unsuitable for a young woman who has been brought up in the seclusion of a town life. Farming involves cows, and I consider that cows carry the maternal instinct to indelicate excess. They seem to regard the universe in general as an imperfectly weaned calf. And then poultry—you must admit that the private life of the domestic barn-door fowl—well, there's remarkably little privacy about it.

SPAR. But, my dear Bavvel——

LUD. And are you quite sure that you are free to pay court to Miss Bomont—that you have no other entanglements?

SPAR. Entanglements? Why, certainly not.

LUD. Think a moment. What about Miss Clifford?

SPAR. Agatha Clifford! You must be dreaming. I haven't the ghost of an entanglement with her.

LUD. I thought I saw you both on rather intimate terms at breakfast this morning.

SPAR. (*indignantly*). She upset a sardine on to my knees.

LUD. I suppose you encouraged her to.

SPAR. Encouraged her! Why, it ruined a pair of flannel trousers.

LUD. Well, I expect her sardine was just as irrevocably damaged. Anyway, you condoned her action; I heard you tell her that it didn't matter.

SPAR. Oh, I had to say that. What else could one say?

LUD. If any one upset a sardine on to my lap I should find no difficulty in keeping the conversation from flagging. The difficulty would be to avoid saying too much. In your case I think you were rather too eloquently silent. The spilling of a sardine on to your lap may seem a small thing to you, but you must remember that women attach more importance to these trifles than we do. Believe me, I have watched your perhaps unconscious attentions to Miss Clifford with interest, and if anything I can do——

SPAR. But I assure you——

(*Enter* AGATHA *and* SYBIL, *door* L. *back.*)

AGATHA. Everything's going splendidly. Every one whom we've asked is coming, and Cook has been given a dark hint to have some fruit salads and mayonnaise and that sort of thing accidentally on hand— Oh, I forgot you weren't to know anything about it. Promise that you'll forget that you heard anything.

LUD. I assure you I heard nothing. I was struggling with some technicalities in a German pamphlet. Dear Miss Bomont, do show me where I can find a better dictionary than this one.

SYBIL. Come along. There's one somewhere in the library.

LUD. And, Agatha—Mr. Sparrowby wants you to help him to dig up some ferns for a rockery he's making at home.

(LUDOVIC *holds door,* L. *front, open for* SYBIL, *both Exit.*)

SPAR. I say——

AGATHA (*cheerfully*). By all means; let's come now. I love rooting up ferns. Here are some baskets. (*Fishes three large garden baskets out of chest.*)

SPAR. But it's nearly lunch-time, and I don't really——

AGATHA. Never mind lunch. There's sure to be something

cold that we can peck at if we're late. Come on; the trowels
are out in the tool-shed. I know a lovely damp wood where
we can grub about for hours.

Spar. But I've got rheumatism.

Agatha. So have I. Come on.

(*Gives him two baskets to carry and leads the way
off by door, R. back.*)

CURTAIN

ACT II

The Hall. Briony Manor.

(Clare *and* Trevor *seated on couch, centre of stage.
Enter* Agatha, *door L., passes behind them. All three
dressed in sheet costume, with hood thrown back, no
masks.*)

Agatha. I say, Trevor, it's going splendidly!

[*Exit* Agatha, *door R. back.*

Clare. If you ask me, it's going as flat as can be. No one
seems to want to dance, and Cook is scared to death and has
only sent us up half the amount of supper that we asked for.

Trevor. There's enough to drink, anyhow; I saw to that.
I went down to the cellar myself.

Clare. Yes, and the result will be that just when we want
to be hurrying every one off the premises they'll be getting
festive and reckless, and your august and awful mother will
run up against half of them on the doorstep, or meet them in
the drive. (*Enter door, R. back, veiled figure, who glides up
to them.*) Hallo, who's this? (Sybil *unmasks and throws back
hood.*) Oh, Sybil, I might have guessed.

Sybil (*seating herself armchair centre of stage*). I fled
away from that tiresome Sparrowby person who keeps on
pestering me to sit out with him. Clare dear, do go and relieve Evelyn, she's played about six dances running.

CLARE. Oh, Evelyn would play all night without feeling tired. (*Rises.*) But one excuse is as good as another, I suppose. (*Walks towards door*, R.)

SYBIL. I don't know what you mean. (*Exit* CLARE, *door* R. *back.*) It's going awfully flat.

TREVOR (*lighting cigarette*). Oh, a frightful fizzle. I think every one is a bit scared at what they're doing.

SYBIL. I know I am. There'll be fine fireworks tomorrow when Her Majesty gets to hear of it.

TREVOR. Fireworks! There'll be a full-sized earthquake. I think I shall go cub-hunting if there's a meet within reasonable distance.

SYBIL. You won't find many of us here when you return. We shall be cleared out in a batch, like Chinese coolies. Trevor, why on earth don't you marry and get rid of this one-woman rule at Briony? With all due respect, your mother is no joke. She's perfectly awful.

TREVOR. Oh, I suppose I shall marry somebody some day, but it's the choosing business that is so beastly complicated. Think of the millions and millions of nice women there are in the world, and then of the fact that one can only marry one of them—it makes marrying an awfully ticklish matter. It's like choosing which puppies you're going to keep out of a large litter; you can never be sure that you haven't drowned the wrong ones.

SYBIL. Oh, but if you go on those lines you'll never marry any one. You should just have a look round at the girls you personally know and like and make your choice from one of them. You'd soon find out whether she responded or not. I believe in grasping one's nettle.

TREVOR. But supposing there are half a dozen nettles and you don't know which to grasp?

SYBIL. Oh, come, we're getting on. Half a dozen is better than millions and millions. And there must always be some one whom you prefer out of the half-dozen. There's Agatha, for instance. Of course she is your cousin, but that doesn't really matter. And in her way she's not a bad sort.

TREVOR. She passed through the hall just before you came

in. If I'm to ask her to marry me I'd better go and do it now before I forget it.

SYBIL (*alarmed*). Oh, don't go and propose to her just because I suggested it. You'd make me feel an awful matchmaker, and I should never forgive myself if it turned out wrong. Besides, I doubt very much if she'd make the sort of mistress you'd want for Briony. One has to think of so many things, hasn't one?

TREVOR. Precisely my standpoint. And if Agatha turned out a disappointment I couldn't give her away to the gardener's boy, like an unsatisfactory puppy. You see, it isn't so easy to grasp the nettle when you really come to do it.

SYBIL. Oh, well, Agatha doesn't exhaust the list. There's Clare, for instance, she's got some good points, don't you think?

TREVOR. You don't say so with much conviction.

SYBIL. I'm awfully good pals with Clare, but that doesn't prevent me from recognizing that she's got rather a queer temper at times; the things that she says sometimes are simply hateful, and she's not a bit straightforward. I could tell you of little things she's done— (*Enter from door centre veiled figure.*) Who on earth is this?

(SPARROWBY *throws off hood and mask and seats himself on small chair facing* SYBIL.)

SPAR. I've been following all sorts of figures about, thinking they were you. But I knew all the time they couldn't be you, because I didn't feel a thrill when I was near them. I always feel a thrill when I'm near you.

SYBIL (*viciously*). I wish you never felt thrills, then.

SPAR. You're dreadfully unkind, Sybil, but I know you don't mean what you say.

SYBIL. Sorry you find my conversation meaningless.

SPAR. Oh, I didn't mean that!

SYBIL. We seem equally unfortunate in our meanings.

SPAR. I say, Sybil, I wish you'd take me a little more seriously.

SYBIL. One would think you were an attack of measles.

(*Enter* MRS. VULPY *with* DRUMMOND, *door* L., *both unhooded. She catches sight of trio and rushes up.*)

MRS. V. (*to* DRUMMOND). Excuse me one moment. (*To* SPAR.) Naughty man, you know you promised me the kitchen lancers. Come along. Hurry.

SPAR. (*rising unwillingly*). But they're playing a waltz now.

MRS. V. They're getting ready for the lancers. Come on.

[*Exeunt* MRS. VULPY, SPARROWBY *and* DRUMMOND, *door* R. *back*.

SYBIL. The Vulpy woman is rather a brick at times. I say, *Trevor*.

(*During* SPARROWBY *duologue* TREVOR *has fallen asleep. Wakes hurriedly*.)

TREVOR. I nearly went off to sleep. Please excuse my manners. I was up awfully early this morning.

SYBIL. Well, do keep awake now. We're in the middle of a most interesting conversation.

TREVOR. Let's see, you were recommending me to marry Clare Henessey.

SYBIL. Oh, well—I don't think I went as far as that. Clare and I are first-rate pals, and I should awfully like to see her make a good marriage; but I'd be rather sorry for her husband all the same. If anything rubs her the wrong way her temper goes queer at once, like milk in thunder-time, and she simply says the most ill-natured things.

TREVOR. That's another ungraspable nettle, then. I told you it wasn't so jolly easy.

SYBIL. But, Trevor, there are surely others, only you're too lazy to think of them.

TREVOR. As to thinking of them, I am not too lazy to do that; it's the further stages I'm deficient in.

SYBIL. Of course I sympathize with your difficulty. I wish I could find you some one really nice, some one who would enter into all your pursuits and share your ambitions and be a genuine companion to you.

TREVOR. I hate that sort.

SYBIL. Do you? How funny. At least, I don't know, I rather think I agree with you. Some women make dreadful nuisances of themselves that way. Well, you don't give me much help in choosing you a wife.

TREVOR. What do you think of Mrs. Vulpy?

SYBIL. What! That woman with nasturtium-coloured hair and barmaid manners. Surely you're not attracted by her.

TREVOR. I didn't say I was. I asked you what you thought of her.

SYBIL. Oh, as to that; not a bad sort in her way, I suppose. Some people call her a rough diamond. If it was my declaration I should call her a defensive spade. But anyhow she's married, so she doesn't come into our discussion.

TREVOR. I want to tell you something, something that concerns you alone.

SYBIL. What is it?

TREVOR. Your hair's coming down behind.

SYBIL. Oh, bother! It's that horrid hood arrangement. I'll fly upstairs and put it right. (*Rises.*) I say, Trev, there's a much nicer sitting-out place on the landing, near that old carved press, where the tiresome Sparrowby person won't find me. Come up in two minutes' time, there's a dear.

TREVOR. Right-oh!

SYBIL. Now don't go to sleep.

[*Exit* SYBIL, *up staircase* L.
(*Enter* AGATHA, *door* R. *back, passes along back of stage.*)

AGATHA. Everything's going swimmingly; it's a huge success.

[*Exit* AGATHA, *door* L. *back.*
(*Enter* RENÉ, *door centre, in evening dress with smoking jacket; carrying bottle of wine, wine-glass, some grapes and peaches. Seats himself on armchair near small table.*)

RENÉ. Going rather flat, isn't it?

TREVOR. Frightful fizzle. I'm so sleepy myself that I can only just keep my eyes open. Was up at the farm awfully early this morning.

RENÉ. Some shorthorn or bantam was going to have young

ones, I suppose. In the country animals are always having young ones; passes the time away, I suppose. I know a lady in Warwickshire who runs a rabbit farm. She has musical boxes set up over the hutches.

TREVOR. Musical boxes?

RENÉ. Yes, they play the wedding march from "Lohengrin" at decent intervals. I'm going to ask you an extremely personal question.

TREVOR. If it has anything to do with spare shirt-studs——

RENÉ (*who is delicately feeding himself while talking*). Don't be silly. It hasn't. I want to know—are you happy?

TREVOR. Immensely.

RENÉ (*disappointedly*). Are you? Why?

TREVOR. One never has any definite reason for being happy. It's simply a temperamental accident in most cases. I've nothing to worry me, no money troubles, no responsibilities; why should I be anything else but happy?

RENÉ. You ought to marry.

TREVOR. You think that would improve matters?

RENÉ. It would elevate you. Suffering is a great purifier.

TREVOR. You're not a very tempting advocate of matrimony.

RENÉ. I don't recommend it, except in desperate cases. Yours is distinctly a desperate case. You ought to marry if only for your mother's sake.

TREVOR. My mother? I don't know that she is particularly anxious to see me mated just yet.

RENÉ. Your mother is one of those proud silent women who seldom indicate their wishes in actual words.

TREVOR. My dear René, my mother may be proud, but where her wishes are concerned she is not inclined to be silent.

RENÉ. At any rate, an unmarried son of marriageable age is always a great anxiety. There's never any knowing what impossible person he may fix his fancy on. As old Lady Cloutsham said to me the other day, *à propos* of her eldest son: "If Robert chooses a wife for himself, it's certain to be some demi-mondaine with the merest superficial resemblance to a lady; whereas if I choose a wife for him I should select some one who at least would be a lady, with a merely superficial resemblance to a demi-mondaine.

TREVOR. Poor Lady Cloutsham, her children are rather a trial to her, I imagine. Her youngest boy had to leave the country rather hurriedly, hadn't he?

RENÉ. Yes, poor dear. He's on a ranch somewhere in the wilds of Mexico. Conscience makes cowboys of us all. Unfortunately, it's other people's consciences that give all the trouble; there ought to be a law compelling every one to keep his conscience under proper control, like chimneys that have to consume their own smoke. And then Gladys, who was the most hopeful member of the family, went and married a Colonial Bishop. That really finished Lady Cloutsham. As she said to me: "I always classed Colonial Bishops with folk-songs and peasant industries and all those things that one comes across at drawing-room meetings. I never expected to see them brought into one's family. This is what comes of letting young girls read Ibsen and Mrs. Humphry Ward.

(*An unearthly long-drawn-out howl is heard.*)

TREVOR (*sitting up*). What on *earth*—?

RENÉ. Only the idiotic Drummond boy, who pretends he's the Hound of the Baskervilles.

(*Enter* AGATHA, *door* L., *runs giggling across stage pursued by* DRUMMOND *in sheet with phantom-hound mask on head. Exeunt both, door* R. *back.*)

TREVOR (*rising slowly*). By Jove, forgot I'd promised to go upstairs. Sybil will be fuming her head off.

RENÉ. We can't get a rubber of Bridge presently, can we?

TREVOR. 'Fraid not. The women would be rather mad if we shirked dancing.

(*Draws himself slowly together and lounges up staircase,* L. *Exit.*)

(*Enter* SPARROWBY, *door* R. *back.*)

SPAR. Why aren't you rigged out like the rest of us, St. Gall?

(*Takes* TREVOR'S *seat on couch.*)

RENÉ. Well, for one thing I'm in platonic mourning, having partially lost a mother, so it would hardly be the thing.

And another reason is that the hood arrangement would ruffle one's hair so.

SPAR. As if that mattered a bit. You're absurdly particular about your appearance and your clothes and how your tie is tied and about your hair. Look at me; it doesn't take me two minutes in the morning to do my hair.

RENÉ. So I should imagine. Isn't there a proverb, a fool and his hair are soon parted?

SPAR. I say, you're beastly rude!

RENÉ. I know I am. My mother was a Whortleford, and the Whortlefords have no manners. I'm sorry I called you a fool, though, because I want you to do something really kind for me. Trevor has suggested a game of Bridge and I don't want to back out of playing. The trouble is that I haven't a coin worth speaking about on me. If you'd be awfully pet-lamb and lend me something——

SPAR. I dislike lending on principle. It generally leads to unpleasantness.

RENÉ. Really this worship of Mammon is getting to be the curse of the age. People make more fuss about lending a few miserable guineas than the Sabine women did at being borrowed by the Romans. I know a lady of somewhat mature age who took rather a fancy to me last season and in a fit of sheer absence of mind she lent me ten pounds. She's got quite a comfortable income, but I declare she thinks more of that lost tenner than of the hundreds and hundreds that she's never lent me. It is become quite a monomania with her. It's her one subject of conversation whenever we meet.

SPAR. Don't you intend paying her back?

RENÉ. Certainly not. Her loss makes her beautiful. It brings an effective touch of tragedy into an otherwise empty life. I could no more think of her apart from her mourned-for loan than one could think of Suez without the canal or Leda without the swan.

SPAR. If that's your view of your obligations I certainly shan't lend you anything. By the way, where is Sybil Bomont? She's been sitting out about four dances with Trevor. It's about my turn now.

RENÉ (*with sudden energy*). Sybil has got a bad headache. She's lying down for a few minutes.

SPAR. Where? I particularly want to see her.

RENÉ. In the billiard-room, and she particularly doesn't want to see any one.

SPAR. But I only want——

(*Enter* CLARE *and* AGATHA, *door* R. *back.*)

RENÉ. Agatha! Sparrowby is complaining that he's got no one to dance with.

AGATHA. Come along, they're just going to try that new Paris dance; I can't pronounce it.

SPAR. But I can't dance it!

AGATHA. Neither can I. Come on.

SPAR. But I say——

[*Exit* AGATHA *dragging* SPARROWBY *off, door* R. *back.*

RENÉ. Thank goodness, he's out of the way. People who make a principle of not lending money are social pests.

CLARE (*seating herself on couch*). This is going to be a dismal failure. By the way, have you seen Trevor anywhere?

RENÉ. Yes, he turned rather giddy with the dancing, I suppose, so he's taking a turn or two out in the air.

CLARE. Is he alone?

RENÉ. Oh, quite. So am I for the moment. Do stay and talk to me.

CLARE. You must be interesting, then. After sitting out successfully with Sparrowby and the two Drummond boys, I feel that there's nothing left in the way of dull and trivial conversation to listen to.

(*While she is talking* RENÉ *hands her half of the remaining peach and resumes his seat.*)

RENÉ. Let's talk about ourselves; that's always interesting.

CLARE. I suppose you mean, let's talk about yourself.

RENÉ. No, I'd much rather dissect your character; I find some good points in it.

CLARE. Do tell me what they are.

RENÉ. You have a rich aunt who is childless.

CLARE. She's a great-aunt.

RENÉ. All the better. That sort of thing doesn't spoil by being kept in the family for a generation or two. The greater the aunt the greater the prospect.

CLARE. And what other good points do you find in me?

RENÉ. I think I've nearly exhausted the list.

CLARE. I don't find you a bit interesting.

RENÉ. Well, be patient for a moment, I'm going to say something quite personal and interesting. Will you marry me? The question is sudden, I admit, but these things are best done suddenly. I suppose it was the mention of your great-aunt that suggested it.

CLARE. The answer is equally sudden. It's "No."

RENÉ. Are you quite sure you mean that?

CLARE. Convinced.

RENÉ. How thoroughly sensible of you. So many girls in your place would have said "Yes."

CLARE. I dare say. Our sex hasn't much reputation for discrimination. I didn't know that marrying was in your line.

RENÉ. It isn't. I dislike the idea of wives about a house: they accumulate dust. Besides, so few of the really nice women in my set could afford to marry me.

CLARE. From the point of view of reputation?

RENÉ. Oh, I wasn't thinking of that. At twenty-three one is supposed to have conquered every earthly passion: of course it's the fashion in statesmanship nowadays to allow the conquered to have the upper hand.

CLARE. A convenient fashion and saves a lot of bother. Tell me, taking me apart from my great-aunt, are you pleased to consider that I should make a satisfactory wife?

RENÉ. Satisfactory wives aren't made: they're invented. Chiefly by married men. But as things go I think we should have made what is called a well-assorted couple. I should have taught you in time to be as thoroughly selfish as myself, and then each would have looked after our own particular interests without having need to fear that the other was likely to suffer from any neglect.

CLARE. There is much to be said for that point of view. It's the imperfectly selfish souls that cause themselves and others so many heart-burnings. People who make half sacrifices for others always find that it's the unfinished half that's being looked at. Naturally they come to regard themselves as un-appreciated martyrs.

RENÉ. By the way, I may as well tell you before you find out. Trevor isn't out of doors. He's sitting out with Sybil somewhere on the landing.

CLARE (*half rising from seat*). You beast! Why did you tell me he'd gone out?

RENÉ. Well, the fact of the matter is, I thought that if those two were left together undisturbed for half an hour or so, one or other of them might propose.

CLARE (*resuming seat*). Oh, that's the game, is it? And has Sybil enlisted your services in this precious stalking move-ment?

RENÉ. Oh, dear, no: I'm merely working in a good cause. Some one's got to marry Trevor, you know, and the sooner the better. Personally, I don't think it's very hopeful, but the whole motive of this otherwise idiotic dance is to head Trevor into a matrimonial ambush of some sort. He's so superbly sleepy that there's just a chance of it coming off, but I'm not sanguine.

CLARE. If he *is* to be rushed into marrying some one, I don't see why I shouldn't be in the running as well as any one else.

RENÉ. Exactly what William was saying to me this morning.

CLARE. William! The page-boy?

RENÉ. Yes, he's rather keen on seeing you Mrs. Trevor Bavvel.

CLARE. That's very sweet of him, but I didn't know he took such an intelligent interest in the matter.

RENÉ. It's not altogether disinterested. It seems they've got a half-crown sweepstake on the event, in the servants' hall, and he happened to draw you, so naturally he's in a bit of a flutter on your behalf.

CLARE. I didn't know we were the centre of so much specu-lation. Mercy on us, what would Hortensia say if she knew that she was nurturing a living sweepstake under her roof!

And is William good enough to consider that I have a fair sporting chance of pulling it off?

RENÉ. I fancy he's rather despondent. He said you didn't seem to try as hard as some of the others were doing. He puts your chair as near Trevor's as possible at prayers, but that's all he's able to do personally.

CLARE. The little devil!

RENÉ. I believe that if the Vulpy woman wasn't handicapped with a preliminary husband, she'd carry Trevor off against all competitors. She's just got the bounce that appeals to a lazy, slow-witted bachelor.

CLARE. There's something I particularly object to in that woman. She always talks to me with just a suspicion of a furtive sneer in her voice that I find extremely irritating. I don't know why Agatha inflicted her on us.

(*Enter* AGATHA, R. *back.*)

AGATHA. What's that you're saying about me?

CLARE. Only wondering what induced you to cart Mrs. Vulpy down here.

AGATHA. Oh, come, she's not a bad soul, you know, taking her all round. (*Seats herself on couch.*) We are all of us as God made us.

RENÉ. In Mrs. Vulpy's case some recognition is due to her maid as a collaborator.

AGATHA. You're all very ill-natured about her. Anyway, this dance was her idea.

CLARE. Yes, and a horrid mess it's going to land us all in. I daren't think of tomorrow. By the afternoon the news will have spread over the greater part of Somersetshire that a costume ball has been given at Briony in the temporary absence of Mrs. Bavvel.

AGATHA. I say, do you think she'll be very furious?

CLARE. If Hortensia is more intolerant on one question than on any other, it's on the subject of what she calls mixed dancing. I remember a county fête at Crowcoombe where she vetoed the project of a maypole dance by children of six and seven years old until absolutely assured that the sexes would dance apart. Some of the smaller children were rather ambiguously dressed and were too shy to tell us their names, and the curate and I had a long and delicate task in sorting the he's from the she's. One four-year-old baffled our most patient researches, and finally had to dance by itself round a maypole of its own.

AGATHA. I'm beginning to get dreadfully frightened about tomorrow. Can't we water it down a bit and pretend that we had games and Sir Roger de Coverley and that sort of thing?

CLARE. We shall have to tone things down as much as possible, but Hortensia will hold an inquiry into the whole matter, and drag the truth out by inches. She'll probably dismiss half the servants and have the morning-room repapered; as for us——

RENÉ. There's a very good up train at 3.15.

AGATHA. But I haven't made arrangements for going anywhere; it will be most inconvenient.

CLARE. On the morrow of an unsuccessful *coup d'état* one generally travels first and makes one's arrangements afterwards.

(*A prolonged howl heard.*)

RENÉ. The idiotic Drummond boy again.

(*Enter* DRUMMOND, *door* R. *back.*)

DRUMMOND. I say, you make nice cheerful hosts, sitting there like a lot of moping owls. Do come and buck things up a bit; there are only two couples dancing.

RENÉ (*tragically*). Yes, let us go and dance on the edge of our volcano.

AGATHA. Oh, don't, I feel quite creepy. It reminds me of that Duchess person's ball on the eve of Waterloo.

[*Exeunt* DRUMMOND, RENÉ,
AGATHA, *door* R. *back.*

(CLARE *remains seated. Enter* MRS. VULPY, *centre.*)

MRS. V. All alone, Miss Henessey? By the way, where is that dear boy, Trevor?

CLARE. I believe he's upstairs, and I don't think he wishes to be disturbed.

MRS. V. I suppose that means that you are waiting to catch

him when he comes down, and that *you* don't want to be disturbed.

CLARE. Oh, please put that construction on it if it amuses you. I shouldn't like to think you weren't enjoying yourself.

MRS. V. Oh, I'm enjoying myself right enough, *Miss* Henessey, watching some of the little by-play that's goin' on. (*Seats herself.*) It is *Miss* Henessey, isn't it? (*Gives a little laugh.*)

CLARE. What do you mean?

MRS. V. Oh, well, only that we've met before, you know, at least I've seen you before, though you probably didn't see me. You were writing your name in the visitors' book at the Grand Anchor Hotel at Bristol, just about six weeks ago.

CLARE. I did stop there one night about six weeks ago. I don't remember seeing you there.

MRS. V. I remember not only seeing you, but the names you wrote in the book: Henessey wasn't one of them, nor Miss Anything either.

CLARE. How clever of you to remember. You seem to have a good head for business—other people's business.

MRS. V. Oh, well, I suppose it was the innocent vagueness of the names you had put down that arrested my attention. "Mr. and Mrs. Smith," London. Your companion had gone upstairs with the luggage, so I didn't see Mr. Smith, and somehow at the time I had a feeling that I wasn't seeing Mrs. Smith—at least not the permanent Mrs. Smith.

CLARE. It sounds rather crude and compromising as you put it, I admit, but the explanation is not really very dreadful. Only——

MRS. V. Only you don't feel disposed to give an explanation at such short notice. You're quite right. Second thoughts are usually more convincing in such cases.

CLARE. Well, to be candid, I don't see that my travelling adventures are any particular concern of yours.

MRS. V. Perhaps you're right. I dare say they more immediately concern the lady whose guest you are. Shall I raise her curiosity on the subject? As you've got such a satisfactory explanation ready, you can have no objection, I suppose.

CLARE. You know Mrs. Bavvel well enough to know that

what might seem a harmless escapade to ordinary judges would not be regarded so leniently by her.

Mrs. V. And Mr. Trevor? He doesn't share his mother's prejudices. You won't mind if I let him into our little secret about the Smith *ménage*?

Clare (*rising from her seat*). Mrs. Vulpy, what particular gratification do you find in threatening to make mischief between me and my friends? It shows you up in rather a bad light, and I don't really see what you expect to gain by it.

Mrs. V. Simply, my dear girl, we happen to be interested in the same man.

Clare. You mean Trevor?

Mrs. V. Of course. I know perfectly well that all you girls are hanging round here for a chance of snapping him up, and I'm clever enough to see which of you is likely to succeed. It won't be Sybil Bomont, whatever any one may say.

Clare. In any case, you can scarcely regard yourself as a competitor.

Mrs. V. Because of being already married, you mean? Well, I don't mind telling you I've more definite news about my husband's condition than I've been pretending to have. He was past all chance of recovery when the last mail went out. I'm too honest to pretend to be anything but glad. If you knew the life we've had! I've been a lonely woman since the day I married Peter, and now I don't intend being lonely any more. As soon as I set eyes on Trevor Bavvel I knew he was just the sort of man I wanted to begin life with over again.

Clare. And do you suppose that you are so obviously *his* conception of the ideal life-mate that he'll throw himself at your feet as soon as he knows you are free to marry him?

Mrs. V. Oh, my dear, most things in life that are worth having have to be worked for. I've made a good beginning by enlisting his sympathy as a fellow-conspirator over this dance. The worse row we get into over it the better. Then, when my husband's estate has been straightened out, I shan't be badly off, and I shall come to this neighbourhood and do a little hunting and give Bridge parties and all that sort of thing. Provided nothing happens in the meantime, I fancy I stand a very fair chance of pulling it off.

CLARE. I see.

MRS. V. Ah, you do see, do you? You understand now why I want your flirtation with Trevor to be nipped in the bud, and why I'm prepared to nip it myself if necessary with that little story of the Grand Anchor Hotel?

CLARE. You are making one little miscalculation, Mrs. Vulpy. Trevor was a public-school boy, and in English public-school tradition the spy and the tale-bearer don't occupy a very exalted position.

MRS. V. Oh, you may call me hard names, but you can't wriggle away from me in that fashion. I've got you in my grip—so! Either you leave the field clear for me or the story of your visit to the Grand Anchor Hotel with a gentleman, whom, for want of fuller information, we will call Mr. Smith, becomes public property.

CLARE. Some one is coming downstairs. Shall we go and see how the dancing is going on? They're playing that Bulgarian March.

MRS. V. Oh, yes, let's go and hear it. I love Slav music, it takes one out of oneself so.

CLARE. Which is sometimes an advantage.

[*Exeunt* VULPY *and* CLARE.
(*Enter down staircase,* L., SYBIL *and* TREVOR.)

TREVOR. I say, it's getting nearly time to call this off.

SYBIL. Oh, nonsense, it's only just ten. They can't be back before eleven. Your mother is delivering an address, and she's not given to cutting her words short on these occasions, I believe.

TREVOR. Well, half an hour more, then. And let's make it go with a bit more fling for the wind-up.

SYBIL. Right-oh! (*Enter* SPARROWBY, L.) Lord, here's that pestering idiot again.

SPAR. Ah, at last I've found you! Are you better?

SYBIL. Better?

SPAR. I was told you were lying down in the billiard-room with a bad headache.

SYBIL. Who on earth told you that?

SPAR. St. Gall.

SYBIL. Oh, René! Never believe a word he says. I'm in my usual health, but I'm frightfully hungry. Trevor, do go and forage for something edible. I'll wait for you here. I was too excited to eat much at dinner, and I know I shan't dare to come down to breakfast tomorrow.

TREVOR. I'll go and parley with Cook.

[*Exit* TREVOR, *door centre.*

SPAR. What have you been doing all this time?

SYBIL (*seating herself on couch*). Oh, don't ask me. Sitting upstairs with Trevor and trying to keep him from going to sleep. I assure you it wasn't amusing.

SPAR. I should never want to go to sleep if I were by your side.

SYBIL. What an inconvenient husband you would be.

SPAR. Oh, I wish you wouldn't be always fooling. (*Seats himself beside her.*) You don't know how much I love you!

SYBIL. Of course I don't; I've only got your word for it that you care in the least bit for me. Now if you were to do something to prove it——

SPAR. I'd do anything.

SYBIL. Well, do something that would give you a name in the world. For instance, paint pictures and have them exhibited in the Royal Academy: it would be something to talk about when one went there.

SPAR. But I can't paint.

SYBIL. Oh, I don't think that matters as long as you exhibited. Of course, they wouldn't sell. Or why not found a religion, like Mahomet and Wesley and those sort of people did.

SPAR. But you can't found religions off-hand. You want inspiration and enthusiasm and disciples, and all manner of special conditions.

SYBIL. Well, then, you could invent a new system of scoring at county cricket, or breed a new variety of fox-terrier.

SPAR. But it would take years and years to produce a new variety.

SYBIL. I would wait—oh, so patiently.

SPAR. *Sybil*, if I was successful in breeding a new kind of fox-terrier, would you really marry me?

SYBIL. I wouldn't exactly marry you, but I would buy some of the puppies from you. I've got an awfully jolly little fox-terrier at home. If you tell her "the Kaiser's coming," or "Roosevelt's coming," she lies quite still, but if you say, "King Edward's coming," she jumps up at once. Isn't it clever? I taught her myself with gingerbread biscuits.

SPAR. Won't you realize that I'm asking you to be my wife?

SYBIL. Of course I realize it; you've asked me so often that I'm getting to expect nothing else. I wish you would vary it a little and ask me something different. Only don't ask me that dreadful thing about "this man's father was my father's only son," it nearly gives me brain fever.

SPAR. I wonder if you have a heart at all?

SYBIL. Of course I've got the usual fittings. It's very rude of you to suggest that I'm jerry-built. But look here, joking apart, do do something to oblige me. Go and dance with poor Evelyn Bray; she's been at the piano all the evening and hasn't had a scrap of dancing herself.

SPAR. If I do, will you give me a dance afterwards?

SYBIL. I'll give you two.

SPAR. (*rising from his seat*). You angel. I wish you'd always be as kind.

[*Exit* SPARROWBY, *door* R. *back*.

SYBIL (*hearing some one coming*). Is that you, Trevor? I'm getting ravenous. (*Enter* AGATHA, *door centre*.) Oh, Lord!

AGATHA. Hullo, Sybil, have you seen Trevor?

SYBIL. No, I think he's dancing.

AGATHA. He hasn't been in the dancing room for about an hour; neither have you. (*Seats herself on chair right of couch.*)

SYBIL. I'm so hot, I'm sitting out here to get cool. I suppose it's the excitement. I say, do go and help Evelyn at the piano, she's getting quite fagged out, poor child.

AGATHA (*acidly*). I've just played them a polka; Evelyn hasn't been near the piano for the last half-hour. If you hadn't been sticking to Trevor like a drowning leech you might have known that.

SYBIL (*furiously*). I haven't been sticking to him, and leeches don't drown, anyway.

AGATHA. Oh, I'm not up in their natural history. I only know they stick like mud. I'll say a floating leech if you like.

SYBIL. It so happens I've been listening to marriage proposals from that pestering Sparrowby all the evening.

AGATHA. I've had the infliction of dancing with him no fewer than four times, my dear, and he kept on complaining that he couldn't find you. Don't be disheartened: accidents will happen to the most accomplished fibbers.

SYBIL. Why is it that plain women are always so venomous?

AGATHA. Oh, if you're going to be introspective, my dear. (*Laughs.*)

(*Enter* TREVOR, *door centre.*)

TREVOR. All I could raise was some cold rice pudding and a bottle of pickled walnuts. If there's anything I detest in this world it's rice pudding.

AGATHA (*going over to table*). I loathe rice pudding, it's so wholesome. On the other hand, I simply adore pickled walnuts. (*Helps herself.*)

TREVOR. Won't you have some, Sybil? (*Helps himself.*)

SYBIL (*rising from seat*). I'm not going to stay here to be insulted. I've been called a liar and a leech.

AGATHA. I said fibber, my dear, not liar.

[*Exit* SYBIL, *door R. back.*

TREVOR. Have you two been having a slanging match?

AGATHA. Oh, no, only poor Sybil is so dreadfully short-tempered, she can't take anything in good part. She's a dear, sweet girl, one of the very best, but I should be awfully sorry for any fellow who married her. That reminds me, Trevor—you ought to marry.

(*Helps herself to another walnut.*)

TREVOR. There's a great deal to be said for that point of view: and as far as I can see there's no particular likelihood of it's being left unsaid.

(*Helps himself to walnut.*)

AGATHA. I suppose the difficulty is to think of any one you care for sufficiently.

TREVOR. Have you anything to say against Mrs. Vulpy?

AGATHA. Good heavens! Mrs. Vulpy? That vulgar, over-dressed parrot, with the manners of a cockney sparrow. I should think she began life in a cheap-jack store. Surely you can't be thinking seriously of her?

TREVOR. I asked you if you had anything to say against her. Considering the short notice you managed very well. Wasn't it you who brought her down here?

AGATHA (*helping herself to walnut*). Well, yes, I suppose I did. Somehow in Folkestone she didn't seem such an awful rotter. Anyway, she's got a husband. No, the woman for you must be one with great similarity of tastes——

TREVOR. On the contrary, I avoid that kind. At the present moment I regard you with something bordering on aversion. (*Stirs frantically in jar.*)

AGATHA. Regard me with aversion! My dear Trevor!

TREVOR. If it hadn't been for our duplicate passion for pickled walnuts this cruel tragedy wouldn't have happened. There's not one left.

AGATHA. Oh, Trevor, not one? (*Stirs mournfully in jar.*)

TREVOR. No, the woman I marry must have an unbridled appetite for rice pudding.

AGATHA (*dubiously*). I dare say some rice pudding, nicely cooked, wouldn't be bad eating. (*Begins agitating spoon listlessly through rice pudding dish.*)

TREVOR. That is not the spirit in which my ideal woman must approach rice pudding. She must eat it with an avidity that will almost create scandal; she must devour it secretly in dark corners, she must buy it in small quantities from chemists on the plea that she has neuralgia. Such a woman I could be happy with.

AGATHA. She might be odious in other respects. (*While talking is waving spoon in air.*)

TREVOR. One must not expect to find perfection.

AGATHA. I wish you would be serious when we are discussing a serious subject. I suppose matrimony is a more serious affair for us poor women than for you men.

TREVOR. How can I discuss anything seriously when you're covering me with fragments of rice pudding?

AGATHA. Oh, you poor dear, I'm so sorry. Let me rub you down.

TREVOR. No, don't you; I won't be massaged with rice pudding.

(*Enter* MRS. VULPY, *door centre.*)

MRS. V. What *are* you two people playing at?

TREVOR. Only trying to find new uses for cold rice pudding. I was firmly convinced as a child that it couldn't be primarily intended as a food.

MRS. V. René is just going to do his nautch-girl dance. He wants you to go and play tom-tom music, Agatha.

AGATHA. Bother René. Why was I born good-natured?

[*Exit* AGATHA, R.

TREVOR. Stay and talk to me, Mrs. Vulpy. I've seen the nautch-dance before.

MRS. V. You are such a sought-after young man that I feel I oughtn't to be taking you away from the others.

TREVOR. I'd rather sit and talk with you than with any of the others.

MRS. V. Dear me! I thought you never worked up the energy to make pretty speeches.

TREVOR. I don't; it's my mere sheer laziness that makes me blurt out the truth on this occasion.

MRS. V. And am I really to suppose that it is the truth that you would rather sit with me than with any of the others?

TREVOR. You are the only woman of the lot that it is safe to sit out with. Perhaps you are not very securely married, but you're not exactly floating loose ready to take advantage of the artless innocence of a young bachelor.

MRS. V. And is that where my superior fascination begins and leaves off?

TREVOR. That's where it begins. I didn't say it left off there.

MRS. V. Now don't try to talk pretty. You know you're not capable of sustained effort in that direction. Nothing is more discouraging than to have a man say that you've ruined his life, and then to find that you haven't even given him after-dinner insomnia.

TREVOR. Oh, I promise to keep awake—only it's rather soothing and sedative to talk to a charming woman who has no intention of marrying one. You don't intend to marry me, do you?

MRS. V. My dear Trevor, I have intended marrying you ever since I first saw you.

TREVOR. They say the road to matrimony is paved with good intentions, don't they?

MRS. V. I have heard it put in a more roundabout manner.

TREVOR. In your case isn't there rather a big obstacle in the road?

MRS. V. You mean Peter?

TREVOR. I suppose he *is* a factor in the situation?

MRS. V. Of course he's my husband, and it's my duty to think of him before any one else. But I am not going to be a hypocrite and waste sentiment in that direction. Our married life has been about as odious an experience as I wish to go through.

TREVOR. Still, I suppose even an unsatisfactory marriage has to be taken into account. There is no First Offender's clause in our marriage system. However uncongenial he may be, Peter remains your husband.

MRS. V. Well, that's the question. Peter was always selfish, but double pneumonia on the top of nervous breakdown may have overcome even his obstinate temperament. Why, at any moment I might get what I should be obliged to call in public "bad news." So you see I'm not so safe a person to sit and make pretty speeches to as you thought. And now I suppose my fascination has melted into thin air?

TREVOR. No, I shall merely have to label you "dangerous" along with the others.

MRS. V. Ah, Trevor, I'm much more dangerous than any of the others, if you only knew it.

TREVOR. Why so?

MRS. V. Because I really want you for your own self. The

others are all after you for family reasons and general convenience and that sort of thing. I want you because—well, I've seen a bit of the world, and I know the worth of a man like you, who can't be flattered or humbugged or led by the nose——

TREVOR. Hush! Some one's coming. (*Enter* WILLIAM, *door* L.) Just clear these things away, William; I should like my mother to find the hall in its usual state. Now, Mrs. Vulpy, I must be going in to the dance. I've shirked my duty most horribly.

MRS. V. Well, let's have a dreamy waltz together, to set the seal on what we've been talking about. We are friends, aren't we?

(*Exeunt* TREVOR *and* MRS. VULPY, *door* R. WILLIAM *gathers up empty plates. Enter* RENÉ, *door centre.*)

RENÉ (*helping himself to wine*). William, can you find me any more peaches?

WILL. No, sir, I brought you the last.

RENÉ (*arranging himself comfortably on couch*). Well, try to discover a fig or banana somewhere, do; and if you remind me tomorrow I'll ask Mr. Ludovic to give you that yellow striped waistcoat that he hardly ever wears.

WILL. Thank you, sir. You don't know of no one wanting a page, do you, sir?

RENÉ. Why, are you thinking of leaving?

WILL. I expect I shall have to leave without having time to do any thinking about it, sir. When Mrs. Bavvel comes to hear about our goings on behind her back she'll behave like one of those cyclops that sweeps away whole villages.

RENÉ. Cyclone, William, not cyclops.

WILL. That's it, sir, cyclone, and I expect I shall be among the sweepings. I've no particular fancy to be going home out of a situation just now, sir. Home life is a different thing with you gentry, you're so comfortable and heathen.

RENÉ. When one comes to think of it, I suppose we are. It's a rather overcrowded profession all the same. (*While* WILLIAM *is talking* RENÉ *is helping himself to* TREVOR'S *Russian cigarettes and filling his case.*)

WILL. Ah, sir, *you* haven't known what it was to be brought up by respectable parents.

RENÉ. Really, William!

WILL. My father is Plymouth Brethren, sir. Not that I've anything to say against Plymouth as a religion, but in a small cottage it takes up a lot of room. My father believed in smiting sin wherever he found it; what I complained of was that he always seemed to find it in the same place. Plymouth narrows the prospective. Between gentry religion and cottage religion there's the same difference as between keeping ferrets and living in a hutch with one.   [*Exit* WILLIAM, *door centre.*

(*Enter the first four in couples by door* R. *back,* TREVOR *and* MRS. VULPY, DRUMMOND *and* CLARE *and* SYBIL, SPARROWBY *and* AGATHA, *prancing through hall and singing* "Non je ne marcherai pas," *which is heard being played on piano off.*)

AGATHA (*to* RENÉ). You slacker! Come and join in.

(*They Exeunt in same order through door* L., *still singing.*)

RENÉ (*to himself*). I'm of far too tidy a disposition to leave half-emptied bottles lying about. Did I hear wheels? (*Rises and listens.*) Stop your squalling, you people. I fancied I heard wheels. (*Listens again.*) My nerves are getting quite jumpy. (*Reseats himself.*)

(*Hall door* R. *thrown open. Enter* HORTENSIA, *who turns to some one in porch.*)

HOR. Ludovic, quick, catch the carriage; I've left my pamphlets and notes in it. (*Catches sight of* RENÉ, *who is regarding her with helpless stare.*) Mr. St. Gall! May I ask what you are doing here at this hour?

RENÉ. Such a silly mistake. Old Colonel Nicholas asked me to go over to Bowerwood after dinner, as I was all alone. I distinctly told the groom Bowerwood, but he drove me here instead, and I didn't see where I was till he had driven off. So I've had to wait here till he comes to fetch me.

HOR. (*who has been staring fixedly at him and at the wine bottles and siphons on the table*). Will you repeat your story, please? I didn't quite follow.

RENÉ. Colonel Nicholas, thinking I might be lonely——

HOR. I hear music!

RENÉ. I've been thinking I heard harps in the air all the evening. I put it down to the state of my nerves. (SYBIL *with hood over head runs through laughing, from door L., and Exit door centre, without noticing* HORTENSIA.) Ah! Did you see *that*! Did you see *that*! (HORTENSIA *stares at doorway where figure vanished. Howl heard off. Enter* DRUMMOND *with phantom hound mask on, door L., runs through and Exit centre.*) Oh, say something or we shall . . . both . . . go . . . mad! (*Sobs convulsively.*)

HOR. (*furiously*). Ludovic!

(*Enter* LUDOVIC, *hall door R.*)

LUD. What is happening?

(RENÉ *has collapsed in fit of pretended hysterics in armchair.*)

HOR. The boy is either drunk or mad! Something disgraceful is taking place in this house!

LUD. Something disgraceful here! René, what *is* all this?

RENÉ (*sitting rigid in chair and staring straight in front of him*). Only were-wolves chasing goblins to the sound of unearthly music. Will some one kindly see if my carriage has come? I refuse to stay another moment in this house.

(*Enter* TREVOR, CLARE, MRS. VULPY, *from door L.* SYBIL *and* DRUMMOND, *door centre, all unhooded.*)

TREVOR. Oh, good God!

(RENÉ *pours out glass of wine and drains it, then lies back composedly in his chair. A prolonged pause, during which* HORTENSIA *surveys sheepish group of revellers.*)

SYBIL (*weakly*). We were having games.

MRS. V. Old English games.

DRUM. Charades.

CLARE. Historical charades.

SYBIL
TREVOR
MRS. V. } (*together*). Yes, historical charades.
DRUM.

(*Enter* AGATHA *and* SPARROWBY, *door R. back, pranc-*

*ing in together singing with fatuous exuberance "Non je
ne marcherai pas." They stop horror-stricken in centre of
stage.*)

HOR. (*seating herself in high-backed chair, her voice trem-
bling with rage*). May I ask who has organized this abomin-
able and indecent orgy in my house? Will somebody enlighten
me?

CLARE. It was something we got up on the spur of the moment; there was nothing organized.

HOR. And what brought people in from outside? I've heard
a contemptibly ridiculous story about Mr. St. Gall's accidental
arrival here; how do you account for Mr. Drummond's presence? Was he also trying to make his way to Bowerwood?

DRUM. (*blunderingly*). Yes.

RENÉ (*decisively*). No. That's my story. I won't be pla-
giarized.

SYBIL. He dropped in by chance.

DRUM. Yes, quite by chance.

HOR. Also on the spur of the moment! A moment, be it
observed, when I happened to be temporarily absent. And
knowing my strong objection to the questionable form of entertainment involved in promiscuous dancing you choose this moment for indulging in an aggravated and indecent kind of dance
which I can only describe as a brawl.

MRS. V. But, dear Mrs. Bavvel, I assure you there is nothing indecent in a sheet-and-pillow-case dance. Lulu Duchess
of Dulverton gave one at——

HOR. Lulu Duchess of Dulverton is not a person whose behaviour or opinions will be taken as a pattern at Briony as long
as I am mistress here. While you are still under my roof, Mrs.
Vulpy, I trust you will endeavour to remember that fact.
Whether, after this deplorable error of taste, you will see fit
to prolong your visit, of course I don't know. Apparently this
monstrous misuse of the bed-linen which is intended for the
sleeping accommodation of my guests was carried out at your
suggestion.

MRS. V. (*bursting into tears*). I think, considering the mental anxiety and strain through which I am passing, with a hus-

band hovering between Johannesburg and Heaven, I'm being most unfairly treated.

[*Exit* MRS. VULPY, *door* L.

HOR. I've refrained from complaining, Agatha, at the inconsiderate way in which you bring brambles and hedge weeds and garden refuse into the house, but I must protest against your introducing individuals of the type of Mrs. Vulpy as guests at Briony. Who is that playing the piano?

SYBIL. I think it's Evelyn Bray.

HOR. Ah! Who also dropped in accidentally, I suppose. Ludovic, will you kindly tell Miss Bray that we don't require any more music this evening. (*Exit* LUDOVIC, *door* R. *back.*) Had we not returned unexpectedly early, I presume this outrageous entertainment would have been kept from my knowledge. I may inform you that the mayor took upon himself to cancel the reception at the Town Hall, at which I was to have delivered a brief address, for the rather far-fetched reason of showing respect and sympathy at the sudden disappearance of Mrs. St. Gall.

RENÉ. I say, that was rather pet-lamb of him.

HOR. Mrs. St. Gall's son appears to treat the incident as of less serious importance.

RENÉ. I came here for rest and sympathy, with the faint possibility of a little Bridge to distract my thoughts; I wasn't to be expected to know that historical charades would be going on all round me. My nerves won't recover for weeks.

HOR. I am a persistent advocate of the abolition of corporal punishment in the Navy and in Board Schools, but I must confess, Mr. St. Gall, that a good birching inflicted on you would cause me no displeasure.

RENÉ. A most indelicate wind-up to a doubtful evening's amusement. I should insist on its being done *in camera*.

(*Enter* LUDOVIC, *door* R. *back.*)

SYBIL. Really, Mrs. Bavvel, we must plead guilty to having planned this semi-impromptu affair just a little, but we thought it would be such a good occasion for making an announcement.

AGATHA. An announcement?

HOR. What announcement?

SYBIL (*looking at* TREVOR). An announcement that I'm provisionally—well, engaged——

SPAR. Oh, Sybil, you angel! Let me announce it! Sybil and I are engaged!

LUD. Engaged! You and Sybil? Impossible. I congratulate you, of course, but it's—most unexpected.

CLARE. You dear thing. Congratulations.

SYBIL (*furiously*). You misunderstand me. I'm not engaged! Do you hear?

SPAR. Oh, Sybil, but you just said you were!

SYBIL. You fool! I was talking about something quite different.

[*Exit* SYBIL, *door* L.

HOR. There seems to be some confusion about this wonderful announcement.

LUD. I gathered that Miss Bomont was talking about something she's engaged on. Anyhow, she distinctly stated that she is not engaged to Mr. Sparrowby.

HOR. In any case this is hardly a fortunate moment in which to make announcements of secondary interest. (*Enter* WILLIAM, *door centre, carrying plate with banana. Stops horrified on seeing* MRS. BAYVEL, *who rises from chair.*) What are you carrying there, William?

WILL. (*miserably*). A banana, ma'am.

HOR. What are you doing with a banana at this time of night?

WILL. It's for her—him, the cockatoo, ma'am.

HOR. For Adolphus? At a quarter to eleven! He's never fed at this hour.

WILL. She—he seemed disturbed and restless as if he was asking for something, ma'am.

HOR. Disturbed? I am not surprised. In the fourteen years that he has lived here he has never before experienced such an evening of disgraceful disorder. Trevor, perhaps you will see that your neighbours who dropped in so unexpectedly will leave with as little delay as possible. Those of you who are at present my guests will kindly retire to their sleeping apartments. William!

WILL. Yes, ma'am.

HOR. Tell Cook to send a cold supper for myself and Mr. Ludovic to the dining-room. Some beef and pickled walnuts and a few peaches.

WILL. (*weakly*). Yes, ma'am.

HOR. Tomorrow I shall have a good deal to say on the subject of these deplorable proceedings. Tonight I am too upset. I left Briony an orderly English home, I return to find it a casino.

(*Exit* HORTENSIA *up staircase* L., *followed by* LUDOVIC, *who holds up his hands in mock despair. The others stand blankly watching them disappear.* RENÉ *seizes banana which* WILLIAM *is holding on plate and exits* R. *eating it. He is followed by* DRUMMOND *and* AGATHA. WILLIAM *Exit, door* L., *leaving* CLARE *and* TREVOR *alone.*)

CURTAIN

ACT III

Breakfast Room at Briony.

(LUDOVIC, *having just breakfasted, is still seated, chair pushed back from table, reading paper.* BUTLER *about to clear away breakfast things.*)

BUTLER. Shall I remove the breakfast things, sir?

LUD. (*glancing at clock*). Is no one else coming down? Where is Miss Clare?

BUTLER. Miss Clare complained of a headache, sir, and had breakfast in her room.

LUD. And Mr. Trevor?

BUTLER. Mr. Trevor breakfasted very early and went up to the farm. Miss Sybil breakfasted in her room.

LUD. Had she a headache also?

BUTLER. She complained of a headache, sir. Mrs. Vulpy breakfasted in her room.

LUD. The same—complaint?

BUTLER. No, sir, anxiety and nervous depression. She made a very big breakfast, sir. I don't know whether Miss Agatha has had her breakfast sent up. She wasn't awake half an hour ago.

LUD. By the way, do you know whether Mrs. Vulpy received any telegrams this morning?

BUTLER. She received one, sir, that she seemed to be expecting.

LUD. Ah!

BUTLER. She held it for a long while looking at it, sir, theatrical like, and then said there was no answer.

LUD. Did she seem less depressed after she'd received it?

BUTLER. She ordered some more kidneys and toast. I should say she was a lot more cheerful.

(*Enter* AGATHA *hastily, door* L.)

AGATHA. Hullo, Ludovic, only you here? I meant to have breakfast upstairs, but I saw Hortensia go out to the rose garden, so I skipped down.

BUTLER. Shall I warm some of the breakfast dishes for you, miss?

AGATHA. No, just make me some fresh tea, and leave the ham and sardines. (*While speaking has both arms on the table.*) I don't see any butter.

BUTLER. Your sleeve's in the butter, miss.

AGATHA. Oh, so it is. And you might bring in some more toast.

BUTLER. Yes, miss.

AGATHA. Isn't there any honey?

LUD. Your other sleeve is in the honey.

AGATHA. Oh, bother. (*Exit* BUTLER, *door centre.*) I say, did you breakfast with Hortensia? Was she very awful?

LUD. She told me she had lain awake most of the night boiling with indignation. She's now in the hard-boiled state of cold vindictiveness.

AGATHA. Mercy on us, whatever shall we do?

LUD. Personally I intend going for a few weeks on a visit to Ireland.

AGATHA. But we can't all go to Ireland.

Lud. One of the great advantages of Ireland as a place of residence is that a large number of excellent people never go there.

Agatha. You're disgustingly selfish; you don't think what is to become of the rest of us.

Lud. On the contrary, it's you that are selfish and inconsiderate. If one of you would only marry Trevor all this Hortensia discomfort and forced marching would be avoided.

Agatha. But how absurd you are, Ludovic! One can't marry Trevor without his consent. No really nice girl would make advances to a man unless he showed himself attracted to her first; and, as regards Trevor, it wouldn't be the slightest good anyway; one might as well make advances to the landscape. We poor women are so dreadfully handicapped. If I were only a man——

Lud. If you were a man you couldn't marry Trevor, so that wouldn't help us. Your sleeve's in the honey again.

(*Enter* Butler, *door centre, with tea and toast.*)

Butler. Is there anything else I can bring you, miss?

Agatha. No, thank you. Oh, tell Cook, in case I should be travelling later in the day, to cut me some ham sandwiches. No mustard.

Butler. Yes, miss. Shall you want the dogcart ordered?

Lud. You had better say the waggonette and the luggage cart; there may be others leaving this afternoon.

Butler. The 3.20 up or the 4.15 down, miss?

Agatha. I'm not quite sure. I'll let you know later.

Butler. Yes, miss.

[*Exit* Butler, *door centre.*

Agatha. If Hortensia is in a never-darken-my-doors-again kind of temper I shall go right off to Town and on somewhere from there. On the other hand, if it's the kind of outbreak that blows over in a week or two, I shall merely go and stay with some people I know at Exeter.

Lud. Nice people?

Agatha. Oh, dear, no. Quite uninteresting. I met them somewhere in Switzerland; they helped to find some luggage that had gone astray. I always lose luggage when I travel.

They have porridge in the mornings, but they live close to the station, so one hasn't got to take a cab.

Lud. Perhaps it won't be convenient for them to have you at a moment's notice.

Agatha. It's not at all convenient for me to go there, but at a time like this one can't stop to think of convenience. Especially other people's.

(*Enter* Sparrowby *cautiously, door* L.)

Spar. I've been afraid to come in before for fear of meeting Hortensia. I'm awfully hungry: I suppose everything's cold.

Lud. As a matter of public convenience I request you to be sparing with the ham; it may be required later in the day for an emergency ration of sandwiches. Have you booked a seat in the waggonette?

Spar. I say, is it as bad as all that? I hoped Mrs. Bavvel might have cooled down a bit.

Lud. She has. She has settled comfortably into a glacial epoch which will transform Briony into a sub-arctic zone in which I, for one, am not tempted to remain.

Spar. (*seating himself at table and beginning to eat*). What an awful nuisance; I don't at all want to leave Briony just now. I say, do you think I'm engaged to Sybil or not? She certainly seemed to say that we were engaged last night.

Lud. I really haven't given it a thought. I don't think it matters particularly. The important question is, is Trevor engaged to anybody?

Spar. I think you're awfully unsympathetic.

Lud. It's absurd to expect sympathy at breakfast-time. Breakfast is the most unsympathetic meal of the day. One can't love one's neighbour with any sincerity when he's emptying the toast-rack and helping himself lavishly to the grilled mushrooms that one particularly adores. Even at lunch one is usually in rather a quarrelsome frame of mind; you must have noticed that most family rows take place at lunch-time. At afternoon tea one begins to get polite, but one isn't really sympathetic till about the second course at dinner.

Spar. But the whole future happiness of my life is wrapped up in Sybil's acceptance of my offer.

Lud. People who wrap up their whole future happiness in one event generally find it convenient to unwrap it later on.

(*Enter* Clare, *door* L.)

Clare. Morning, everybody. Have you brave things breakfasted with Hortensia?

Agatha. No, only Ludovic. He reports her as being pretty bad. It's a regular case of *sauve qui peut*.

Clare. Such disgusting weather to travel in. Fancy being cooped up in a stuffy railway carriage all the afternoon. Anything in the papers, Ludovic?

Lud. Very possibly there may be. Agatha and Sparrowby have kept me so pleasantly engaged in discussing their plans that I've scarcely been able to grapple with the wider events of the day.

Agatha. Oh, I can always read and carry on a conversation at the same time. I suppose I've got a double brain.

Clare. Why don't you economize and have one good one.

Lud. (*rising*). If you two are going to quarrel, I'm off. Other people's quarrels always make me feel amiable, and a prospective Parliamentary candidate can't afford to be amiable in private life. It's like talking shop out of hours. (Ludovic *walks towards door* L.)

Spar. (*jumping up and following him*). I say, Ludovic, I want to ask you—do you really think——

[*Exit* Ludovic *and* Sparrowby, *door* L.

(*Enter* Mrs. Vulpy, *door centre*.)

Mrs. V. Is the coast clear? I'm scared to death of meeting that Gorgon again.

Agatha. Had breakfast?

Mrs. V. Nothing worth speaking of. Oh, is there tea? How adorable. (*Seats herself at table*.) Well, has anything happened?

Agatha. The luggage cart has been requisitioned, and if you want anything in the way of sandwiches or luggage labels an early order will prevent disappointment.

Mrs. V. Gracious, what an earthquake. And all because of a little harmless dance. If any of you girls do succeed in marrying that young man, you'll have to break him of the farmyard habit. A husband who is always going to earth is rather a poor sort of investment.

CLARE. As long as one marries him, what *does* it matter? One can afford to be neglected by one's own husband; it's when other people's husbands neglect one that one begins to talk of matrimonial disillusion.

MRS. V. Other people's husbands are rather an overrated lot. I prefer unmarried men any day; they've so much more experience.

CLARE. I don't agree with you. Isn't there a proverb: "A relapsed husband makes the best rake"?

AGATHA. You're positively disgraceful, both of you. We used to be taught to be content with the Ten Commandments and one husband; nowadays women get along with fewer commandments and want ten husbands.

MRS. V. It's no use scolding. It's the fault of the age we live in. The perfection of the motor-car has turned the country into a vast prairie of grass-widowhood. How can a woman be expected to cleave to some one who's at Lancaster Gate one minute and at North Berwick the next?

AGATHA. She can stay at home and lavish her affections on her babies.

CLARE. I hate babies. They're so human—they remind one of monkeys.

(*Enter* SYBIL, *door* L., *throws herself into chair* L. *centre of stage.*)

MRS. V. Well, it's no use taking a tragic view of yesterday's fiasco. There are thousands of as good men as Trevor in the world, waiting to be married.

SYBIL. That's just it; they don't seem to mind how long they wait. And when you come to have a closer look at the thousands there are very few of them that one could possibly marry.

AGATHA. Oh, nonsense; I don't see why one should be so dreadfully fastidious. After all, we're told all men are brothers.

SYBIL. Yes; unfortunately, so many of them are younger brothers.

AGATHA. Oh, well, money isn't everything.

SYBIL. It isn't everything, but it's a very effective substitute for most things.

MRS. V. By the way, tell me which is the nearest and cleanest way to the farm.

AGATHA (*who is about to leave room*). Through the white gates into the fir plantation, and past the potting sheds. You can't miss it. (*Suddenly turning back and sitting down abruptly.*) What do you want to go there for?

MRS. V. Merely to say my good-byes to Mr. Trevor, and while he is showing me round the farm buildings I dare say I'll find an opportunity to tell him how badly he's treated you all, and what an uncomfortable situation he's created, and generally work on his better feelings.

SYBIL. You might as well work on superior blotting-paper. (*Exit* MRS. VULPY.) I don't trust that woman a little atom.

CLARE. I believe she's had bad news from South Africa, and she's keeping it dark and going for Trevor on her own account.

SYBIL. He spoke very curiously about her to me last night, asked what I thought of her and all that.

AGATHA. Exactly what he did to me. I say, can't we stop her?

CLARE. Are you proposing to use violence? If so I think I'll watch from a distance; when you used to play hockey you were noted for hitting more people than you ever aimed at.

SYBIL (*jumping to her feet*). Hortensia's voice!

(CLARE *and* SYBIL *scurry out of the room by door* R. AGATHA *blunders into the arms of* HORTENSIA, *who enters by door* L.)

AGATHA (*trying to look at her ease*). Oh, good morning. Did it rain in the night?

HOR. I lay awake most of the night; I did not hear any rain. (*Rings bell.*)

AGATHA. Oh, I'm *so* sorry you didn't sleep well. Oak leaves soaked in salt water and put under the bed are an awfully good remedy. Let me get you some.

HOR. (*coldly*). Thank you, we don't want any more decaying vegetation brought into the house. My sleeplessness was not due to insomnia. Under normal circumstances I sleep excellently.

AGATHA. I feel that I ought to explain about last night.

HOR. You will have to explain. Every one will have to give an account of his or her share in the disgraceful affair, including the servants, who seem to have connived at it. I have ordered a gathering of the household for 4 o'clock in the library, which you will kindly attend. (*Enter* WILLIAM, *door centre.*) William, at this hour of the morning I expect the breakfast things to be cleared away.

[*Exit* HORTENSIA, R.

AGATHA. William, tell John that I shall have to leave here well before four to catch the 4.15. I've got lots of luggage to register at the station.

WILL. Yes, miss; the waggonette's ordered already.

AGATHA. I expect it will have to be the dogcart as well; there will probably be a lot of us wanting to catch trains this afternoon.

WILL. Yes, miss. What I envy about you, miss, is your play-going way of taking things.

AGATHA. Play-going way?

WILL. Yes, miss. You just sit and wait till things has been brought to a climax and then you put on your hat and gloves and walk outside. It's different for those who've got to go on living with the climax.

AGATHA. I hadn't thought of that; I suppose it is rather horrid.

[*Exit* WILLIAM *by door centre, carrying off breakfast things on tray.*

[*Exit* AGATHA, *door L.*

(*Enter* LUDOVIC, *door R. He takes newspaper packet off table L., opens wrapper, throws himself into a chair and begins reading.*)

(*Enter* RENÉ, *door R.*)

RENÉ. Ludovic! Aren't you all feeling like a lot of drowned kittens?

LUD. I don't know what a lot of drowned kittens feel like. I hope I'm not looking like a lot of drowned kittens.

RENÉ. Oh, don't talk about looks. (*Looks himself carefully over in the mirror.*) I felt so jumpy last night that I scarcely dared put the light out. I had a hot-water bottle in my bed.

LUD. A hot-water bottle? Surely it's too warm for that.

RENÉ. Oh, there was no hot water in it, it was merely to give a sense of protection. I suppose there's a general stampede? (*Seats himself, chair centre stage.*)

LUD. The house resounds with the cutting of sandwiches and the writing of luggage labels.

RENÉ. And what does *he* say to it all?

LUD. Who? Trevor? He made a strategic move to the farm at an early hour.

RENÉ. I believe he was so sleepy last night that he doesn't really know whether he proposed to Sybil or not.

LUD. Sybil did her best, but that miserable Sparrowby ruined whatever chance she had.

RENÉ. I've no use for that person; he's just the kind of idiot who comes up to you in a Turkish bath and says, "Isn't it hot?" Meanwhile, what are you going to do?

LUD. I shall pay a long-projected visit to an old chum who lives in Kildare.

RENÉ. Nonsense, Ludo, you can't. Nobody really lives in Kildare; I don't believe there are such places. And old Spindleham is really at the last gasp. The *Western Morning News* says he can't live out the week.

LUD. Under present circumstances, René, I've no intention of standing.

RENÉ. Oh, don't be so provoking. Go and see Trevor and tell him he must marry Sybil. Explain the circumstances to him. A wife is a sort of thing that can happen any day. But a Parliamentary vacancy is a different matter. There's your career to think of.

LUD. He will naturally retort that his whole future happiness has got to be thought of.

RENÉ. Oh, damn! what about my whole future income?

LUD. My dear René, the question is, whether we have not hunted Trevor into the wrong net. I have just met that Vulpy

woman in full cry up to the farm, and something in her manner tells me that she's running a trail of her own.

RENÉ. But her husband——

LUD. I asked her if she had had any news of him. She was
careful to tell me that she hadn't received any letters this morning. She was equally careful *not* to inform me that she did get
a telegram. I fancy that telegram announced her promotion to
the rank of widowhood.

RENÉ. But you surely don't think that Trevor would——

LUD. That's exactly what I do think. We've tried to badger
and harry him into a matrimonial entanglement with all sorts
of eligible and likely young women, and it's quite in the nature
of things that he'll turn round and perversely commit himself
to this wholly impossible person. You must remember that
Trevor is a fellow who has seen comparatively little of the
world, and what he's seen has been more or less of one pattern. Now that he's suddenly confronted with a creature of
quite another type, with whom he isn't expected to interest himself, naturally he at once becomes interested.

RENÉ. Well, if this stumbling-block of a husband of hers has
really been good-natured enough to migrate to another world,
everything is plain sailing. Trevor can go ahead and marry the
lady—after a decent interval, of course.

LUD. Absolutely out of the question. I should never forgive
myself if such a thing happened.

RENÉ. But why—haven't we been moving heaven and earth
to get him married?

LUD. Married, yes, but not to Mrs. Vulpy. After all, Trevor
is my only brother's only son, and if I can help it I'm not going
to sit still and let him tie himself to that bundle of scheming
vulgarity. Besides, a woman like that installed as mistress of
Briony would only mean a prolongation of Hortensia's influence. Trevor would be driven to consult his mother in everything, from the sheer impossibility of putting confidence in his
wife.

RENÉ. I think we're being absurdly fastidious about Trevor's
wife. We've given him heaps of opportunities for marrying decent nonentities, so I don't see why we should reproach our-

selves if he accidentally swallows a clumsier bait. Anyhow, I don't see how you're going to stop it if there's really anything in it.

LUD. That's just what's worrying me. To speak to him about it would be to clinch matters. With rare exceptions the Bavvels are devilishly obstinate.

RENÉ. Well, it would be rather a delicate subject to broach to her. She would scarcely relish being told that she's impossible.

LUD. I should put it more tactfully. I should tell her she wouldn't harmonize with local surroundings, that she has too much dash and go, and—help me out with some tactful attribute.

RENÉ. Too flamboyant.

LUD. I asked you for tact, not truth.

RENÉ. Too much individuality. I don't know what that means. But it sounds well.

LUD. Thank you, that will do nicely. A woman always respects a word that she can't spell.

RENÉ. You'd better jot it all down on your cuff. You'll forget it in a sudden panic when you're talking to her.

(*Enter* BUTLER, R.)

BUTLER. Colonel Mutsome.

(*Enter* COL. MUTSOME, R.)

[*Exit* BUTLER, *same door.*

COL. How do you do? (*Shakes hands with* LUDOVIC, *bows to* RENÉ.) What unpleasant weather. Quite damp. I hope dear Hortensia is well. I've a great admiration for Hortensia. I always say she's the first lady in Somersetshire.

RENÉ. Everything must have a beginning.

COL. I hear our member is not expected to live. (*Seats him-self in chair,* R.)

LUD. I saw something to that effect in the local papers.

COL. I suppose we shall be having an election in a few weeks' time. Is it true that you are the prospective Party candidate?

LUD. I saw it suggested in the local papers. There has always been some idea of getting a Bavvel to stand.

COL. I suppose you would accept!

LUD. That will depend very largely on family considerations.

RENÉ. Of course Ludovic means to stand. I caught him yesterday being ostentatiously sympathetic to the local chemist, a man with a hare-lip and personal reminiscences and a vote. No one listens to the personal reminiscences of a man with a hare-lip unless they've got some imperative motive; when the man also has a vote the motive is unmistakable.

LUD. René, as a private secretary, you would have to be very private.

COL. I suppose you subscribe to all the principal items of the Party programme?

LUD. Oh, I believe so—and to most of the local charities. That is the really important thing. It is generally understood that a rich man has some difficulty in entering the Kingdom of Heaven; the House of Commons is not so exclusive. Our electoral system, however, takes good care that the rich man entering Parliament shall not remain rich. It is simply astonishing the number of institutions supported by involuntary contributions that a candidate discovers in his prospective constituency. At least he doesn't discover them—they discover him. For instance, I don't keep bees, I don't know how to, and don't want to know how to. I don't eat honey. I never go near a hive except at an agricultural show when I am perfectly certain there are no bees in it. Yet I have already consented to be vice-president and annual subscriber to the local bee-keepers' association. On consulting a memorandum book I find I am vice-president of seven bell-ringers' guilds and about twenty village football clubs. I cannot remember having been so enthusiastic about football when I was at school. I am a subscribing member of a botanical ramble club. Can you imagine me doing botanical rambles? Of course you quite understand that there's no bribery in all this.

COL. Oh, of course not. Bribery is not tolerated nowadays.

LUD. At any rate, one gives it another name. Let us call it altruism in compartments; very intense and comprehensive where it exists, but strictly confined within the bound of one's constituency.

Col. I suppose you're sound on religious questions? There is no truth in the story that you have leanings towards agnosticism?

Lud. My dear Colonel, no one can be Agnostic nowadays. The Christian Apologists have left one nothing to disbelieve.

René. Personally I am a pagan. Christians waste too much time in professing to be miserable sinners, which generally results in their being merely miserable and leaving some of the best sins undone; whereas the pagan gets cheerfully to work and commits his sins and doesn't brag so much about them.

Col. I trust you are only talking in theory.

René. In theory, of course. In practice, every one is pagan according to his lights.

Lud. René, as a private secretary, I'm afraid you would become a public scandal. I shouldn't dare to leave you alone with an unprotected deputation.

(*Enter* TREVOR, *door* L.)

TREVOR. Morning, Ludovic. Hullo, Colonel, I didn't know you were here. (*Shakes hands with* COLONEL MUTSOME.) Morning, René. I distinctly heard you all talking politics. (TREVOR *seats himself in chair, centre stage.*)

Col. Politics are rather in the air. It seems we are threatened with a Parliamentary vacancy.

Lud. By way of meeting trouble half-way, Colonel Mutsome has come to ascertain whether there is any probability of my standing.

Col. I should have expressed it differently.

Lud. Things do not point at present to the probability of my becoming a candidate, but the Colonel has taken things betimes and has been doing a little preliminary heckling.

Col. Not heckling, exactly. My position as Vice-Chairman of the local Party Association gives me some opportunity for gauging opinion down here. Collectively the Government has, perhaps, lost some of its prestige, but individually I think Ministers are popular.

Lud. Including the irrepressible Bumpingford.

Col. Oh, certainly. Rather an assertive personality, perhaps, but of undeniable ability. He comes into the category of those who are born to command.

LUD. Possibly. His trouble so far is that he hasn't been able to find any one who was born to obey him. So you think Ministers are in general popular?

COL. Compared with the leaders of the Opposition——

LUD. One should be careful not to say disparaging things of Opposition leaders.

COL. Because they may one day be at the head of affairs?

LUD. No, because they may one day lead the Opposition. One never knows.

COL. There is the question of Votes for Women.

LUD. Personally I see no reason why women shouldn't have votes. They're quite unfit to have votes, but that's no argument against their having them. If we were to restrict the right of voting to those of the male sex who were fitted for it we should have to enlarge Hyde Park to accommodate the protesting hordes of non-voters. Government by democracy means government of the mentally unfit by the mentally mediocre tempered by the saving grace of snobbery.

COL. You will be very unpopular if you say that sort of thing down here.

LUD. I have no intention of saying it. Some poet has remarked, "To think is to be full of sorrow." To think aloud is a luxury of sorrow which few politicians can afford to indulge in.

COL. (suddenly). By the way—was there some dancing at Briony last night?

LUD. (in nervous haste). Oh, no, just some Shakespeare readings and a little music. I wonder you haven't asked me about land values.

COL. I was coming to that.

TREVOR (eagerly). It's rather an important question, particularly down here.

LUD. Most important.

RENÉ (same eagerness). It's quite one of the questions of the immediate future. An aunt of a Cabinet Minister was speaking to me about it only last week. She said it kept her awake at nights.

COL. Really—I quite understood that there was a Cinderella dance——

LUD. Oh, no, dear no, nothing of that kind. Some Shakespeare reading, in costume.

COL. In costume—but how very interesting. What scenes did you give?

RENÉ. The Ghost scenes from what-do-you-call-it.

COL. The Ghost scene from "Hamlet"? That must have needed a lot of rehearsal.

RENÉ. No, we had a lot of ghosts, so that if one forgot his lines another could go on with them.

COL. What an odd idea. What a very odd idea. But they couldn't all have been in costume.

RENÉ. They were, rows of them. All in white sheets.

COL. How very extraordinary. It couldn't have been a bit like Shakespeare.

RENÉ. It wasn't, but it was very like Maeterlinck. Whoever really wrote "Hamlet," there can be no doubt that Maeterlinck and Maxim Gorki ought to have written it, in collaboration.

COL. But how could they? They weren't born at that time.

RENÉ. That's the bother of it. Ideas get used up so quickly. If the Almighty hadn't created the world at the beginning of things Edison would probably have done it by this time on quite different lines, and then some one would have come along to prove that the Chinese had done it centuries ago.

COL. (*acidly, to* TREVOR, *turning his back on* RENÉ). How is your cold, Mr. Trevor? You had a cold before we went to Worcestershire.

TREVOR. That one went long ago. I've got another one now, which is better, thank you.

COL. We had such a lot of asparagus in Worcestershire.

TREVOR. Yes?

COL. We got our earliest asparagus in London, then we got more down here, and then we had a late edition in Worcestershire, so we've had quite a lot this year.

RENÉ. The charm of that story is that it could be told in any drawing-room.

COL. (*rising from seat*). I think I saw Hortensia pass the window. If you don't mind I'll go and meet her.

LUD. Let me escort you.

[*Exeunt* LUDOVIC *and* COLONEL MUTSOME, *door* R.

RENÉ (*lighting cigarette*). You've heard the story that's going about?

TREVOR. That we held unholy revels here last night.

RENÉ. Well, *à propos* of that; people are saying that you and Sparrowby proposed to the same girl and that Sparrowby threatened to break your neck if you didn't give way to him; and that you gave way rather than have any unpleasantness.

TREVOR. What an infernal invention. I am damned if I let that go about.

RENÉ. I don't see what you can do to stop it.

TREVOR. I might break Sparrowby's neck.

RENÉ. No one could have any reasonable objection to that course; Sparrowby is one of those people who would be enormously improved by death. Unfortunately, he is your guest, and on that account it wouldn't be quite the thing to do. He's sure to have a parent or aunt or some one who'd write letters to *The Times* about it: "Fatal ragging in country houses," and so on. No, your only prudent line of action would be to marry the girl, or any girl who came handy, just to knock the stuffing out of the story. Otherwise you'll have to take it recumbent, as the saying is.

TREVOR. I'm not fool enough to rush off and perpetrate matrimony with the first person I meet in order to put a stop to a ridiculous story.

RENÉ. My dear Trevor, I quite understand your situation.

TREVOR. You don't.

RENÉ. Of course I do. You don't want to interrupt an agreeable and moderately safe flirtation with a woman who has just got husband enough to give her the flavour of forbidden fruit. I'm not one of those who run the Vulpy down just because she's a trifle too flamboyant for the general taste. As a wife I dare say she'd be rather an experiment down here, but I've no doubt you'd be tolerably happy. She'd be more at her ease at a suburban race meeting than at a county garden party, but still—you could travel a good deal. And if you find her sympathetic it doesn't matter so very much whether she's intelligent or not. But all that is beside the point, because she's not available. Inconvenient husbands don't come to timely ends in real life like they do in fiction. If you seriously want to put your foot down on the gossip that is going about, and make an end of this uncomfortable domestic situation, your only course is to go straight ahead and propose to the first available girl that you run up against. If it's the bother of the thing that you shirk let me open negotiations for you—my mission in life is to save other people trouble, on reasonable terms. (RENÉ *becomes suddenly aware that* TREVOR *has gone to sleep, and rises angrily from his seat.*) Of all the exasperating dolts! I don't know how match-making mothers manage to grow fat on the business; a week of this would wear me to a shadow.

[*Exit* RENÉ *in a fury, door* R.

(*Enter* LUDOVIC, L.)

LUD. Hullo, is René here?

TREVOR. He was, a minute or two ago. I think I heard him leave the house.

LUD. Has anything been heard of his mother? So many distracting things have been happening that I clean forgot to ask about her.

TREVOR. By Jove, so did I. He'll think us rather remiss, but anyhow he seemed more concerned about finding me a suitable wife than about retrieving his lost parent. Have you heard anything of the story that he says is going about?

LUD. (*seating himself*). About last night, you mean?

TREVOR. Yes, that Sparrowby and I proposed to the same girl, and that Sparrowby bounced me into taking a back seat.

LUD. Ah! no—at least, probably what I heard had reference to that. What an unpleasant scandal. Unfortunately, the fact that Sybil is leaving Briony in such a hurry will give colour to it.

TREVOR. Was it Sybil, then?

LUD. I suppose so. I think I heard her name mentioned. What shall you do then?

TREVOR. Do? I don't know. What do you suggest?

LUD. My suggestion would be so simple that you are not likely to accept it for a moment. If one shows people an intricate and risky way out of a difficulty they are becomingly grateful: if you point out a safe and obvious exit they regard you with resentment. In your case the resentment would probably take the form of going to sleep in the middle of my advice.

TREVOR. I wasn't going to sleep! I was wondering which particular girl you were going to recommend to my notice. There seems to be a concentration on Sybil Bomont.

LUD. It's scarcely my place to fill in the details for you; I suppose matrimony is an eventuality which begins to present itself rather prominently to you, and when you've settled that point the details soon fit themselves in. If the Bomont girl doesn't meet with your requirements there is your neighbour Evelyn Bray, whom you entangled in last night's entertainment—I shall never forget her face when I told her that Hortensia didn't require any more music—and there's Clare Henessey; you used to get on famously with Clare.

TREVOR. Clare and Evelyn are very good sorts——

LUD. (*raising his hand*). Good sorts— Oh, my dear Trevor, you are still in the schoolboy stage as regards women. The schoolboy divides womenkind broadly into two species, the decent sort and the holy horror, much as the naturalist, after a somewhat closer investigation of his subject, classifies snakes as either harmless or poisonous. The schoolboy is usually fairly well informed about things that he doesn't have to study, but as regards women he is altogether too specific. You can't really divide them in a hard-and-fast way.

TREVOR. At least there are superficial differences.

LUD. But nothing deeper. Woman is a belated survival from a primeval age of struggle and cunning and competition; that is why, wherever you go the world over, you find all the superfluous dust and worry being made by the gentler sex. If you are on a crowded P. and O. steamer, who is it that wages an incessant warfare over the cabin accommodation? Who is it that creates the little social feuds that divide benighted country parishes and lonely hill stations? Who is it that raises objections to smoking in railway carriages, and who writes to house-masters to complain of the dear boys' breakfast fare? Man has moved with the historic progression of the ages. But woman is a habit that has survived from the period when one had to dispute with cave bears and cave hyenas whether one ate one's supper or watched others eat it, whether one slept at home or on one's doorstep. The great religions of the world have all recognized this fact and kept womankind severely outside of their respective systems. That is why, however secular one's tendencies, one turns instinctively to religion in some form for respite and peace.

TREVOR. But one can't get along without women.

LUD. Precisely what I have been trying to impress upon you. Granted that woman is merely a bad habit, she is a habit that we have not grown out of. Under certain circumstances a bad habit is first-cousin to a virtue. In your case it seems to me that matrimony is not only a virtue but a convenience.

TREVOR. It's all very well for you to talk about convenience. What may be convenient for other people may be highly inconvenient for me.

LUD. That means that you're involved in some blind-alley affair with a married woman. Precisely what I feared. Men like yourself of easy-going, unsuspecting temperament, invariably fall victims to the most rapacious type of cave woman, the woman who already has a husband and who merely kills for the sake of killing. You pick and choose and dally among your artificial categories of awfully good sorts and dear little women, and then some one of the Mrs. Vulpy type comes along and quietly annexes you.

TREVOR. I seem to have been annexed to Mrs. Vulpy by popular delimitation. Critically speaking, she isn't a bit my style, but I don't see anything so very dreadful about her. She's a trifle pronounced, perhaps—she tells me she had a Spanish grandfather.

LUD. Ancestors will happen in the best-intentioned families. Every social sin or failing is excused nowadays under the plea of an artistic temperament or a Sicilian grandmother. As poor Lady Cloutsham once told me, as soon as her children found out that a Hungarian lady of blameless moral character had married into the family somewhere in the reign of the Georges, they considered themselves absolved from any further attempt to distinguish between good and evil—except by way of expressing a general preference for the latter. When her youngest boy was at Winchester he made such unblushing use of the Hungarian strain in his blood that he was known as the Blue Danube. "That," said Lady Cloutsham, "is what comes of letting young children read Debrett and Darwin."

TREVOR. As regards Mrs. Vulpy's temperament, I don't fancy one need go very far afield.

LUD. Oh, no, Greater London is quite capable of turning her out without having recourse to foreign blending.

TREVOR. Still, I don't see that she's anything worse than a flirt.

LUD. Oh, on her best behaviour, I've no doubt she's perfectly gentle and frolicsome; for the matter of that, the cave hyenas probably had their after-dinner moments of comparative amiability. But, from the point of view of an extremely marriageable young bachelor, she simply isn't safe to play with. I don't want to run her down on the score of her rather common personality, but I wish to warn you that she is one of those people gifted with just the sort of pushing, scheming audacity— (*Enter* MRS. VULPY, *door centre.*) Ah, good morning, Mrs. Vulpy (TREVOR *looks round and jumps to his feet*), just the sort of pushing, scheming audacity that makes them dangerous. Once we let them wriggle their way into the Persian Gulf they'll snap up all our commerce under our eyes.

MRS. V. You dreadful men, always talking politics.

LUD. Politics are rather in the air just now.

MRS. V. I feel as if we were all in the air after the dreadful explosion of last night. I am just wondering where I am going to come down.

TREVOR. It seems an awful shame, driving all you charming people away. My mother goes to absurd lengths about some things.

Mrs. V. It's poor us who have to go the absurd lengths. I shan't feel safe till I have put two fair-sized counties between Mrs. Bavvel and myself. Oh, Mr. Trevor, before I leave you *must* show me the model dairy.

Trevor. Right-oh, I'll take you there now if you like.

Mrs. V. Do, please. I just love dairies and cheese-making and all that sort of thing. I think it's so clever the way they make those little blue insertions in Gorgonzola cheese. I always say I ought to have been a farmer's wife. We'll leave Ludovic to his horrid politics.

Lud. Before I forget, Trevor, go and get me those trout flies you promised me, and I'll have them packed. Mrs. Vulpy won't mind, I dare say, waiting for you here for a few minutes.

Trevor. Right you are. I won't be a second.

[*Exit* Trevor.

Lud. I hope you don't despise me too much.

Mrs. V. Despise you! Oh, Mr. Ludovic, what ever should I despise you for?

Lud. For being fool enough to put confidence in you as a fellow conspirator.

Mrs. V. Why, I am sure I have been loyal enough to our compact. If the results haven't been brilliant, you can scarcely blame me for the breakdown.

Lud. The compact was that you should help in an endeavour to get Trevor engaged to one of the girls of the house party. I don't think I'm mistaken in saying that the game you are playing is to secure him for yourself.

Mrs. V. Never more mistaken in your life. Really, you seem to forget that I'm a married woman.

Lud. Your memory is even shorter. You seem to forget that you received a telegram this morning to say that your husband is dead.

Mrs. V. Whatever will you say next? You don't know what you're talking about.

Lud. Oh, it's correct enough; I read it.

Mrs. V. (*raising her voice*). How dare you intercept my correspondence. The telegram was marked plain enough,

"Vulpy, c/o Bavvel." You're simply a common sneak.

Lud. I didn't read the intelligence in your telegram. I read it in your manner. You've just been obliging enough to confirm my deductions.

Mrs. V. Oh, you're trying amateur detective business on me, are you? (*With sudden change of manner.*) Now, look here, Mr. Ludovic, don't you set yourself against me. Why shouldn't I marry Trevor? You said yourself two days ago that it was a pity I wasn't a widow, so that I could be eligible for marrying him.

Lud. Of course, I spoke jestingly.

Mrs. V. Well, it isn't a jest to me. I have had a wretched, miserable time with my late husband; I can't tell you what a time I've had with him.

Lud. Because you have had a miserable time with the late Mr. Vulpy is precisely, my dear lady, the reason why I don't wish you to try the experiment of being miserable with my nephew. You are so utterly unsuited to him and his surroundings that you couldn't fail to be unhappy and to make him unhappy into the bargain.

Mrs. V. I don't see why I should be unsuited to him. Trevor is a gentleman, and I am a lady, I suppose. Perhaps you wish to suggest that I am not.

Lud. You are, if you will permit me to say so, a very charming and agreeable lady, but you would not fit in with the accepted ideals of the neighbourhood. You have too much dash and go and—in—indefinable—characteristics. I don't know if you've noticed it, but in Somersetshire we don't dash.

Mrs. V. Oh, don't fling your beastly county set and its prejudices in my face. I am as good as the lot of you and a bit better. I mix in far smarter circles than you've got here. Lulu Duchess of Dulverton and her set are a cut above the pack of you, and as for you, if you want my opinion, you're a meddling, interfering, middle-aged toad.

Lud. You asked me a moment ago why you shouldn't marry Trevor. You're supplying one of the reasons now. You're flying into something very like a rage. In Somersetshire we never fly into a rage. We walk into one, and when necessary we stay there for weeks, perhaps for years. But we never fly into one.

Mrs. V. Oh, I've had enough of your sarcasms. You've had my opinion of you. You're a mass of self-seeking and intrigue. You're mistaken if you think I'm going to let a middle-aged toad stand in my path.

(*Enter* TREVOR.)

TREVOR. Here are all the flies I could find. Sorry to have kept you waiting, but I had to hunt for them.

LUD. Don't mention it; we've been having such an interesting talk, about the age toads live to. Mrs. Vulpy is quite a naturalist.

Mrs. V. I've got all my packing to do, so we'd better not lose any more time.

TREVOR. Right you are, we will go off at once.

[*Exit* TREVOR *and* MRS. VULPY, R.

(*Enter* AGATHA, L.)

(LUDOVIC *flings himself down savagely at writing table.*)

AGATHA. Have you seen Trevor anywhere?

LUD. He was here a minute ago. I believe he's now in the dairy.

AGATHA. The dairy! What's he doing in the dairy?

LUD. I don't know. What does one do in dairies?

AGATHA. One makes butter and that sort of thing. Trevor can't make butter.

LUD. I don't believe he can. We spend incredible sums on technical education, but the number of people who know how to make butter remains extremely limited.

AGATHA. Is he alone?

LUD. I fancy Mrs. Vulpy is with him.

AGATHA. That cat! Why is she with him?

LUD. I don't know. There's a proverb—isn't there?— about showing a cat the way to the dairy, but I forget what happens next.

AGATHA. I call it rather compromising.

LUD. It's a model dairy, you know.

AGATHA. I don't see that that makes it any better. Mrs. Vulpy is scarcely a model woman.

LUD. She's a married woman.

AGATHA. A South African husband is rather a doubtful security.

LUD. Then you can scarcely blame her for taking a provident interest in West of England bachelors.

AGATHA. It's simply indecent. She might wait till one husband is definitely dead before trying to rope in another.

LUD. My dear Agatha, brevity is the soul of widowhood.

AGATHA. I loathe her. She promised she would try to get Trevor to put an end to all this muddle and row by getting him engaged to——to Sybil or any one else available.

LUD. How do you know she's not trying now?

AGATHA. Oh, I say, do you think she is?

LUD. I think it's quite possible; also I think it's quite possible that Trevor is discoursing learnedly on the amount of milk a Jersey cow can be induced to yield under intelligent treatment. Frankly, I consider these milk and egg statistics that one is expected to talk about in the country border on the indelicate. If I were a cow or hen I should resent having my most private and personal actions treated as a sort of auction bridge. The country has no reticence.

(*Enter* SYBIL, R.)

SYBIL. Well, I've packed.

AGATHA. Oh, dear, I haven't begun. I know I shall be late for the train; I'm always late for trains. I must go and dig up some foxglove roots in the plantation to take away with me.

SYBIL. I refuse to let you bring more than five cubic feet of earth mould and stinging nettles into the carriage.

AGATHA. Don't excite yourself, my dear. I'm going by a down train and you're going by an up, I presume.

SYBIL. Don't be a pig. You must come with us to make a four for Bridge; there'll be Clare and myself and you and the Vulpy. Otherwise we'll have to have let that wearisome Sparrowby in, and I'd rather have a ton of decaying hedge and compressed caterpillar in the carriage than have Sparrowby inflicted on me for three mortal hours.

AGATHA. I'm not going to upset all my visiting plans just to suit your Bridge arrangements. Besides, you said the last time we played that I had no more notion of the game than an un-born parrot. I haven't got such a short memory, you see.

SYBIL. I wish you hadn't got such a short temper.

AGATHA. Me short-tempered! My good temper is prover-bial.

SYBIL. Not to say legendary.

LUD. Please don't start quarrelling. You're making me feel amiable again.

(*Enter* MRS. VULPY, R., *trying not to look crest-fallen.*)

MRS. V. I never knew a dairy could be so interesting. All the latest improvements. Such beautiful ventilation—and such plain dairymaids. What it is to have a careful mother.

LUD. You weren't very long in going over it.

MRS. V. Oh, I had to rush it, of course. I must go and super-intend my packing. It doesn't do to leave everything to one's maid.

SYBIL. Hortensia! It's no use bolting, we're cornered.

(*Enter,* R., HORTENSIA *and* COLONEL MUTSOME.)

MRS. V. Good morning, Mrs. Bavvel. (*She bows to the* COLONEL.) (*Pause.*)

COL. Mrs. Bavvel has just been showing me the poultry yard. I've been admiring the black minorcas. How many eggs did you say they've laid in the last six months, Hortensia?

HOR. I don't think Mrs. Vulpy is much interested in such matters.

MRS. V. Oh, I adore poultry. There's something so Omar Khayyám about them. Lulu Duchess of Dulverton keeps white peacocks. (*Pause.*)

COL. Such a disappointment to us not to have had Mrs. Bavvel's lecture last night. All on account of Mrs. St. Gall's extraordinary disappearance. People are talking of a suicide. Others say it's a question of eluding creditors. Her debts, I be-lieve, are simply enormous.

HOR. One must be careful of echoing local gossip, but from the improvident way in which that household is managed one is justified in supposing that financial difficulties are not un-known there.

COL. In any case, I feel convinced that we shan't see Mrs. St. Gall in these parts again.

(*Enter* RENÉ, *door* R., *followed by* TREVOR.)

RENÉ. I've found my mother!

COL. Mrs. St. Gall found? You've seen her?

RENÉ. No, but I've spoken to her. She was having a bath when I got back, so we conversed through the bath-room door. Touching scene of filial piety. Return of the prodigal mother, son weeping over bath-room door-handle. We don't run to a fatted calf, but I promised her she should have an egg with her tea.

COL. But where had she been all this time?

RENÉ. Principally at Cardiff.

COL. Cardiff! Whatever did she want to go to Cardiff for?

RENÉ. She didn't want to go. She was taken.

HOR. Taken!

RENÉ. She was doing a stroll on the Crowcoombe road when Freda Tewkesbury and her husband swooped down on her in their road car. They live at Warwick, at least they've got a house and some children there, but since they've gone mad on motoring they spend most of their time on the highway. The poor we have always in our midst, and nowadays the rich may crash into us at any moment.

COL. Your mother wasn't run over?

RENÉ. Oh, no, but Freda took her up for a spin and then insisted on her coming on just as she was for a day or two's visit to Monmouth and Cardiff. Freda is always picking up her friends in that impromptu way; she keeps spare tooth-brushes and emergency night-things of various sizes on her car. Of course, you can't dress for dinner, but that doesn't matter very fundamentally in Cardiff.

LUD. But surely your mother might have telegraphed to say what had become of her.

RENÉ. She did, from Monmouth, with long directions about charcoal biscuits for the chows' suppers, and again from Cardiff to say when she was coming back. Freda gave the wires to her husband to send off, which accounts for their never having reached us. None of the Tewkesburys have any memories.

Their father got a knock on the head at Inkermann and since then the family have never been able to remember anything. I love borrowing odd sums from Tewkesbury; both of us are so absolutely certain to forget all about it.

Hor. And it was on account of this madcap freak that last night's function was postponed and my address cancelled.

Col. This promiscuous gadding about in motors is undermining all home life and sense of locality. One scarcely knows nowadays to which county people belong.

Hor. I trust that Mrs. St. Gall showed some appreciation of the anxiety and alarm caused by her disappearance.

René. I don't know. I wasn't in a position to see.

Hor. Altogether a most extraordinary episode—a fitting sequel to last night's Saturnalia.

Col. Saturnalia! At Briony?

Hor. Advantage was taken of my absence at Panfold last night to indulge in an entertainment which I describe as a Saturnalia for fear of giving it a worse name.

Lud. Perhaps we are judging it a little too seriously. A little dancing——

Hor. Dancing of a particularly objectionable character, in costumes improvised from bed-linen.

Col. Bed-linen!

Hor. To an accompaniment of French songs.

Col. *French* songs! But how horrible. I was told that it was merely Shakespeare readings.

Hor. I regret to say that some of the servants appear to have lent themselves to the furtherance of this underhand proceeding. Among others it will be my unpleasant duty to ask Cook to find another place; I shall give her a good character as a cook, but I shall be very restrained as to what I say about her trustworthiness.

Trevor. But, mother, isn't that being rather extreme? She's an awfully good cook.

Hor. I put conduct before cookery.

Trevor. After all, she did nothing more than make two or three supper dishes for us; she couldn't be expected to know that there would be French songs to follow.

HOR. It was her duty to consult me as to these highly unusual preparations. I had given my customary orders for the kitchen department and they did not include chicken mayonnaise or pêches melba. Had she informed me of these unauthorized instructions that she had received the mischief would have been detected and nipped in the bud.

TREVOR. I think it's scarcely fair that she should be punished for what we did. (TREVOR *rises and goes to window*, R. *centre*.)

LUD. I confess I think it's rather unfortunate that such an eminently satisfactory cook should be singled out for dismissal.

HOR. Scarcely singled out, Ludovic; two or three of the other servants will also have to go.

COL. One must see that one's orders are respected, mustn't one?

(*Enter* WILLIAM, L., *with card*.)

WILL. (*to* LUDOVIC). The reporter of the *Wessex Courier* would like to speak with you, sir.

LUD. Tell him I am unable to see any pressmen at present.

WILL. (*handing card to* LUDOVIC). He's written a question which he would feel obliged if you'd answer, sir.

HOR. What is the question?

LUD. He wants to know if I intend standing in the event of a Parliamentary vacancy. (*To* WILLIAM.) You can tell him that I have not the remotest intention of standing.

(RENÉ *groans tragically*.)

WILL. Yes, sir.

[*Exit* WILLIAM, L.

HOR. Really, Ludovic, I think you are rather precipitate in your decisions. Differing though we do on more than one of the secondary questions of the day, I am nevertheless inclined to think that the Briony influence would be considerably augmented by having one of the family as Member for the division. Subject to certain modifications of your political views, I am distinctly anxious to see you representing this district in Parliament. I consider this impending vacancy to be a golden opportunity for you.

LUD. There are some people whose golden opportunities have a way of going prematurely grey. I am one of those.

COL. I must say we rather counted on having you for a candidate. I think I may voice a very general disappointment.

RENÉ. There are some disappointments that are too deep to be voiced.

(*Enter* WILLIAM, *door centre.*)

WILL. If you please, ma'am.

HOR. What is it?

WILL. Adolphus has laid an egg.

RENÉ. Oh, improper little bird.

HOR. An egg! How very extraordinary. In all the years that we've had that bird such a thing has never happened. I must admit that I'm rather astonished. See that she has everything she wants and is not disturbed.

WILL. Yes, ma'am.

[*Exit* WILLIAM, *centre.*

(*Enter* CLARE, R., *with telegram in hand.*)

CLARE. My great-aunt, Mrs. Packington, died at nine o'clock this morning.

(TREVOR *goes into fit of scarcely suppressed laughter.*)

COL. A great age, was she not?

HOR. A great age and for longer than I can remember a great invalid. At any rate, a great consumer of medicines. I suppose her death must be regarded as coming in the natural order of things. At the same time, I scarcely think, Trevor, that it is a subject for unbridled amusement.

TREVOR. I'm awfully sorry, but I couldn't help it. It seemed too—too unexpected to be possible. Please excuse me. (*Goes to window and opens it. The others stare at him.*)

CLARE. The fact is, I was Mrs. Packington's favourite niece. There were things in her will which I couldn't afford to have altered. On the other hand, as I dare say you know, Mrs. Bavvel, she had a very special dislike for you.

HOR. I am aware of it. We had some differences of opinion during my husband's lifetime.

CLARE. It was a favourite observation of hers that you reminded her of a rattlesnake in dove's plumage.

Col. Oh, but what unjust imagery!

Clare. She hated Briony and everything connected with it, and I had to keep my visits here a dark secret.

Col. How very embarrassing.

Clare. Not at all. I like duplicity, when it's well done. But when Trevor asked me to marry him it did become embarrassing.

(*All the others start up from their seats. Enter* William, *L., stands listening.*)

Hor. Trevor asked you—to marry him?

Clare. Two months ago. Mrs. Packington wasn't expected to live for another fortnight, but she'd been in that precarious condition, off and on, for five years. At the same time, I couldn't risk letting Trevor slip; he'd have forgotten everything and married some one else in sheer absence of mind.

Trevor. I don't altogether admit that, you know. A thing of that sort I should have remembered.

Clare. Anyhow, we married on the quiet.

Trevor. By special licence. It was rather fun, it felt so like doing wrong.

Lud. Do you mean to tell us that you are Mrs. Trevor Bavvel?

Clare. Of Briony, in the County of Somerset, at your service.

René (*shouts*). William!

Will. Yes, sir.

René. Has that journalist man gone?

Will. A minute ago, sir.

René. Quick, send some one after him. Stop him. Tell him——

Lud. That in the event of a vacancy——

René. Mr. Ludovic Bavvel——

Lud. Will place himself at the disposal of the Party leaders.

René. Fly! (*Almost pushes* William *out of the door*, L.)

Clare. And, William—tell John to bring up some bottles of Heidsieck.

Will. Yes, miss, ma'am.   [*Exit.*

SYBIL. You dear old thing, you've taken all our breaths away; I always said you and Trevor ought to make a match of it. (*Kisses her.*)

AGATHA. I shall put up evergreens all over the house. (*Kisses her.*)

HOR. On a subject of such primary importance as choosing a wife I should have preferred and certainly expected to be consulted. As you have *chosen* this rather furtive method of doing things, I don't know that there is anything for me to do beyond offering my congratulations, which in the nature of things must be rather perfunctory. I congratulate you both. I trust that the new mistress of Briony will remember that certain traditions of conduct and *decorum* have reigned here for a generation. I think without making undue pretensions that Briony has set an example of decent domestic life to a very large neighbourhood.

CLARE. My dear Hortensia, I think Briony showed last night what it could do in the way of outgrowing traditions. Trevor and I have had plenty of time during the last two months to think out the main features of the new *régime*. We shall keep up the model dairy and the model pigsties, but we've decided that we won't be a model couple.

(*Enter* JOHN *with four bottles of fizz.*)

JOHN (*to* CLARE). If you please, madam, will the waggonette and luggage cart be required as ordered?

CLARE. No, I don't think any one will be leaving today. I shall expect you all to prolong your visits in our honour. Oh, of course, I was forgetting Mrs. Vulpy has to go up to Tattersall's to see about some hunters. Just the dogcart then.

HOR. I shall require the carriage for the 4.15 down. There is a conference at Exeter which I think I ought to attend.

JOHN. Very well, madam. [*Exit*, L.

[*Exeunt* HORTENSIA *and*
COLONEL MUTSOME, R.

AGATHA (*holding up glass*). You dear things, here's your very good health, and may you have lots and lots of——

RENÉ. Oh, hush!

AGATHA. I was going to say lots of happiness.

RENÉ. Oh, I was afraid you were going to lecture against race suicide.

LUD.
SYBIL
MRS. V.
RENÉ
⎬ (*speaking together*). "Mr. and Mrs. Trevor Bavvel." (*They drink.*)

TREVOR. Thank you all, and here's to the success of the future Member for the Division——

CLARE. Coupled with that of his charming secretary.

    (LUDOVIC *and* RENÉ *bow.*)

    (*Enter* WILLIAM, *centre, with enormous pile of sand-wiches.*)

WILL. Please, Cook thought that as the sandwiches wouldn't be wanted for this afternoon you might like them now. Those with mustard on the right, without on the left, sardine and egg in the middle. And, please, I'm asked to express the general rejoicing in the servants' hall, and Cook says that if marriages are made in heaven the angels will be for putting this one in the window as a specimen of their best work.

CLARE. Thank Cook and all of you very much. (*She whispers to* TREVOR.)

TREVOR. Of course, certainly.

CLARE. And tell John to open some Moselle in the servants' hall for you all to drink our healths. We're coming in presently to get your congratulations.

WILL. Yes, ma'am; thank you, ma'am.

    (WILLIAM *turns to go.*)

CLARE. And, William——

WILL. (*turning back*). Yes, ma'am.

CLARE. How much did you win on the sweepstake?

    (WILLIAM *turns and flies in confusion.*)

CURTAIN